AUSTRALIAN RAIN

E. R. G. BREWSTER

MINERVA PRESS
WASHINGTON LONDON MONTREUX

AUSTRALIAN RAIN

Copyright © E. R. G. Brewster 1994

All Rights Reserved

No part of this book may be reproduced in any form,
by photocopying or by any electronic or mechanical means,
including information storage or retrieval systems,
without permission in writing from both the copyright owner
and the publisher of this book.

ISBN 1 85863 123 8

First Published 1994 by
MINERVA PRESS
2, Old Brompton Road,
London SW7 3DQ.

Printed in Great Britain by
B.W.D. Printers Ltd., Northolt, Middlesex

AUSTRALIAN RAIN

ABOUT AUSTRALIAN RAIN

All characters in this book are based upon real people, some characters mirror these people closely, while others have developed into more (or less) than they are by the events of the story.

Most of the events in this book are taken from real life, however in the interests of the story some have been added, while a few have been omitted.

Every opinion expressed is bias; not least my own, however I have tried to be fair to all characters and where this is not noticeable it is one characters' bias towards another. All the characters included here are of equal importance to myself as the reporter of events, regardless of how large or how little a role they play, or appear to play; though I don't understand any as well as I do my friend and constant companion Al.

Australian Rain was begun in earnest in October 1990 in Auckland. The first draft was very erratic and highly emotional as it spewed forth through my pencil in three stressful weeks. I lost a lot of weight; and like Al I can't afford to lose any!

Draft two followed immediately and was typed in five weeks.
There was then a long break while I tried to earn enough money to survive and then the third and fourth drafts were written in Wellington between November 1991 and January 1992. There again followed another break until the fifth draft happened between July 1992 and February 1993 in Sudbury and Bristol; and now I know that I dislike word processors, even if they are very convenient.

After a lot of work in between drafts; with a fair amount of residual pain and bad memories, this is my attempt at a novel. I cannot judge it now, having lived through it six times I am numb to what happened; maybe that's for the best.

There have been two things which have surprised me greatly with the production of Australian Rain. Firstly, that I was able to write so many words and that anyone should call me a writer. Secondly, how many people laughed at me for doing something that they themselves are not able to do. Some are still laughing. I find this very strange and feel a little sorry for them.

Finally I would like to thank all those people who have helped me along my way between 1989 and now; you know who you are, I could not have done it alone.

Special thanks to Kate Stone and Daphne Brasell at Brasell and Associates in Wellington for all their encouragement and faith they showed to me.

Very special thanks from Al to Steven for giving him a life and a future and for some wonderful memories.

E.R.G. BREWSTER.

To my friend and brother
for the love and understanding that you gave unselfishly to me.

to laugh; and then to cry,
to feel the pain of a crisp new dawning,
to dream for freedoms, of mind and of soul,
to long for the return of a new Sutton Hoo man.

AUSTRALIAN RAIN

Contents	**Page**
Introduction	xi
Cold Hearts, Hot Heads And Tears	17
Australian Rain	62
A Dream, Once Dreamt, Is Forever Lost	179
Adelaide	265
Twisted Mind, Wasted Life	312
Meet Me At Heathrow	347

INTRODUCTION

Melbourne, 19th July 1990

From within the dome of a small green tent, on a camp site beside a busy and noisy dual-carriageway at the edge of a large industrial estate on the eastern outskirts of Melbourne; he lay on his sleeping bag with pen in hand and an almost blank sheet of paper in front of him. The undulations of the ground beneath him making it less than comfortable; as anyone who has ever been camping long-term will know. Again and again he tried to turn his thoughts into words and record them on to his paper in the hope that it would help him to understand what had, and what was now happening to him. Time and again he felt into every dark corner of his mind in the hope that he could drag out something; anything, that would make some sense.

"Maybe I am mad?" He said in a severely depressed tone. He didn't really believe that, though it was a question that he had asked himself so many times, without answer. He had to wonder why and how it was that he was now spending his second winter in a tent in Australia? Was it not a little more than strange? He scribbled down some words, only to cross through them with a series of heavy blue lines which made deep troughs in his paper. With each stroke of his pen his heart sank a little more. With each stroke the pain weighed heavily upon him. It was a sad and desperate attempt to make some sort of sense of himself, his feelings, his past, present and though he could admit to having one, his future.

The familiar pitter-patter of rain on what had become his little home was an almost constant sound.

"My home? Why does it feel more like a prison? How can it rain so much here? I've never seen it rain on Neighbours." He shook his head in disbelief and was almost amused by the thought that most people at home in East Anglia thought that it was always warm and dry here.

"If only they knew." He shivered.

Suddenly! The walls of his tent leaned to the side at a thirty degree angle as a gust of wind caught it and brought it folding down on him, like a sandwich made of nylon and cotton, with him as the filling.

"Oh God not again! Please, no more."

It happened so often and he always dreaded that this time would be the time that the fabric would no longer stand up to the savaging wind. His mind, black with worry, confusion, loneliness, played tricks on him in his desperation to escape the nightmare within which he felt he was permanently trapped. He was drowning in an ocean of emotions, miles from the shores of love. He couldn't swim.

Slowly, as the wind reduced, the flexible fibreglass frame would right itself and for a while longer he could breath easily again.

From outside of his little home came the continuous thunder of traffic as it rushed past on the highway. The never ending noise of the traffic that was slowly driving him insane; along with life in his tent, in the cold and damp of a Melbourne winter.

"What on Earth am I doing here?" He asked himself, another question that he had asked himself every day for more months than he could, or cared to remember and still he had no real answer for himself. So far from home. So far from his friends.

The dim light which came from his gas burner cast an eerie shadow over his hand and onto the paper, the low heat from which failed to fight off the cold. The gentle hum of the butane as it flowed from the canister and into the stark blue flame was a comforting sound; though it made him realise just how alone he really was; it was the only sound to be heard within his tent, apart from his tired and forlorn breathing.

"I'm here to get out of debt!" The thought sprang into his mind with all the impact of watching a firework exploding into the darkness of a chilly November Suffolk night.

"This was how Columbus must have felt when the thought of a round Earth first entered his head." He tried and failed to convince himself that this was fun, something that he wanted to be doing.

"Yes, I'm here to get out of debt, I must remember that." He had already sent four thousand dollars home and only needed another fifteen hundred to be free from the financial burden of his past. "After all, that's why I came back to Australia this year," he thought half-heartedly, not believing that for a second. He was so desperate to convince himself, fool himself, that this was what he wanted to be doing instead of being in East Anglia close to his brother.

"Yes! Isn't that what I told everyone when they asked why I was coming back down here?" It was nothing but an illusion that fooled no one, let alone himself. None the less, it was an illusion that he needed to believe in for now. The illusion that this country had captured his imagination and enthusiasm so much that he wanted to see more of it. His debts had been such a convenient excuse for him to keep running from those horrific first few months of 1989. Australia had been such a convenient place for him to run to, because he needed as much distance as he could get and it would have been difficult to get much further from Suffolk without leaving the planet!

His memories of the previous year were still haunting him. After all the time that had past they still intruded so much into his thoughts.

"Is there nothing that I can do without prompting some memory of yesterday?" He lost himself for a moment as he recalled a scene or conversation from his past with amazing clarity, like an old movie playing over and over again in his crazy mind, a constant reminder of pain. He was living in a nightmare and he didn't know how he could awaken himself from his tormented sleep.

Imagine if we were now told that the Earth is flat. It always was and always will be, and all the pictures from outer space of a round Earth had been distortions caused by the Ozone layer; and now that the Ozone layer is disappearing we now have a true picture of a flat world. Yes, it is a stupid thought, but imagine if it was true. Imagine how shattering that would be. One of the most unquestionable, unshakeable facts had now become fiction. Everything else that you had ever believed in would have to be called into question. All your 'facts' would have to be re-examined just in case they too were false.

Before January 1989 his world was round, but then became flat, very flat. All his hopes, plans and dreams disappeared and he had been running ever since and could not find a reason to stop. What was he running from? What does anyone ever really run from? He was running from a shadow that never left his side, a dark stranger, a constant companion, his own shadow, his own mind. He knew that, but that didn't make accepting the answer any easier. It was an answer he could not deal with, which was compounded by the thought that he could never see an end to it. He had resigned himself to the frightening thought that he would be running for a very long time yet, maybe always. Like a ball rolling down a hill, once it starts it cannot stop on its own. A frightening thought because he was so far from the land that he called home, the land that he loved. So far from the people he loved, too far from his brother. A daily existence of life in a little green tent in a land in which he did not belong, alone. No plans, no hopes, no dreams. Only fear and loneliness to accompany him. His only friends in Australia no longer wanted him to come to their home. No longer was he welcome there and that made the loneliness and isolation seem even worse than it probably was. He was alone in a city of nearly three and a half million people, with only a seemingly distant date of August 22nd that would break the monotony; the day that he had to leave Melbourne and fly to Auckland, to all the uncertainty that a new place always brings, the uncertainty that comes with a breakdown in routine and the loss of familiar surroundings. The uncertainty of whether or not one will be able to find work and accommodation. The uncertainty of learning how to fit into a new society, a new culture, a new system. How long would he stay there? A week? A month? Six months? Unanswered questions. His head was drowning in a flood of unanswered questions.

"Oh Australia, my land of hopes, my land of opportunity, my land of isolation. How could I have known of the disasters you had in store for me, both real and imaginary? How could I have known of the true loneliness and isolation and confusion? When can I go home? Where is home?" Questions he had asked himself a thousand times and he was no nearer to an answer. He had returned to East Anglia last November and found himself feeling that he no longer belonged there. He no longer fitted into that little niche in life that had once been his. He was no longer needed. He had spent so long getting used to life in the southern hemisphere without even realising it and it had not occurred to him that it would also take time to readjust to life at home. He was horrified at how much he thought had changed, when in reality nothing had changed, except for him. His life was totally different upon his return than it had been before he first departed for Australia. He went back with too many false ideas of what was waiting for him there. Too many hopes. Too many dreams. He was so naive and so very wrong. Had he honestly expected everything to be the same? So much had happened in the past eleven months and that had frightened him. He had tried to be strong upon his return home and tried to pursue whatever vague plan he had dreamt up in order to keep his mind occupied, but somehow his plans went wrong and that was why he had run back to Australia. That was why he was to find himself lying in a tent in yet another winter; his fourth winter in a row, his fourth winter in two years. He had no idea how much Australia had changed him. How much isolation had changed him. After all that had happened in his life, in his mind, he should not have been so surprised.

The rain eased off and the noise of the raindrops hitting the nylon fly-sheet softened to an intermittent dull drip.

"No leaks this time, good. I'm not sure how much more of this I can take before I crack totally. Oh Christopher, I am trying to be strong. I am trying to get better. It's just..." He paused and wondered what it was. The isolation he felt weighed heavily upon him, he had not experienced such a pronounced void in his life before. Life had become a sterile existence. "It's just... I miss you. I wonder if you know? Really know?"

Living out of a backpack and in a tent was not fun. It had never been fun, nor was it easy, especially in the winter. He had long ago discovered that he was not cut out to be a traveller and he had no desire to become one. He had long ago stopped pretending that he was enjoying this. As the days drifted into weeks and the weeks into months he began to realise that what little inner strength he had, he was now losing quickly. Time was supposed to heal, or at least rearrange memories, but nothing seemed to be happening in his mind. He thought back to an event at work two days ago which showed him so clearly just how close he was to falling apart. Two days ago he spat the dummy, as they say down here in Dandenong. So what? Everyone loses their temper once in a while. Why should he think that he was any different? For him, the problem was that he had 'spat' it at someone who had become his closest friend, after Christopher. He let Paul have his anger. Paul, who was supposed to be special to him. He had never behaved in such a way before and it left him feeling totally ashamed. He was totally shocked and surprised by his actions, as was Paul. He would never have expected such an outburst from Al and Al could see in Paul's eyes that he was not only offended by his behaviour, but also hurt. Of course he apologised and Paul knew him well enough to know how badly he felt, but for Al it should never have happened and he could not forgive himself for it. Life had just become too much for him to cope with. He did not, could not understand why, after such a long passage of time he still felt so much pain. Was there never to be an end to it?

COLD HEARTS, HOT HEADS AND TEARS

Sudbury, 27th April 1989

The second half of April had been a disappointment; cool, dull and showers every day. It had followed such a mild and dry winter and was as bad an April as it could have been. It reflected his mood; and more than that, it amplified it. Al was walking back from Sudbury for what was probably the last time; in two days he would be sitting on the plane and leaving this country. He met his father at the bottom of the hill. It seemed that they always passed here. For so many years they would walk past each other and not say a word, not even a nod of acknowledgement. Now they indulged in shallow conversation then his father mentioned that his mother had been taken into hospital again. He interjected the statement into the weak excuse for a conversation as if he was passing comment on the weather forecast for the day. Al continued home and tried to understand the family that he belonged to. He was an outsider in a family full of outsiders. The horse chestnuts were coming into leaf on the hill and spring; which had threatened to start at the end of January, was now held in check. Al recognised a face in a car that drove past towards town, he gave a wave, no wave was returned. Above him the clouds gathered grey and white-grey, it wouldn't shower before he got back to the house.

"Hi Fatima," he said when she finally got around to answering.
"Hi Al. What can I do for you?"
"Nag-nag is in hospital again." Nag-nag was their pet name for their scatty mother.
"What? I saw Baba in town. He didn't say anything."
They had been brought up to address their father in Turkish, though none were Turks and none had ever been there.
"You're honoured that he spoke to you aren't you?"
"If I see him I won't let him get away without talking to me. Are you going to go to Bury to see her?"
Al didn't answer immediately. He was thinking how strange it was for his sister to be virtually disowned because she married an Irishman. Asha had got past that stage after she married a native East Anglian and produced a son. Al laughed. He hadn't done so badly

really; ignored since the age of thirteen, yet living under the same roof, but the past few years there had been the occasional communication since he had moved to Ipswich.

"What are you laughing at?" Fatima asked.

"Oh nothing, just thinking of something. Yes, I'll get the ten o'clock bus from town. Are you going to meet me?"

"Yeah, I'll meet you at the bus station."

It took an hour to get to Bury, Bury St. Edmunds to give it its full name. The last Angle king of East Anglia; but not the last East Anglian king, was buried here after being killed in battle against Swein of Denmark in 869 near Hoxne. Al did not mind the journey, in fact he relished it. He saw it as one last opportunity to look at the medieval market town of Lavenham. It was always a precious sight to behold, no matter how many times he saw it. The assemblage of such fine half-timbered buildings from a bygone age and in such large numbers were the very essence of East Anglia. Al and Fatima got off the bus opposite the old gaol and walked the remaining mile or so to the hospital.

"I hate hospitals. I hate that smell," Al said, half under his breath.

Fatima laughed as she reminded him of the time that they were going to give blood.

"Do you remember? You went white at the thought of having your thumb stabbed for a blood test!"

"Yes, I remember and I don't need reminding!"

They entered the building and passed through the waiting room. They knew where they were going in the maze of the hospital, they had been there many times before. The stair well echoed to the sound of footsteps going both up and down and to the whispers of conversations which were deliberately lowered in tone. Walking into the cardiac care unit they found exactly what they knew they would. Nag-nag was sitting in her bed looking around the ward, being very nosy. As soon as she saw Fatima and Al she had her audience and was off.

"Now don't you two make me laugh, or you'll make the wiggly line on that bloody monitor go too fast and they'll tell me off," she said pointing to the screen. The line increased its speed as she got excited. "See that man over there," she pointed her finger in a less than discreet manner. "He was snoring all bloody night, he kept me awake. I was going to get up and push his pillow over his face, that would have shut him up! And that woman there," she waved her finger in another direction in just as subtle a way. "She kept farting all night! Oh it stank!"

Al and Fatima were creasing themselves laughing as their mother said all that without taking a pause for breath.

"Don't you two laugh, it was really bad. I thought that I was going to choke. And see that man there." She pointed to the remaining bed which was empty. "Well he had a heart attack in the middle of the night and all the doctors and nurses rushed around, giving him needles and electric shocks and everything; but he snuffed it!"

She had to be the fittest heart attack patient they had ever seen, full of energy and in everyone else's business. Al looked at Fatima with the 'she's the same old dragon' look.

"And do you know what?" Nag-nag continued.

"What?" Fatima answered.

"They've got more poisonous snakes in Australia than they have non-poisonous ones. It's the only place in the world like it and I bet that you didn't know that!" She said very proudly. In a day in hospital she had become a leading authority on venomous snakes.

"I'm still going to Australia tomorrow. You know, Australia, the big island on the other side of the world? Tomorrow, no matter what; and it doesn't matter how many venomous snakes they've got, because it only takes one to kill you! I could go out tomorrow on the heaths here in Suffolk and get bitten by a venomous snake, but that has never stopped me has it?" That wasn't quite true as the vipers would still be in hibernation, despite the mild winter. Nag-nag didn't have an answer, but her mind was ticking over trying to find one, so Al carried on while he still had the advantage.

"Anyway, I hope that there are a lot of snakes, so I can cook one on my fire in the outback, miles from anywhere!"

"Oh my God, you're scared of worms!"

"Yes, but snakes aren't slimy and horrible and they have a lot of meat on them."

Nag-nag pulled a face and made them both laugh.

"Besides, the plane could crash long before I get there!"

"Oh shit, don't say that. I'll be worrying all the time now."

"You'll be worrying all the time anyway! Just think, the train could crash before I get as far as London, or I could get run over on my way for the bus in the morning. We're all going to snuff it, only for some it will come sooner rather than later."

"Don't look at me like that!" She answered defiantly.

She sat in her bed like Queen Muck receiving court, grey hairs protruding from her white chin. Small round eyes darting this way and that.

"And another thing," she was off again, "they're all drunk out there and they're always fighting. Don't you laugh boy. I know what I'm talking about because I've been there. I've been to Wagga Wagga and it was just a dirt track that went there!"

She was proud of her royal trek to the remote settlement of Wagga Wagga so many moons ago. How many times had she told them about it? They had lost count.

For an hour she carried on like that. Al and Fatima were tired, they couldn't keep up with her. Al looked coldly at his mother sitting there. There was nothing wrong, she just tried to stop him from leaving.

"Oh well Nag-nag, I'll see you in six months; if I'm still alive!" Inside he hoped that he wouldn't be; what reason did he have to live? Everything he had known and wanted had gone and getting through each day was getting harder and harder, though helped with more than a little alcohol.

"Well I might not be here when you get back!"

"You've been promising that for years and you're still here! There's nowhere for you to go anyway. Him upstairs won't have you and him down there wouldn't, otherwise he'd be out of a job! They'll put a lid on your coffin and you'll scream out I'm not ready yet! It's only Australia, not another planet. I'll still be able to hear you nagging!"

Fatima and Al left the hospital, hardly saying a word. She looked at him and he knew what she was thinking. He took offence.

"Well what the fuck should I do? Stay here?! If I did that I would never be able to do anything would I?"

Fatima didn't answer him. He was right and she knew it. They both knew how Machiavellian Nag-nag could be.

"Even if she was really ill, I'm still going tomorrow."

"That not fair Al."

"Life's like that!"
"But she's your mother." Fatima pleaded.
"I'm her son, what difference has that ever made to anything?"

It seemed that morning would never arrive, but finally it did and Al was up at six thirty. He had no reason to be up so early, but he had spent most of the night lying there awake, thinking of Steven.

He had already packed, so there was little else to do other than have breakfast. He walked to the end of the garden and looked at all the plants that he had planted over the years. The Sorbus was now beginning to look like real tree and it would give a good display in May and October. The leylandii, which was only eighteen inches tall not too many years ago were now over six feet and had been cut twice a year for a couple of years.

"I hope they don't prune the Sorbus," he said himself, knowing full well that the act of pruning to his parents was mutilation to him, but then, when they watched Al prune a plant they always thought that he got carried away. In the tall Crataegus behind the garden; which once formed part of the original hedge which was left behind from when all this was farmed land, perched a pair of greenfinches. It reminded him of the winters when he would spend hours watching the birds from his bedroom window. At any one time there might be well over a hundred birds feeding and during the season over sixty species would visit the garden. Hours of watching the wildlife through the lonely years of adolescence.

Time moved along and at quarter to nine he said goodbye to his father, an uncomfortable goodbye. His father said that he would miss Al. Al found that unlikely and a very strange thing to say.

He stood waiting for the bus and hoped that he would see someone he knew, which he didn't. He was disappointed about that. He needed someone to say what a great adventure it would be to go to Australia. He needed to be told how lucky he was.

At the end of the road he saw the old red double-decker come around the corner and he prepared himself for this last journey on a route which he had travelled so very many times before.

"Single to Ipswich please."

"Single?" The driver questioned.

Al nodded yes, paid and then climbed the stairs and sat at the front of the bus. The bus trundled its way between the houses and fields, up and down valleys and through small villages. He was aware of everything, like never before. He was seeing things for the first time after a lifetime of seeing them. He sat motionless, staring out of the dirty windows which were clouded with condensation. He felt a strange sickness as the bus climbed the hill out of Hadleigh and passed close to the school where Steven would be inside teaching. All he saw was seen in a strange slow motion, like in a dream that would never end. The end of the journey could not come soon enough and he was pleased when Tony finally met him at the old cattle market. For ten days they had been so impatient, and now it was a close run race between anticlimax and exaltation as they walked the two miles to where Tony had been living for the past few months. They had so much time on their hands until they had to get the train to London and the thought of being en route to Australia was still inconceivable. Going to France for a day trip, would have made more sense, but they were not going to France.

Midday was a long time in coming. It was time to take a walk to the station, but there was no hurry and if they missed this train and had to get the next one, it would not have mattered. Al's eyes were everywhere as they walked through the town. All this had been part of his life for the past four and a half years and now it was slowly slipping away into his past. It was such a massive chunk of his life. Gone. Part of him was dying as he took each step. There was no going back. No way to recapture those years and re-live them. It all felt like such a waste to him.

They sat in the station cafeteria drinking coffee and eating chocolate cake and as they did another piece of Al's heritage was drifting away as he looked around the Victorian railway station. He reflected on his history lessons and all the hours they spent covering the Industrial Revolution. The tunnel at the end of the platform had been dug by hand; he couldn't imagine that there would have been need of dynamite as there was no hard rock to cut through and so many fossilised giant deer, horse and hippopotamus had been found during it's construction, he had seen their remains in Ipswich museum many times, he hadn't realised that Ipswich had a museum until he had moved to the town.

"I wonder why more people don't visit Ipswich museum? It should be a regular school trip."

"What?" Tony asked. He had no idea what was going on in Al's head. "What are you on about Ipswich museum for? You're on your way to Australia!"

A train arrived from London. Al missed seeing the class 47 diesel locos that used to pull these trains, they seemed to have more character than these electric engines. It stopped for a minute then moved out of the station towards Norwich.

"They speed up so quickly don't they."

Tony just looked at Al. He thought it best to ignore Al's odd comments.

A train departed for Felixstowe and another for Cambridge and a third left for Lowestoft. The sun broke through the cloud for a few minutes and seemed to lift the atmosphere of the station and everyone who sat there waiting for their train. The bells started to ring, another train was coming through the tunnel. Al loved the workings of the railway network, he could spend hours in train stations whiling away time, not that he would consider himself to be fanatical; he couldn't see the fun in taking down train numbers or anything that extreme. A new Sprinter emerged from the darkness of the tunnel and the bells fell silent. It was on its way to Blackpool.

"I've never been to Blackpool Tony. I wonder if the illuminations are worth the effort of going there?"

"I don't believe you. Here I sit barely half a day away from flying out of Heathrow for Australia, hardly able to believe that we're actually going there and what are you on about? Ipswich Museum, British Rail and bloody Blackpool! Are you off your face or what? In two days you'll be in Australia not Blackpool!" Tony wasn't sure if he really wanted to be going to Australia any more than Al wanted to go. For both of them it would be a period to escape their individual situations.

The London train arrived and Tony was pleased, he hoped that a bit of East Anglian countryside would stop Al's mind from drifting into the obscure depths of depression.

The Orwell estuary was quickly left behind and within ten minutes the train roared over the bridges across the Stour flood plain. In the shallows a few mute swans fed. There used to be many more, but gradually they were being killed off by fishermen's discarded lead shot; a slow poisonous death. The train raced past orchards and small woods, fields and water and then Colchester appeared as they began to slow down. The town stood at the top of the hill just where the

Romans had put it more than nineteen hundred years ago. It dominated the surrounding countryside, with Jumbo, as the Victorian water tower is called, standing tall and red-bricked, crowned with a green roof. Another sight that he had seen far more times than he could remember. Jumbo could be seen from several miles away and he remembered how often he would cycle the fifteen miles from Sudbury and think how he would soon be in town when he was able to see it. Tony attempted to make conversation, but failed. Al was not happy about leaving his homeland and he was lost in feelings of disbelief rather than excitement.

The train began to slow down just outside Liverpool Street Station and inched its way lethargically towards a platform. Doors began to open and people jumped from the train before it had come to a halt. Those who jumped a little too soon made a less than dignified entry into the station. There was no hurry, so Tony and Al strolled along the platform and entered the underground. People passed almost at running speed; Londoners were always in a hurry! The tatty posters on the walls caught Al's attention and the litter on the floor was shameful. Around them hundreds of people with blank expressions on their faces, making them seem almost androidean; how bored these creatures were. How depressed they looked. Each face could tell a story. Hundreds of stories passed him by, but none had anyone to tell their stories to and no one had time to tell them. There was a rush of warm air as they entered the platform. The warm sweet-smelling air blew across Al's face; it was almost as sweet as strongly scented summer flowers, it was familiar and in a strange way, refreshing.

"Probably electrocuted rats," he mused.

Tony looked at him, not quite sure if he had heard Al correctly, so he said nothing.

Al laughed as he pictured an army of rats trying to outrun a worn out tube as it clattered and jerked along the rails; some getting away, some squashed and some cooked.

* * * * *

The wheels of the aircraft touched the ground for the final time. It had not seemed as far as either had imagined, but then this was not the end of their journey, but the beginning. Tony looked at Al, he could see that he still wasn't here with him. God knows what the hell he was thinking now? Tony worried for his friend, but had no idea how he could help him.

Passengers filed along the aircraft and into the terminal. It was early, four o'clock. Outside it was as dark as it was in Al's mind. He was afraid? He was glad to have Tony with him. Yes it was good to be with a friend and not to be alone. They escaped the aircraft for the last time and followed sheepishly with the flow of people. Were they really in Australia? That thought flew around their heads; seemingly impossible, as the plane had from London, across the world. No, it was no dream.

"I'm nine thousand miles from East Anglia," he said to himself, though it did not really mean that much to him. He had never seen that sort of distance and could not imagine it. His world map, flat, with Australia on the bottom right and East Anglia centre top was just a flat map, without proven or logical meaning.

"What was that Al?" Tony was tired, he also was not quite sure what it was that he was doing here. He wanted to stop drinking. He wanted to think about his future. He wanted to make sense of himself in order to make good use of the time to come. They both had their reasons for running.

"We're so far from home." Al sounded almost surprised. Tony didn't answer. He just looked at Al, unsure of what to say. He was worried. How long would Al remain calm? Nothing had really changed, only the place. They were still trapped in their problems and the act of crossing the world was not going to change a thing, they brought their problems with them. Being where they found themselves was not going to alter very much, it was merely a little room in which they could breath and find a little space to sit and think, without the immediate pressure of the real world and real life.

It was Friday evening in Ipswich. Friday evening, shopping, then sitting in front of the television watching Wogan; eating turkey escallopes, chips and peas with mayonnaise, lots of mayonnaise and a bottle or two of Becks beer. For three months Al had been caught in this trap. The trap of past happiness encased in the reality of the pain of the here and now, all from the events of one night in January. His mind had shattered into a jigsaw of pieces, remnants of hopes, love, dreams, desires and fears. Remnants of his life, his future, leaving him unable to do anything other than run. He still wanted to be with Steven, he still thought of him, longed for him, despite all the pain that resurfaced by having such thoughts he still wanted Steven.

Al and Tony joined the queue at Immigration. There were hundreds of weary-eyed passengers standing quietly in untidy lines waiting to be processed. Someone whispered and a dozen tired eyes turned to look. Children sat on cases, rested heads against fathers shoulders. Al didn't feel tired, but wanted to sleep, yes he could sleep, but where? This early shift must be a good shift to work as an Immigration Officer, heavy limbed people all too tired to give any trouble as they sedately answered whatever questions they were asked. Al moved a little closer, he began to feel guilty and primed himself for the inevitable difficulties ahead. His crime was to have a British passport with a Turkish name.

Tony was called forward by a stern looking official, he picked up his pack and moved to the counter. Al shuffled forward to the 'wait behind this line until called' red line. Tony was interrogated, but Al could not hear what was being said, he imagined; or rather half imagined... never finishing one thought before his mind flew off on another tangent, he imagined all sorts of things, all sorts of difficulties. Tony was waved though. He had fooled them. He had got through the net. Like a very clever spy passing through tough security and melting into the shadows behind the Iron Curtain. The officer directed Al to come forward, without a word, he watched Al gather his pack and bag and rush forward.

"Don't keep him waiting Al," he looked at the officer. "Good morning," Al said as cheerfully as someone who was travel weary and nervous could sound.

The immigration officer looked up from his computer terminal and at Al as if he had just been sworn at. He said nothing, then continued typing Al's visa number into the machine.

"Oh my God, I've done it now, he won't let me into the country."

He looked around the official's desk; he was always nosy; something that he had inherited from his mother, then at the person in the queue on his left who was having a hard time gaining entry.

"Are you with the chap who has just gone through?"

"Yes, that's right." Al answered a little apprehensively.

"You do realise that you're not allowed to work don't you?"

"Oh yes. We've both got more money than the Embassy in London recommended." Al fumbled in his bag searching for his travellers cheques, credit cards; all five of them, and cash. He had his passport handed back and was told to pass through to customs.

Within ten minutes they were standing in the lounge of the airport looking for the train which would take them into the city. There was no train and this confused Al. He had imagined such a young and wealthy country being far more advanced than the one he had left behind two days ago. How could there not be a rapid transport system here? After looking for a bus they decided to wait out the night at the airport. There was not going to be much open in a city that didn't even have a rail link to its airport.

"I guess I ought to phone home to say that the plane didn't crash. Are you going to phone anyone Tony?"

"No, there's no one to phone."

Al found that strange, but also understood. He was really making the call to reassure himself that home wasn't so far away after all. He phoned his sister Asha. The phone rang, it was so quick. She answered, her voice was so clear. He didn't have much to say, just a short and very predictable conversation that millions of people have everyday upon their safe arrival at their destination, devoid of feeling and real emotions, "I'm here, good flight, safe flight." He felt as if he was just down the road, not the other side of the world.

Outside, the darkness of the night began to give way to the light of a new dawn. Tony and Al felt more than a little excitement as they stood outside in the crisp air, waiting. Waiting for their first Australian morning. Al's body began to lose the weariness that had been grinding him down for the last few days, indeed months. His body began to take on new life. He became charged with an energy, an excitement, an expectation as the sun rose above the vast flat land. Little by little the landscape yielded to its secrets, its beauty, its magic. The scene unfolding before them held their minds captive as the first rays of morning sunlight found their faces and warmed them. Al felt as if he was floating somewhere between heaven and paradise and for a while there was not one painful thought to trouble his tortured mind. It seemed like the most beautiful sunrise that he had ever seen and somehow he felt freed by it. The air was still and fresh, it was held in suspension like an unspoken promise between two people in a forbidden love. A promise of tomorrow and for tomorrow. A promise for always. The sands, red and gold, stretched out before them, they were littered with dry bushes and trees. The sun, huge, growing larger, rose into the sky.

"This is Australia," Al whispered into the morning air. "I'm in Australia."

"Tell me this is real Al." Tony stood at his side, as he had been at his side for many weeks throughout his nightmare. He also could not quite believe that they were where they were.

* * * * *

It was a cool day in mid April when Al had had the idea of going to Australia. What an idea that was! Driving along the A12 through Essex, the radio turned up loud to mask the noise of the concrete road with Tony and Al trying to talk above the din of both.

"What are you up to Al?" Tony asked. He knew that something was going on.

"Nothing. Why should I be up to anything?"

"Come on. I know you better than that. You're up to something with a grin as big as that on your face." There was no fooling Tony, but Al didn't quite know how to make his announcement.

"You know me Tony, always cheerful!"

"Pigs shit! What's up?"

"I'm going to Australia," he said quickly.

"What?!"

"I'm going to Australia," Al replied.

"I'll give you a lift to London. I don't think it's going to rain today and by the way I'm going to Australia. What the fuck are you up to now?" Tony said very matter-of-fact. They drove back onto tarmac and turned the radio down, there was no need to continue shouting.

"There's no reason to stay here, so I may as well clear off."

"Yeah, that's fair enough, but Australia? When did you decide that?"

"Last night. I was looking through an old atlas which my sister stole from school. Europe is far too close and my French isn't much cop and that's the only other language I speak. America is so cheap to get to and from and I'd just jump on a plane and come back, besides it's full of Yanks! So there isn't really much left that will be far enough away, relatively cheap to get to and where they speak English."

"And when are you planning to do this?"

"I don't know. Two or three days time. I'm going for my visa today and I'll look around for a cheap fare, then go!"

"I think you'll find it's not as easy as all that. These things have to be booked up in advance, it's not like jumping on a train to London or a ferry to France." Tony wasn't sure how to react. "I think you had better think this over a little."

"I have. I'm going."

Within three days of flicking through the pages of a stolen school atlas, he had his visa and air ticket. In such a short time his insane idea had become the here and now and although just as insane as before, it was now reality.

* * * * *

They tired of the view outside in the bright, but still cool morning, returning to their luggage which they had left for so long. In any other airport security would have taken it away and probably destroyed it in a controlled explosion. Here at the edge of such an isolated continent, life had not caught up with the horrors of living in London, among other cities and no one seemed the least bit bothered. The cafeteria was now open and they decided to eat before heading into the city centre. Now this could have been anywhere in the British Isles, the same food, the same set up, the same Anglo-Saxon face behind the counter. They had 'the lot'. Bacon, egg, sausage, mushrooms, tomatoes and toast and a cup of coffee and all for just six dollars; two pounds seventy, once converted back into real money! They ate; now tired from their journey. The airport took on a new lease of life as people began to spill through the doors as another day of departures and arrivals really got under way.

"It still doesn't sound possible to get from London to Perth in just twenty three hours, with stops. The world must be so small."

"No, it doesn't sound right does it?"

"And I know about gravity and all that, but I just can't picture in my head a round planet with us here upside down. I've never been upside down before and I can't imagine being so now." Al said, leaning over to his right and tipping his head down so he would be the right way up, but that didn't feel like it was the right way either, just upside down and uncomfortable. "I'm glad Newton was right about gravity Tony." Al's face red with the rush of blood, the result of his scientific experiment which followed in the footsteps of Newton, both involved food. Newton and his apple, Al and his fry up!

"We had better make tracks into the city Al."

"Yeah, O.K. Tony, but first I want to pinch this knife, fork and spoon. I haven't brought any with me," Al said as he wrapped the cutlery in a serviette and slipped it into his bag, feeling extremely guilty and having every reason to do so. "We've got to get value for money haven't we? Even Queen Maggie would be proud of us."

"Shit man, good thinking." Tony said, as he made his way to collect a clean set from along side the till. Al sunk down in his seat and became one with the furniture. Less than four hours after arriving in Australia they had committed their first crime, maybe they belonged in Australia after all?

They decided to take a taxi into the city. Al hated using taxis, he hated the way the meter always added up to a massive total, but Tony had already asked how much it would cost, Tony was good with people, he could look after himself. Al was just the opposite, self-conscious and little, nay, no self esteem and totally unable to approach anyone in order to get what he wanted. How the hell did he think he was going to get on in Australia alone? It was just as well that Tony had agreed to come out with him. But that would not last for long. Not that Al had any thoughts of being alone at the moment. He was happy to be with Tony and thought no further ahead than he had to. For a while longer he was safe from himself.

The streets of Perth were wide and strange, there was room for four, sometimes six lanes of traffic, sometimes kerbed, sometimes not. Few roads had footpaths. Along the verges there was grass, patchy, yellow, brown, dead. The houses were strange wooden affairs, bungalows not houses, large sheds with windows, white, paint peeling. Gardens were barren, unkept, many had a tree or two in a corner, tall, wide, exotic, but not like any garden Al had ever seen. He recognised a few of the trees, their foliage was not the lush green of home, but grey-green, blue-green, and yellow-green. It was so different, quite unlike Neighbours. Wasn't this how America looked?

The city centre stood tall, modern, wealthy. Marble, glass and concrete. How could this be so different from Britain? There was a common history and culture. At what point in the chain of city evolution had Australian and British architecture and planning diverged? The buildings stood like monoliths against the surrounding suburbs and appeared to be a contemporary version of a prehistoric monument on a bleak moor. It was unlike anything Al had seen before. So clean, so stark and so few people walking along its wide streets.

They walked around for a while, hoping to see a directional sign for the tourist information office, but there was no real hurry. They looked around, it was all so new to them and they soaked up the sights.

"I'll go and ask those workmen where the tourist bureau is." Tony said, leaving Al with their packs.

"Tony isn't going to have any trouble here is he?" Al thought, as he wished that he could deal with strangers as easily as Tony made it seem. "I'm going to have to learn how to communicate with people and learn bloody quickly! God help me when Tony and I split up." Tony came back. Al watched his movement. His James Dean walk, his cute smile, his dimple. His friend.

"I've been so lucky to have him around. I'm glad he came out here with me."

They found the tourist office and sat outside until it opened and then inquired about camp sites and then had to find out which bus they needed to take in order to get to the nearest site. They headed towards the main shopping area, but became confused by all the malls and arcades which were not on their map. They stood studying the poorly photocopied plan, trying to work out what was what and where was where.

"Good morning."

Startled, they looked up from their poor excuse for a map. A well dressed middle-aged man stood beside them, he wore a friendly smile. They felt a little less alone in a strange city.

"Welcome to Western Australia, can I help you with something?"

"Yeah," said Tony who was not the least bit put out by being approached by a stranger. "We're looking for the bus information bureau."

The man gave them the directions they needed, they were not far, just as they thought.

"You've obviously just arrived. Where are you from?"

Al let Tony do all the talking, he felt safer like that.

"Yeah, we got in at four this morning. From England." Al

cringed when he heard that.

"East Anglia, you traitor, not England."

"Is there anything else you need to know?"

"No. We just need to get out to a camp site."

Al watched Tony as he calmly dealt with this man without any emotion. Al always felt threatened, no matter how innocent the approach was. Was there such a thing as an innocent approach? Wasn't every approach a potential pick-up? Wasn't everyone after something? Nowhere was safe from these queers who saw every man as fair game. Al remembered the time at Victoria train station, just after he had seen Daphne off at the coach station, she was going back to Dunstable and he would follow later in the evening after the concert he was going to had finished. After all day in London he needed to go to the toilet; he hated to use public toilets, but he had no choice now, he was busting. He thought it strange at the time when he thought he imagined being followed down the steps and he thought it stranger still when with many vacant urinals this man chose the one next to him. Al, staring at the pebble dash, paint flaking away, embarrassed and annoyed. It hadn't occurred to him that many homosexuals use public toilets as pick-up joints. He had never heard of such a dirty habit. Now, many years later, and much, much wiser, he hated these people. He hated the thought that maybe he was supposed to be like them, he was after all, one of them. How could he be homosexual when he hated gays? Everyone was now suspect to him and he retreated deeper and deeper into himself, building walls around himself which grew taller and thicker daily. He had to keep the world at a great distance, only allowing a few trusted friends close. He was becoming homophobic to the extreme; love being such a sharp and double-sided knife. Yes, how to deal with people?

"O.K. then. I hope you both enjoy your stay in Western Australia," he smiled and left them.

Al returned to the current conversation from nightmare thoughts of his past and the deep-seated mistrust of everyone whom he had no proof of being able to trust.

"Could you imagine that happening in London, Al?"

"I couldn't imagine it happening anywhere in East Anglia, let alone London."

The chance meeting with their first native Australian left them both with a good warm feeling. They imagined that the sea of faces around them belonged to people like this man; kind, helpful, friendly. This was a good country.

Within the hour they were at a camp site seven kilometres out from the city along the Great Eastern Highway. It was still early and they were unable to put up their tents until someone packed and left, so leaving their packs in the office they went for a wander around the streets. There wasn't anything amazing to see, only that it was all so new to them. The space and barrenness was bewildering. Even the name of the road, the Great Eastern Highway, sounded as if it had come straight out of some romantic bygone age of great adventure, long since lost to a brave new modern world; the age of greed and progress and waste.

The sun rose higher in the sky and it was getting hot. A far cry from the drizzle and cold that they had left behind. Like stepping out of the depths of winter into the height of summer. Winter had lasted too long for both of them. Returning to the camp site they were now able to put their tents up.

"I'm going to get some food before I unpack." Tony said. It was a kilometre to the nearest shop and after so many hours, day and night, at each other's side Al stayed and Tony walked away. Time alone at last. Al unpacked and within a short time his tent was pitched and he was in his shorts. He wanted to make as much use of the available sunshine as he could. Thinking that he would be helpful he decided to get Tony's tent set up for him, but after several failed attempts, he became wound up and then gave up, so he retired to a picnic table in the sun and attempted to write what he felt. He was calm, very calm and that was worth noting. He closed his eyes and took a deep breath. The air was different here. The sounds were different too. It was a different type of warmth here. Scenes of East Anglia flashed through his mind. The smell of an estuary on a summer's evening, the sound of salt water lapping on mud, sand and gravel. The screams from a small flock of waders as they circled and dived along the tidal edge before landing and hunting for one more feed before the sun fell beyond a wooded hill. He sighed. Memories of estuaries and summer evening inevitably meant memories of Steven. He scratched at the surface, beneath which lay the pain. It was all so far away now, at least in physical distance, if not in time or thought. Al sensed someone close by, looked over to his bright green tent and saw Tony standing over the wreckage of his own.

"I did try to fix it, but as you can see I couldn't figure it out. So I left it!" Al's voice was lazy and without concern, he was busy sitting in the sun.

"Yeah, I can see that. What have you done to it?"

"Not a lot... as you can see!"

Tony arranged, then rearranged his poles and nylon, at first being as confused as Al.

"Oh I get it."

"I take it you've figured it out?"

"Yeah. It helps if you don't try to put it up inside out." Al turned his head and pulled his sunglasses down onto his nose, looking over the top of them at Tony's tent rising to become a massive dark green igloo made not of ice, but from man made materials. He was too relaxed to feel stupid, he hadn't felt this relaxed for months. Sitting with his eyes closed as he soaked up the sunshine, his skin hot, close to burning, it felt so good.

"I think that I'll go to the shop now. Did it turn out to be a long kilometre or a short one?"

"I'd say that it was a mile, if not more, so it's a long one!" Tony smirked.

Neither of them could picture a kilometre, but they both knew that there was one point six of them in a mile. Why had Australians converted to metric when they were an island and so far from the real world?

Al walked along the highway, looking into gardens as he went. They were barren, dry yellow grass, few flowers, few shrubs. A strange laughing from the top of a mature Eucalyptus tree burst into the heat. Al stopped to look for the source, he knew it to be a kookaburra. Looking up into and through the blue-green leaves which formed a massive domed canopy he could see the strange unshapely brown and white bird. A couple of parakeets few past chattering. He reached the food market; definitely a long kilometre, and went through the process of converting kilos into pounds and ounces and dollars into pounds and pence. A mixture of excitement and confusion filled his head. He tried to tell himself that this should be the greatest adventure of his life, but it wasn't and it certainly did not feel like it. At the forefront of his mind was Steven and being so very far from home, much further than he wanted to be.

It seemed like no time at all, but they had already been in Perth for three days. Three days of relaxing in the sun, quietly talking things over and wandering around the city without any regard for time as it ticked past and drifted away. Time was one thing that they both had plenty of. There was no urgency of having to do anything, though they were both equipping themselves with boots which covered their ankles and hopefully prevented snakes from biting them! There was an anticipation of a journey; lamps, stoves and water bottles were looked at and then bought, though neither mentioned any journey. No talk of anything further than the following few minutes. Al and Tony were happy in the stability which came from being together. Their surroundings were becoming more familiar and they were feeling less like strangers now. Both were glad to have each other's company and the bonds of friendship grew stronger with the passing days. They became at ease with their own problems by understanding each other's. It helped to know that they were not alone, either physically or mentally.

April was now May and the sun shone bright and strong. They soaked up the ultraviolet rays like they were going out of fashion, so much warmth. It seemed like last summer had never happened, so long ago now.

A young Australian chap pitched his tent beside them on the fourth day and sat talking to them for a while. He and Tony decided to go to the pub in the evening. Al didn't want to go, he had had enough alcohol to last him a life time. He was never any good with it and thought that Tony needed to adopt the same attitude for a while until he also got his alcohol problem under control. Alcohol could change someone so much, it was an evil drug with a wonderful taste which was hard to resist. It took away so many problems, only to replace them with others before the original problems returned with soberness.

Al sat in the evening sunshine before it fell behind the tops of the Eucalyptus and into the Indian Ocean. As the night fell the mosquitoes arrived. Al was glad of his lamp and he lay in safety inside his tent and read until he fell asleep.

He was woken suddenly, about eleven, by voices outside his tent in the darkness which rested with but a whisper of air movement. He had been in a deep sleep and it took him a few seconds to adjust to his surroundings, remembering why he was in a tent and then recalling the knowledge that he was in Australia. His senses returned to him. The voices, there were two, a man and a woman. The man was Tony, drunk. The woman, also drunk, was unknown.

"Tony's picked someone up at the pub. How could he do that? He's got a girlfriend at home, a girlfriend whom he says he loves."

For the following couple of hours a new noise was added to the sounds of the Australian night. Al felt sick at the thought of Tony cheating on his girlfriend. His head echoed with that thought and the memory and knowledge of Steven's actions.

* * * * *

It had been a strained day with long, dark, tense silences. The atmosphere was so thick it could have been cut with a knife. As always, Steven dealt with the problem by pretending that it did not exist; but if it did, then it was so trivial that he need not concern himself with it. Trivial to him, was not necessarily trivial to Al; and seldom was. Al tried to pretend that there was nothing wrong, bottling up his confusion and anger just as he always did. His stony silence was clear indication that there was plenty wrong. They avoided confrontation during the day, but the scales of control and calmness tipped that night. Steven sat in bed reading. The atmosphere grew blacker than black. Al looked coldly at Steven as he sat there in that bed in which Al was just the most recent sex partner of Steven. No matter how much work Al had done in the house and garden in the past four and a half years it still was not a home for him.

"How can you just sit there and act as if nothing is wrong?"

Steven was a little startled, he didn't expect this now. He looked up at Al who stood there shaking with confusion. Looking as lost as a new boy at a large school.

"What do you mean Al?" Steven answered. Al looked into Steven's eyes, he had that 'I haven't got a clue what you're on about' look in those bright blue eyes which made Al melt, made him weak at the knees. Steven knew only too well what Al was on about, Al was so predictable, but Steven knew how to handle difficult situations. He had learned that in the classroom, teaching disruptive pupils.

This situation had manifested itself from the arrival of a letter from Helga, an ex-girlfriend with whom Steven had a six month relationship many years ago. Helga's letters were always more in keeping with a current lover than one relegated to the annals of history. They were so often sexually explicit and Al found it unreasonable of Steven to allow it to carry on. It had been carrying on for many years, often through letters which were sent directly to his school, when Steven had already told Al that there would be no more. He had lied. It was just one of a series of lies which Steven told to Al, knowing full well that Al would believe everything he said. It was always just a matter of time before the lie was discovered and then the pain from the deceit would magnify the abuse of the act. Al insisted, as he always did, that if he was good enough to be living with him then he should be good enough to have his feelings taken into account and not brushed aside on the whims of an ex lover.

"I don't understand why you have to lie to me so much, or why you think far more of people who walked out on you than you do about the person who stands by you day in, day out, year after year. Can I be worth so little?"

"I do value you Al. You know that I do."

Al came back with a very sharp, "no I don't!"

"She won't write anymore Al."

"You mean she won't write here and you'll be more careful in future." Al was suffering badly, things had never felt so desperate before. He could not allow himself to believe that things would be alright just because Steven said they would, even if it was exactly what he wanted to believe. "I've been with you so long Steven, this just isn't fair. Not even I deserve to be treated this way. Shouldn't I expect anything from this relationship?"

Steven said nothing. How could he answer without making this situation worse? What could he say to defuse it? He was trapped in a relationship with Al that he only wanted to be short term and fun, but somehow he had let it drag on year after year. He could never find a way of saying that it was over without hurting Al. Hurting him was the last thing he ever wanted to do. Year after year passed by with the convenience of always having someone there, always being able to rely on Al's presence. It wasn't all bad either, sometimes he was really glad of Al's company, Al's natural happiness and optimism. Sometimes, he even loved Al, really loved him. But mentally and physically Al wasn't fulfilling, no one person could ever be both, or indeed for very long for Steven. He always wanted more and ended up with far less. He didn't understand Al's need to feel, as he put it, special. Steven knew that he could not do that for him, because Al wasn't special, at least not in the way that Al needed to feel. Al wanted too much from Steven and Steven could not fulfil those needs.

"You are important to me Al," Steven said meekly, and honestly.

"Am I!? Am I really? I suppose I should just accept everything you say, accept it all as it is and just be grateful that you don't screw around behind my back?"

Steven said nothing, he just sat in his bed looking at Al. His eyes lost in the glare that Al was giving him. He looked down in silence. In shame. Al went cold at Steven's silence and action. The words that Steven did not say sent an icy shiver through his body. For nothing more than a second Steven's eyes had cried out in immense pain to Al. A piercing scream of "help me" and "I'm sorry my love." The sight of Steven's eyes burned onto Al's retinas where their beauty and betrayal would always stay, a reminder to carry with him for the rest of his life. A reminder each time he closed his eyes and cried for Steven.

For minutes there was no sound, not even the sound of their own erratic breathing to break the silence. Al looked at Steven, Steven did not return the look. Al shook, he wanted to speak some words of love, there were none there, no words of any kind. In silence they were both terrified, though for different reasons. The room was cool and growing cooler, or was it just their body temperature which was dropping below that of the room. The room was dark, though a lamp was on beside Steven. A silence which lasted forever gave Al time to understand what Steven's eyes had told him, he knew what it meant, but still could not fully comprehend the thought that was flying around and around in his head. He stopped shaking and with a coolness and calmness of mind and voice he asked the question that he didn't want to ask. The question whose answer he did not want to know.

"You have cheated on me haven't you?" he said, almost in a whisper.

Steven looked up to Al, who was standing against the wall, which was half supporting his weight, He looked at Al, then down again at the quilt. His refusal, or was it inability to say anything angered Al. It hurt him.

"You have cheated on me!" It was no longer a question. It had happened and Al knew it and could not pretend otherwise. "Answer me! Don't just sit there, tell me the truth for once in your miserable life!"

There was another seemingly long pause. Tears rolled down Steven's face, he kept thinking not of how to lie, not of how he should have lied and been more careful, but of how he had hurt Al in the worst way he could have. He had sickened himself because he had always known how Al loved him. He never had a reason to doubt Al's feelings and even if he could not love Al in the same way that Al needed, then the least he should have done was not to have hurt him. Now at this moment, when he could see Al's world crumbling around him; a result of his actions, he realised how much he loved Al after all. He loved Al for always being there for him, for his company, his laughter, his love, his body. It was too late, Steven had just destroyed the very thing that he had been searching for all his adult life. How had he been so callous, cruel and stupid?

"I'm sorry Al," Steven whispered, his words tortured with emotion and truth.

Al stood there trembling, his mouth open, stunned. He wanted to cry, but there were no tears. He wanted to scream, but there was no sound. He felt sick, gasping for breath. He had heard what Steven had said, but somehow it didn't seem possible. He stood waiting for Steven to tell him that it wasn't really true, but he wasn't going to do that. The past four and a half years began to flash through Al's mind over and over again. He was confused. Distraught.

Yes, yes, yes, rang through his head again and again. Steven sat quiet and still in his bed, there was nothing to say. The horror of reality froze him, there were no words of comfort, no words to make right past wrongs.

"You couldn't have done, Steven. When could it happen?"

Al didn't want to hear the answer any more than Steven wanted to furnish it. A painful silence hung over them, it couldn't last and it didn't. If Steven had had any doubts about Al's reactions, then they were quickly dispelled.

"When!?" Al screamed. He screamed because it was an impossible question to ask. The impossible and most feared. He looked at Steven sitting in his bed and all he could see was the person he loved, the person he had trusted not to hurt him by doing this. Al wanted to hate him. He felt that he should be hitting Steven or something, anything. He should be making Steven hurt as much as he was hurting, but all he really wanted to do was to hug him.

The silence stood over them, heavy and dark. Dozens of answers and possible results from those answers went around and around in Steven's mind, searching for the right thing to answer which would make things better, or at least make it seem less bad. The right answer had not yet been written. Al's voice interrupted each thought like a giant bell sounding danger. When! When! When!

"It was only once," Steven said in a whisper, immediately realising the folly of his answer.

"What do you mean ONLY! It should have been never!" Steven's answer had had the worst possible effect. Had Steven been thinking as clearly as he was trying to, he would never have said only, he knew full well how it would incense Al who would see it as nothing more than a political statement of damage limitation. Was Steven serious in his attempt to play down this situation that he had caused? Al hoped not. Steven hoped that he could.

"Who was it Steven?"

"No one you know."

"Who!" Al screamed.

"I can't remember his name."

"Bullshit! You have sex with someone behind my back, you wouldn't forget that name in a hurry. You'd see that face and hear that name each time you'd touch me!" Al was shaking from head to toe. He did not want to know any more, but he had to know everything. He could not let it be. It was no trivial matter for him.

Steven didn't move a muscle, he watched Al as he got sucked deeper and deeper into his very own hell. Swallowed up, deeper and deeper and no hope of escape. What had he done? He tried to show Al that he did care by not waiting for him to ask the next, obvious question.

"It was a long time ago Al. It didn't mean anything," he said after some deliberation. He knew how bad that would sound to Al, but there was no better way of saying it.

"What? When?" Al asked quickly.

Steven looked helplessly at Al. He saw a young man whose world was crashing down around him while he sat watching from his bed, knowing that it was he who was undermining the foundations to life as Al perceived it. He watched Al's face soaked by the tears which were now streaming down from those dark eastern eyes of his, each teardrop carrying the pain from a thousand cuts. Al couldn't tell if Steven was as cold as he appeared to be, that wasn't possible, was it?

"When I went to Edinburgh, while you were at Daphne's." Steven answered Al's question.

Al had heard what Steven said, but something was missing, something was wrong with the answer he gave. The knife once again began to twist inside his head, Steven's words went around and around. What was it? What didn't sound right? Then the penny dropped.

"That was eighteen months ago! You bastard. You disgusting pervert! You cheat on me and that's not enough. You have the nerve to put your filthy hands on me. You've used me for a year and a half! What gave you the right to do that?"

Steven swallowed hard. It was all true and he knew it.

"What gives you the right to play God with my life?" Al's throat went dry, he thought about all those months, the falseness of it all. So much time had been taken from him, stolen, wasted, lost. He cried, his back slid down the wall and he sat in a wreck on the floor. Through his tear-filled eyes he looked around the room at the wardrobes which he had spent many months building. The wallpaper they had hung together, the carpet he had laid. What was it all for? Intruding into today was that bed from the past, which wasn't past after all and in it Steven sat playing at God, presiding over life itself, Al's life.

It was a hellish time for both of them. The minutes ticked past and the hours drifted away, leaving both behind in a situation which neither of them knew how to handle. Al's mind and body drained of energy. He just sat there staring at the opposite wall. He wanted to find himself waking up from this terrible dream and find out that that was all this was, a terrible dream. A trick of an over-active imagination. Steven in bed, not moving, terrified of inflaming the situation if he made the wrong move at the wrong time. He could not see that things had gone far too far for that.

Eventually, when the silence was broken, it was Al who spoke. His words floating gently over the pain in an almost apologetic tone.

"But I love you, Steven." Simple words, true words. Words and emotions from the heart and soul. Words which were stronger than the pain and anger. Steven broke down, crying uncontrollably. He didn't need to hear what he knew to be true. No matter how bitter Al could sound, Steven knew what lay below it all.

Slowly Steven got out of bed and knelt beside Al.

"I am so sorry Al. I didn't ever want to hurt you. I didn't mean to do that, I'm sorry." He reached out slowly, carefully, tenderly, resting his hand on Al's arm and cried.

* * * * *

"How did you pretend for so long Steven?" Al buried his head in his sleeping bag and clasped his hands over his ears in an attempt to shut out the horrendous noise from three metres away.

"Steven you bastard, why did you do it? What did I do to deserve such punishment? I loved you Steven, I loved you. I still love you. I want to be with you now." The tears that now flowed from his eyes were the same tears that he had been shedding now for four long months.

It had been a few weeks since he had last been in such a desperate state and now he realised just how stupid it was to be nine thousand miles from home. Christopher wasn't here to help him now, he wasn't here to pick up the pieces. "What the fuck am I doing here? It hasn't changed anything has it?"

The noise continued to carry from Tony's tent. An elderly couple in a nearby caravan were woken by the girl's yelp. Al's mind was being lacerated by the pain of his recent past. With no one here to turn to and he was drowning in his confusion. Another scream crossed the night. Of desire, or satisfaction? More likely pain from the sound of it, it reverberated around the camp site.

"Hell Tony, what are you trying to do? Fuck her to death?" It began to sound like mating time in the jungle and more and more people woke to their noise. A caravan door slammed not too far away. The noise continued.

"Poor Aussie slag, she's obviously got more than she bargained for with Tony."

Al could not cope with this situation which brought his past back to haunt him in the most graphic of ways. His thoughts and feelings were so confused that he could not finish one line of thought before his mind was departing on another one without reason. He crawled out of his sleeping bag, dressed and left his tent. He started to run through the camp site. The sounds of passion fading behind him. He reached the sanctuary of the empty and silent road.

It was the early hours of the morning, or was it night? That vague time before one o'clock which partygoers see as part of the evening before and workers on the morning shift see as a ridiculous time in the morning to be awake. Everything was still. Everything was silent. The night was black. The air was cool, but not cold, but his face felt cold for it was wet with the moisture from his tears. The only noises to break the silence of the night was the sound of his feet pounding against the tarmac and that of his very erratic breathing. He ran out onto the highway with no idea where it was that he was heading to.

Perth now took on a new image; no longer the warm, sunny and friendly city that he had got used to so quickly, now it was so very different in the domain of the night. The streets took on a hostile ambience. A dark, silent and inhospitable world where who knows what was lurking in the shadows on every corner?

Al stopped running, but only because he was not fit enough to carry on. He spent the next few hours wandering the streets of the inner city suburbs, with no idea of where he was once he left the main highway. A soft breeze whispered across his face in the wide, empty and dark streets. He was lost and alone, both physically and mentally. This was isolation. He could not remember where the camp site was. He had turned a few too many corners and become disorientated. He couldn't even remember what it was that had made him leave the safety of his tent. Where was Tony? Where was Christopher now he really needed him? How many times had he really needed him in the past few months?

"Oh Christopher, my strength, my love, my brother. I wish I could be with you. I wish I could have told you how I really felt instead of spending so much time pretending that I was coping. I'm so sorry, I wasn't trying to deceive you. Just trying to be strong." But Christopher was out of reach. Al was alone and totally lost and trapped in a state of hysteria. He wanted to stop walking. He was tired, but he didn't stop. He recognised a building. He had seen it earlier in the night. He had been here before. By five o'clock he found himself close to the airport. There were quite a few cars on the road now. Passing him by and creating eddies of cold air and dust as they went. He entered the building. Heavy duty carpets on the floor, people walking in all directions. He looked around, for nothing in particular, but his eyes met with a row of telephones, two of which accepted credit cards. Al walked towards one. He decided immediately and without hesitation or consideration that he would phone Steven. Had he been the slightest bit rational he would have realised what a bad mistake that would be. But then, had he been able to think in a rational and logical manner he would not have been wandering around the streets of Perth at that time of the morning; indeed, he would not have been in Perth in the first place.

The terminal building was lit up brightly against the darkness of the night, though it was now beginning to give way to dawn. The light hurt his tear-filled eyes and it took a little while to adjust. His hands fumbled in his wallet as he searched for the credit card which had the largest amount of credit on it. He swiped the card through the slot at the side of the telephone and nervously pushed the buttons; international access code, Great Britain, Ipswich, Steven. A moment of silence followed. This telephone which he was holding in Perth was going to connect him to Steven in Ipswich. He panicked and as the phone began its first ring, he hung up. His mind was racing around and around and nothing at all made any sense. He was frightened, though of what he did not know. Maybe the thought of hearing Steven's voice after so many weeks? It must have been nearly four weeks since he had last been to see him. He calmed a little, the desire to speak to Steven over-ruled his fears and confusion. 0011 44 473 and as he pushed on the last six digits he held his breath until he heard it ring. It rang. It was as if it was only a few miles away. He went cold. His body shook with anticipation and with fear. A new dilemma queued up in his head along side all his other problems. The latest being what the hell was he going to say if Steven answered the phone? He ignored that thought. He just wanted to hear the voice of the man he had lived with for seventeen hundred days. His thoughts were abruptly interrupted.

"Hello, Steven Brown."

Steven's voice went around and around in Al's head and for a while he couldn't speak. His mouth formed shapes, but no sound would form. Steven sounded so clear, so close, so real, almost as if they were together in the same room.

"Hello Steven, it's me," he answered rather lamely and stating the obvious. It sounded as if it had been years since he had spoken to Steven.

"Hi Al. How are you?" Steven asked nervously. It was obvious from his tone that he did not want to speak to Al and Al thought that the enquiry was a little shallow. Did it matter how he was? Just so long as he was out of the way?

"Steven, I miss you." Al wasn't planning to say that, indeed he wasn't planning anything. Somehow those words just came out. It was natural. It was true.

There was a long and heavy silence on both sides of the globe. Steven did not want to hear that and he avoided giving an answer to it.

"Where are you, Al? Are you phoning from Sudbury?"

Al paused, he hadn't expected that question. Steven should have just assumed that he was. He couldn't lie to him, not now, not ever.

"Um, no. I'm not in Sudbury."

"Are you in Ipswich?" A tone of concern as alarm bells began to ring inside Steven's head. Was Al coming around now?

"No," he answered.

"Where are you then?" The concern in Steven's voice being replaced by curiosity. He paused. He didn't want Steven to know, but he couldn't lie to him.

"I'm in Perth."

Steven thought that it was strange for Al to be in Scotland. The only people Al knew up there were in Edinburgh and they were Steven's sister and her boyfriend.

"What are you doing up there? You don't know anyone up there."

"No Steven. It's the other Perth."

Steven was silent on the other end of the line. What other Perth was there in Britain? The only other one he knew of was in Australia.

"The Perth down here." Al filled in the gap for Steven. "In Australia."

Steven thought about Al's statement. It didn't make sense. Al couldn't be in Australia, but why should he say that he was, if he wasn't? No, Al wasn't playing a game. This was no trick. He could never have lied to Steven and Steven knew that. He loved him too much, even if he was angry and trying to hate him.

"Al?" Steven was frightened by whatever it was that he was up to. He was frightened for Al. Who could he turn to out there? Who was there to help him? Steven was really beginning to see what it was that his actions had reduced Al to; a distraught, unstable, unpredictable mess. "What are you doing in Australia?"

"I don't know. I thought I wanted to be a long way from you, but I don't. I miss you, Steven." He began to cry. He wanted to be with Steven again. "Please give me another chance." Had it all been Al's fault? He was now believing that it was. "I promise not to hurt you again... and you can see whoever you want and do whatever you want. Just let me be with you... Please."

Steven gave no answer, he did not need this, not now, not ever. He didn't understand how it could be that Al found himself in Australia. It was extreme, even by Al's standards. How could he answer Al's pleas? They could never be together again. It was over. He didn't want the complications that would come from saying yes to Al, but at the same time he desperately wanted to say yes. He wanted to say yes because that would have been the easiest thing for him to say at this moment and it would allow Al to get a flight back to East Anglia, where once again he could be near friends. The conversation continued, though mainly through pauses and silences which made it more and more desperate, more and more painful. Al was in a mess and out of control, Steven knew what he was like and could picture him so clearly even if he was half a world away. Steven's tone hardened, he grew colder and colder, more and more distant, which only served in making things more final and distressing for both of them.

'Out of credit' began to flash on the telephone display and the line to Ipswich fell silent, then was replaced by a dull telecom tone which smacked of finality, hopelessness and isolation.

Around Al people marched towards the check-in counters, departed through their relevant gates. A mass of attaché cases and sombre suits. Minds focused on reading through business papers one last time before the mid-morning meeting in some other Australian city, in some other time zone. The buzz of the receiver rang in Al's head as he hung onto it in a weird hope that Steven was actually still there. Waiting for him to talk again. Waiting to hear his voice again. His head leaning against the perspex of the telephone booth, listening, crying, shaking. The feeling of isolation and rejection made him numb.

Now it's over and there's nothing left to say,
I leave, close the door, tomorrow won't be just another day,
This life of mine had been turned upside down,

Once here, now gone and never to be again.

We laughed, and then we cried,
Cold hearts, hot heads and tears,
Cold hearts, hot heads and tears,
Cold hearts, hot heads and tears,
I look back onto all those lost years.

Such pain cuts deeper than my knife,
I'll run, I tried and failed at being strong,
No distance can be far enough away,
Something once alive inside has now died.

We laughed, and then we cried,
Cold hearts, hot heads and tears,
Cold hearts, hot heads and tears,
Cold hearts, hot heads and tears,
I look back onto all those lost years with you.

It's over, and there's nothing left to say.

"Why couldn't you say that you'd try once more?" He cried.

* * * * *

In the late evening in Ipswich, Steven too was hanging onto the receiver, holding onto an empty hope that he was still able to hear Al.

"Why didn't I say yes to whatever Al had wanted, just so I could get him back to East Anglia so he could be helped?" He cried at the thought of Al alone in Australia. So far from home. So far from friends. There was no one out there for him to turn to. He grabbed a coat and left the house, feeling more than just empty. He walked through the town centre, with each step he recalled snippets of conversations past, a mishmash of memories, of pain. A cold wind blew through the streets, unusually cold for May. It had been a sunny day, a sign that at long last spring was here and summer was not far off, but this evening it was drizzly and depressing. The weather seemed to be a harbinger which he only now recognised, too late.

He passed the swimming pool and remembered the last time that they went swimming together, or rather the last time that they were going to go swimming together.

It was a few weeks after that hellish night and both Al and Steven had tried to continue with things as best they could, in the only way they knew how; Al by pretending that it hadn't happened and Steven pretending that although it had happened, it just didn't matter. Either way the end result was that they were making themselves ill. Not eating properly. Not sleeping. Sinking deeper into the abyss of dead love, no hope, no future.

Al was sitting in the dining room watching Steven get ready to go swimming. Steven was unaware of Al watching his every move. He looked to him, a little startled by Al's glazed expression.

"Why don't you come with me Al? A swim will do you the world of good. Go and get your things, I'll wait for you." He genuinely wanted his company and Al felt good about that, even if he knew that it was but a passing need and desire. Al didn't feel like going for a swim. He didn't feel like doing anything, but so strong was his desire to be a part of Steven's life, to be involved in whatever it was that he was doing, that he found himself smiling and running up the narrow Victorian staircase to fetch his towel, trunks and bag.

They walked towards the pool. Not much conversation and the atmosphere still a little on the tense side, but after the previous few weeks it wasn't so bad. It was cool outside, but not cold; the winter had been mild and dry. Al found anywhere depressing when it was cold and wet, especially Ipswich, so weather-wise it had been a good winter.

They were within a hundred metres of the swimming pool when Al realised that Steven's invitation had nothing to do with him trying to find a way forward together. It wasn't an attempt to mend the broken fences, nor was it a gesture of letting Al know that he was wanted. Being with Steven was a mistake that was too much for Al to cope with when he noticed that Steven was looking over at a youth on the other side of the road. Al tried to ignore it, Steven often looked at other men in a blatant manner which Al found offensive, especially now. He should have been used to it, but he wasn't and he could never get used to it, or accept it. They carried on walking, Al getting angry as each second passed and Steven still looking, totally oblivious to Al's presence, almost unaware that he was being so obvious. They were further away from what Al termed 'the piece of meat' that had caught Steven's eye and in order that he could keep looking at him, Steven turned to look over his shoulder. Al could no longer ignore Steven, who was looking in the opposite direction in which they were walking. What he had thought to be an attempt at reconciliation had turned into adding yet more insult to injury.

"I'm going back." Al turned and walked back the way they had come. Steven didn't even bother to ask why?" Was it a deliberate attempt to widen the chasm between them, making it impossible to bridge?

It took a couple of minutes to get back to Steven's house. Al had never felt that it was his home and never referred to it as such. He slammed the door shut.

"How the hell does he have the nerve! What am I still doing here? He's just a cock-happy queer and there's fuck all here for me. There never has been!"

Al was more angry with himself than Steven. Steven couldn't help himself, it was just the way he was, but Al? No, he knew what was what, but he refused to believe what was going on in front of him. He naively thought that Steven would change, could change. The more he thought about this evening and the events of eighteen months ago the more incensed he became. Within minutes he stormed up the stairs and entered Steven's study. He pulled open the middle draw on his desk. For a few seconds he paused. He looked down into the clutter of loose papers, photographs and... and diaries. Slowly, very slowly his hand moved forward and in amongst the litter. Searching, searching, until he found a small red book. A diary. Gently he lifted it out of the drawer. Ran his hand over the cover, wiping away flakes of dust, before carefully laying it on the desk. He moved in and searched for another, found one and went through the same process, treating it as delicately as one handles a thin-shelled egg, a new born baby, a lolly that has melted free from its stick. Six times he eased from the drawer a little red book, until all six rested in a stack on the desk, cleansed of dust. Before him, in six volumes were the most intimate, most painful, most heart-felt feelings which came from deep within Steven. Things which he could not bring himself to discuss with anyone, but he had let Al read all of them, apart from three pages which Steven had torn out one night when Al had started to ask questions, which obviously touched a raw nerve. Al had guessed what it was about and because it was something he didn't like and didn't want to know about he shut it out of his mind, but was also hurt that he wasn't trusted.

 Al picked up the diary with the missing pages. Outwardly, five of the six looked the same. The one with the missing pages was one of the five and Al knew which one of the five it was. It felt dark. It held secrets. Dark heavy secrets and although the words were no longer to be found inside amongst its pages, Al could feel it was still there. He sensed it. It was his sixth sense. Like the times he would dream of violent Earthquakes days before a major quake would happen. If only he could have developed this and used it. He might have been able to avoid the situation he was now in. He might have seen it coming. He lifted the diaries, gently, carefully. In his hands were nine years of emotions. Carefully he carried them down the stairs and into the dining room, placing them on the carpet by the fire. Al cried as he gently cut the string binding from each batch of sheets. Eight pieces of string in each book were cut enabling him to separate the sheets of Steven's words without tearing a single page. He filled the open grate with page after page, then brought a box of matches from the kitchen and sat in front of the fireplace. Taking a match from the box he hesitated before running its firm sulphurous head along the side of the box. It flared up like a massive incendiary device. Its orange-yellow flame swayed in the down-draft from the chimney flue. The match shook in his hand, the flame moving gradually along the little piece of pine leaving a charred and shrivelled contortion behind in its wake. It burned shorter and Al slowly moved it towards the edge of a sheet of the diary. All these years and he had not dreamt of doing this, even though he would have liked Steven to get rid of them. A small yellow flame slowly took hold and grew like a disease across the paper. The match burnt Al's finger and thumb, he dropped what was left of it, a plume of grey smoke rose from it and mingled with the flames from the ever growing fire. He sat in silence. Eyes locked onto the scene in front of himself. Unhappy and ashamed, as the flames spread until line by line they engulfed every word in a hot orange-yellow furnace. A wall of heat rushed out from the grate, heating Al's face to the point of pain, then began to die leaving behind a heap of fluffy black ash. As the last puff of grey smoke melted away, he knew that he had done wrong, but he was lost so deeply in his own unhappiness that he no longer understood the difference between right and wrong.

 It was such a long hour until Steven returned from the swimming pool and Al greeted him at the door with words that he would never have expected to hear.

"Steven," he hesitated. "I've... I've burnt your diaries." Tears in his eyes as well as love, though the love was hard to see through the pain.

Steven looked at him in disbelief, Al couldn't have done that? Al couldn't lie to him either. He walked through to the dining room and saw the grate full with the remains of burnt paper. It could have been any paper. He poked around in the ashes, nothing was recognisable. Al followed sheepishly into the dining room. Steven went upstairs. Al heard the drawer slide open, he heard papers being moved, pushed here and there. Then silence.

He came slowly down the stairs and looked with incomprehension at Al who was just standing there, not gloating, not ashamed, totally without any expression.

"Why Al? Why did you do something like that? You had absolutely no right to do that!" It was rare for Steven to raise his voice to Al, though he often felt like doing so. Al looked at Steven, shook his head. He didn't understand any of this. He didn't understand how a month ago he had everything and now it was all falling away from him without reason, without sense, as masonry falls from a neglected Norman castle, a Roman fort slipping onto the North Sea.

"I'm not proud of it Steven, I'm not even glad I did it. I know it was wrong, but rightly or wrongly I felt that I had reason to do it."

Steven didn't understand, that showed Al how wrong the relationship was, not that it made it any easier. Even if he and Steven had totally different ideas of right and wrong it didn't take away the fact that he loved him.

"We were going out for a swim. At your invitation. A few weeks after I find out that you've cheated on me and you proceed to gorp at someone in the street; not just look, but gorp in such a blatant manner. Do you really have no idea how dirty I feel because of your actions?"

Steven looked hard at Al, then softened his gaze. Al was obviously coping far worse than he had realised, but what could he do to help?

"How can you be so bloody insensitive?" He paused and let Steven digest those thoughts. Steven really had no idea of Al's feelings, he was as guilty as Al in only seeing what he wanted to see. "I know there are no excuses for what I've done, I'm not trying to justify it, or excuse it, just explain it. It doesn't make sense, nothing makes sense anymore. I'm sorry Steven. I really am sorry. All I really know is that I feel so utterly and totally confused and dirty and lost and I need you to help me. I need you to take this pain away for me."

Steven arrived at Julian's flat, knocking on the window as he walked to the door. Julian answered.

"Hello Steven, come in," he said in his usual cheerful manner. "What brings you here at this time?"

"Guess." Steven answered bleakly.

"Oh no. What's he done now?" It was as much an enquiry about Al's well-being as it was about any problem he had caused. All their friends had tried hard to maintain a neutral position in the middle of the mess that Al and Steven had found themselves in, which wasn't easy. They went into Julian's bed-sitting room. A piano in one corner, harmonium in another. Stacks of books and records filling up any and every gap around the room.

"He's just phoned. He said he was calling from Perth airport."

"He was probably at Heathrow. I expect he went up for the day. Why on Earth would anyone want to go up to Perth? He doesn't know anyone up there, does he?" Julian tried to make light of the situation. He laughed, Steven didn't respond.

"That's what I said, but he said it was Perth... Australia."

"Oh don't be silly! Maybe he was at an airport and maybe it was Perth, but Australia! Come on Steven, even that's a bit extreme for Al."

"I know it sounds stupid, but he is there. I know he is, Julian, he can't lie to me and something bad must have happened for him to call and beg me to give him another chance like he did. I haven't heard from him for so long and he sounded as bad as he ever has. What can I do?"

"Well, if he really is in Australia, which I very much doubt, there isn't an awful lot you can do. He can take care of himself. He'll be alright. In a couple of days he'll probably turn up in Ipswich and say he got a one week return or something. If, as I've said, he is in Australia."

"You really don't think he's there?"

"No I don't. Not Al, no."

"Maybe you're right Julian. It's just that he sounded so bad and I have been a bastard to him. I wasn't fair, I can see that now. I never gave him the chance to say no more, because I never told him the truth. I guess I miss him. I wouldn't want him back, but I really miss him. It's all very well picking someone up for the night and sex with someone new is exciting, but I'm so lonely the rest of the time. He's always been there for me. Reliable, dependable Al. I do something, say something, or hear something that he liked and a whole flood of memories come back and I'm torn between thinking I'm such a bastard and I'm glad it's over. But he's always there, in a tree, by the river, sitting in a chair, at dinner, in a song, in bed, he's always there."

* * * * *

He hung the receiver back onto the telephone and turned, crying, towards the exit. City business men and women en route to Sydney and Melbourne stared at Al as they walked past. Al had no concern for them. He was alone, tears running down his face. He bumped into a few very astonished people as he left the building. How many times in the past few months had he felt that he was at the lowest point in his life? He was feeling it once again. How much more was there? Surely things could only get better?

As he exited through the glass door he bumped into a well-dressed and very attractive business woman. Her eyes met with Al's. They were full of hopelessness. It was as if she seemed to understand what Al was going through and knew that there was nothing she could do to help. Her eyes burned a feeling of hope into Al's mind, to the very core of his being. A feeling that somehow this wasn't the end of everything he knew and understood. A feeling that he would never forget.

The fresh morning air hit Al's face as he ran from her seeing eyes. He ran without looking and fell onto the pavement, cold and alone, shaking and crying. The pain he was feeling was ripping him in all directions. The distress from a situation that he could not deal with. One of the many feelings that life has to offer that can only be understood through experience in life. An experience from the rich and varied tapestry of life. A bitter tasting flesh from the most beautiful looking fruit that everyone wants to eat, but no one wants to

[handwritten: a transparent style, decently controlled, slipping to hint at its own unease]

taste.

He picked himself up from the cold paving slabs and walked slowly along the road. He began to realise that nothing looked familiar to him. The direction in which he was now walking was not the same way in which he had come. His head spinning with one thought and one thought only, Steven. Again and again the fragile and brief conversation; it wasn't so brief, lasting over twenty minutes, ran time and again through his thoughts. A tape with automatic replay was at work and Steven's voice could be heard as clearly as if he was standing next to him. Despite his current situation of being lost and confused he was now surprisingly calm. The sun rose over the horizon, above the roof tops and trees. In the near distance was the rumble of some early morning traffic and a strange wattle-wattle of some bird, calling unseen from high up in the Eucalyptus canopy. The crows and kookaburras were laughing at him from a great height. The cool morning air emphasised his loneliness and the strange bird calls accentuated just how far he was from home.

By seven o'clock he had found his way back to the camp site. He remained calm, almost as if nothing at all had happened. It was like a fuse had blown and shut down a circuit in his crazy mind, now being quite matter-of-fact about the day ahead. The day ahead? He would have breakfast and leave Perth.

The air began to warm as he sat in the doorway of his tent eating. The first rays of light to make it over the trees on the camping ground found his face and rested there a while. It felt pleasant. Tony was still asleep as the morning dew began to dry from the tents, leaving them with that brand new look of straight out of the plastic bag. The grey-blue leaves glistened as the last drops of moisture evaporated in the gentle breeze. They hung like fingers of satin from the branches and whispered light shadows on the grass below. Al crawled into his tent and began to pack, taking care not to make any noise which was avoidable.

"Is that you Al?" Tony called from inside his tent.

"Yes, I didn't realise that you were awake. It's a beautiful morning out here."

"I wasn't," he said, making it clear that it was Al who had woken him. "What are you doing? It sounds as if you're packing."

"Yes. I've decided to leave Perth this morning."

"What! Why? Hang on Al. Don't you go tearing off. I think we ought to talk about this." Tony was alarmed about Al's sudden desire to leave. He had not said anything of the sort yesterday. What had happened to cause this?

Tony was quickly dressed and appeared from within his dark green dome.

"What's wrong Al? Why are you going?"

Al thought about the question before answering. He looked at Tony. He had been a good friend, but he could not rely on him forever.

"It's time to move on. I just need to be alone now. If I was an Arab I would say... It is written." He said those last words in as Arab-like a voice as he could, actually sounding more Russian than Arab. He smiled, but Tony could see right through it.

"Fuck that! Sometimes I don't understand what the fuck you're on about. When you die you ought to donate your brain to medical science, it would keep them puzzled for a few years. And you're not a fucking Arab so why the hell are you going, Al?" Tony was angry and afraid for Al's safety.

"I just need my space now. I always said I'd go."

"I know that Al, but it's just that it is a bit sudden. A bit sooner than I had anticipated."

"There's no time like the present. Strike while the iron's hot and all that crap. You know me Tony, not exactly one of the world's most rational people, am I?"

"Yeah, and don't I know it!"

Tony was disturbed by this apparent calmness and control. Al was never calm, nor was he in control. He was afraid for his friend, but he could not stop him from doing whatever it was that he had planned, or not planned as was probably the case.

"Does it have anything to do with last night?" Tony asked, looking Al straight in the eyes. If he could get Al to talk, really talk, then maybe he could get Al to change his mind?

"No, Tony," he replied, returning his gaze. "It's just me, isn't it." Whatever had happened last night, which may or may not have triggered the events of this day were no more than that, a trigger, not the cause. Al felt sorry for Tony for last night. He felt sorry for his girlfriend. He was however, in no position to judge his friend and would not do so. Tony was his friend and that was all that mattered.

He too had problems and Al was unable to help him with them. He didn't understand them. He didn't understand his own. They sat in the sun for a while, thinking over last night in the bright Perth morning. They were losing something here, something they both needed, but maybe it was for the best in the long run. They shared the moment with no more questions and no reproaches, while it lasted.

"I phoned Steven this morning." Al said in passing interest.

"Why?" Tony was alarmed.

"Why?" Al laughed. "That's a silly question to ask me. I'm the last person who would know the answer to that sort of conundrum."

"Are you alright?"

"Yeah Tony, I'm alright." Al sounded surprised by the question.

"I mean alright?" Tony's tone was deliberate and full of emphasis on alright.

Al nodded. He understood exactly what Tony meant. Tony gave a sigh of relief and smiled, showing off his cute dimples and boyish looks.

"You knew that I'd go off on my own."

"Yes I know, but after just four days? It's a bit soon. Can't you wait until tomorrow? I've got to be here for..." Tony stopped short of saying her name and Al got the picture anyway.

"No Tony. I think it's best if I just go while I feel O.K." At least Al knew that Tony could take care of himself and even if he ended up feeling guilty about leaving him behind he wouldn't have the worry of Tony being alright.

They sat quietly together for a while. Enjoying the morning and a few precious last moments together. The sort of silence that under its weight true friendship doesn't buckle beneath, unable to stand the pressure of silence and stillness. They thought about college days, they had met there three years earlier. Occasional chance meetings in Ipswich, with never enough time to stop and talk for more than a few minutes. Then it was that their paths crossed again, at a time when they were able to help each other and for the past three months they had spent so much time together. Neither would have guessed when they met that they would have found themselves in Australia together, or under such circumstances.

"What did Steven have to say?" Tony resumed the conversation.

"Not a lot. What could he have said? He doesn't believe that I'm in Australia." Al laughed. He could see the funny side of it now. He could picture Steven's face when he told him. "He thinks I'm in Scotland!"

"It must have cost you a fortune to phone and I bet that you were on for more than a couple of minutes."

Al smiled at that and told Tony of the wonderful invention called credit cards.

"I feel really sorry for Steven. He's going to end up old and alone now. One day he's going to wake up and realise that life has passed him by and all the fun he thought he was having will have gone. He'll realise it's all over. He'll never find anyone who'll take the crap that I did and for all my bad points at least I loved him and I wasn't just after whatever I could get from him."

Al finished his packing. Tony ate breakfast and by ten o'clock Al was ready to leave.

"Oh well Tony. I guess this is it. I'm going east. Maybe I'll see you in Kalgoorlie in a few days?"

"Yeah," Tony said vaguely. "I'll look out for you Al. Take good care of yourself won't you... and try not to panic too much." He smiled again, flashing those dimples which glowed golden in the morning light against his red cheeks. They exchanged a long handshake, then Al left Tony sitting by his tent as he walked off towards the highway. Tony's heart sank as he watched his crazy friend leave on an adventure into the unknown.

"If you are real God, please look after him. He's not a bad bloke and he needs all the help he can get. Don't do anything stupid Al. Don't!"

Al was soon out of sight. He wanted to look back to Tony, for reassurance, but he had to be strong and self-reliant and if he had looked back he knew he would have cried and shown Tony that he did not really want to go and that he didn't know what he was doing. He needed to know that Tony at least thought that he was alright.

Reaching the highway and put his pack down. There was still so much empty space in it. He wondered why they were made so big? Didn't he have everything that he needed? In the sky it was blue in all directions. Not a cloud in sight. Another beautiful Australian day.

"Dear Sarah and Christopher, Well here I am upside down in the world and I'm impressed with the little I've seen so far. Perth is so clean and modern and the natives are friendly. It's 28°C and I'm enjoying the sun. I can't really believe I'm here yet. I wish you were here with me. There are parrots and kookaburras flying around and palm trees along the river. Tony and I are being really lazy, but so what! We're in a camp site about four miles out from the centre, not far from the airport. Take care, lots of love, Al."

"Steven, I'm sorry that you don't feel that you need to help me. I'm also sorry that you feel that it is so easy to throw me to one side and kick me when I'm down. I'm leaving Perth today and look forward to reaching the barren Nullarbor, it will be kinder to me and I should find peace there. I love you and did not deserve the treatment you gave me. One day you'll realise what a rotten bastard you have been. Love, Al."

"What the hell am I going to do now?"
He didn't even try to answer that one. His last link with a friend, with security, was now severed. Now he was really going to be alone. Al tried not to judge Tony. What right did he have to do so? Was he so perfect that he was in a position to judge? It seemed to Al that Tony was only letting himself down and Al felt that he could not stay and watch his friend self-destruct on alcohol and promiscuity. Nothing Al could do would help Tony, anymore than anything that Tony could do would help Al. For both of them, they had to look inside themselves for the answers to their problems.

"This is a chance of a life time. Thousands of people would love to be in my place. This is going to be fun." He wasn't really fooling himself, but he tried just the same. He scribbled a sign, N 94 EAST. There wasn't a lot of choice. North and south of Perth there seemed to be a lot of space that didn't really go anywhere and to the west was the Indian Ocean, next stop South Africa. East seemed to open a whole can of worms; so many possibilities. Before too much time had passed a car stopped and Al got in. The driver was a young chap, maybe a little younger than himself, and was from the Rhondda Valley. They had a chat about Wales and Australia and after a ten minute drive Al was left at the side of the road in Midland. The thought of standing at the side of the road in Australia sounded wild to Al. Who would have thought that he would ever have found himself here? After four days here the novelty had not worn off. A few minutes passed before he had another lift. This time with a Scot.

"Are there many Australians in Perth?"

"Put it this way, there are a hell of a lot of Brits!" His driver answered with a laugh.

They reached the outskirts of the city and began to climb up a ridge. Perth stretched out behind him on that massive sand plain. Now they were entering bush. It was so different from anything he had seen in Europe. It all looked so dry and the trees were not of the lush greens of home, but of a beautiful, cool, blue-grey-green. It all looked so wild, primitive. This was the Australia he had always dreamt of. At any moment Skippy would come bouncing out of the trees to see him and say 'tut tut tut tut'! Mile after mile of trees, a few patches cleared for cattle. After twenty minutes he was left at the side of the road in what seemed to him to be the middle of nowhere in particular at all. Al watched as the car disappeared along a dusty track and over the hill. He looked around, there were no cars on the highway, just bush in all directions. He looked back to the track. The dust had soon settled and the only trace of a car passing were the tracks in the soft red sand. Gradually he realised the predicament he was in. There was nothing here. This was not Suffolk. There wasn't going to be a village over the hill and around the corner. The fuse that had blown in his mind in the early hours of the morning had not been replaced. He didn't give a damn and maybe it was better that way.

"Oh well, that's what life is like! I can't do anything about it now so why worry?" This was not Al talking, though it was his voice. He picked up his pack and just started walking up the hill. If he had been the slightest bit rational and practical he would have been worried. Almost as if this was normality for him, he strolled along the road looking at the different species of Eucalyptus and the many other plants that he didn't have names for.

"At least there's plenty of places to put up a tent for the night," he consoled himself. Not that he'd ever camped away from hot and cold running water before, or alone. He was content as he wandered along the road, unconcerned about the next minute, hour or day. Half an hour past and then someone stopped for him. He was a young chap, though older than himself and the first Australian that he had met to talk to. He was going to Kalgoorlie and Al thought that it must be his lucky day and prepared himself for a couple of hours journeying. He had grossly under-estimated just how far this part of Australia stretched. Indeed how far the whole of Australia stretched and as for kilometres, well! They meant absolutely nothing to him. On his map it was a distance of seven centimetres. That couldn't be far? It wouldn't be far on the scale of maps which he was used to, but this wasn't what he was used to.

The landscape changed from hills and bush into flat, dry prairie. He was in the wheat belt. In the first instant the vastness and harshness of this open landscape was impressive, but soon the novelty began to wane and his European eyes grew tired of the bleak land. It seemed that Australia had not heard of the American dust bowl as the farming practises they were employing here would ultimately achieve a similar result before too long.

By mid-afternoon they stopped at a small and unfriendly township called Southern Cross. Outside of the car it was hot, the air dry and laden with dust. Grant didn't have a lot to say for himself and as Al wasn't in the mood for conversation this suited him fine. A hot coffee helped lift the boredom from Al's mind. He forgot about the events of this morning and only thought of the here and now with a cold and calculating tunnel vision. Not one thought side-tracked from this moment in time.

They pressed ahead with their journey. Stopping again a few kilometres outside of the settlement. There were three other cars at the side of the road and people standing around watching a dog which had been hit by a car. They got out to look at the dog as it dragged its back two legs behind it. Grant decided to drive back to Southern Cross and get someone to come and help it. Help for this animal meant a bullet in the head, it was hurt that badly.

After that they once more raced through the nothingness of flat wheatlands and slowly the scenery changed back into bush, behind them the flat open fields merged into the horizon and were gone. Time was passing faster than the kilometres and Al realised that they would not make it to Kalgoorlie until after dark. This thought worried him. He who had wandered most of the previous night alone in Perth was worried about arriving in a small inland town alone. It wouldn't even be night, just late evening and dark. His tunnel vision broadened and allowed him to imagine panicking because he had nowhere to stay.

"Can you drop me off at the next rest area please?" he asked casually.

"What for?" Grant was surprised by this request. "Maybe he needs a piss," he thought.

"I think I'll stay out here and see some of the real Australia. That's what I came for," he lied. He came to run away, die if possible.

"But there's nothing out here."

"Yes, I know. That's why I like it so much. No people." A few more Ks down the road and Al got out of the car.

"Are you sure that you want to be left out here?" Grant asked.

"Yes, I think so. Never done this before, so I may as well do it now."

"Well, good luck. I think that you'll need it."

Al didn't understand what Grant meant, so he thanked him for the lift and said good-bye, then stood coughing in the cloud of dust left by the car as it sped away. It merged into the horizon and was gone.

"Now that was really stupid, wasn't it!"

It was the middle of nowhere. It was just bush and more bush and he didn't even know just how far he was along the little line on his map. Al looked around, the ochre sand stretched endlessly in every direction. The blue-green of the Eucalyptus leaves contrasted starkly with it and the blue of the sky. Mile upon mile of red soil, mile upon mile of bush. He was really alone now.

AUSTRALIAN RAIN

Boorabbin, 4th May 1989

"Oh well, looks like I'm here for the night," he said nonchalantly as he turned around and merged as one with the bush, lost so quickly from the view of anyone who might have passed that way, not that there was anyone else about. He had a compass, not that he bothered to use it, taking note of the position of the sun in the sky and the time was enough. If he got lost? Tough! Who would be there to care? He wandered off, only having to walk for ten minutes before he found a space suitable for his tent, which he quickly pitched. He looked around and wondered what he would do now, there wasn't much that he could do, so he walked off and explored the area, taking note of anything which might look a little different, which would help him find his way back again. The trouble was that everything looked the same. No extra large trees, rocks or anything that was so obviously different. His stomach rumbled. Food? He hadn't given a thought to food, or water. Making his way back to the tent the first thing he did was to have a drink of water, he had not had a lot of fluid during the day and he knew how quickly he dehydrated.

"Less than half a gallon left. That won't last long."

He searched his bag for food. What was left? A piece of bread, rice and curry powder.

"Not exactly prepared to go bush are you!"

"Oh well, never mind. Curried rice for tea. How does that sound to you?"

"I think that sounds bloody awful to be honest. What about meat and veg?"

"Well, if you can go out there and find some meat and veg, then I'll be happy to cook it for you. If not..."

"Actually, curried rice sounds O.K."

"Good! That's settled then."

Cooking rice uncovered in a frying pan was wasteful of water and curried rice alone was not so good. At least he would have bread for breakfast, but then what? Did it matter? It wasn't right that he should not be bothered by his lack of food and preparation, but he just did not care. Tony was right, he wasn't himself.

He couldn't think why on earth he had left the security of a car and a town at the end of the journey. Sure, he would have panicked, but there would have been showers, milk and real food to be had in the morning. What he was doing was silly and potentially dangerous. It was a way out, not an easy way, but... He was so calm that had anyone seen him they would surely think that he did this sort of thing all the time; an expert at going bush?

The evening drew in close. His fifth night in Australia, but also his first in Australia. There were no safe city sounds here as the bush began to fill with the strangest noises that he had ever heard. He looked out from his tent; it was still warm, but he could see no life from which the sounds were omitted. He ate his food, he must have been hungry as it did taste rather good. He lit his lamp and as soon as he did a thousand insects seemed to gather at his side, so he zipped up his tent taking refuge inside.

He was feeling as calm as he had when he left Tony this morning and he was glad of that.

"Poor Tony. It wasn't fair to leave him like that, but I couldn't stay around knowing what he was doing. It wasn't really because of him that I left anyway. Last night was just the tip of the iceberg." Al wrote down his thoughts as they occurred to him, some obscure and seemingly nothing to do with his life now, many from his childhood, his adolescence. If he thought it, he wrote it. All played a part in forming the person he now was. All could hold a clue to what he should do. Here, he had no distractions. He could think.

The strange noises outside, merged into an orchestra of sound that drifted around in the darkness as he wrote late into the night. There would be no intrusion here. He felt alone, he was alone. It was what he needed, it was what he got. It was safety.

It was early when he awoke, but not too long before light began to break. The air rang with the sound of crow and raven from perches high in the canopy of damp blue Eucalyptus. In less than a week in this strange and wondrous land it had become a familiar, though still a peculiar noise. Al could not help but smile each time he heard it. In his head he could picture the large black birds falling down from the trees as they called, ah-ahh-ahhhhhh. The last note extra long and fading to an end.

He lay listening to the noises, then peered outside at the half-dark and sighed. The sun rose and once it was high enough for its light to pass through the tops of the trees and find his tent, it soon became warm. Al, feeling calm, relaxed and totally unpressured, decided that there was no urgency in leaving here. He would spend this day in the bush.

He pulled open his tent, the sunlight poured in. Outside the last of the morning dew burned away to leave all dry once more. The light lay on his olive skin, warm and good.

"I'll get a decent tan here," he said to himself as he lay naked, basking. There was no other soul around for miles, hours maybe, but he would not lay outside of his tent, as that, for him, would not be proper. Nudity was a private thing and only persons of dubious morals would strip in public. Steven indulged in such things. Steven, even if Al did not want to believe it, even if he loved him, was one of those people who fitted into Al's 'of dubious morals' category.

Twenty four hours previous Al had been wandering lost and distraught around the streets of Perth. Making a desperate phone call halfway around the world. He had left a good and trusted friend behind and run off to where he found himself now. In contrast, here, he was miles from anywhere that remotely resembled anything from home, lying naked in the hot sun; if inside a tent, reading 'The Origin', as if he was without a care in the world. Every half an hour he turned himself in order to get an even tan without burning.

"Now I know what it must be like to be an oven-ready chicken!" he joked with himself.

The day began to drift. He returned to his writing and his thoughts turned to Steven. Calmly he thought of the man whom he loved and tried to understand what had happened, when it had happened; and why? It didn't make sense to him. How could it? He stopped and thought as he watched the bush for any sign of life. None to be seen, apart from plants. He began to tan in the pouring sun. The heat was radiating, raining.

"Yes it is raining! This is Australian rain." He sat up and looked at the blue sky. It was a different shade of blue from the skies at home. The sun was certainly bigger in the sky here. He felt, but could not admit to it, that Australian rain was also the pain and isolation he was feeling. The pain was from Steven. The isolation from being so far from home and friends. The harsh environment was merely a reflection of his own mind and that was why he felt calm and safe.

Comfort in the torment of being at the edge of existence as he understood it. Alone. No one on this planet knew where he was. No one.

The day grew hotter and drifted along, taking Al with it. Not having a care in the world, he relaxed. His water had long since finished and he was unconcerned. There was no more food to eat, save for rice and without water it wasn't really much good to him. They were minor details which for a brief moment had occupied a few cells of thought in his mind and then as with the time that passed him by, so did his thoughts.

Dressing, he left the tent. His skin warm beneath his shirt and shorts; warm, but not burnt. His semi-Mediterranean skin took quite a lot of ultra-violet before it burned. He stretched and looked around. The small red-sanded clearing lay still. The grey of Eucalyptus bark stood like an old charred graveyard, the aftermath of a most violent explosion of heat, many, many years ago. The blue-green leaves cast a thin shadow onto the floor of the wood. Dappled yellow-blue light came through the gaps and speckled the sand in hot brightness and warm dull patches of shadow. Looking around, he found a heavy stick and picked it up after checking for spiders and other crawlies.

"Hunting!" he said to the bush. "Kangaroo, wallaby, maybe a snake or lizard? Knowing my luck it will be nothing more exotic than a bloody rabbit!" And so he headed off into the bush. Avoiding twigs which lay on the ground which would have given his approach away, he zig-zagged his way deeper and deeper, quietly into the bush. The firm damp sand was noiseless beneath the soles of his trainers. Eyes darting first one way and then another, scanning rocks, leaf litter, tree trunks. He hunted, further and further from his tent, as if he had done this everyday of his life, as if he knew what he was doing.

"Ah-ahh-ahhhhh." A crow called down from a high branch. Too high and too hidden to be able to throw a rock at it. Al stood still and silent, looking, always looking. He was no hunter and there was nothing to be seen to hunt even if he was.

"So much for the plagues of kangaroos and rabbits," he turned. "Shit! Which way did I come?" He looked at the ground. So skilful had he been at being quiet that there were no broken twigs, moved leaves, kicked rocks, or even slight traces of a footprint left behind in the firm sand. The bush looked wild and untouched by humans since the dawn of times but of course he knew that it wasn't so. This stand of forests was not as wild as it appeared at first glance. How many forests, untouched by man, only have trees of the same age?

He had hunted for an hour and now he searched for his way back to his tent for another hour and still he had not returned. He was hungry and hot. He was thirsty. It had been too many hours since he had his last taste of water. He wanted some water now. His lips dry, his head light. Yes, he was thirsty and he did realise that he had to drink soon, but much to his surprise he didn't really care. If he had been all emotional and irrational he could have understood this unbothered attitude of his, but he was calm, cool and logical and still he didn't care. It was unlike him. He continued the search for his little green tent and though the green was a bright shade, it did not stand out amongst the greys and blue-greens. It was another hour before he found his mobile home, an over-heated ball of nylon. A wall of heat hit him as he unzipped it. To his amazement and horror, inside, an army of giant ants had eaten their way through the groundsheet and were searching for food. Al was struck with horror!

"You little bastards! You may as well fuck off because I've got nothing for you! Do you think that I'd be out here wandering about in the hope of at least catching a snake, if I had any food in here?"

Al leaned inside and began the war of regaining his home from the invading armies. He hadn't realised that ants could grow so large; over a centimetre in length and even more robust than the species he was used to.

Hot, tired, hungry and thirsty, he lay in his tent trying to forget about food and water; that proved difficult with the noises being made by his stomach and the dryness of his throat, getting sore. Being hungry was worse than starving and he knew that he would not starve for many days yet, he ate too much under normal conditions to starve easily now. Not that he had fat reserves anywhere on his body, being the skinny little runt that he was.

"I wish you were here Christopher. I need to talk to you." He repaired the floor of his tent. "Not that I'm ever truly open about my feelings with you. It's not right. I'm always on aware of everything that you've done for me and I want you to be proud of having me as a friend. I shouldn't spend so much time trying to impress you, it never happens anyway. You've seen me at my worst and you still love me, why? I came here to die, but I'm still here. I don't like the way I've been feeling and I don't see a future without Steven. More to the point, I don't want one. It was stupid to trust anyone quite so much. It was stupid to build my life around him and it was stupid to think that it would last forever. Naive? Yes, I suppose so, but stupid mainly. I trusted him Christopher, I believed him! I gave him a hard time, but why shouldn't I have expected a little more from him? I gave enough myself. What the hell am I doing in Australia? I can't believe that I chose to be here. It just isn't like me, is it? Oh Tony, by the way I'm going to Australia. What A cretin! No wonder he gave me such a strange look. I bet he's worrying about me now. I'm sorry Tony. I'm sorry. I'm lucky that I've got such good friends, though they must be really pissed off with me now. They were always there for me, all of them, but for so many months? It's just as well that I've come down here, I can't be a nuisance to anyone now. Just as well I didn't have to rely on my parents, isn't it!"

* * * * *

"Why don't you go to Cyprus instead?" Al's father said, sat on the edge of the worn out three-seater sofa.

Al looked at him in disbelief. He understood only too well where this conversation was going to lead. Why, after nearly fourteen years of barely saying a word to Al, did he want to start playing the part of a concerned father?

"What for?" Al snapped. Oh yes, he knew the answer well enough. He sighed, he had better go along with the charade a little longer, there might be a way out of the inevitable ending which would follow. "I don't know those people out there, even if they are related to me. They're all strangers and besides, I don't speak any Turkish."

Al was right, he was his father's son, but they were almost like strangers, let alone all his uncles, aunts and cousins. His father couldn't; and more importantly would not understand that Al was different. Al was an East Anglian, his father thought Al was Turkish. Al loved a man, lived with him for four and a half years, his father wanted Al to marry a good Turkish girl; or even English if it meant he would produce children, lots of children, preferably boys. Al had to escape this situation with his parents as much as running from Steven. He was nothing but a caged bird, both of the two worlds he had known up to this time were gone. Still he longed for one. Still he loathed the other. He had to be alone. He had to. The thought of going to Australia next week grew ever more urgent. The minutes ticked past and as they went he began to believe that he had in fact done the right thing by buying a ticket to Perth.

"We only want you to be happy son." His father proclaimed. "Son?!" Al screamed inside at the sound of that word. He couldn't be serious. To be his father's son his father had to be a father to him, not a stranger who stood aloof from reality, who saw only what he wanted to see and dismissed all else out of hand.

"We only want what's best for you... We want you to get married and have children."

Al saw red. If he had had any love in his heart for his parents then he would have been devastated by this, the most direct and open dismissal of his feelings. His heart was filled with contempt for the people who had brought him into this world and viewed him as an object, a piece of property, something that should be obedient and live a life that was totally and utterly unnatural for him. He had heard it all before. He wanted no part of it.

"If that's a condition of borrowing some money from you, then I don't want it. You don't give a fuck about what I want. You don't give a fuck about my happiness. You just want me to be a monkey dancing to a Turkish tune. I'm not Turkish, I'm East Anglian and I love a man. I've been living with him for nearly five years because I love him. It's not some perverted phase that I'll pass through, it wasn't a game. I loved him!" Al stormed out of the house, leaving his mother crying and his father totally disgusted. It was a slur on his manhood if his son was a poof.

It was cool and misty, much of April had been like that; it had been a disappointment after such a mild winter. He walked along the river, no one else about, not even fishermen. The willows stood tall and silent, there wasn't even the gentlest of breezes about to stir the branches which were just beginning to break bud. The dark water of the Stour, glass-like in the pale light. A moorhen called from the reed bed across the river, whittuck, whittuck, whittuck. A splash, followed by ripples from where a fish had jumped, probably a gudgeon, chased by a perch. Al was full of hate. He had grown up in this small market town, totally alone. The people he lived with didn't love him, they tolerated his presence only because to send him away would have caused questions to be asked. No, it wasn't through love that they had kept him, love would have demanded that they sought to understand and help, or at least talk about homosexuality in the hope of changing his mind. Why had there been no one to help him? How had he gone through school and wasted his last three years there? Didn't anyone ask themselves questions at the beginning of upper school of how had such a promising pupil could so suddenly become a disruptive, lazy and disinterested body? He didn't blame his parents for not being happy about his sexuality, but with the passage of time could they not have accepted it? Why, after living with Steven for so many years was their only reaction to the end of that relationship one of an assumed chance to make him 'normal'?

* * * * *

"Maybe it was for the best that I came here. The distance is good, but I miss East Anglia. I miss you Christopher. Shit! I've only been gone a week. What will I be like after a month? Do you think you'll still be alive in a month?" He stared into the bush, the jungle of grey bark which barred his view beyond ten metres in any direction. There was no answer in the leaf litter, the setting sun or the cooling air. No glimmer of hope that one day he would be able to live life without the incessant reoccurrence of thought which began and ended with Steven, punctuated with a longing for Christopher and East Anglia. He was in his living hell, which people at home called a holiday. Would they want to be feeling as he was? Would they choose to put themselves in a situation where they had no food or water and no way out to the next town; however far that was, other than by walking with a twenty kilo weight on their back? Depression began to return, heavy, dark and foreboding. He fought it off with the blasé attitude of 'I don't give a fuck!'

Night fell, insects filled the air and he closed his tent.

Lying awake and watching the flame dance around inside the smoke-coloured glass, waiting for the night to pass. The night passed but slowly, the tent hot with the light on until the gas ran out and the flame expired into an orange-yellow glow before fading into darkness with everything else around him. That was two o'clock, that was early, too early and waiting for time to tick past and eager for the arrival of the dawn can make a long night much much longer. It was a long night. It was a dry and hungry night and Al shook from not having eaten for so long. He did not like being hungry.

Tiredness got the better of him, but it wasn't long before dawn that he had finally got to sleep, only to be woken by the sound of crows and ravens. He emerged from the warm tent into another beautiful, but cool and damp Australian morning. The bush echoed with the sounds that were beginning to ring with familiarity. He sat, still and silent and watched the tiny droplets of moisture lifting from everything it had rested on during the night, as the air warmed and the sun began to rise. His stomach growled and he packed his home away into his rucksack and headed for the road.

Reaching the edge of the bush at the roadside his eyes adjusted themselves to unhindered light. The tarmac reached out through the bush, seemingly to the very edge of the Earth herself. He looked west towards Perth. Nothing. Just a dead straight road which disappeared into the distance and even though it was still early morning it was warm enough for the heat haze on the tarmac to give the impression of a giant lake not far away. Had he not driven through that lake two days ago he might have believed that it was real. He turned east, towards Kalgoorlie, it was a mirror image of what lay to the west. An empty road stretching tirelessly to the horizon and beyond.

"Oh," was all Al could say. It had to be the understatement of his life, if not the century! His heart sank a little lower into his chest and he stood there looking, looking at nothing, thinking nothing. He was dwarfed by the enormity of his situation. He was but a diminutive figure at the side of the road surrounded by thousands of acres, no, millions of acres of bush. Mentally and physically he felt broken. This had to be the last straw, the straw that broke the camel's back.

"What's the point? I can't walk all the way to Kalgoorlie. I couldn't last that long in this heat and it's not even hot yet!" Slowly he once again looked west and back to where he thought that he should be going. Nothing had changed.

"Tony might be at Kalgoorlie. I did say that I was heading there. If I don't go and he is waiting for me..." His face wore the expression of a daunted person, fixed rigid as if it had been there for the whole of his life.

"It would be good to see him..." Now, after a couple of days of being calm and nonchalant a tear began to form at the corner of his eye. He swallowed a dry and grated swallow.

"Oh well, I'll just have to start walking."

He picked up his pack, it felt heavier now and he started to walk.

He had no idea how far he had to go, it had to be less than a hundred kilometres and surely as soon as someone drove past they would stop and give him a lift? The tarmac was soft beneath his feet, but at least it was easy to walk on. He walked, ten minutes became twenty, twenty minutes drifted into half an hour. After an hour a car passed and kept going. Al hardly noticed it until it was long gone.

"Thanks mate. No, I'd rather walk, thanks all the same." Another half an hour and the sun rose still higher into the sky. The Australian rain poured down upon him and his head heated up.

"Ha ya goin'?"

Lost in his world of stewing brain and sweat Al was rudely and suddenly interrupted by an old man, around seventy, on a bicycle who had the strangest and strongest Australian accent that Al had ever heard.

"Slowly, very slowly." Al said in answer to his question.

"Where ya from?" The old man demanded.

"East Anglia." Al answered politely, but did not stop walking. He dreaded stopping for anything, for fear that he would not be able to motivate himself into movement once more. The old man cycled slowly beside him.

"Is that Pommy or wha'?"

"No, it's East Anglian! Cheeky bloody Colonial." Al snapped.

"Hum!" He was dismayed and disgruntled with Al's answer.

They continued in silence for a little way.

"Well! what ya doin' out 'ere?"

"Walking." Al answered curtly.

"Yeah, but why?"

"Because I want to go east."

"Oh."

Another silence fell upon them as they continued. The old man thinking long and hard about this strange East Anglian; whatever that was, he didn't understand why anyone should be out in the middle of not very much at all, walking.

"How far east are ya goin'?"

"I'm not sure yet. I thought I might head off north east towards Ayers Rock."

"Fair dinkum?"

Al wasn't sure what that meant, but it sounded like a question so he just nodded vaguely.

"Why d'ya wanna go there?"
"Because it's there."
"Ain't nowt but a rock."
"It is not nowt but a rock, it happens to be the world's largest monolith."
"Well yeah, I know tha', but it's still a bloody long way to walk to see a bloody rock, even if it is the biggest!" Al was making the old man a little irate, who in turn was making Al less than sociable.
"You should get yaself a bike... It's the best way to travel. I've been doin' it for years."
"Yes, I'm sure there are plenty of bicycles around here. Maybe I should pop into the bushes and get one?"
"No need to be like tha'!"
"Well here I am, God knows where in Western Australia, miles from anywhere, trying to walk somewhere; and to get there as soon as possible, and I find that I can't even be alone out here. Not just that! All you can say is that I should get myself a bike! Great advice for here wouldn't you say!" Al was red in the face, as much for his outburst as for the heat. He continued to walk. His throat hurt. The old man cycled behind for a little way and then caught up again.
"Ya got nuff tucka?"
"Yes."
"Wha' 'bout wa'er?"
"Yes thank you." Al lied, lifting his empty water bottle up in such a way that it looked as if it was half full.
"Ya won't get a lift out 'ere. Too many driver been attacked." The old man looked at him, waiting for a response which was not forthcoming, then cycled off. "Still, ya may be lucky," he called.
"Oh great! That's all I needed to hear. Why on Earth did I lie about the water?"
Within a minute the old man and his bicycle were swallowed by the heat haze and were gone, leaving no sign that they had ever passed that way.
"Stupid old coot!"
He was alone once again. Growing larger and larger, the sun rose higher into the sky and the day became even hotter. The old man had long since gone and would not have been far from a town now. Al was really thirsty and scolded himself for lying about the water.
The bush was thick on both sides of the road and he could not see

much more than a few metres into it, even so it offered no protection from the burning rays of the sun. The rain was getting hotter. Beneath his feet the tarmac lifted with each step he took, then slurped back to the road surface, slowly reforming into that black permanence. At the side of the road grew a creeping plant which had small water-melon type fruits hanging swollen along its vines.

"Should have bought a plant book instead. It's all very well knowing what the birds are, but I can't eat them. I can't even see them!"

He kept walking. His pack felt heavier by the minute and beneath his hat his head stewed in the heat. He licked his lips, barely able to produce enough saliva to moisten them, they were cracking through dryness.

"How could Steven say he loved me when he hated the thought of being with me? How could he make love to me knowing that I would have hated him near me if I had known? How could he lie to me like that? How do my parents think that they love me when all they want is for me to marry and have kids? That's not love. If they only knew what they did to me. What it was like growing up alone."

"Ah-ahh-ahhhh."

"Yes you bastards!" Al shouted up at the trees, spinning around as he searched the tree-tops for the source of the sound. "You want me to die so you can have your dinner. Well you can all fuck off! Go on, fuck off, because you're not pecking my eyes out!" He waved his arms limply, it frightened not one of the crows that watched unseen from their perches.

The crows continued to mock and hound him as with each step he reminded himself that he was a little nearer to his destination. Each second felt like an hour. Each hour like a day. There was so little traffic on the road and what few cars there were might as well not existed as they sped past at high speed.

He had left the bush not long after sunrise, it had been cool then, relatively. Now it was midday. The sun high above, almost directly above, with no escape for him. He felt a cool breeze as another car raced past him. One second beside him, the next second so far away. He looked through it and into the distant haze and then noticed the red brake lights illuminate. The car skidded to a halt.

"Oh my God! It's really stopped." He tried to run, but the weight of his pack, the lack of food and water and the heat got the better of him and he continued to struggle slowly forward as if he had all the time in the world.

It took him another couple of minutes to come close to the car and as he did so he could see a middle-aged woman get out and walk towards him.

"How long have you been out here?" Her voice was so soft and warm and caring. Al felt that it was the most beautiful sound that he had ever heard.

"I started walking at seven," he answered between pants. She was well dressed. "A solicitor or state politician," Al thought as he looked at her in awe and gratitude that she had stopped for him when others had just driven past.

"There's not exactly too much traffic on this road at the best of times, is there?" She smiled.

Al smiled back, not answering. It was one of those questions where an answer was not really necessary. He lifted his pack into the boot of the car and then walked around to the passenger door. His body sank into the soft, cool seat in the air-conditioned vehicle.

"It's good to be able to help each other once in a while," she said in her mellow tone.

Al's body felt as if it was melting in the comfort of the car. He turned to look at the rear seat, lying across it was a fifteen or sixteen year old boy. He stirred, lifted his head briefly, then fell asleep again.

The bush was now nothing more than a blur of grey-green as they travelled at a hundred and forty kilometres an hour. He could not see the crows that had been pestering him, though he couldn't see them when he was out there walking either. He felt smug at the thought that he had escaped them, though in his head; which still spun through lack of water and excess heat, he could still hear them.

"Where are you from?" Al eventually asked.

"From Perth. We left there this morning. I have to get to Norseman before my daughter appears in juvenile court. She ran away and the police caught her at the border and took her back to town."

Al stared out of the window, at the heat. He would not have lasted too many more hours and only now that he was in the comfort and safety of the car did he realise how tired and thirsty he was.

"We're running a bit behind schedule because we stopped to help a farmer earlier on. His tractor had got stuck on a level crossing and a train had hit it." Al was shocked by this, by the way the woman was talking about it so calmly, as if it happened every day. He stared at her in the most unbecoming manner. "He was lucky that he escaped with only a few cuts and shock," she added.

Al's view of the bush changed as he sat there in comfort. The sun poured through the canopy of the trees and made it look so lush and exciting. It had seemed so barren while he was out there, being roasted in the heat. Every now and then they passed a dead kangaroo at the side of the road. He had not seen anything while he walked and despite the almost abundance of carrion, there was a noticeable lack of live wildlife of any description.

By car, Coolgardie was not too far along the road. By foot, it would have taken Al many hours. As they arrived in what was nothing more than tiny remnant of the gold-rush city that it had once been, Al had never been as glad to reach somewhere as he was now. At one time this town had been home to tens of thousands of hopeful prospectors and traders. Hopeful of riches and glory, or just glad to be able to make a living in the harshness of the Australian outback.

"I'm going to be stopping for petrol here," Laura said as they headed towards the far side of the township. "Then I turn off in a different direction to the way that you need to go. I think that your best bet is to ask someone who stops for petrol if they wouldn't mind giving you a lift. Kalgoorlie isn't far and I'm sure that no one would mind."

Al didn't like the sound of approaching total strangers and asking for a lift. It didn't sound like a nice thing to do. They arrived at the petrol station. Beyond it was nothing. It was the end of Coolgardie and this was his only chance for a lift. The car slowed to a halt.

"Look, you can ask that chap with the Range Rover. He looks like a decent sort."

Al got out of the car and walked towards the Range Rover. He didn't feel at all comfortable about doing this, but he felt that he had little choice but to do what Laura had suggested, especially as she watched him as she filled her car with petrol. He felt even more uncomfortable when he remembered that a green Range Rover had passed him over an hour ago and that this was more than likely it.

"Excuse me Sir," Al said in his most conciliatory voice, "but are you going to Kalgoorlie?"

The man, tall and reserved to the point of sternness, was startled by the approach of this tatty looking boy. Without thinking, he answered, "yes".

Al, who was extremely nervous and unused to talking to strangers was surprisingly quick to exploit the situation in which he quite rightly deduced that he had the upper hand.

"I've just been dropped off by that lady over there..." he waved his arm in the general direction of Laura, who was watching them talk, "and she said that I should come over here and ask if you wouldn't mind giving me a lift to Kalgoorlie."

The man looked over to Laura and then back at Al. He was so startled by this intrusion into his privacy that he answered neither yes or no and Al immediately seized upon his indecision.

"That's alright then?" He paused for no more than a second. "I'll go over and get my luggage. Shall I put it on the back seat?"

"Yes." He answered Al's last question before realising what he had said yes to and stood wondering how he had picked up a hitch-hiker when he didn't want one!

Al walked back to Laura, said thank you and goodbye, then loaded his pack into the back of the Range Rover. For once social pressure was working to his advantage, probably for the first and last time in his life. He sat in the car and waited for the driver to return from inside the station building, almost proud of himself for pushing and manoeuvring the situation to achieve the result he wanted and needed. He tried to work out how it had happened when he knew how bad he was at talking to strangers, then realised that just as the man had yielded under the gaze of Laura and Al's quick talking, Al had only asked in the first place because of the pressure he felt from Laura. It seemed that both he and the man were victims of the same fate.

"No Al, it wasn't really much to do with you was it?" he said to himself as the sense of pride faded away and the man returned.

It was a painfully quiet journey to Kalgoorlie. The man who gave Al a lift was an Englishman; and very aloof. How had he allowed himself to give a lift to this common hitch-hiker? It was beyond his comprehension and beneath his social standing. Al was glad of the lift, he was still suffering the effects of heat exposure, but at the same time he was incensed by the attitude of this man he was travelling with.

"If he's too good to bother talking to me, I'll talk to him," Al thought and then proceeded to talk and talk and talk. He asked so many questions of the man, to which he only got a stare in response to the first few, but slowly he began to get monosyllabic answers, then short sentences. Al dug around his brain for every scrap of stored information about the flora, fauna, history and geology of Australia, asking questions which the man was unable to answer.

"So you think you're better than me? You obviously don't know so much about a good many things." Al smiled to himself at the achievement of bringing someone down to earth with a bump.

The man; who never gave his name, just a hard fixed glare, was becoming visibly uncomfortable. He was a civil engineer and when Al found this out he started on about construction methods as employed by the Romans, Normans and modern construction. He was speaking quite generally and for the last ten minutes of their journey they actually indulged in a conversation. Al was impressed with the change in attitude of this snob and it was all down to Al being stressed out through heat and irritated by a very proper Englishman.

Kalgoorlie was unlike any town Al had ever seen, but not so different from many remote Australian towns; or to be more precise, cities; as from this week the twin towns of Kalgoorlie-Boulder were a officially a city. Not that it looked much like a city as far as Al's eyes were concerned. It spread out for mile after mile, though it only had a population of around thirty thousand people. Its streets were wide, up to six lanes wide; and sprinkled with a fine red powder which Al instantly recognised as typical outback soil. Along some roads, but not all, were paths which were nothing more than dusty lines worn into the ground by the passage of people and time.

In the town centre were some fine wooden colonial buildings, which would not have looked out of place on the set of an American western; a few horses and John Wayne would not have looked out of place at all and apart from the noise and smell of the V8 engines it would have appeared that time and progress had not caught up with this part of Australia.

By the time he had reached a camp site and put his tent up his head was burning and swaying in the heat. He drank a litre of cold water, then another and then a third. He felt bloated, but still in need of more liquid. For over half an hour he stood in the shower, dust washing away from him and lungs breathed in water vapour from the hot steam. He began to feel better, if not quite right.

Hungry, but not so thirsty, he walked the three kilometres back into town. Walking wasn't so hard now, without a backpack and with enough water.

"I need a saucepan, with a lid. I won't be so wasteful of water again." He wandered around the shop, basket in hand, oblivious to the people around him who stared as he talked to himself. "Coffee. I really missed not having any coffee to drink..."

For an hour he walked around the supermarket discussing what he did and did not need to have and it was not much longer until he sat in the doorway of his tent drinking orange juice while he waited for his four rashers of smoked back bacon, three eggs, two slices of fried bread, two fried tomatoes and a pile of mushrooms to cook.

He smiled as he ate and watched a young man unpack a tent from a heavily laden car.

"English," he scoffed as he watched him clumsily erect his tent as the taste of the last piece of bacon was chewed, savoured, then swallowed. He cleared his pots then slept soundly and happily.

* * * * *

Tony had spent the whole of the day that Al left Perth in the camp site. He had watched Al walk out of sight and he was worried for him. Sat in the sunshine where Al had left him he thought about his actions of last night.

"I'm sure that was the real reason for his leaving, but even more important than that was the phone call he made to Steven. He must have been in a terrible state to do that and what state was he in after the call? Where had he spent last night? What was he going to do now? Why was he so calm? This means trouble."

His concern grew stronger and stronger. Guilt crept in, he had let his friend down. Tears formed in his eyes and he fought them back. He sniffed hard, stood up and ran in the direction in which Al had gone.

"Al!" he shouted as he turned the corner and saw, three hundred metres away, Al was getting into a car.

"Al!" He ran as fast as he could. The car door shut and the noise

*Al wanders off into the bush —
the letting go...*

of the surrounding traffic drowned out Tony's frantic scream. He looked on in horror as the car began to move out into the traffic and head off along the highway. He reached the end of the road, puffing, sweating. He could still see the car and he ran along the highway for a while before losing sight of it and realising that he was too late. The feeling of defeat hung heavily upon Tony. Never had he felt so useless, so hopeless, so inept. He sat at the side of the highway, head in hands. Numb with the sense of loss. Cold with the feeling of fear.

"Hi, Tony?" A girl's voice called him from outside of his tent. She stood waiting for him to answer as behind her the sun began to sink in the sky.

"Tony? It's me, Lucy." Inside the tent Tony stirred from his sleep. It took him a while to recall the events of last night and this morning.

"Are you in there Tony?"

"Yeah, come in Lucy," he said as he pulled on a pair of boxer shorts.

She entered his tent.

"Are you alright?" she asked, staring at his almost naked body.

"Not really."

"What's wrong?" She sat beside him on his sleeping bag, touched his arm gently.

"Al's gone. I'm worried about him, Lucy. He can't look after himself in the state he is in."

"He'll be alright, it's not a third world country you know."

"No, it's not that. He's so screwed up and I'm partly to blame."

"Don't be silly Tony. We all have to live our own lives, besides, and I don't mean to sound heartless, there isn't much that you can do now, is there?"

"I know, I just wish that I could."

"You're a good bloke."

He looked at her in the dimming light of the tent. He had allowed Al to go because he wanted to have sex with this girl. She gazed back at him, at his body.

"I've got a surprise for you. I wasn't going to let you have it until later tonight, but you need cheering up a little."

"What's that?" Tony was not more than vaguely interested, he smiled a little.

"Close your eyes and give me your other hand."

Tony felt silly, but went along with her little game, opening his eyes wide when he felt his hand moving under Lucy's denim skirt and up her legs.
"You've got no knickers on!"
"I knew you liked denim and I thought that you might like this."

Tony lay awake listening to the crows and kookaburras in the trees. Lucy had gone, as she had yesterday, in the early hours of the morning. The sun was up and shone brightly through the nylon flysheet.
"Where are you Al?" He lay there, half expecting an answer. "How far did you get?"
By nine thirty Tony had packed his tent and was leaving the camp site, getting some strange and disapproving looks from other holiday-makers as he went. Instead of turning east towards Kalgoorlie he walked along the highway until he came to the ring road and waited for a lift south. He thought that there was no chance of meeting up with Al again, so there was little reason to go chasing after him and anyway he feared the worse for Al.
"He won't last long out there on his own and it will all be my fault for letting him go. With friends like me he doesn't need enemies."
How could Tony really blame himself for anything that might or might not happen to Al? He had tried to stop him, though he had been too late, but it was that last minute chase along the road after Al that had left him feeling so desperate. That moment when he saw Al getting into the car and no matter how loudly he called, Al could not hear him. No matter how fast he ran he could not catch the car. It felt like failure.

* * * * *

Al slept for a few hours, waking refreshed, though still a little thirsty. It was a good feeling to wake up and still feel clean. It was a good feeling to wake up and know that you had a pile of fruit, fruit juice and enough food to have at least another large fried breakfast. He dressed and looked out of the tent at not much at all. A few people were returning to prepare their evening meal and that English boy was still unpacking and reloading his car. He had a bike on the back of the estate and Al thought that maybe having a bike would be a good idea. There would be no worries about trying to hitch a lift. No worries about having to walk for hours in the heat and he would be able to carry more water. The problem was money. He had just over a hundred dollars a week, so there wasn't really enough to spend on a bike.

"I better go and check the other camp sites in case Tony has arrived," he thought as he ate a banana, zipping up the flysheet.

He passed by the chap whom he assumed was English, and being very nosy he thought he'd stop for a chat.

"Hello," he said, much to his own surprise. When had he last spoken to someone without needing to?

"Hi." David answered somewhat abruptly.

"What's his problem?" Al thought. "Where have you arrived from?" Al wasn't much interested now, but thought that he would ask anyway.

"I came along the coast from Perth and up through Norseman. What about you?"

"I came straight across along the main road."

"Oh, so you're heading east?" David sounded a little more interested now.

"No. I'm going up to Leonora then across to Ayers Rock."

"Have you got a four-wheel drive?"

"A what?"

"A four-wheel drive. You won't get across in an ordinary car."

Al hadn't realised what a four wheel drive was at first. He was puzzled that anyone would think that he had any such thing.

"No, I don't have a four-wheel drive. I'll just keep to the main road, hitch where I can and walk the rest."

"What? There's no road across there and you certainly won't be walking across. It's as remote as it gets out here."

"No, that's not right. I've got a road marked on my map and there are a few towns on the way." David got out his map and sure enough there was a thin red line marked on and Al pointed to it. "See, there's the road and its got the towns marked on, there, there and there."

"I hate to disappoint you, but you've got a lot to learn about Australia. That red line is a dirt track and those towns are in fact cattle stations and some might be miles from the track, some might be deserted. You couldn't walk it because there isn't any water and as for getting a lift, well, don't even think it."

"Oh, I see."

"You'll be going across the way I go, through Norseman. If you like you can come with me as far as Ceduna. That gets you across the Nullarbor and you can please yourself then." Al was surprised by the offer. He certainly hadn't expected it.

"I'm going to see if my friend has arrived first, but if he hasn't then sure. It sounds easier than standing at the side of the road."

"We'll share the petrol fifty-fifty," David added.

"O.K." Al left it at that and went off to check if Tony was in town. He wasn't. Returning to his tent after leaving a message for him should he come into town in the next couple of days.

A flock of galahs flew past screaming, Al woke and listened. They flew back and rested in a large Eucalyptus tree behind his tent, they chatted and he thought that he may as well get up, it was morning after all. He had slept late and he was pleased that he had been woken as his throat was dry and he needed to have a good long drink.

He pushed his head out into the world and looked up to the gathered parrots, grey and pink and plump.

"I wonder if they taste as good as budgerigars?" Not that he had ever eaten a budgerigar, he would never have eaten one of his own birds. They were loved pets, but more than that, they were money.

"Melopsitticus undulatus, or good food," he remembered both the Latin and the English translation of the Aboriginal. His tent was still in the shade of the trees and it would stay that way for another half an hour, so he decided that he would shave and shower and then come back for breakfast once the sun had warmed things up a little. He kicked at the grass as he walked across the field. It was a sad affair of tufts of yellowish-green spikes lost in a sea of red sand which had already stained his trainers red.

He shaved carefully and slowly. He still wasn't used to wet shaving, he had only been doing it for a week and he didn't like the thought of having, not one, but two small, but still very sharp blades in his hand. Each time he drew the razor across his skin he closed his eyes for fear of seeing what a mess he was making of it. As it turned out it was probably a better way of learning to wet-shave as he was relying solely on touch and not what he thought he saw in the mirror.

"That's not too bad," he said as he looked at the little drops of blood on his neck. No matter how careful he was, he always drew a little blood there. He stared in the mirror and for a moment he thought he saw Steven standing behind him, watching him as he shaved, as he would have done in Ipswich. It frightened him that even the most mundane of things could be tainted with thoughts of the man he still loved, especially as he was trying to run away from him. He stared hard into the mirror. It was only himself. But now he tried to picture Steven there, he wanted to see him there. He wanted him to be here. Wasn't he on holiday? Camping? Didn't he and Steven always go on holiday together? Didn't they always share a tent? Where was he now?

"G'day." An Australian man came into the toilet block and interrupted him.

Al turned suddenly and answered, packing his things up and disappearing into a shower.

"Too much time alone and too much time to think... and too many memories."

He had timed his shower just right as when he returned to his tent the day was warming it up, but not unpleasantly. He breathed deeply and smelt the bacon which sizzled in the pan as he wiped his mushrooms and cut the tomatoes in half. The bacon began to curl and turn pink, he pushed it to one side of the pan so he could cook some fried bread. Everything had to be timed right, he didn't want cold food and he had no grill under which he could keep things warm. Food began to pile high in the pan; tomatoes at the bottom, then mushrooms, bacon and fried bread. Three eggs squeaked and popped as they cooked quickly in half of the pan. He flipped them over for a few seconds while he started to put everything out onto his plate. He looked at it and shook his head disapprovingly at the plastic plate. Water boiled for his coffee, eggs were out and breakfast had begun.

"Lemon and ketchup," he said wistfully, hankering after two other things he wanted, which would round off his breakfast quite nicely.

He took his time eating and rested for a while as he thought about the day ahead.

"I wonder if Tony will arrive today? I guess that he's still in Perth with that girl. I hope he does come. I need to let him know that I'm alright and it wasn't his fault. He blames himself, I'm sure of it."

Al let almost an hour drift past as he lay in his open tent, thinking. It was still early and he had decided to visit a gold mine and be a real tourist for the day. There was little other movement on the site and eventually he set off. He had a map, but it was of the kind that he hated, photocopied and even worse, not to scale.

He watched the ground ahead as he walked, he watched for the snakes that were said to be everywhere, kicking the red sand over the tops of his trainers.

"My feet will be filthy by the end of the day," he was not pleased by that thought.

"Would you like a lift?" A man called from a pick-up that slowed beside him.

"That's really kind of you to offer," Al was a little taken aback, "normally I'd jump at the offer, but I'd quite like to walk, thanks all the same."

"No worries mate. Take care of yourself."

Al was feeling quite pleased and relaxed after the chance encounter with one of the locals. Like Perth, it seemed that the natives were friendly. However, after an hour he wished that he had accepted the lift as it became painfully apparent that the map was nowhere near a uniform scale.

"Hi." David said, as he caught up with Al. He was riding his bike.

"Morning," Al answered.

"Where ya going?"

"I thought that I'd have a look at a gold mine. Something that I've never done before."

"Yeah, me too. I'll come along with you."

Al didn't mind this too much as it gave them a chance to get to know each other before they set off on the journey to Ceduna. David, as Al had guessed, was from England. He had come out to Australia as a teenager, alone. Al couldn't imagine doing something like that at the age of sixteen, but maybe that would have been easier than arriving at the age of twenty six with a host of expectations and preconceived ideas.

They arrived early for the next gold mine tour and sat having a coffee, talking. David was shy, almost to the point of making Al seem quite chatty; which he was, but usually only with people he already knew. Al couldn't work out how someone who had left his family and home behind at such an early age could not be extremely extrovert. David seemed much less confident than himself, but that was probably an advantage for Al, it meant that he didn't have to be too much of a social creature if he didn't feel like it.

It was mid-afternoon by the time the tour had finished. David had left Al, returning to the camp site and Al took a walk into town. He enjoyed being able to just wander about looking at the things around him; architecture, parks, gardens and of course people. A flock of galahs were gathered in a park, picking around on the grass. Al stood watching for several minutes thinking how strange it was to be in a country where parrots flew wild; true, East Anglia now had a native breeding parrot of its own, the Indian ringneck parakeet had settled down to the good life in the Kingdom. The galahs waddled about, occasionally lifting their heads to make sure they were safe, checking for danger, then continued to pick at the grass.

"How can they say that galahs are a pest? I think that they look quite cute here in a town. How can I only have been here a week? It feels like a year." He continued to look around.

Kalgoorlie had stood still; by all appearances, in colonial times. For Al this meant it was interesting, unusual and wonderful. The Exchange Hotel commanded a prominent place on a corner of the main crossroads. It was big and brash, almost to the point of ugly. Its 1900's shape was uniform and yet irregular from most angles and like most of the other buildings of the period, wood had been widely used and balconies stretched the full length of the buildings. Some had ornate wrought iron balcony rails; a product of the Victorian empire era.

For three hours Al wandered about, dodging the sun, looking. He was pleased to have something to do while he waited for Tony to arrive, or until he decided what he was going to do with himself. If Tony didn't come then the next few days would be spent travelling across to Ceduna, but then what? He had this idea that he would go to Ayers Rock and that in itself was alright, but then what would he do? He still had over five months to fill.

Tony didn't arrive in town and Al sat on a tree stump in the early morning sun, his backpack at his feet, ready to go. David was still sleeping and while Al waited he read, but wasn't really able to concentrate. In a way he was glad to be moving on, it gave his mind something to think about other than himself and Steven. It was too easy to think about Steven and wonder how he was? What he was doing? Who he was with?

"Just remember that this is fun Al."

A flock of galahs screamed and circled overhead, then flew off towards the airport. Time passed and David got up and ate. Al watched him from across the grass, a distance of thirty metres or so. He wasn't sure how this trip east was going to work out; David wasn't the easiest of people for Al to talk to and Al assumed that it would be a strain.

They journeyed south towards Norseman. David drove slowly, but Al didn't mind, he found the bush so impressive. He couldn't begin to comprehend how many millions of acres of trees there must have been here. It was unlike anything he had ever seen, there was nothing in Europe on this scale, except for mountain ranges. The trees gave way to salt pans, large and silver in the sunlight, shinning like gems in a jeweller's shop. Al wanted to get out of the car and touch one. He wanted to run barefoot upon this strange sight, to feel the salt crystals beneath his feet, between his toes, to shout like he was having fun. David was uninterested, he glanced over at them and said "nice" and then carried on looking at the road, the road which stretched off far into the distance; as it would do so for a few days yet. David wanted to drive around Australia, not to look at it, he just wanted to be able to say; as so many people could, that he had done it. All he wanted was to clock up the kilometres and do some fishing along the way. He didn't know what he wanted out of life any more than Al did.

The journey continued. David played some tapes; at least some of his choice in music was shared by Al, though not much, and they talked a little, but Al didn't find David the easiest person to talk to and eventually he gave up, instead he chose to just stare out of the window and listen to the music.

Many hours and four hundred kilometres later they arrived at Balladonia roadhouse. They would spend their first night here, but Al decided that he would not spend any money. The camp site was nothing but a dusty patch of cleared bush, not particularly flat either. For this, they were supposed to pay a five dollar fee? Al decided that if there was no grass, there was no way that he would pay, so they set up their tents and collected some firewood from the nearby trees.

David and Al sat by the fire, above them darkness arrived and from it a host of stars lit the night's sky. The heat from the day disappeared and was replaced by a fresh chill, which was kept at bay by the fire. Al collected his food from his tent and sat cooking. He looked over towards the source of a noise and watched in horror as a bull-terrier walked into his tent. Al hated dogs, he was terrified of them; ever since that day he and some of his friends had been attacked by a bull-terrier; that too had been someone's darling little pet that wouldn't hurt a fly. The only thing he hated more than the dogs, were their owners; selfish, inconsiderate, ignorant. He tried to be brave and shoo it away. The dog ignored him.

"Why doesn't the owner come and get his bloody mutt? Typical dog owner, a selfish, irresponsible dick-head!"

Eventually a man came and collected his dog, behaving as if the dog and himself had every right to do as they pleased and ignore anyone else's wishes. Al was more than a little wound up by this and it was only the smell of food cooking that began to relax him. Much to Al's relief the dog wandered off to bother someone else.

Awaking as light arrived, Al lay warm in his sleeping bag. Outside he heard the sound of a crow falling from its perch, he smiled. He looked up at the cotton inner tent, the shape of the dome; he was in Australia and what's more, he was in a pretty remote part of it. That sounded totally odd to him, but yet, because he knew what the soil was like, what the trees were like, it also didn't feel strange at all.

"The air would be full of birds singing in East Anglia, but there's nothing but an odd crow here."

He stayed in his tent longer than he wanted to. He was listening to the silence as he imagined that bull-terrier waiting outside his tent for him. He heard no movement, then looked out of the tent. The patch of dirt was still. None of the other campers had got up and there was no sign of any dog. Al went for a shower and refused to pay for that; on the pretext of he shouldn't have to put up with a dog on the site. He was conserving money by cutting out unnecessary expenditure so he could spend it on something else at a later date.

Al began packing before David had even got up and by the time David had got up he had had two coffees. Al didn't know how he had lasted two mornings in the bush without a coffee.

"So uncivilised." He said, almost in disbelief that he had done that.

David went off for a shower; he paid three dollars for his, then sat by the fire with Al before packing. Al couldn't imagine a more unlikely person that he could be travelling with. They had nothing in common, nothing that Al was aware of anyway, except for that small amount of music, but that wasn't going to help them across to Ceduna. They were going to spend so many hours together, so what the hell would they talk about?

By nine thirty they were on their way once more. Along the same road, with the same scenery; the same sky, trees, red sand at the side of the road. Al concentrated on studying the land and its plants, not that he could see an awful lot from the window of a speeding car, but that wasn't important. Like an artist using great sweeps of colour to give the impression, a suggestion of a scene, Al watched and absorbed the feel of that scene upon which he stared out at. He still found it different and interesting enough to keep his mind occupied, keep his mind from thoughts of Steven.

For hours they drove along, a few words here, a few words there, disintegrating into nothing, but not so bad that the lack of conversation was too deafening. Al was strangely relieved to be in this non-communiqué situation, it was comfortable and gave him space.

After a whole day of heading across flat plains, unchanging flat monotonous landscape, they suddenly found themselves heading down a steep ridge. The cliff stretched out on both sides of them on a typical Australian scale; massive, or bigger than massive, or even bigger still. At the bottom of which was another vast plain and in the distance, though out of Al's range of sight, he knew that there were yet more cliffs and then the Southern Ocean.

"This is amazing. All this was once under the ocean, whether it was an under-sea cliff, or land movement created it, I don't know."

"Don't be silly, this was never under water."

Al looked at David, at the person who had no interest in stopping to look at salt pans, at the person who had no interest in stopping at the viewpoint on the top of the ridge, who's only interest was in driving around Australia, so he could say that he had done it; and thought what was the point?

It was late afternoon and half an hour after they had descended the ridge when they found a dirt track, which must have been infrequently used, so they left the highway and headed towards the base of the ridge which they had been following.

"Yes! This looks like a good place to stop for the night." Al said, quite happy to be camping miles from anywhere, rather than a patch of dust that you were supposed to pay for.

"Yeah, it looks alright." David answered.

"Miserable lord of understatement!" Al cursed to himself. Al had his tent up in a matter of minutes and then searched for firewood from along a gully filled with rounded boulders which ran down from the ridge. It was obvious that during heavy rain, water would feed into this channel from higher up, but close to where they pitched there was no sign of water; the gully stopped abruptly. Al looked for a sink hole, but found none. He knew that some massive cave systems existed in this area of the continent, he suspected that below them was one such system. He continued to collect wood and stepped from rock to rock proceeding along the water-worn route. A few pools of water lay still and rancid in dark sun-free pockets. He wondered when it had last rained, because surely even if it was in the shade the water would still evaporate due to the heat? Returning with an armful of wood, he saw that David had finished pitching his tent and was collecting wood a little further back. Al looked at him and thought how silly he was to be here with someone who he didn't know instead of being here with Tony. He would love to be out here in the wild with his friend.

As darkness fell, the fire grew large against the blackening landscape, a beacon for everything for miles around. Above them, a gallery of brightly shinning stars began to take to the stages of the heavens in a spectacular display, the like of which Al had never before seen. A chill soft breeze blew across the plain and sent some orange-yellow flames dancing into the night around them. Al watched David, his face glowing orange-pink in the heat and against a background cloth of black. Away on the highway a lone vehicle roared across the plain, its headlights beamed into the sky in front of it as it sped along, slowly disappearing into the silence, distance and darkness. The smell of steak and onion; and of the wood burning, filled the gully with aromas which had probably never touched this air before, or so Al liked to think; an old fool, a romantic fool. Al gazed up at the myriad of tiny white dots, countless millions of them, that filled the sky above.

"I don't think that I've ever seen so many stars before."

David looked up, thoughtful, restful and almost rested after another day of driving.

"Yes, the skies down here are really spectacular."

A meteor shower raced across the sky and burned out. Al's heart lifted into his mouth and for a moment he was speechless; it wasn't often that Al was speechless. He had only seen that twice before and both times were in Sudbury. It reminded him that he was so far from home.

"I think I'll get up early and watch the sun rise tomorrow, watch it come up over the plain." Al said to himself thoughtfully.

"Give me a shout, I wouldn't mind seeing that myself."

Al looked at David, it seemed unlikely that he would want to do something like that when he hadn't wanted to stop and look at salt pans or at the view from the top of the ridge.

Sometimes talking, but mainly in silence, they sat on rocks by the fire, staring into the flames and feeling good to be warm in a cold place. The patterns in the heavens changed and the fire began to die down as hour after hour passed.

"It's gone midnight David. I'm going to bed now."

"Don't forget to give me a call in the morning."

Al woke at four, it was still dark outside and he had plenty of time before sunrise. He stretched out his arms, he didn't like being locked up in a sleeping bag, he found it too restrictive. His hands touched both sides of the tent. It was wet. He listened, and thought he could hear drizzle falling.

"Oh that's great! It only rains a couple of days every year and today has to be one of them!"

He stayed in his tent until after it was light, there seemed little point in getting up to watch the rain, though that would have been worth seeing in a place like this.

When he eventually grew bored and looked out of his tent, he popped his head out into another one of those clear Australian mornings that he expected would always be there for him. It had not rained at all, it was just the sound of the breeze and the touch of the heavy dew that had made him think that rain had fallen. He dressed and emerged from his tent, he stretched his body hard, so hard it pulled him to his greatest extent before he might snap. Beneath his feet the red soil was wet and the leaves and stems of the plants were heavy with moisture. This was how all these plants were able to

[handwritten annotation at top: the prettiness of landscape, the relaxed prose — the leisure of the read — opens the characters gently. he goes for setting and familiar metaphor. Unhurried, the relaxed ... into the ~~quantity~~]

survive out in these harsh conditions. There was so much water around in the morning dew that they would have no trouble in absorbing some of it.

The air was still cool; and damp, the sun was still hidden behind the ridge. Al collected some more wood and it seemed that he was the only thing that stirred in an otherwise silent world. He stopped and for a couple of minutes just stood still and listened. Nothing stirred, nothing broke the silence except for the sound of his own breathing. Tiny droplets of water hung to the tips of leaves, motionless, fixed, an air of permanence, of always, of forever and ever more. Time itself seemed to be standing still. David was still asleep in his tent and away in the distance the road had not yet been woken by racing tyres, rubber on tarmac, hot on cold. Al bent down by the ashes left behind by last night's fire. It was still a living entity. He could feel heat radiating out towards his body, pushing the chill of the morning away from him. He poked at it with a stick, revealing some pieces of orange glowing wood. Sometimes life was worth living, while moments like this lasted.

"Steven would like it here, he'd love the chill of the morning and the wildness of this place... You should be here with me Steven. You should be here to feel this. Oh I still love you."

He caught himself drifting down a line of thought that he had been too many times before and along which he did not want to return. He wanted to be near to him, not to think of him from the other side of the world. He smashed some of the larger pieces of wood and piled them onto the hot grey ashes. It began to smoke as it dried and he put on all that he had collected and he didn't have to wait long for the flames to burst through the twigs and twist and push their way around each piece of wood, consuming them like a hungry beast gorging itself on warm meat, flesh, dripping blood. Al filled the pan with water and waited for it to boil so he could make a coffee. The first coffee of morning, so important, the most needed.

"I wonder where Tony is? I hope that he is alright."

Al sat drinking his coffee and eating his food, thinking thoughts about Steven and Tony. Thoughts which served no purpose other than to make him lonely.

"Why could I not share this with someone I love, instead of a stranger with whom I have so little in common?"

The ridge stood in front of him. A barrier blocking his way

forward, but not one that could not be overcome. Just like the problems in his mind, an enormous obstacle, but one which in time could be removed, would be removed, one which he would conquer. The boulders, black and rounded by the action of water stood silently waiting for the next time that they would be washed by a running stream. They were not limestone as much of the underlying rock was. Neither were they sandstone, the source of the bright red soil. Whatever they were, they sat there in silent judgement of Al. They knew the right answers, they had stood the passage of time and still they were there, but they told him nothing and yet everything.

"Be still with yourself," they screamed silently at him.

Al took a walk along the ridge when David finally got up.

Neither felt like talking, neither had much to say to each other. There was a little used track which they had followed from the road and it continued up the side of the ridge towards the top, Al followed it, though he didn't have time to continue to the very top. He just walked along looking at the flora and to his surprise there were a number of plants in flower and dozens of butterflies floating around them. They all appeared to be of the same species, a type of fritillary, he supposed. The sun broke over the ridge and warmed the tiny, but obviously not so fragile insects, on their haphazard journey from one plant to another, not a care in the world. It was always better to see a plant in its native environment rather than a botanic garden, it was more fascinating, more informative to see the austere geographical situation in which he now found himself. On the side of the ridge the rock strata was clearly visible, it was easy to recognise the different sedimentary layers. All around were fossilised sea shells; clam like, white and hard.

"And how long have you been sitting high up on this ridge? How long before that had you been buried in the sands at the bottom of the great sea?"

He collected a couple and thought that he had better go back and pack. He did not want to find David waiting to go, but that was unlikely to happen.

The morning air began to warm, but in the shade the last of the chill air hung around. David was still by the fire and Al sat and had another coffee.

"Here you are David, fossils from the bottom of a great ocean, from millions of years ago."

David could see that what Al had handed him were indeed fossils, but he still had trouble believing that all they could see was once under salt water. Because David could not imagine the picture that Al painted for him on the formation of this vast plain, he became unimpressed and threw the fossils over his shoulder. Al looked at him in disbelief and was glad to pack and leave, he looked forward to the end of the day's journey, he looked forward to the knowledge that at the end of this day it would be their last full day of travelling together. He was longing for a conversation. It didn't have to be a deep and analytical discussion, indeed it would be better for him if it wasn't, for Al was no great brain. He just longed for something stimulating, something to make his mind do some work. All they had were music cassettes which played the same music as before and long silences which were the same silences as before.

By early afternoon they had stopped for lunch at a point where the highway came close to the sea. Al stood looking down the huge cliffs to the cold water far below. A strong wind blew and carried with it salt. The air was clean and invigorating, it didn't get much cleaner than this, fresh from the Antarctic, which was the next piece of land to the south. In each direction the cliffs stretched to the horizon and beyond. Nowhere could Al see a way down, not that he wanted to go down there, down to the crashing waves and cold water. This was certainly something for Steven to see, something that he would have enjoyed; that was something which Al must have thought and felt as he stood staring into the wild cold breeze.

Within minutes of getting back onto the road, it seemed to Al that they had never stopped. All too soon it was the same monotonous journey. For four hours they travelled east, with little conversation, just the same tapes playing again and again.

"It will be dark in half an hour David, we'd better find somewhere to stop overnight."

"Yeah," David answered, bored with the journey, but carrying on until he found a suitable place to turn off the highway. Al pitched his tent while he could still see and let David make the fire. The night arrived quickly. They had changed time zones and gone a long way east in the past three days.

Al went over and sat by the fire, around them the trees stood to a height of no more than ten metres and they kept the breeze out of the clearing that they had found, causing the smoke from the fire to drift up aimlessly into the darkness. Al didn't have much food left, but he wasn't bothered, he had fruit to eat and coffee to drink.

"Do you believe in life after death?" David asked as he pushed the last of his food into his mouth.

Al sat looking into the flames, thinking about the question.

"No, or at least I hope there isn't any. Once is more than enough."

The water boiled and Al made a second cup of coffee and looked up through the overhanging branches of a nearby tree and up at the sky.

"If there is reincarnation and I have to come back, I'd like to be a tree."

"That's daft. You'd get cut down."

"A tree in a botanic garden. A specimen tree, never to be removed. Maybe a Carpinus betulus, yes I like hornbeam. There's a beautiful young hornbeam by the information centre in Wolves Wood; a nature reserve at home; and at the back of the wood there are some old trees where I..." He stopped to think a little. "Ginkgo biloba would be another possibility, it's a beautiful tree, but maybe a Metasequoia glyptostroboides."

"A what?"

"Metasequoia glyptostroboides. A deciduous conifer from China. It wasn't catalogued until 1947, I think? It has a very good shape and bark, and in the spring the new leaves are a wonderful soft green."

"I'll take your word for that. They all look the same to me."

Al looked vaguely at David and thought that they probably did all look the same to him. He found it sad to think that people like David existed.

It was dark, pitch dark. Al could barely make out the white cotton inner tent. It must have been early, about one, maybe two, when he was woken by an eerie sound which was halfway between howling and crying. Outside in the darkness, not far from his tent he could hear movement, a scuffling and scratching. Whatever it was out there, there were many more than one of them.

Al was frightened by the unknown. A yelp echoed around the tent. Dingoes? Al had never seen a dingo and had not thought that they would be a problem to him. Weren't they supposed to be solitary animals? Hadn't they crossed the dog fence yesterday? Weren't they the safe side of that dog fence? A dog scratched close to the tent, bushes rustled, voices rang through the darkness. There were at least half a dozen of them. The case of the dingo that took a baby at Ayers Rock, which had been on the news so much at home, came back to him like it was yesterday.

"That was just one, there's a pack out there and now it's me who's going to be dragged off into the bush, never to be seen again and eaten by a pack of dogs." He broke out into a cold sweat. He lay in his sleeping bag, unable to move, absolutely terrified. Horrified in the knowledge that any second now they would begin to tear through his tent and then tear him to pieces.

"I should have made the fire up before coming to bed." Suddenly the risk of causing a bush fire seemed so trivial, too trivial to have taken any notice of it.

"If I light my lamp and gas stove the light and noise will frighten them away," but he was so scared by the thought of a pack of dogs attacking him that he could not even reach his arm out to grab hold of his lamp and matches. His mind was telling his body to move, but his body would not obey. He could only lay there and wait for them to come and get him, as he pictured in his mind the sight of a dingo ripping through nylon and cotton and coming straight at him. In his mind his image of a dingo grew and grew until it was similar in size to a black bear. He could almost feel sharp, ever-so-sharp teeth, sinking deeper, deeper, into his flesh, ripping at him.

Ah-ahh-ahhhh. The sound of a crow was the next thing that he heard. It was morning, the crows were awake. He felt his throat, it had not been torn open. He looked around the tent, there were no holes in it, so no dingo had come through. He felt his face.

"I'm alive! Aren't I? I feel strange, but that doesn't mean that this is life after death. Does it?"

The crow flew off and all fell quiet again. All seemed to be in order around his tent, so he dressed and crawled out into the cool and still of the morning. He looked into the grey damp stand of Eucalyptus and then over to David's car; he hadn't bothered to put his tent up and had slept inside his car and now it was fogged up with condensation and he was still asleep inside it.

"Of course I'm alive... I must be?"

To any stable person the question of whether or not you had been torn limb from limb would not arise; it would be too absurd. But to Al, who was not a stable person; troubled by the knowledge that Steven had sex with someone else; something that he believed would never happen; by the knowledge that he had lied for so long; something else that he believed would never happen; by the loss of his business; from being so many miles from home and his friends, it did not seem the slightest bit absurd. Had he fallen asleep, passed out, or been killed? He didn't know how big a dingo was. He wasn't even aware that they hunted in packs, so how would he know if they hadn't done the deed?

He walked off into the bush, touching the trees, their bark. They were real. They were damp, as they always were in the morning. He stopped and listened. Silence.

"Why is it so quiet? It's never quiet in the bush. Where are all the crows?"

He thought about the feelings he was having and then laughed at his stupidity. He laughed at himself, but still he wasn't totally convinced that he wasn't right!

"Have a coffee and something to eat and you'll feel a lot better."

That sounded like a more reasonable thing to think and do, so he took a handful of twigs back to the fire and put some water on to boil. The sound of the twigs crackling into life woke David and he wound down a window and poked his head out.

"Umm, good to see the fire going. I'm cold in here. Is there any water for a coffee?"

"Yes, it's on."

"Good."

"David... Did you hear the dingoes last night?"

"No. What dingoes?"

Al proceeded to tell David about the events of last night and how he wasn't sure if they had ripped him to pieces or not and David proceeded to have a good laugh at Al.

"Don't you know how small a dingo is?"

"No, but I know how small a bull-terrier is and I've seen what one of those can do to an alsatian and to people!" Al snapped back.

David continued to laugh and Al realised that he was alive, because if for no other reason had he been dead he would not have to put up with this idiot for another day!

After that, Al was eager to pack and get moving. It was the final day of their journey together and by lunch time they had reached the small village of Penong. After so many hours of mainly uneventful journeying it was a source of amazement for them. They stopped for something to eat and looked around the wide dusty streets, which were in a poor state of disrepair. It seemed to Al that someone had dumped a load of tarmac and rolled it out to whatever size they fancied, no kerbs, no paths and here and there small clumps of yellow-brown grass grew.

"How do people live out here? It would drive me nuts. They haven't even planted trees everywhere in an attempt to make it a little more civilised."

"I couldn't live in a dump like this, I love Sydney too much," David answered.

"It's so barren, so different from East Anglia. It's horrible."

"It's worrying to think what the people must be like from living in a hole like this. There's nothing for them to do apart from farming and drinking. Come on, let's get moving."

Now Ceduna was a real town, a population of a few thousand people and lots of shops. Al was so happy that their journey together, so often silent, was over. They arrived at the camp site which was across the road from the beach and just around the corner from the main road and all the shops.

"It's going to be so good to be able to do something other than sit in a car watching the scenery go by. There's so much to do here: walk on the beach, go into town and buy food, post a letter..." Al felt a sense of freedom, a freedom which comes from no longer being dependent on someone else. A freedom which would allow him to spend time alone. They set up their tents. Al had already decided to stay here for at least two nights and then went for a long, long hot shower before facing the chore of doing his laundry. The grime of the long journey washed away into the great unknown of the town sewer system; which probably meant straight into the sea.

He was surprised to find that the town had a pier. Not like the great British Victorian piers, with amusements and side shows, but nonetheless it was a pier. A short wooden construction which was once used for tying up boats, but it had probably been many years since it was last used; there was now a large modern port at the other end of the bay which handled the grain, fish and minerals.

It was here in Ceduna, a not so sleepy little town, but so many miles from any other town, that Al came across his first group of Aborigines. It was a sight that he neither expected... nor wanted to see. He came to Australia with so many naive attitudes and preconceived ideas. Ideas which came from his studies in primary school about this great island continent down under. Ideas which had been reinforced through television programmes, but nothing had prepared him for the sight that now presented itself to him. On a lawn by the beach, under the shade of some Norfolk Island palms lay twenty or more Aborigine men, women and children, all drunk. Flies buzzed around them and landed on their faces without let, or hindrance. Al was disgusted with what he saw, but more than that he was sad for them. Was this the reason that they turned their backs on their traditional way of life? Was white man's life really so appealing? They looked so lost and out of place in this little town, a lonely outpost of western civilisation. It seemed to him that they were trapped between modern society and an ancient and noble past, an abyss into which Al would find that so many of Australia's indigenous people had fallen. He turned his back and walked away, saddened by what he had seen.

* * * * *

Tony had reached Bunbury by mid afternoon. It had taken three lifts and he now found himself with the people from the final one. Berryl and Brad were travelling around Australia with their two children, Jason and Beth.

"Why don't you share a caravan with us? It will be much cheaper for you than staying on your own." Berryl said. Tony wasn't too sure about these people, they seemed a bit too much like they were on the take to his mind.

"We could all travel together along the south coast and over to Melbourne." Tony liked the sound of not having to wait for a lift each time he wanted to go somewhere, so he agreed.

Two days and a hundred dollars later they were ready to move on. For two days they had done very little other than eat, drink and sleep. Tony thought that this would be a one-off thing and anyway he enjoyed a good drinking session, but as they travelled south to Albany and east to Esperance he came to despise these people. Parasites, living off the state with no intention to do anything other than eat, drink and travel.

Berryl was fat and ugly. Now it seemed to Tony that everyone had the right to be both fat and ugly, but she abused that right and it wasn't hard to see how she got to be in such a state with all the junk food and alcohol she consumed and there was never a waking moment when she would be without a cigarette in her mouth, only ever without one when she slept. She sat like a beached whale in the passenger seat, ripples of fat oozing over the edge. Rolls of fat squeezing out over the tops and from the bottoms of ill-fitting garments. Her face totally round, poxy skin plastered over with poorly applied make-up and the saddest thing of all for Tony was the fact that she was only thirty-four and even though that meant she was a massive thirteen years older than Tony, he knew that it wasn't really old.

Brad was a similar case, though not quite so fat. He epitomised Tony's preconceived impression of a fat, lazy, drunken Aussie male. Never did he cook food, wash the dishes or clothes. In fact the only thing he would do was drive the car.

The kids, Jason and Beth, were like their parents, fat. It was obvious that Jason was a carbon copy of his father and Beth, one of her mother. Tony thought that it was both sad and amusing that these children were looking at images of how they themselves would one day look.

They travelled further and further east. Tony regretting taking the offer of this lift as each hour dragged on. It was proving to be an expensive few days, but it wasn't a few days, now it was a week since he had left Perth, over a week since he had last seen Al. How was he? Where the hell was he now? Over a week since he had last had Lucy. He still couldn't believe how easy she had been, or was it he who had been easy? He still wasn't sure who had picked up who? They had driven since early morning from Norseman, stopping only once, for lunch. Now they were at Eucla and Tony was longing to get away from them. Brad and Berryl took the kids and went to get a room for the night at the motel.

"I'll see you over there, Tony said. "I need a piss." He made his excuses and went to find out if he could get a lift with a truck driver, overnight, tonight. After several beers and a lot of talking, a truckie agreed to take him as far as Port Augusta. Unknown to Tony, this man with whom he was going to travel throughout the night had only left Perth eighteen hours ago and Perth was more than nine hundred miles away. Now, after a huge meal and a few hours rest he was going to drive all night to Port Augusta which was over five hundred miles further on.

Tony took his pack from the car and didn't bother saying to the fat freaks; which was how he thought of them, that he was leaving. He was tired of travelling, but the thought of getting away from those people was too great to resist.

In the darkness the truck thundered along an almost empty road. In two hours they had seen two other trucks, one bus and a car and hit a few kangaroos. Each time they hit a roo the truckie cheered and said how wonderful Australia would be if they could kill all these fucking pests off. Tony was having trouble keeping awake. The driver offered him some pills, Tony declined.

"They'll keep you going for hours mate. I couldn't do this job without them. Do you smoke?"

"Thanks." Tony said, as he took a tin from the driver and rolled himself a joint.

The journey seemed to go much quicker once he was almost as stoned as the driver and the lights from the oncoming vehicles, few though they were, gave him much amusement as he insisted that they were reflections from the eyes of giant kangaroos.

Around two o'clock the next morning, Tony, high as a kite, but not as high as his driver, passed through the sleepy town of Ceduna. Nothing moved in the town as the truck rumbled noisily from one side to the other. Unknown to Tony, that in the camp site not two hundred metres away, Al lay awake in his tent. They had both travelled many hundreds of miles since Al's sudden and worrying departure from Perth and here by chance their paths crossed, but neither was aware of that fact.

The truck continued out of the town and on through the obscurity of the bush and grain farms, thundering ever further east. Tony rolled both of them another joint; he didn't like it when this Aussie drove the truck at speeds which were well over the official speed limit and rolled a joint at the same time. Each time he felt the stony shoulder of the road every time the truck started to wander about the carriageway he felt sure it was only a matter of time before they would crash; and although Tony was stoned, he wasn't so far gone that he didn't care about living. The journey continued much the same for another five hours until they were nearing Port Augusta and then daylight arrived. The morning was sobering as Tony began to come down from his high. He hadn't slept and he was feeling rough from the lack of sleep, but he was pleased that he had left those horribly obnoxious and fat people yesterday and he was equally pleased to be getting out of the truck here and not carrying on to Adelaide in it. He noticed that he had just passed a camp site and it wasn't much of a walk back from where he had been dropped, so he moved his weary limbs along the road and set up tent, not bothering to pay; he figured that it was too early to ring the office bell, he just crawled inside and slept.

* * * * *

Al sat on a rock by the shore and lazed in the sun. The sea was calm with just a gentle lapping of small waves on the soft golden sand. The water almost looked inviting, but not quite. In the shallows, shoals of tiny fish darted in unison, first one way and then another. He sat and let the day drift along, taking him with it. Morning turned into afternoon, afternoon ran into evening and evening merged with night as the air was bathed with the smells from the bay; fish, salt, ozone. Above him a glittering parade of stars filled the heavens. They looked so close, almost close enough to reach up and touch. He enjoyed moments like this, though he always knew that they would end with the same thoughts of Steven and how he should be here to enjoy this with him. Sometimes it hurt, sometimes it was much worse. After unwinding after days of uneventful travelling; apart from the horrors of last night, Al decided on an early night followed by an early morning. Unusually for him, he was asleep within minutes, but was rudely woken just before midnight by what sounded like a World War Two air raid siren. He shot bolt upright in his green dome and it took a few seconds before he could even remember that he was in Australia, let alone the small town of Ceduna. His heart was beating rapidly and his breathing was deep and erratic.

"Oh my god, it's an air raid! Who the hell would want to bomb the shit out of Ceduna and why?"

He couldn't think that Australia had any enemies, but the world still wasn't so logical and rational, even if Gorbachev was in control of the U.S.S.R. Bush was still there and unafraid to bomb anyone that he wanted to bomb. Al got dressed as quickly as he could and emerged from his tent. David was already standing there.

"What's going on? Is it an air raid?"

The noise from the siren was deafening and Al had to shout his question. David laughed.

"That's what I thought when I came over here and heard it for the first time. They use them for fire sirens over here. You can hear it for miles, so it's a sensible way of getting the fire crew here and letting everyone know that there's a fire."

"Yeah, I bet you can hear it for miles. I should think that everyone has heard it now, so why don't they turn it off?" Al thought how lucky he was that he hadn't been around in London during the blitz; imagine that each time you heard the siren you would have the fear that you would not live to see the next day. It must have been horrific. It was something that Al could never appreciate as a kid. He was fed up of hearing about the Second World War and how people suffered for his generation. He felt a little different now. The siren continued to yell for another ten minutes before it was switched off and wound down.

"At least if there is an air raid I'd not be able to miss the warning!"

The excitement over, the crowd that had gathered began to disperse and Al returned to his tent. Now he was wide awake, whereas before he had been dead to the world; but not dead to sirens! Hours drag slowly at night when laying awake waiting for either morning to arrive or tiredness to send you to sleep. He began to nod off, but the noise of a large truck going through the town shook him as he began to drift. Unknown to him that it was the truck in which Tony was travelling.

Al was up as soon as daylight arrived. He hated lying in his sleeping bag when he could be out in the sunshine, especially early morning sunshine, which he more often than not had to himself. He was pleased that the mundane task of laundry had been taken care of yesterday, that meant he only had to spend a little time cleaning his tent and boots; but that could wait until later, much later! Instead he chose to sit beneath a palm and write a letter, drink coffee and eat.

"Dear Sarah and Christopher, I've travelled a lot of miles since Perth and now find myself in Ceduna. I was pleased to leave Kalgoorlie - not enough to keep me interested. The journey across the Nullarbor was uneventful apart from being woken up early one morning by a pack of dingoes outside of my tent in the bush, I thought that I was dog food! I'm now sitting under a palm by the beach with no one else about and another hot sunny day beginning. Take care, I miss you. Lots of love, Al."

Out to sea a ship was disappearing into the horizon, through that area of water between the ultramarine near the shore and the dark grey of far away. Seagulls combed the beach for dead fish and any other tasty morsels that they might find. Others raided around rubbish bins, pulling at paper which might hold the remains of a burger, chiko or spring roll, or some chips. Indian mynahs waddled on the grass and pecked around the trees, always on the look out for the opportunity of a free meal. Al sipped his coffee and watched with not more than vague interest. It all only served to remind him that this was not home.

Feeling that he had been cheated out of almost a whole night's sleep and still waking up before dawn, he resolved to doing as little as possible during the day ahead. Once again it would be hot enough for shorts and a short-sleeved shirt; the latter he would discard as the temperature began to rise, in order to allow as much sunlight on his back, which, from what he could make out by twisting himself in front of a mirror, was no longer white.

"I don't understand how my life has changed so much in such a short period of time?"

He looked over to a mynah which was being brave and searching for food nearer and nearer to him.

"It must be good to be a bird. To have the freedom of the skies and not have anyone tell you what you can or can't do. No broken hearts for you my little feathered friend." The mynah looked at him and chortled, nervously stepping first forward and then backwards.

"Well, much as I'd like to, I can't sit here all day. I need some exercise." He said, getting up to return his cup and postcards to his tent before walking along the beach, which he still had to himself.

A trail of footprints stretched out behind him for much further than he could see. A train moved in the sidings at the port far ahead of him. On the waterline a variety of pieces of seaweeds and shells bobbed up and down each time the water came in and then went out again. The sand, firm beneath his feet, shells crunched and broke into a collection of small pieces; they would break into yet smaller pieces with the action of the waves against themselves and the sand. His mind drifted, his heart sank and the sun rose in the sky.

* * * * *

It was December 31st. A very ordinary December 31st. Just like any other December 31st. Al had no strange feeling of impending doom, there was no feeling of a calm before the storm. He had no reason to suspect that there was anything wrong on this, the last day of the year. It had been a good year and the next one was going to be even better. It was about four thirty or five and it was already dark outside. The afternoon air was cool on his face as they walked along the street to where the car was parked. Above them, the stars were thinly masked by some patchy cloud and it was going to be a dry, cold and frosty night. There would be ice on the road coming home tomorrow morning. A shiver ran down his back at the thought of ice. Steven looked at him and smiled. Al was happy.

Along the other side of the otherwise quiet road, a middle-aged couple walked along without talking. It was such a familiar walk; how many times had they walked it in the past four and a half years? Al had no idea.

It was quiet and the only sound to break that quiet was the sound of their feet hitting the paving slabs rhythmically as they walked. The tiny soft red-bricked Victorian terraced houses looked warm and inviting; some of their chimneys puffed out small clouds of grey smoke which seemed to be dancing a path through the black of night.

"Humm." Al sighed aloud, lost in his own thoughts and happiness; almost smugness. "I don't think that there is anything as comforting as a bright open fire on a cold winter's evening."

Steven looked at him and again smiled. His eyes were bright and Al melted in his gaze.

"Except for you." Al added. He could see that Steven was happy to be with him at moments like this.

It would have been much nicer to be sitting by the fire, on the floor and lost in thoughts which would mean nothing in particular, just watching as the flames danced their Swan Lake and disappeared into the flue and out of sight. Steven was thinking similar thoughts to Al, he did not want to be going to Hadleigh tonight.

As they walked along the path they peered over the low walls into the gardens; which were no bigger than a dinner table, to see what new plants had appeared since they last looked. Despite the small size of the gardens they were full of interest as most of the inhabitants took more than a passing interest them. There were always plants in flower in the street, especially in Steven's garden and it was especially good to see them during the winter months when everything else looked so drab. Any of the gardens that they passed which had not been weeded, or in which the soil had not been turned over recently giving it a healthier tended look, were met with a light hearted tut-tut.

Steven unlocked the car door and got in as Al walked to the other side. He got in and pulled the door, but it didn't close properly; it never did, it always needed to be slammed shut. They buckled their seat belts, click, click. They said nothing, content in each other's company. The streets were nearly empty of traffic, which was strange at this time of the afternoon and as the engine fired up, it seemed that it broke the silence of the winter's evening. They drove through Ipswich and out to the west, the route was a familiar one to both of them. Steven had once lived in Hadleigh and now worked there. Al had lived in Sudbury, which was another twelve miles further on and for two years he had commuted along this road to and from work. He was part of this area, he knew every lump and bump along the road like the back of his hand. He knew the landscape, which he loved with an intensity and passion which was hard for most people to understand.

Hadleigh is just ten miles from Ipswich and in the daylight one can see the broad rolling hills and little valleys that are so typical of much of eastern East Anglia. Wherever you are in this land you can always see small clumps of woodland, small streams and slow flowing rivers, small villages with half-timbered cottages painted in shades of cream, beige and Suffolk Pink. Suffolk is full of sleepy little villages, yet it is only sixty miles from central London. Despite the darkness outside of the car Al could picture the view with amazing clarity. He loved East Anglia. He loved being part of it. It was in his blood and this was where he always wanted to be. To live and to die in his country, a country in which he still believed in and not in the thought of its reduction to regional status under generations of Saxon, Norman and German monarchs. East Anglia has no mountains, or towering cliffs. It's an undramatic landscape, but so stunningly beautiful that it takes one's breath away just as a dramatic landscape would. It was the land of Thomas Gainsborough and John Constable and just by looking around any fool could see that it was not by chance that they became two of the world's greatest artists; the greatest as far as Al was concerned. It was the land in which they were raised that nurtured them. The Stour valley is like the embers of a fire, there are no flames to burn you, but a constant heat which warms you. A warmth that pours into your heart and soul even when you leave it for some other land, for it becomes part of you and you part of it. A gentle land of fens, broads, woods and heaths. Its meandering rivers cutting softly through the hills formed by an ice age long ago. A savage coastline which changes each year as the sea smashes away at it; still destroying the city of Dunwich; what little there is left of it. Once a great city with dozens of ecclesiastic houses, including an Abbey, Priory and Friary, now a small gathering of cottages and a pub and a wall from the last of its great churches which stands on a lonely sand cliff amidst a few graves and wind beaten trees waiting for the grey sea to take it. The only safe waters are those of her magnificent estuaries which open wide against the rich green of the woods and fields. An ancient kingdom which was in existence long before the country it now forms part of. A land where noble peoples have been leaving their mark for centuries; The Celts, Romans, Angles and Danes were all here long before the Normans arrived to oppress the peoples of Britain.

Hadleigh is a small market town, which has luckily escaped a lot of the urban renewal that Sudbury and Ipswich have suffered, especially through the architecturally stale nineteen sixties, there are still large groups of half-timbered houses, dating mainly from the early sixteen hundreds. It was so easy to take all this heritage for granted and whenever Al caught himself adopting this smug attitude he would reprimand and remind himself how lucky he was to have been raised here. Moving from southern to eastern East Anglia was the best thing his parents had ever done for him. People in the south are totally ignorant of the fact that they are part of East Anglia.

Steven's mother lived in Hadleigh and it was to her house that Al and Steven now travelled. She was expecting them for dinner and then they would see in the New Year together with Steven's sister Susan, her boyfriend David and their younger brother Jonathan. It was infrequent that the family were all together; once, sometimes twice a year and these gatherings could occasionally be slightly on the stressful side of kinship, however, Al enjoyed their company, mainly because he was always made welcome, never was he made to feel like an outsider. Steven would not have had the same welcome from Al's parents that was certain. They couldn't have the neighbours knowing that their son lived with another man. Imagine the shame of it, how would they ever be able to lift their heads in public if the 'whole world' knew that their son was a poof?

It didn't take long to get to Hadleigh; despite Steven's deliberately slow driving. He didn't like this sort of get together, he found it too much of a strain to be with his family, he was quite intolerant of them and he would much rather have spent time with friends than family, but once they were all together, talking and having a few drinks he soon forgot about that. For the first hour they did not have to struggle for conversation, David had passed his final examination and was now Dr. David and this gave them something to discuss and when conversation did slacken off they each slipped back into those shallow questions which are instantly recognisable as not the slightest bit genuine and very disinterested. The sort of questions which should only be used at cocktail parties and yuppie housewarmings.

Dinner was not long in coming and that gave them all something else to talk about. They sat around the large old mahogany table, passing plates and bowls this way and that, until each person had seen everything at least once. This was by far Al's favourite part of the evening; dinner was always a large affair and totally disproportionate to the number of people seated at the table and this met with his total approval. Eating was Al's biggest hobby; after Steven, though to look at him you would swear that he hardly ate a thing and that was his excuse for eating so much, for fear that he would waste away and disappear if did not consume huge quantities of calories.

The room was cluttered with all manner of things, photos of children; there were no grandchildren yet, nor were there likely to be from any of Mrs. Brown's three children in the foreseeable future, if ever. Plates stood on the dresser, glasses, a bowl of fruit. Pictures, dark with age adorned the walls and dull curtains hung on both windows.

"Ooh-ah!" Mrs. Brown exclaimed in an alarming manner. "I've got some crackers left over from Christmas... I nearly forgot." Her Ipswich accent came through loud and clear and Steven looked to Susan as if to say, "oh no," as his mother went to the cupboard to fetch the crackers. She returned to the table with a large box and handed crackers out to everyone. Most pulled with a fizzle; a wet fart, as crackers do. So they sat around the table wearing silly hats; Steven's and David's ripped.

"It's because your heads are too big!" Al laughed at them as he put his on with as much dignity as he could, but it was too large and it slipped over his face, much to the amusement of all.

"Much better Al," Steven said, getting a dirty look from Al once he had removed the silly paper thing which filled him with indignation. They read the so-called jokes, which no one understood to be funny, but it was something to amuse themselves with as they waited for New Year which was still hours away.

Dinner came and went and Mrs. Brown went through to the lounge to sit down while the kids cleared the table, washed up and made coffee. They took their time in the kitchen, though there was a lot to clear.

"I think mum used every pot and pan in the house." Susan said to Steven.

"Yeah, of course!" Jonathan piped up, it was rare for him to say anything.

"She's got to get out of this big house. It's too much for just one person. Steven said, looking around.

Their mother had been trying to sell the house for over a year, but it was big and needed work done on it. It wasn't easy to sell, even if the housing market was booming.

By ten o'clock Al, Steven, Susan and David were sat on the floor in the lounge playing the game of 'Scruples', while knocking back a few gin and tonics. Mrs. Brown sat knitting and chatting to them about people they had known only vaguely more than twenty years ago. They would say that they didn't remember the people in question and she would answer, "Oh yes you do, they lived by so-and-so and went with that lad from the corner house..." the way mothers and grandmothers have a habit of doing, while the man on the television talked away to himself with no one's attention; but to everyone's annoyance, as it was too loud. Jonathan sat in a chair reading The Independent and occasionally he would interject some witty comment into the conversation, which he never directly paid any attention to. He was so quiet and if asked a question he usually answered it with an indistinct "erh" or "umm" and even Mrs. Brown would joke, "was that an erh or an umm sonny?"

The game continued and Al amused himself watching Steven, Susan and David discretely looking at their watches; so subtle they were, so clever, about as subtle as a punk rocker would be in a flute concerto. They asked their questions, some of which were a little close to the mark and Mrs. Brown stopped talking so she could hear the answers. Al knew Steven and how he would answer and likewise Steven knew Al, but for Al it was interesting to find out what Susan and David thought of him. They were a bit wide of the mark and he found that quite revealing, he had summed them up better than they had him and he was pleased about that.

Behind Susan, and opposite Al, the fire was giving off a nice warmth as the large piece of applewood began to burn properly. Al felt tired in the heat, though it might have had something to do with the quantity of alcohol that he had drunk. He wasn't the only one who had too much alcohol. Mrs. Brown had overdone the sherry and had started to giggle at things which were most obscure.

The evening wore on, but seemed to be going at half time as they still awaited the New Year, even so, it was a cordial affair and with far less tension than at some previous gatherings. Al was happy. He looked forward to the New Year and what it would bring; or to be more precise, to what he thought that it would bring. He felt like a king with the world just sitting there ready for the taking. All the hard work that he had put into his little landscaping business was now paying off and from next week he would have his first full-time employee. He had a friend who worked for him part-time, because the work had snowballed and he hadn't expected that at all. This coming year would see him put another two and a half thousand pounds into new tools and machinery and he would even buy some land on which to open a small garden centre. 1989 was going to be such an exciting year and the most important thing as far as Al was concerned was the fact that he was with Steven. This summer would be their fifth year together and although they had their ups and downs;

and what couple doesn't, whether heterosexual or homosexual? Al loved Steven, he was devoted to him, he was unwise enough to worship him and build his life around him, but that didn't matter because he knew that no matter how bad things had seemed at times in the past, Steven did love him and they would always have each other.

The second hand ticked up towards the twelve.

"Five, four, three, two, one. Happy New Year."

They raised their glasses to one another and toasted their health and happiness.

"Any excuse for a drink," Al said what some of the others thought, but dared not say. Steven pushed him lovingly, it was the only contact that he'd dare with his family around. He was happy.

* * * * *

It was so easy to remember the things that he would have rather forgotten, but four months wasn't such a long time, even if at times it felt like it was. He had walked to the far side of the beach and sat in the sun for rather longer than he had planned, so long that he could recall and picture events like they happened yesterday.

"Time for dinner, yes stomach?"

He saw David heading off towards the pier with his fishing rod as he arrived back in town, without saying anything to him he headed off to the supermarket, unsure of what exactly he needed rather than wanted. He would be heading east in the morning so he did not want to find himself carrying too much food, but more than he had been carrying when he had left Perth; he didn't want to find himself in the bush with nothing to eat again.

The sun began to sink below the bight as he ate his chicken, rice, courgettes and calabrese. It was easy to eat well and be travelling, if one chose sensible foods, not pre-made, over-processed, or over priced. He rested for a while, he felt good to be here, but quite happy to be moving further east. On the move again before he grew too familiar with his surroundings and began to panic. The air was warm and the sky began to darken. Al walked across the camp site and towards the beach. He thought that he should say goodbye to David as he was certain not to be up in the morning when he would leave.

At the end of the pier stood three people fishing. Shadows of people growing into the darkness of night. Under his feet the boards sighed and moaned as he walked lightly along towards where David stood. Beneath the pier the sea lapped at its supports, making a calm sea sound choppy.

"Alright Al?"

"Yeah. Have you caught anything?"

"A couple of tiddlers, but nothing worthwhile yet."

"Don't you get bored waiting around for hours?"

"No, I love fishing."

Al couldn't imagine anything so boring as waiting for a fish to bite the hook at the end of a line, though he was quite happy to sit still on a mountain, in a wood, by a river and just let hours drift past as he thought things over; maybe fishing wasn't so different after all?

"I'm leaving tomorrow."

"Which way are you going?"

"Straight across to Port Augusta, then north."

"I'm going to stay here for a couple of days and then go along the coast and do some more fishing."

"I'm going to bed now. I'll be leaving quite early, so I don't expect that I'll be seeing you again." Al found himself wondering why this conversation was taking place? Why did he feel the need to explain what he was doing? Leaning on the rails of the pier, he looked into the darkness below. The water was not the clear blue that had been there during the day, it was now a murky green-black, uninviting, cold.

The town was quiet as he packed. David was asleep. Forty metres away the waves lapped tirelessly against the soft sand and the smell and taste of sea air filled his lungs. Al set off to the edge of town, every few metres having to swat at the flies which were already out in abundance. It was warm and the frantic waving of his map at the flies only served to make him hotter and irritable, but his whole body crawled as those flies kept trying to get into his eyes, ears, nose and mouth. He reached the outskirts of the town and no cars had passed him. At first he thought he should stand and wait, but he didn't like the thought of being a sitting, or rather a standing target for those dirty winged insects, so he kept walking, leaving the town behind as the morning pressed on.

He had been walking for more than an hour when a car stopped, but Al declined the offer of a lift to Port Lincoln as he had already made up his mind to head inland and east. He watched the car drive away and then decided that he should have taken it and travelled around the peninsula, which might have been more interesting. It was too late now and he wasn't going to cry over the lost opportunity. He marched on, at war with the army of flies, unceasing in their attacks.

It was hot, very hot and he was glad that he had a full gallon of water in his pack. Even so, it was hot and he was without the protection of shade, he knew that he would not last long today before he would begin to suffer. There was nothing new to look at as he proceeded east. The bush was very much the same as he had seen day after day and he wondered just how much of Australia was forested?

It did not occur to him that what he was doing was not too sensible. Why should it? He was just walking along a road because he wanted to get somewhere. He had been walking for two hours, walked around sixteen kilometres and so few cars had passed. Where were all the villages in this country? If he had been in the remotest parts of East Anglia, he would have walked through a handful of villages and would now not be far from a town. Where were all the farmers and hunters and foresters? Didn't people live in the countryside here? To his relief a car stopped. A preacher and his wife were heading to Wirrula for a funeral. He would be fly-free for an hour and was glad of that though he felt a little uncomfortable and conversation did not flow freely and although he was very grateful for the lift, he was glad to be dropped at the side of the road once again. Looking around, he noticed he was the odd one out. A collection of cars, shiny, clean, stood along the road edge and a mass of people stood around in small groups, talking quietly. All were dressed for the funeral. The whole town was closed up and Al meekly walked through the crowds trying to avoid any eye contact if he could. He tried hard to look unhappy, or at least not happy. He dreaded his normal reaction, which was to smile at people and cheerfully say hello to anyone he met in the street. Once the crowd was well behind him, he took refuge from the sun and from the masses of eyes which were on him. He laughed. He laughed because he tried too hard to be sombre, he reacted uncontrollably and felt embarrassed, but he couldn't help himself. He could not control the laughter that welled up from deep inside and the more that he tried to make himself stop, the worse he became. He tried deep breaths; it worked for hiccoughs so why not for laughing? He drank water; that also worked for hiccoughs, but not for laughter. Al controlled himself by feeding his face. Food worked wonders for him!

He was reluctant to leave the cool shade that he had found for the heat and flies and the endless fear of having to walk nearly four hundred kilometres which still separated him from Port Augusta. Eventually he resigned himself to the knowledge that he had to go and sorted himself out and set off again. He was so thankful when he heard a car coming from behind. He could hear that it was going slowly and although he assumed that it was going to stop for him, he thought that it didn't look good to show that was what he had assumed, so he turned around, thumb sticking out and his sign held at driver level. As he saw the sight behind him, he was struck dumb with horror. His mouth fell open, his face flushed purple. The car with which he was trying to hitch a lift with was a hearse, not only was it a hearse, but it was the hearse which was being used for the funeral there. Still standing there, staring. A fly tried to enter his mouth so he closed it and hid his sign and thumb behind his back. The hearse passed by and the people in the following car went red with trying not to laugh at Al's situation. He turned, tucked his head down and continued walking as a hundred pairs of eyes turned to look at him from the cortege as it passed at little more than walking pace. It seemed to take forever to leave his side.

It was getting too hot for Al and he was beginning to think that it was going to take a couple of days to cover the remaining three hundred and eighty kilometres. The only sign of life was that of the flies, which would not leave him alone for a single minute. For as far as Al could see it was dry and barren. The wheat had been harvested and the stubble stood in the fields waiting to be ploughed in or burnt off; he wasn't sure what they did to it here. There was a severe drought and a new crop would be delayed until rain eventually arrived. Al recalled 'The Grapes Of Wrath', not that he had paid any attention to his English lessons, but little bits of the coursework went in and he surmised that the American mid-west landscape was not vastly different to this part of Australia; be it the land, the buildings, farms or people. Here and there along the road the Eucalyptus trees grew to six to ten metres, but little more. They afforded little protection against the burning rays of the sun. Time was passing, but Al paid no thought to time. He thought it better if he ignored time altogether.

A car raced past, the first since Wirrula. It stopped at the side of the road in a cloud of dust about two hundred metres ahead of Al, then turned around and came back. Al could see that there were already four people in it, but they made room for him.

"We've been to a funeral at Wirrula, we saw you there. Have you been walking all this time?"

"Yes, I was just resigning myself to the prospect of walking all the way to Port Augusta." Al said nothing about Wirrula, he didn't want to remember his embarrassment.

"What on Earth do you want to go there for? Is there something there that I don't know about?"

"The road north starts there!"

"Yeah, that's the only good thing about the place, it's easy to get out of in any direction!" They laughed.

"I take it that there isn't really much to the place?"

"Even less than not much!"

"Oh well, I'll stay a night and have a look around."

"Well we're not able to take you far, just about another twenty Ks from where we picked you up."

"That's O.K. that's another twenty Ks that I don't have to walk."

"What happens if you don't get a lift?"

"I'll walk there. I won't have a lot of choice will I?"

They were amazed by Al's determination; or were they amazed by his stupidity? Whatever it was, they were impressed. Very soon they stopped at the side of the road where a dirt track led to a farm and a few houses and grain silos. Al said thanks and once again started to walk. He could have been on another planet it was that far removed from anything he was used to in East Anglia. The distances that he could see were huge. It was so dry, so dead. The massive fields had no hedges to break the effects of the wind and the frail red soil was blowing away. Surely it was a slow death of the land, it was disheartening to see. It would not be much longer before it was of no use to man nor beast.

The plague of flies grew worse as the day grew hotter. It was twenty eight in the shade, but Al was in the sun. His skin felt like it was crawling with insects, sucking at his sweaty body, as he repeatedly swung out at them. Now he thought that he understood what it must be like as he recalled the television reports of the starving masses in Africa, flies all over the poor children's faces; at least Al had the energy to fight them off.

It was but ten minutes since he had resumed walking when he was rescued by a young woman and her two children. Al was more grateful than any words could express. This was the second time that a woman had picked him up in the middle of not very much at all and it reinforced his belief in the friendliness of the majority of the people in this land down under. It was just like the television commercials at home. Maybe he would be able to join in someone's barbie on a beach one day, just like he had been led to believe. Once again he was away from the flies, even if it was not going to last for long. She told Al that she was only going as far as Poochera and that she lived on the farm with the people who had just dropped him off. Al had to listen carefully, her accent made it difficult for him to understand. To Al, it sounded like a mutation between a strong Bob Hawke whine and a deep Texas drawl. It was odd, to his ears it was awful. She was a little younger than Al, but looked much older. Al figured that living in this harsh environment had taken its toll on her looks. In the back of the car her two young sons sat chatting away, but Al couldn't understand a word. This was the most foreign country he had ever been in, apart from Wales; he could only say two words of Welsh and one of those was not polite!

They arrived in the sleepy little town of Poochera where they turned away from the highway and headed for a friend's house. She got out of the car and told Al that she wouldn't be long. Al watched her disappear into the small wooden building, white flakes of paint falling from the weatherboards. He sat in the car and waited. The two boys sat in the back, the eldest one talked to Al and Al tried to work out what it was he was saying. The youngest child sat eating from a half empty packet of crisps. Al looked around at the lifeless streets and was feeling good about making a little more progress towards his destination, slow though it was. He noticed that she had left the keys of the car in the ignition and he was shocked by this. He could have stolen the car and taken the kids with him.

"What if I had been a child molester? I bet she would not have done this if she had known that I am homosexual. No, I'd be branded the dirtiest type of pervert and I just could never be trusted around kids, could I?" He was bitter by the thought of how he was judged by his sexuality and not by the person he was. He hated the preconceived ideas held by so many people about how he was supposed to be, what he was supposed to do.

The woman reappeared from the house, Al looked up at her as she stood chatting a little longer to an old woman. He was glad that she hadn't been long, he didn't know what to do with one kid who he could understand, let alone two who he couldn't.

"I'll take you to the servo. It might be easier to get a lift from there."

"O.K. Thanks very much."

She dropped him off and as soon as she had gone, the flies began another onslaught. Al looked around, there was nothing here except for a garage.

"Easier than what?" He thought.

He took a break from the heat and went to buy a litre of milk and a can of drink for later, but consumed it all in a short space of time. He wanted to eat something, but was not game enough to try to eat anything with the flies that were buzzing around. The thought of food and flies made him lose his appetite anyway.

It was now early afternoon and he had been travelling for several hours. It was too hot for him and his body was sweaty and sticky like it had never been before, he felt uncomfortable and longed for a shower. Sitting in the shade he smeared his arms, legs and face with fresh sunscreen and insect repellent.

"That will stop you little bastards for fifteen minutes or more!" He hoped, "not much more than three hundred kilometres left," he said looking at his map.

"Six days if I have to walk." He began to accept that there was going to be little chance of a lift out here, or at least not today and not to Port Augusta. He wasn't particularly bothered by the prospect of having to walk.

"Good character building that's what it is. Make a man of me and all that crap!"

He stood up, picked up his pack and set off along the road as if it was no big deal. He began to feel like he had been doing this for most of his life and it almost seemed natural to be walking along a highway in a remote part of Australia, which only ever reached a town, eventually. It was normal to be constantly waving his arms about in a continuing war with the flies. Had it really been less than two weeks? It wasn't long since Al had left East Anglia, but time didn't mean anything out here. Not as he understood time anyway. It was a different set of rules out here. And what about Steven? Where was he now and what was he doing? Did he yet believe that Al was in Australia, or still that it was some sort of trick?

"Bastard!" He said under his breath. "I wish I really hated you; I do hate you! You're nothing but a cock-happy queer." He was beginning to get himself worked up for no real reason and it made him feel even more daunted by the distance ahead.

"Don't think about him. He's not worth the effort is he? He's scum and you hate him, so forget him." The problem is that one cannot forget someone if they are trying to hate them. That person commands too much of their thought to be able to forget; and love and hate are just opposite sides of the same coin. One emotion, two extremes. Al desperately needed to believe that he hated Steven, it might make it easier to accept the situation that he was no longer with him. He loved Steven, but did not want to admit to it in the brightness of daylight.

A fly flew into his ear and he jumped about trying to get the little shit out. His spine had a shiver racing first down it and then back up again. He started to scratch at himself furiously all over his face and body.

"Fuck! Fuck! Fuck! Fuck! I hate this! I hate you flies! I hate you Australia! I hate you Steven!" He spun around screaming as he hit out at the air, at the flies, at nothing.

"I love you Steven," he whispered into the heat and a tear began to form in his eye.

* * * * *

Things had been calm; though still tense, for a couple of weeks. February was now well under way and the uneasy status quo that had been in existence now came to an end.

Steven was in the lounge watching television and Al was in his study working. For no apparent reason Al knew that it was time to leave. He didn't want to leave, but he could no longer live under the same roof as Steven, sleep in the same bed as Steven, never being sure of what Steven had been up to during the hours that they were not together. He could bare it no longer. Packing a small bag with enough clothes for a few days he walked slowly down the steep narrow Victorian staircase. Steven sat upright when Al entered the lounge.

"Where are you going Al?" He said, concern in his voice.

"I'm leaving," he said calmly, without malice, without bitterness, but added, "isn't that what you wanted?"

"You can't go now. Why don't you wait until the morning?"

"Oh yes, you'd like that wouldn't you. You'd like me to leave when it was most convenient and comfortable for you." Al walked to the door and opened it. Steven rushed over and pushed it shut.

"Steven, this isn't easy for me. I don't want to leave, I don't want to be away from you, so please don't make it harder than it is."

"Stay until the morning Al. Please."

"And you'll be happy for me to leave tomorrow will you? What if I change my mind? You'll still be stuck with me.

" Steven didn't want Al here any longer than he had to endure him, but was too much of a coward to make him leave. He could not live with himself if he had made Al go and there was still a part of him that loved Al. Al was reliable and dependable even if he wasn't physically exciting to look at.

"Tell me where you're going, then?"

"I'm no concern of yours any longer. This is that you've been waiting for, you'll be free of me at last."

"But Al, I'll worry about you."

"Look Steven, it's me walking out on you. You're the injured party and I'm sure that you can find someone else to comfort you."

Al pushed Steven back and left, pulling the door shut behind him. It slammed shut and the sound from it echoed through his head like a bomb exploding. It smacked of finality. It was cold and dark as he crossed the road to his van. He fumbled with the keys and started the engine, then raced down the road like a rally driver, tears streaming down his face.

In fifteen minutes he was parked in Wolves Wood; the nature reserve near Hadleigh in which he used to work, hidden from the road by naked trees, he sat alone and frightened in the dark. The night was almost quiet, the only sounds being the occasional click from the engine as it cooled down and the sound of the thin branches rubbing against each other in the gentle breeze.

Steven sat behind the closed door, crying. The sound of the door shutting was also echoing through his mind as he relived pictures of happy times, so many happy times that he and Al had shared, though they were mixed with many painful memories, but none of them seemed significant compared to the pain he felt now.

He stayed by the door for an hour in the hope that Al would come back. He wanted him back now, even if he would not want him tomorrow. The telephone rang. He ignored it. Al wasn't coming back, he knew that now. This was it. For a month they had tried to get on as if nothing had really changed, but it hadn't worked. Al had tried so hard, Steven knew that. It hadn't been easy for him.

"Hello mum."

"Hello Steven, how are you?"

"Al has just left. Can I spend the night at your house? I don't really want to spend the night here."

Mrs. Brown hesitated before saying yes. This was the first time that anything had been said to suggest that Al was anything other than Steven's friend and lodger, though she was well aware of what was what. He packed his things for tomorrow's lessons and left the house; which felt hostile and less than homely, empty.

There was a tapping on the window, Al turned to look, it was Christopher.

Al wound the window down and looked at him, not quite sure of what had happened.

"Al? What's wrong? What are you doing sitting out here in the cold? We don't bite you know."

Al looked at him unsure of what to say. He didn't remember driving to Acton.

"I've left him Christopher."

Christopher could guess that and he wanted to say something, but didn't know what he could say that would help his friend.

"It's probably for the best Al. Come on, come inside and warm up."

"Can I take you up on your offer?"

"Of course you can stay here Al. We're your friends aren't we?"

It was warm inside and Sarah was just about to put their son to bed.

"Why didn't you come in? Honestly! Sitting out there in the cold.

We don't bite you know," Sarah said.

* * * * *

Around him the red sand laden with small stones stretched away. Where was the humus rich peat and clays of home? Even the thought of the grey chalk soils of the western parts of East Anglia would have been a welcome sight, anything but this red, red, red. The endless red. The dry fields were far drier than he could remember during the 1976 and 1983 droughts at home. This wasn't natural. He didn't belong here and he knew it only too well. Standing still for a few minutes, trying to regain his composure and determination to go on. He started to walk. The stones crunched against each other under his boots as he marched forward. Wherever there was a tree which afforded a little shade he altered his pace to make the most of it and compared to the extreme heat in the sun those little pieces of shade felt positively cool.

"You do realise how stupid it is to be out here in the midday sun like this don't you? This isn't the sort of place where you can stroll out on a Sunday afternoon and not have to take account of it being hot. You're not in Suffolk now, you wally. This is the middle of nowhere in particular, in Australia!" He didn't know whether to laugh or cry at his situation, his stupidity, his determination? He shook his head and half laughed. It was better than letting it get to him.

"Mad dogs and Englishmen..." he said, then shouted. "and East Anglians!"

Searching around in the dark, it's so dark in my mind,
Trying to hide from you, but I have first to escape myself,
Australian rain burns deep into my soul,
Tearing my heart apart,
Australian rain burns in my mind,
She won't let me forget my pain.

How can I run, when I'm running from myself,
Where can I hide, when I'm not hiding from you,
How can I love when I'm longing to love you,
How can I live when I'm longing to die,
Why can't I cry,

Why can't I break down and cry, and let this pain out.

I'm running across this lonely land, I can't outrun my mind,
Another thousand miles between us, another step nearer you,
Australian rain burns deep into my soul,
Tearing my heart apart,
Australian rain burns into my mind,
She won't let me forget my pain.

Desperate times lead to desperate acts,
I've never felt so low,
The pain of a crisp Perth morning,
The understanding in the airport building,
Strange how people can sense your pain,
Cruel how those times hurt the most,
I'll tell myself I'll be strong tomorrow,
And in time this pain will go,
I'll tell myself that it didn't matter,
And that it all meant nothing to me,
And I'll laugh, Ha! at my time with you,
But what do I tell myself now?

Australian rain won't you burn out my heart,
Let me sleep in your rich red bed.

It had been two hours since he had left the relative safety of Poochera. He had no idea how far he had walked and what was more, he no longer cared. All he was sure of was the fact that he was getting nearer to his destination and that he was hot, and when a car stopped and he found it hard to react to the prospect of a lift, he continued to stroll along the road until he reached it. A tall smartly dressed man got out, about forty, forty four, he had a wild tawny coloured growth of a beard.

"Hi, my name is Oliver. I saw you at Wirrula earlier today. I must say I didn't expect to see you still walking."

"No, neither did I. My name's Al."

"I was at the funeral."

"I think the whole town was at the funeral from what I saw."

Oliver smiled and asked Al where he was going. Al told him

where he hoped to go.

"That's good. I can drop you there. I'm going to Lameroo, that's the other side of Adelaide."

A sense of relief came over Al at the thought of getting to Port Augusta by the end of the day, even if it was still a few hours away.

Al and Oliver talked and talked, strangely Al was relaxed in his presence and it almost felt that they had met somewhere before. Oliver was a preacher, but did not preach to Al, only questioned. He questioned Al's reason for walking in outback Australia on his own. He questioned Al's reasons for not being in his home country when it was so obvious that he wasn't whole hearted about this tour of Australia. He questioned Al's hate of God and the establishment and Al said all that forgiveness nonsense stuck in his throat. The conversation got deeper and deeper into the whys and wherefores and at one point Al almost mentioned Steven's name, but stopped himself just in time, thinking that society can only accept so many things and homosexuality was not one of them, no matter how deep and genuine the individual's feelings are. Al was not about to stand up and be a defender of homosexuality and risk being labelled as one of the stereotypical queers that he also disliked. He wasn't about to conform to what either side wanted him to be.

Oliver was good for Al. He met him at the right time and he was receptive to Oliver's questions. Questions which made Al question every answer that he gave. He was able to see things from another point of view, even if he could not accept that point of view.

"You're so angry and unless you look at why you're angry you won't ever deal with it. It will make you hateful," Oliver said.

"I'm trying hard to be hateful, but it's not as easy as I once thought."

"No, you don't want to be hateful. You just want some help. God is always there to help you. You can trust God."

"I wouldn't trust God any further than I could throw him! I won't accept anything that man-made religions preach, they manipulate and destroy."

"How do you mean?"

"Well let's face it, they are all very much for the white middle classes aren't they? They all want you to conform to an ideal that doesn't exist, An ideal that is easily manipulated. None of them like self expression, or any questioning of what you are told as hard fact.

Anything that does not conform is suffocated and destroyed and at the end of the day it's just an emotional crutch and a way of easing your own conscience when you do wrong."

"But we all need forgiveness, because we all make mistakes."

"I can't accept that someone you trust can screw around behind your back, knowing full well how you feel about that, not to mention the risk of catching something, then they can say to God that they are sorry; and yes they might even mean it, then, according to religion, God will forgive them. Never mind the person who has been hurt. Shouldn't it be they who do the forgiving? Shouldn't they be asked? It's they that pay the price for it, not some high and mighty bloody God!"

Oliver was about to answer when the car started to pull violently to the left. They stopped at the side of the road, got out and had a look at the tyres. Neither Oliver nor Al could see anything obviously wrong, so they continued on their journey, but it happened again.

"We'll have to go back to Wudinna and get it checked out." Oliver said.

They drove slowly back to the town, which luckily they had only recently passed.

"There's a bulge in the tyre," the mechanic said. "It's because of the heat."

Neither Al nor Oliver could see a bulge, but there was something wrong and they had to have something done about it. Oliver had a remould fitted and before too long a delay, they were on their journey again. Barely eight kilometres from the town the same thing happened again. Al swallowed hard and waited for Oliver to get understandably angry, but he didn't. He simply turned the car around and went back to town. Al was impressed by Oliver's calmness. Getting upset would not improve the situation, so why get upset was Oliver's attitude, but keeping calm in potentially stressful situations was easier said than done; especially for Al. He always flew off the handle.

Oliver decided that it would be better to get a new tyre, he did need some anyway and it seemed the best thing to do now and it was what he should have done in the first instant. They were sent to another garage and were told that they would have to wait an hour before they could be dealt with.

"That's alright." Oliver said, it was a break from driving, though *his journey from lift to lift, glancing encounters with mundane folk..*

it would make his arrival home much later.

"Do you want me to run you back to the highway to see if you can get another lift?"

"No, I may as well wait. Lifts haven't exactly come easily today and I'm happy with your company," Al answered.

"And I'm happy with yours, Al."

Wudinna was another one of those dusty little outback towns, where although there were many houses, there didn't seem to be the corresponding number of people to go with them. They stood outside the garage and chatted about nothing in particular, neither felt like resuming their previous conversation now that they had lost the flow of the argument. Oliver told the mechanic to put two new tyres on, the other front tyre wasn't so good, but it would do as a spare. They watched the new and expensive tyres being fitted and Oliver paid the bill before they settled back into the car ready for the rest of the journey.

As they left the town neither spoke, for fear of something else going wrong. It was many kilometres before they felt like breaking the silence and by now it was just beginning to get dark and Al had only reached halfway between Ceduna and Port Augusta. The thought of getting out of the car and setting up his tent for the night crossed his mind. It sounded less bad than being left somewhere in a strange town in the dark and not knowing where the nearest camp site was to be found; but on the other hand, did he really want to be walking along this same road tomorrow morning with the flies buzzing around him in the heat? No, he didn't like the sound of that at all.

It had gone nine by the time they reached the outskirts of Port Augusta and the first thing that Al saw was a camping ground. That made him feel a lot better, safer. Oliver drove in.

"I'll wait with you, until they say that they have room for you."

Al thought that was unnecessary, but amiable of him, so he rang the bell, the office was in darkness. While they waited for someone to answer, two English nurses arrived, they wanted a caravan for the night. They were on a working holiday and were just about out of money, so they were heading to Sydney in the morning to get some work, if they could find someone to share the petrol money with them. Oliver took out his wallet and gave the girls a fifty dollar note, much to Al's amazement.

"Here you are Al, take this because you might need it one day," Oliver said, offering a fifty dollar note to him.

"No thanks. It's really generous of you to offer, but I have all the money that I think I'm going to need and you've been good enough to me as it is."

Another two people joined them and they too were British. Al found it a little more than odd to think that he found himself in a situation in a little railway town on the edge of Australian civilisation and out of six people, who by chance just happened to be in the same place, five of them were British. On reflection, he realised that he had come across more Australians this day than during the past two weeks and during all of that time he had bumped into far more British people than he would have thought possible in the whole of his stay here.

The office door opened. Al paid for one night and Oliver said that he had to go now, he still had over five hundred kilometres to drive before he would be home.

"Thanks for the lift Oliver; and your company and conversation."

"Take care of yourself and try and avoid walking in the remote parts of this country. Hitching isn't as easy as it once was. Crime is increasing and people are becoming richer and more selfish."

Al watched as Oliver got into his car and drove away.

"What a really nice man," Al said to himself.

"Hey, I like your friend. I didn't think that he was going to give me some money," one of the nurses said.

"Yeah, but you took it, didn't you, and I bet you've got plenty of money left," he thought.

"I've never met him before today. He picked me up near some trees and lots of flies."

"That could be anywhere in Australia," she laughed.

"It felt more like nowhere in Australia!"

"Well if I thought I'd be given fifty dollars from everyone I hitched with, I'd sell the car and hitch all the time." The girls laughed, Al wasn't impressed with them.

"I'm going to put my tent up. I'm tired." With that he left them at the office and headed into the camp site.

The camping area was lit by just two lights and the grass sloped down from the office. At the bottom of the hill was a small shower block. Al walked along and looked for a spot near to a light. He stopped in his tracks when he saw a large dark green dome tent which looked exactly like Tony's. His heart lifted at the thought of seeing Tony and he was ready to go over to it and call his name, but the thought that there must be hundreds of tents like this one in Australia stopped him and he didn't want to call out Tony's name and then find that it wasn't his tent, or him inside.

"I'd feel like a right wombat then, wouldn't I?"

He began to pitch his tent under a large wattle tree, not more than three metres away from this tent in which he hoped to find Tony. He was a little noisier than normal in setting up camp, hoping that the occupier would come out and see what the reason was. No one came out and his tent was up. He sat in the doorway, watching.

"If it is Tony's, he probably won't be in it anyway. He'll be in town, in a pub."

Al was frustrated in his inability to call out Tony's name. To ask if there was anyone inside. To find out who was in there. He stood up and walked over to the track which split the camp site in two, standing halfway between the tent and the light, his shadow cast upon the dark green dome. He stood there for half a minute, paced up and down and then convinced himself that even if there was someone in there it would not, could not be Tony. What would the chances be of bumping into Tony here?

He returned to his tent and put some water on for a coffee. He wanted something stronger than coffee, but he hadn't had alcohol for a few weeks now and he did not want to buy any. From inside of the tent, on which Al was keeping vigil, the noise of a zip could be heard. Whoever was inside, would soon be outside. Al's mouth dropped open, he shook with anticipation that it could possibly be Tony; and fear that he was about to be disappointed because it wouldn't be him. Slowly the flysheet zip began to rise up and the gap at the bottom grew larger. Al could see no hand, still he couldn't see if it was Tony or not.

"Hello Tony. You took your time coming out," Al said with a huge grin and sigh of relief the instant he saw that it was indeed Tony, his friend who he had not seen for ten days. It seemed so much longer to him.

"Oh my God! Where the fuck have you been? I wondered what sort of person would deliberately make a noise at this time of the night and then purposely stand near the light making a shadow on my tent and you were the only person I could think of! How long have you been here?"

"About half an hour. I came in from Ceduna today. What about you?"

For the next hour they caught up with what each other had been doing and how they were faring up to the nomadic life in Australia. Tony told Al how he had managed to get through more than half of his money and he would start to look for work as soon as he got to Sydney. Al couldn't imagine how Tony could have got through more than sixteen hundred dollars in less than two weeks; and he didn't ask, or judge. They were joined by an Australian chap who had had his tent stolen while in Western Australia and was now trying to get home to Canberra. Tom asked Tony if he could share his tent and Tony said yes. Al was shocked by both the question and the answer. He was glad that he wasn't asked. He was also impressed by the seemingly natural way that Tony had said yes; without hesitation. Al would have been too suspicious of anyone asking to share his tent. Al told them about the two English nurses with whom he had just been talking and then took them over to their caravan so that they could arrange a lift to Sydney in the morning. Al was more than a little disheartened by the thought that Tony would be leaving so soon. Any hope that he may have had that they might have spent a few weeks travelling together were now gone.

They sat by their tents, talking, asking questions, being together, until it had gone midnight. Al was totally shattered after the day's journey and could no longer keep his eyes open. Tony looked at Al, he didn't want to leave him, but he felt that he had to go and look for work. Al seemed to be coping well enough, he certainly looked better than he did when Tony had last seen him.

"Will you give me a call when you get up Al?"

"Yeah, sure. Half seven too early?"

"No, that's fine. It will give us a little time together in the morning."

"That will be nice." Al had a sad tone in his voice.

"Yeah." Tony looked at Al as an older brother might look at a younger brother, his face filled with concern and love. "I didn't think that I'd ever see you again Al. I'm glad we bumped into each other here."

"Me too. Good night."

Tony answered and watched Al disappear into his tent, as if he was making sure that Al was safely inside and out of harms way.

All too soon it was morning and Al called Tony and Tom, made them all a coffee and shared out his food. It felt good to be in a position to give instead of taking; he never felt comfortable when he took, it was never easy for him. Tom left them alone for a while. Al continued eating.
"Are you alright now, Al?"
"Yes Tony. As alright as I'm ever likely to be," he joked.
"I feel bad about leaving you so soon..."
"Don't be," Al interrupted. "I left you after just four days in this country!"
"Well now you mention it, are you going to tell me why you left?"
Al looked at Tony and was silent for a while.
"One day, I guess. When time is on our side." Al was thoughtful and still more than a little confused about the events which led up to his hurried departure from Perth.
"It was because of me, wasn't it?"
"No Tony, it wasn't because of you. When I understand what happened I'll try and tell you about it."
"You will take care of yourself won't you Al? And I'll see you in Perth in October, unless we bump into each other again."
Tony packed and far too soon he was loading his things into the car and was going. Al tried to pretend that he wasn't bothered, but it hurt to think that was going so quickly after they had found each other. He felt cheated by circumstances which had only allowed themselves a few hours together. Briefly Al had thought about going to Sydney with Tony, but for some reason he considered that it was best if he stayed independent from him, to become self dependent. The car left, Tony looked back and waved. Al waved. He went for a shower, there the tears he shed for his friend; and for himself as they lost each other once again, could not be seen by the world.

Al stayed in Port Augusta for a couple of days. He didn't feel that there was any attraction for him; just as he had been told on his way here, but he could not motivate himself to get moving so soon after watching Tony go. He used the time wisely and relaxed in the sun, his tan was quite strong and deep now. He kept a record of his thoughts and still sent a lot of postcards to East Anglia. It was his way of keeping the feeling that he was close to his friends. He longed to hear Christopher's voice. He could have phoned at any time, it would have been so easy, but he thought that if he allowed himself to telephone once then he would make a habit of it. Each time he opened his wallet he would see Christopher and Sarah, a wedding photo that never left his side, an unfailing source of strength.

Restless, lonely and alone, he packed his tent. This town held no attraction for him now that Tony had gone. How routine all this was becoming, how normal, how ordinary. He had so quickly grown used to life in a tent, a life which involved many hours of walking along roadsides in some strange and remote areas, more remote than he would have been able to imagine three weeks earlier. He had accepted that his shirts were never ironed, only washed and folded, he had accepted that he couldn't go to a wardrobe and choose from a collection of shoes, trousers, shirts. Routine life in a house in East Anglia no longer felt possible. It already seemed like nothing more than a wishful dream. He heaved his backpack up off the grass, and though he had not got used to how heavy it was, it was now easier than two weeks ago. Leaving the town he headed towards the Stuart highway, the road north through the centre of Australia. The main road? The only road, to Alice Springs and Darwin. It sounded quite exciting to him, though he didn't know why. He could not recognise that his excitement was a way of dealing with the loss of Tony. In this excitement he felt good and the sight of the road disappearing into an arid and hot, barren landscape, was not going to change his mood. He walked along the road, but stopped. The idea of walking until he got a lift didn't sound so good and he decided to wait at the side of the road and see what would happen. It wasn't wise to set off towards Woomera and hope that someone would stop for him. It had been barren enough coming over from Ceduna and most of that was either bush or farmland, out there was desert. No, he would wait for a lift. He stood there looking around at nothing in particular and he noticed the back of a traffic sign which was covered in writing. He couldn't see what it said so he took a mosey over and started to read it.
"The worse place on Earth to hitch, David. U.S.A."
"Gone for the bus, Richard. U.K."
"Gave up after three days, Karl. Germany."

"Gone to Sydney instead, Steve. Canada."

The back of the sign read as a catalogue of failed lifts. Travellers who had waited in the heat, some for days, only to give up and leave. The sign was covered from corner to corner with black marker pens, names and messages from people from many lands.

"Oh well Al, looks like you're in for a long wait. Still, not everyone who did get a lift would have had time to write on the sign."

Nothing was going to depress him today. Nothing. And if he did have to wait all day, so what?

He walked back to his pack and watched a couple of cars pass him by.

"Please take me with you. I'm car trained," he said through his smile as he held out his sign to a passing car, with no effect."

"Within two hours, I'll be heading north!"

Determined words, but they were only words, it was beyond his control.

The sun rose higher and he knew that he had done the right thing when he filled his water canteen to the top. He stood thinking about the distances he had travelled, he had never been so far in Europe as he had now been in Australia, but the distances were nothing more than figures. He had covered a great distance, but he couldn't picture it in his mind. This was the here and now for him, but at the same time it was not reality, it was as a dream to him, at times as a nightmare.

Within forty minutes a car stopped. Al was surprised by this, as it drew behind it a horse box. He opened the door of the car and to his horror, sitting on the floor was a dog.

"Put your pack on the roof," Graham said.

Al nodded and tried to find a space on the already overloaded roof rack. He tied his pack on and then got into the car. Graham held the dog, while Al settled in, then pushed the dog down by Al's feet. Al didn't like this, but it was only going to be six hours to Coober Pedy, so he told himself to be brave. The dog snarled. Al was worried, courage didn't come easily.

The car struggled into movement, it was well overloaded; one horse, one pony, the horse box, the rear seat, boot and roof rack full with heavy luggage. The dog snarled again and Al sat motionless. The car stank with the smell of the dog; and maybe with Graham as well.

Eventually the car reached top gear and the journey began. Al mentioned the messages on the back of the sign and Graham laughed.

"Yeah, most people don't pick up hitch-hikers, they think it's too much of a risk. I don't care though because I carry this." He reached under his seat and produced a gun, pointing it at Al. Al swallowed hard, his face drained white, he went cold. He had never seen a hand gun before and never had he expected to have one pointing at his face.

"So don't even think of trying anything."

Graham returned the gun under his seat and Al hoped that it was the last he saw of that. He would not have dreamed of trying anything, even if there had not been a dog at his feet, even if Graham had not been twice his weight. If Graham honestly believed Al would try anything, why had he stopped for him?

The scene outside the window was different from the parts of Australia Al had already seen. There were fewer trees here and what he had expected to be desert was in fact clothed in scrub and spinifex grass, dotted with salt bush, but it still appeared to be a much more hostile environment than the crossing from Perth. They headed north at little more than eighty kilometres an hour, but given the weight on tow, that was quite good. All seemed well until a tyre burst on the horse box. They pulled off the road and Al found himself trying to jack up a horse box with two horses in it, in the middle of the weirdest landscape his imagination could have conceived as real, in the heat of the late morning with an army of flies at his person. It took over half an hour to change the tyre before they could get on with their journey, stopping at the roadhouse at Pimba. Graham filled up with petrol and asked about getting the tyre fixed. When told how much it would cost he said that it was too expensive, so didn't bother.

"You've got too much weight on this side of the float because you've got different size tyres. That's why it blew." The garage hand said.

"Oh well, it's been like that for years and it's not been any trouble before." Graham answered. He failed to mention that yesterday he had had two tyres burst and they sat flat on top of the float with the one from today.

Al and Graham went for a drink in the café and Al was surprised and a little impressed that Graham had a non-alcoholic drink, he said it was because he was driving. Al didn't think that Graham would have let that bother him.

"That kid didn't know what he was talking about. It's just bullshit that they hand out in order to try and rip people off." Graham said, referring to the young lad in the garage. Al knew nothing of such things, but after seeing what happened with Oliver a few days ago, he would have been inclined to listen to what he had been told.

Minute after minute, mile after mile, they headed north, nearer and nearer to Al's destination for the day. There was mallee and spinifex for as far as the eye could see; the deep colour of the ochre sands stretched to the horizon and beyond, like a warm carpet beneath the scrub. Every now and then along the side of the road lay a dead kangaroo. Where were they all? Al had not yet seen one wild mammal, marsupial, or reptile. Each time they passed a carcass, a swarm of flies seemed to explode from it and into the air, like a handful of dust whipped up by a rogue eddy of wind on an otherwise calm day. Occasionally there would be a massive wedge-tailed eagle feeding along side the flies on the free meat. It was an impressive sight to watch as they jumped into the air and spread their wings as they moved from out of the path of the oncoming car. Al had never seen wild eagles this close before, in fact he had only ever seen them once; while on holiday in the west of Scotland, with Steven.

Inside the car the smell still smelled and the cause of the smell still sat at Al's feet. Graham had grown tired of conversation and had turned to playing cassettes, which Al thought were obviously an acquired taste; it was the crudest type of pub music that he had ever had the misfortune of hearing. Each line had a shit, or fuck, or cunt in it, often a combination of the three and the theme of each so-called song was alcohol or sex and once again, usually both.

"I assume that one has to have a long and brainless life in order to appreciate this music," Al thought to himself. He found it sad and beyond comprehension. It made him feel out of place. Was this what a real man was like? They continued the journey, it had been two hours since they had last stopped and now another tyre burst. It was the same side as before and obviously the chap at the garage was right. They got out and Graham climbed up on top of the horse box.

"I thought so," he said.

"What's that?" Al queried.

"That was the last spare that we put on there. All these are flat."

Al looked up at him, not quite believing what he was hearing.

"One hears of people like this all the time, but you never think that you will ever meet one, let alone be foolish enough to travel with one!"

There they were in the Woomera Prohibited Area; where the British Army used to test rockets and bombs, with two horses and four flat tyres and no spares.

"I'll go back to Glendambo roadhouse and take all the flats and get them fixed. I'll get some bigger sizes too." It was about twenty-five kilometres back to Glendambo and Al stayed with the horses because Graham thought that someone might steal them!

"Who in their right mind would want to steal a horse box with a flat tyre and two horses out here? What was he on?" Al scoffed to himself. "But then who in their right mind would set off on a three and a half thousand kilometre journey with the wrong size tyres and no spares!"

Graham passed down the flat tyres to Al and then unhitched the float. The car turned and disappeared into the distance with the dog and the tyres. The same car which held all Al's luggage, passport, travellers cheques and money. He stood there looking down the empty road with only the clothes in which he stood, no water and no protection from the sun, in one of the hottest parts of Australia, with two horses.

"You stupid bastard! You do realise what you have done, don't you?" He started to laugh, though at what he didn't know. "Oh well, it's too late now and there's nothing you can do about it."

Very soon he began to feel the heat. There was only a slight breeze, but the air was so hot that it gave no respite. The sky was blue from one horizon to the other and the heat haze washed every direction with water.

"I could always jump on a horse and go riding off into the sunset." The only problem with that was he had never been on a horse and he would have no idea how to drive one. "How do you change gears on a horse? Do they have a handbrake?" Out in the heat the flies were more aggressive than he had previously encountered. He walked to the rear of the float to hide in the shade that it cast, but the stench made him step backwards into the sun again. It was putrid. He held his breath and looked over at the horses. There was one large horse, white with black patches and a smaller pony, brown with big sad eyes.

They were both suffering badly from the heat which so quickly built up inside their small packing crate on wheels. Their coats were dirty and looked as if they were covered in white fungus; fluffy like mealy bugs on a plant, they had already been in this box for thirty six hours and they wouldn't be let out until they reached Alice Springs. He walked away, suddenly the thought of being in the heat of the midday sun with no hat and no water didn't seem like such an unattractive proposition to him. At least he had that choice.

Would he ever have imagined at any time in his life that he would one day find himself walking along the side of the road looking at plants, flowers, soil, here in Australia? More especially in this part of Australia. He knew the outline of the country and he knew a few dozen towns and cities, but here in this central bit he only knew of Port Augusta and Alice Springs and roughly where Ayers Rock was. He knew that there was a railway which used to follow an old camel trail, but which had been replaced by a new track because the old one used to keep getting washed away in the floods and he knew that there was; whether still or used to be he didn't know, an overland telegraph north to south through the centre. It was a lot more than the average European would have known unless they had made the effort to read up on the area, but Al had not done that. What he didn't expect to see were thousands of square miles of purple, yellow and white flowers where he thought was desert and they weren't the flowers of plants that suddenly appeared after the rains had come, these were plants which were always there. It wasn't a desert as he knew of them. He walked into the scrub, continuing his own botany lesson, taking mental notes of everything, from flower arrangement to unusual methods adopted for survival in this environment. He wanted to see some of the fauna of the area, but the only fauna to be seen were the flies and he had already seen enough of those to last a lifetime.

A car drove past slowly and a couple of old wrinklies stared out at him with idle curiosity. Al opened his mouth and stared at them, they drove off quickly, outraged at his cheek.

"Stupid old bags! You want to know what's going on, but you won't stop and ask if I need any help will you? I bet you'd be horrified if you broke down and realised how many people drove past you without offering to help. Oh yes, I keep forgetting that every hitch-hiker is a murderer and rapist, but no car is a potential coffin is it?!"

He continued his studies as the sound of the car faded behind him.

"Field studies are much more interesting than sitting in a classroom."

He had been in the heat for more than half an hour. He had no way of knowing how hot it was, all he knew was that it was very hot. He looked up and realised that a car had stopped and a man sat looking at him.

"What's wrong?" the man called out to him.

Al looked at the symbol on the car as he walked over to the road.

He was a ranger for this area.

"I beg your pardon?" Al answered. He had heard the question, but just wanted to make him ask it again.

"What's wrong?" The ranger asked again.

Al looked at the flat tyre which was so painfully obvious to anyone within a hundred metres of it.

"I thought I'd stop and have a wander around, look at the plants, you know, getting to know the area and all that sort of thing. After all it's not everyday one gets the chance to be in the middle of Australia."

He gave Al a contemptuous stare, but said nothing, he realised that he deserved ridicule after a question like that.

"I see you have a flat tyre. Are you alone out here?"

"Oh yes, just me and two horses."

The ranger thought that Al was getting too smart for his good. Al's head was getting too close to boiling point to care very much, he just felt that this man was an idiot asking idiotic questions of him.

"You can't go wandering off out here. We don't know what's out there still. Your lot fired all sorts of missiles out there."

"My lot?"

"You are English aren't you?"

"No I am not! I'm East Anglian."

He looked at Al oven more contemptuously than before.

"Where are you going?"

"Coober Pedy, I hope."

"Are you travelling with a friend?"

"No, hitching."

He looked at the horse box and thought it was unlikely that someone with horses would stop for a hitch-hiker when caravanners never did.

"Where's your luggage?"

"That's a bit of a long story, but I hope that it's in Glendambo and will soon be on its way back here."

Al started to talk to the ranger as if he was a real person. If he had had his luggage with him he might have been able to get a lift with him and he could have left the horses to roast out here on their own. But he didn't have his pack and he was bound to stay and wait in the heat for as long as he had too, no matter how long it was. He was at the mercy of Graham and he didn't like being at anyone's disposal at all.

The ranger satisfied himself that Al wasn't up to no good and he was in fact waiting for his luggage to return from the roadhouse, along with some spare tyres. He said goodbye and left. Al stood and watched a potential lift disappear north over the crest of the slope.

Long after his brain had come to the boil and was simmering gently, he saw something in the distance through the heat haze. A few minutes passed before the dark object took on a distinct form and as it grew larger against the ochre, grey and blue background he saw Graham's car with his luggage and the tyres on top.

"At last! I bet he's been for a drink as well, while I've been out here cooking with the horses and flies." They changed the wheel and to Al's surprise Graham had got the correct size and had got all the spares fixed. The journey continued and after fourteen hours on the road they still had not arrived in Coober Pedy.

Outside it was dark. Nine o'clock had been and gone and outside in the darkness the air was not just cool, but cold. Al could feel a draft from somewhere which was uncomfortable on his bare legs.

"We're nearly..."

"Nearly there?" Al interrupted.

"...out of petrol." Graham said, finishing his sentence. Al looked at him, at the fuel gauge and then out of the window at the darkness.

"Oh dear. Why am I not totally surprised by this? This wanker has got to take the prize for the world's biggest dick-head. He had a collection of fuel cans on the top of the car and he didn't even bother to fill them up at Glendambo!" Al couldn't react too much to this situation and he was far too tired to get upset by it. "Oliver would not let this bother him would he?"

They passed a sign at the side of the road. Lit up by the headlights against the dark of night outside. C.P. 40.

"I don't think we'll make forty Ks." Graham said.

Al didn't answer. He was preparing himself for the moment that they would come to a grinding halt in the middle of nothing but darkness. What should he do? There were two options. One, to stay and wait until morning before walking to town, and two, get out and walk while there were no flies about and it was cool.

Al and Graham didn't speak. The radio and tape were off. There was no noise other than the sound of the engine and the squeaks which came from the float. Al could feel his heart beating like a hammer against an oak beam. Time ticked on and neither breathed too deeply for fear that somehow that would affect their fuel consumption. The fuel gauge needle was still sitting well below empty; where it had been for twenty minutes. The car struggled up a long slope. They were pulling too much weight, but as they rounded the crest of the hill they could see, lit up in the distance, a small town against a black background. It reminded Al of some tacky Christmas card with all the stars high above it. C.P. 20. It was still so far away. It might as well be on the other side of the world right now. Surely they couldn't make it?

C.P. 10. It was so close now and becoming closer. It would not be too far to walk from here.

C.P. 5. The lights were brighter and the town was bigger than Al had at first thought. They turned off the highway and into the town. They had made it, but there was no sign of life. The first thing Al saw was a camp site, so at least he knew where he was heading. Stopping at the garage Al opened the door and a rush of cold air came at him. It was bitterly cold on his bare arms and legs. Graham filled up the car with petrol and Al walked along the road to the camp site.

"I smell of dogs," he said, longing for a shower. He was so relieved that the day's journey was finally over, it had felt like it would never be.

There was a stony track leading towards the camp office and he shivered in the night air as he walked along it in the darkness. Opening the door and entering the small room he was surprised to find a Greek family running the camping ground, he thought that all the Greeks were in Melbourne. They were friendly and smiled at the late arrival and Al was pleased to see some happy faces.

"How do you have a family name like Kemal if you are from

Britain?" The mother asked. She was surrounded by two daughters and a niece from Greece.

"My father is Cypriot," Al answered.

They seemed to like Al's answer and chatted with him, finding out if he was planning to stay in Australia, if he wanted to stay in Australia, if he was married? The eldest daughter and her cousin smiled silently at Al. Al felt like he was an object on a supermarket shelf which they couldn't quite decide whether to buy it or not. They smiled even more, though trying to be a little coy.

"It must be true..." Al thought as he looked at them, "all Greeks like big noses. Sorry girls, but you're barking up the wrong tree with me!"

He did not want to leave the warmth of the office, but the thought of a hot shower and something to eat tempted him even more, so he braved the cold desert air and pitched his tent under a light on what could only be described as weathered bed-rock. No, that was an exaggeration, it hadn't even begun to weather! After a few minutes of cursing and bending all of his pegs, he set up and headed for the shower and then did some laundry while he could be bothered to do it.

His stomach growled to him and he remembered that he hadn't eaten since seven this morning.

"Oh shit! I've got that pork chop in my pack. I bet that it doesn't smell too good now."

He was right, it didn't smell good at all, but he refused to throw it away. Instead he just cooked it until it was well and truly dead. He didn't like his meat dead, but he thought that it was wiser that it was the meat and not he that died tonight. Food poisoning was not an attractive proposition right now.

He was tired after the long, ever-so-long journey, but he could not sleep. Beneath his sleeping bag and foam mat the stones were hard and were many, it was positively uncomfortable. The past few days seemed to have been so short, so many hours since Ceduna and yet where were they all? He thought of Oliver and hoped that he got home safely and thought of Tony. What was he doing in Sydney? Had he got a job? Would he be alright?

"Take care Tony, sometimes I think that you are in a worse state than I am. At least I can understand why I'm being so stupid, but you, you haven't got a clue have you? Don't drink too much my friend, you can't run forever." Wise words from someone who could not sort out his own problems, but then it was always easier to see another's situation clearer than ones own. One step backwards can make all the difference.

* * * * *

"Huh, just my sodding luck," he said as he saw the London-bound train disappearing into the tunnel as he crossed the river.
"If East Anglia is so flat and so boring then why the fuck have we got tunnels on our railways? Bastard Saxons are too stupid to know anything about my country. The stupid pratts don't even know where it is, they all assume it's just Norfolk and Suffolk. What wankers they are!"

He crossed the road and bought a ticket to London. He wanted to go somewhere beyond the city, but he didn't yet know where, probably Wales but he would decide that in two hours. There was an hour to kill; kill being the operative word in his mind at the moment, before the next train south. After just a few hours work he had to run. The pressure of working with Jane, his trainee, trying to be pleasant and helpful when all he wanted was to be alone and to be anywhere, other than close to Ipswich, it was too much. Once again he dropped Jane off at home and told her to read about ornamental shrubs. She didn't mind, she was still getting paid for it and it was better than digging soil that was heavy with plant growth.

It was a cool day, but not cold for the time of the year. The sun was shinning as brightly as she could while being so low in the sky, not that Al was moved by the warmth provided. He walked along the river, totally oblivious to the world which passed around himself. The Gipping was dark and dirty, it looked as cold as he was feeling, the surface was glass-like, unbroken by even the gentlest of ripples until a seagull swooped and splashed in for a small dead fish which drifted along on its side. The traffic rumbled and rolled over the bridge and behind him the horn of a ship sounded loudly from within the wet dock. Al stood there, staring, staring through the dark water below, slime-green-brown.

"Hey Al!"
A voice called him, but he didn't hear.
"Al!"
He looked around to see Tony approaching.

"God man, you look like you're going to jump?!"

Al managed a half smile, he was pleased to see Tony, even if he couldn't show it. How long had it been since they had last seen each other? Wasn't it just one chance meeting since college, eighteen months ago?

"Shit man, you look really rough. What's up?"

Al thought that Tony had a wonderful way with words and inside, deep inside, he laughed. "Life."

They stood chatting for a few minutes and caught up on some of the things that had been happening since they had last seen each other. Tony had been to Thailand, moved around Britain, spent lots of time with friends and had a really good time. Al had set up a business, which he no longer wanted, found out that the person whom he very foolishly worshipped, had been screwing around behind his back, which he didn't tell Tony and he had also had his stomach pumped out after trying to O.D., but he didn't mentioned that either.

"I wish I had more time, but I've got to get a train to London. I'm going to Sussex."

"There's another twenty minutes until the next train. I just missed the previous one."

They walked across to the station, where Tony bought his ticket and then they sat in the warm and almost silent cafeteria drinking coffee.

The train rolled in a couple of minutes late, as was normal on this line and as they sped towards London Al listened to Tony and all the profound thoughts he had since his five weeks in Thailand. Al assumed that he had become enlightened on whoopy weed and was still on a high after all this time.

"I can't work out the tubes. I have to go to Victoria for my next train." Tony said.

"I'll come over with you. I'm not in any hurry. This way."

Al led Tony into the network of tunnels and the crush of people. So many people had trouble with the tube and that was something that Al could never understand.

Tony decided to stay in London with Al for an hour and a half, taking a later train out. They went for some food and wine and sat talking. Tony didn't like seeing Al like this, it was so unlike the Al that he knew. He felt that he had to do something to help him, though he didn't know what he could do except give him some time, which was the best thing that he could have done.

In a little over three hours; the time that they had shared, Tony had lifted Al out of his severely depressed state, though he still wasn't alright. Tony boarded his train.

"I'll be back in a week. Give me a call and we'll go out for a drink."

"O.K. I will." He watched Tony's train crawl out of the station and then walked out into the streets of London.

There was a cool-wind blowing and the air held onto the smell of diesel like a summer garden hangs onto the sweet scent of honeysuckle an a balmy evening. He walked to keep warm and to keep busy, not to get anywhere. Buckingham palace stood like a huge monolithic oddity in a conurbation of oddities. It was strange to think that all he saw was part of East Anglia: Al figured that if England didn't recognise the treaty of Wedmore, which pushed East Anglia back to the course of the river Lea, up to Bedford, along the Great Ouse and up Watling Street, then neither would he; and the border would still be the Thame-Thames confluence.

Three hours later, bitterly cold and still undecided about what to do, he headed back to Liverpool Street for the return journey to Ipswich. Maybe all he had needed was a change of scenery and a friend to be with. It had been good to see Tony and maybe he would give him a call in a week or so.

* * * * *

The following morning he had not died of food poisoning, so he set off to explore the opal capital of the world. The first thing that was painfully noticeable was the almost total lack of grass and trees. Out from the town lay a moonscape scene. Dry, rocky and barren beyond belief. By ten o'clock he was diving for whatever shade he could find. The heat was burning and this was late autumn. Imagine what it must be like in summer!

"I'm going to look like a real wog if this carries on!" He joked with himself.

Hot and dry was just how he liked it. Unfortunately, that was just how the flies liked it too and whatever it was that he did or did not expect Coober Pedy to be, it certainly was not it. A shabby and dull little town with a charm all of its own. Drunken Aborigines on the street corners, with dogs and flies hanging around them. The dusty air making one long for a drink every few minutes. It wasn't the sort of place that he could ever find himself living. Every other shop was selling, or rather was trying to sell, opals. They were in darkness until a potential customer stopped to look into the window and then a hand would slide around from a corner at the back of the shop and push the light switch on. Instantaneously the colour of the opals took on a new brilliance and intensity. It seemed to him that he was the only tourist in town. No one else was looking in the shops that he passed and no one was buying. The coloured pieces of stones looked nice enough, but Al could not see what all the fuss was for? They didn't look nice enough to pay the amounts that they were asking. It was clever marketing of coloured stones which put a price tag onto the things in order to make them desirable, to create a market for something and nothing, without which the town would die a slow death, visited only by passing traffic and foolhardy tourists.

There was little that he wanted to do or see here. He would have taken a walk out of the town, but for the flies which were really pissing him off, instead he made for the church across the road, a retreat from both flies and heat. The red dust swirled around his feet as he walked, gradually turning blue trainers red. He opened the door and a wall of cool air hit his face. Outside, the temperature could soar above fifty, or drop below freezing, but inside, in the underground church it would remain a pleasant temperature, barely changing from month to month. The cool air was much needed, it had the same sort of effect as immersing one's body in a bath of hot water after a day of walking on cold exposed mountains. It was sheer bliss.

The small church was silent, almost deafening. The dim light gave a strange and almost sensuous warmth and atmosphere to the underground cavity. The dull colours of the walls and their unevenly hewn roughness appeared soft and mellow and were relaxing after being in the blazing sun and the vividly stark colours outside. Al sat quietly in the cool still air. His thoughts turned to Steven and to the events of his recent past. He was afraid of whatever might lie ahead. He felt alone. His hands and body shook with the emotions he felt, the feelings that he had managed to keep buried for the past few days. A tear rolled down his cheek. He sniffed and tried to pull himself together.

"Why the hell did I ever come so far from home? So far from my friends?"

He had the feeling that there was someone watching him, he turned to look, but there was no one there.

"Arif."

He spun around, but there was no one where the voice had come from and who knew this name? Only Tony and he was in Sydney. He went cold with fear.

"Don't be afraid of me Arif."

What kind of trick was this? Who was here?

"I know that you think that you hate me and that you are at war with me, but I am your friend and I am here to help you."

Al's blood ran hot. His fear rapidly turned to hatred. He knew who it was now and he hated the thought that he dared to call himself a friend.

"You bastard! Now dare you abuse the word friend by saying that you are a friend of mine. What the hell have you ever done for me except encourage your followers to use others as if it didn't matter because you would be there to say it didn't matter. You're a wanker and when I get my hands on you I'll ring your fucking neck!"

"I am your friend Arif and that is why I am here now. You are not at war with me, only yourself. You need a friend to help you deal with this pain that you feel. Don't turn it all onto yourself in anger. You are not alone."

The strangest feeling came over Al. A feeling that something had just passed through his body. It was as if his body had little substance, allowing things to move freely within him. Like a body moving through water, the water was resistance, but not enough to stop it. But how could anything that felt so real and full of life, pass through his body?

Al sat back and relaxed. He was now calm. All the tensions and anxieties and even the hatred were gone.

"I want to go home," he cried.

"So why don't you?"

Al shook his head. "I'm scared."

"It would be easy for you to get on a plane and return, but do you think that that would be wise? Do you think that you could deal with the situation there?"

"No, but I don't want to be here and I don't want to feel like I do anymore. If you are who I think you are then you could stop this feeling for me." Al pleaded.

"I know about the pain you are feeling Arif, but I cannot do what you ask. You will carry this pain for many years, even long after you think that you have accepted the situation. There is a reason for everything Arif, though you will not understand it now. Maybe you will never be ready to understand it."

"I don't understand," he screamed from pain and confusion.

"I know, but I can only guide you and tell you that you will never be alone."

Al said nothing. He just thought that he couldn't get much more alone than he was here in Australia.

"But I love him."

"I know Arif. And I know that your love runs deep and a love like yours will hurt even deeper. You must remember that your love is a gift from me and true love can never be wrong or dirty because it is my gift to you, though there are people who will try to tell you otherwise. Do not listen to them for they have lost sight of the truth. They assume the things which fit neatly into their corrupt and narrow view of what this life is about. Pity them for it is they who are alone and not yourself. Listen to me Arif and listen well, because you will not fully understand what my words mean, but an event will come to pass and then you will understand. Firstly you must remember that I am your friend and not your enemy. I will guide you and lead you to people who will help you when you need help. You will never be alone, though at times you may feel that you have been totally deserted. I will be at your side, but I will not interfere in your life. I will not live your life for you. I do not punish, or reward. Ask yourself how you can be alone when your brother has you in his heart? He worries for you and though you do not realise it, you are a special person Arif."

"Christopher has been good to me. I love him very much. I miss him."

"And he loves you Arif, far more than either of you will ever admit."

Al sat still and in awe of the voice that was all around him and inside of him. He sat as a child would sit and listen to a parent's voice while being read a story.

"One day you will be in East Anglia again and you will be with

Steven. You need to talk together. You both have questions which need answering."

"When can I go back and know that I won't feel like this?"

"I will send you a sign. A sign that you will recognise. A sign that cannot be overlooked. But do not search for it Arif, for if you look then you will tell me that you are still are not ready."

"I don't understand." Al trembled.

"I know. But you will when the time is right. One day Steven will love you and you will love him and it will be a love long fought for and hard won, but a love that will last forever."

"I don't want to be with him again. I love him, but he hurt me and I don't want it to happen again."

"You allowed yourself to be hurt Arif. You trusted him and only let yourself see the things that you wanted to see. You do not hate him. It is yourself that you hate and that anger will get you nowhere my friend. Do you think that he is not living his life without you? He is not running across Australia, but he is running, just as you are. He is hurting, but in a different way and for different reasons. He is living his life with only passing thought for you, but is that selfish, or just his way of coping?"

A pause of calmness filled the space between them.

"I was selfish. I expected too much." Al said in whispered reflection.

"No! For what did you ask that was not your right to ask? Honesty? Love? Respect? Is it really selfish to need to feel worthy, special, or wanted? Did you make him do the things that he did? Did you give your love to him at any price? I think you know that the answer is no. Here you are in a small town, thousands of miles from your home and he is with his new love, a new love that will give him but a moment of excitement and then leave him with an empty feeling. You know how superficial that kind of love is. Do you think he knows how lonely and sad he is?"

Those words cut through Al like the sharpest knife. The thought of Steven having sex with someone else. But he did not become angry, he accepted it for what it was. For what Steven was.

Al felt a horrible sense of loss, a sense of being left behind. His body felt strange, he was feeling himself again. The loss of Steven and now the loss of this person whom he didn't want to accept existed. Al knew, he could feel that he was leaving.

"Remember, I will always be with you and you will find your sign when the time is right. For those times when you feel that you are alone remember the love of your brother and you will be alone no longer."

"You're going aren't you? Will I meet you again?" A feeling of urgency hung on his words.

"We will meet twice more."

"When will I stop feeling this pain? Why can't I die?"

"You must never attempt to take your own life again. That is not the right way. Death will come soon enough. It always does."

A flash of bright light raced through the chamber and then disappeared with a bang as the door closed again. It echoed around the stone walls. Voices. Noisy people. The silence was shattered and 'He' was gone. Al turned to look sternly at the source of the disturbance. His face wet with tears.

"How dare you come in here in such a riot!"

The visitors stayed for a few minutes of chaos and then left. Silence once again fell in the cavity. Al sat silent and still, looking and listening. Nothing.

"Are you there?" He whispered. Nothing stirred and his words faded into the nothingness. "Hello. Where are you?" He stood up and searched nervously through the man-made cavern. He could find no one, but who was he looking for anyway?

"Come on Al, pull yourself together. You don't really believe you have just had a conversation with God, do you?"

"But the voice was real. It wasn't in my head. It wasn't Steven or Tony, so who the hell could it have been?"

"You've spent too much time in the sun, that's all it is. Your mind is playing tricks on you."

He was frightened by the unknown and did not like being so unsure of what may or may not have taken place. He began to panic. Walking backwards through the hollowed rock, stumbling. Al turned and dashed for the door, pulling at it, it was heavy. He stepped out into the real world and the brightness of the sunlight hurt his eyes and for a moment he couldn't see for squinting. Passing through the town he was suspicious of every face he saw along the dusty street. Who was doing this to him? Which person was it? Why would they do this to him? Returning to his tent, he hid inside even though it was like an oven beneath the nylon. He was frightened, but he wasn't sure why?

It was crazy.

"I'm having a breakdown, that's what is happening. Yes, it was my imagination that's all. There's no one here trying to trick me, just my own mind. Surely I can't believe that I have just spoken with God, can I?"

He searched for reasons to disbelieve what had just happened. Yes, he could be going through a breakdown, but could he really imagine the physical effects on his body. Was the power of suggestion really that strong?

"They would think I was right off my rocker if I told them back home about what has just happened. It's just too silly to be true!"

Al satisfied himself that what he had just experienced was only a trick of his own tormented mind and nothing more than that. It was easier to believe that he was mentally unstable to that extreme, rather than accept that God could be real.

He wanted to leave this dusty little town and put a large distance between him and it, but he was almost out of money and would have to stay another day before he could change his travellers cheques. He should have taken note of the dates on which Australian public holidays fell.

His tent was unbearably hot for him so he took refuge in the laundry; it was cool in there, while he thought about his next move.

"Tuesday morning I'll change some money then head off to the Rock. I should be able to spend a few weeks looking around there? That still gives me a day to kill here and there's nothing to do except fight the flies."

Repasting himself with fly repellent he braved the heat again and returned to town, walking through to the far side and into the wastelands which surrounded it. With no tree cover, an abundance of flies and not really much to see, he couldn't keep himself interested for long.

"Dear Sarah and Christopher, I'm in a strange little dust bowl called Coober Pedy. This is where most of the world's opals come from. Not much to see, except flies and it's too hot in the sun (there aren't any trees to shade beneath, no grass either). Some of the buildings are cut into the rock, which is a cooler way of spending the days and a warmer way of spending the nights. Heading north to Ayers Rock tomorrow (500 miles). I miss you, lots of love, Al"

"My dear Steven, It's been a long time since I wrote that awful postcard on the day I left Perth. I meant it then, I'm sorry now. I've travelled 1700 miles since then and now I'm at Coober Pedy. Would you believe me if I said that I have just had a conversation with God? I guess not. You'd wonder what I'm up to now? Maybe I have lost my mind as I would like to believe - it's easier to understand that. He told me things about you that I didn't really want to know, but I want you to know that I don't hate you. Sorry. All my love, Al."

It was ten o'clock and Al sat at the side of the highway waiting for a lift. The flies were getting plenty of exercise playing dodging the map with Al as he swung his map at them through the dry dusty air. He was bored with this game, he just wanted to sit and read until a lift came along. He wanted to get north and see Ayers Rock. That strange and unique phenomenon that symbolised outback Australia. High in the clear blue sky there were half a dozen hawks soaring on warm air thermals and all around him the dry scrub stretched to the horizon and beyond.

"I don't want to walk anywhere today," he said loudly for the whole world to hear, though there was no one around to hear his proclamation.

He took 'The Origin of Species' out of his pack and attempted to read, but the flies would not allow him to concentrate for long. He knew that he was going to be in for a long wait, so took a wander into the scrub and looked at the plants which were in flower. He recognised most of them, even if he could not put names to them, Latin, English or Aboriginal. One or two he had not seen before, that, or he had forgotten them already, but that was not likely. Time was not dragging too much and after just two hours a battered old car pulled up for him. Two hours out here did not seem so bad at all given that only three cars had passed him. The driver was an Aborigine and on the back seat sat his four year old son, who began picking holes in Al's sleeping mat as soon as Al pushed his pack over the seat.

He thought that he would be able to find out something about the Dreamings from Bruce, but Bruce apologised, saying that he knew little of his history. He had grown up on the fringe of western civilisation and now he was part of it.

"I should learn about it I know, then I can teach my children about their ancestors, but it's not easy to find the time, working in the opal mines and looking after the house and kids. My wife works at the hospital all day and then has other things to do as well. I guess we're Aussies now." Bruce laughed at the thought of being an Aussie when so many whites in the cities would squirm to think of an Aborigine as Australian and therefore a legitimate part of their society.

They journeyed north into the sun, past dead kangaroos, wedge-tailed eagles and more red sand. In front of them a road train blocked their way. Bruce pulled out to overtake. Al thought that it was lucky that the roads were straight for miles out here. They pulled over into the oncoming lane, there was nothing else in sight. Al looked out of the window towards the trailers that they were overtaking. One, two, three, four trailers. They thundered along and looked bigger than they were and they blocked the sun out from where he sat in the car, casting a dark shadow and swirling sand and plant debris in their wake. Al watched in horror as the truck moved across the white lines and came closer to the car. The trailer loomed ever closer and Bruce moved nearer the edge of the road. The car could go no faster. The truck kept moving closer and Bruce had no choice but to slam on his brakes and leave the road.

The road train sounded its horn and thundered away as they came to a rapid, dusty and bumpy halt on the road verge.

"Are you alright mate?" Bruce asked Al. then looked back to see if his son was alright.

Al looked at him, shaken, but silent.

"It happens now and then. They say the only good Abo is a dead one. Don't look so shocked mate, there's a lot who still think like that."

Al hardly said a word for the rest of the journey, which only lasted another fifteen minutes. Bruce turned off at Marla and headed along a track to Mintabie, to the mine, leaving Al behind to continue his journey north.

"Are you going north?"

Al turned to see a young man who was obviously part Aborigine sitting in a Toyota four-wheel drive.

"Yeah." Al called to him.

"Jump in then mate."

Al couldn't believe his luck. Marla was just a collection of buildings, not even resembling a village, let alone a town and he had got a lift in just a few seconds.

"I'm going straight through to Alice Springs."

"That's great. I was going to go across to Ayers Rock, but I might as well see Alice first and then come back to the Rock."

As they went north the scenery began to change in a way that Al could not have imagined. There were hills here; and even mountain ranges. Not Alp type mountains, but nonetheless mountains. It was no longer the flat wilderness that he had become used to and trees flourished here. Tall trees, not stunted bush-like growths and it looked distinctly wet compared to the dry open scrub. In places there were pools of water and even rivers to be crossed, and what's more the rivers had water in them! The so-called desert was bright like a florist's shop, flowers everywhere. The rotting carcass of a kangaroo or cow littered the roadside and although they didn't stop to take a look, Al could imagine the stench would not have been to his liking. The wedge-tailed eagles did not have to use their hunting skills since the advent of the motor vehicle. They were now scavengers of the open highway.

Al looked at his map of Alice Springs and found a camp site at the southern end of the town where the road, railway and river all squeezed through a gap in the ridge. It sounded scenic and he asked John to drop him off there when they arrived. It would be dark by then and Al did not want to walk back from the town centre.

"Yeah that's good. Don't you go walking near the river at night."

"Why's that?" Al asked.

"You get a lot of Aborigines there at night, many are drunk and they would rob you before you had chance to get away."

Al didn't like the sound of this town called Alice. He had visions of a charming colonial outback town built of wood, but with the street life of Los Angeles, not what he had expected at all.

John dropped him off at the camp site and waited until he made sure that there was room. There was and John drove away. Al looked around, the camp site was lit up and all around was a tall fence.

"Feels like a concentration camp." He wasn't sure if it was to keep the Aborigines out, or the campers in. He set up camp near the river side of the grounds, close to some other tents which were more like mobile homes than tents. Some old people looked at him, but did not answer when he smiled and said hello.

"Miserable old bags," he said beneath his smile.

They were in a group. Several large tents and several large cars. One old woman was struggling with a heavy box, so Al stood up and walked over to help.

"Can I help you with that?"

She looked at him and shook her head and continued to struggle. Al walked away and let her get on with it.

"Serves her right if she has a heart attack!"

There was little to do and even less that he wanted to do after the long journey, so he had a shower, did some washing and ate before the day and evening had gone. Sometimes he found his sleeping bag so luxuriously comfortable when he collapsed into it at the end of a day. Days like this.

Waking with the sunrise he crawled out of his tent to watch another beautiful daybreak. He felt a bit of a fraud to be standing here in what was very nearly the centre of Australia watching the sun rise over the tops of the hills. Behind him the River Todd was running quite fast. Al figured that he should count himself lucky to see water here. There could not be many days in the year when the river ran. Over on the far bank he watched some Aborigine children walking along, looking bored, trying to find something to fill their attention, just as kids anywhere in the world will do. The gap by which he was camped was in fact a gap and not a small gorge as he imagined it would have been. The railway and road filled the space not used by the River and all three fitted between the ridges which rose steeply on each side.

"Right then Al what are you going to do with this day?" He couldn't answer himself. He was lost in visions of Suffolk and remembered how green it was compared to the grey of here.

"It's summer there now, not that it's cold here, but May can be such a good month and it will already be light until late in the evening. It will be Whitsun soon and we'd be thinking about our holiday around now wouldn't we Steven? Probably Wales or the Peaks for some hill walking." He stopped himself from thinking any further down that line of thought, he didn't want to get himself into another state where he would start to believe that he was talking to God! Heaven forbid!

"No, don't be fooled too easily Al. So many people find God at times like this. At times when they need an emotional crutch to lean on. They end up becoming religious freaks and you don't want to be one of them, don't give in... But I know what I heard and I know what I felt. Just because it doesn't make sense to me it doesn't mean that it didn't happen and if I ignore the possibility of God being real then I put myself in the same position as all those people who say that Darwin's theory of evolution is just a theory because not every link in the evolutionary chain has been proven. Proof? How can they expect indisputable proof after millions of years of change; climatic, chemical, physical change. Those people would have us believe that there could never have been hundreds of millions of North American passenger pigeons just because they are now extinct and it sounds totally incomprehensible that any animal or bird that was so numerous could be exterminated by man in such a short period of time. But, on the other hand I can't assume that everything is real just because it seems that way. However, just because I cannot hold something in my hand and see it, it does not allow me to dismiss it as false."

He argued the possibilities with himself and was no nearer explaining the events at Coober Pedy. It puzzled him and he didn't like that. It made him vulnerable.

It was about three kilometres into town and this was one of the things which Al already hated about Australian towns. At first it seemed like a good idea to have lots of space between buildings, but he had quickly come to realise that he preferred the small cluttered towns of home. It was never far to get out into the country; less than a ten minute walk from anywhere in Sudbury to green fields and trees and meadows, but here in an Australian town suburbia stretched much further and it meant that driving everywhere had become a way of life. Cars, and the dependence on cars, was another thing that Al disliked. He didn't think it was right to be dependent on a motor vehicle to go to school, do the shopping, go into town. In these towns a car was needed and with cars the town could spread further, it was a vicious circle and talking of vicious, that was the other thing that he really disliked here; the number of dogs which were left to roam the streets unsupervised. On his way into Alice Al had to pass four dogs which to him all looked menacing. It made his blood boil.

Alice Springs was not the town that he had prepared himself for.

It was not the twee remnant of colonial outback Australia, lost in a time of its own in the middle of the world's driest continent; or rather the largest island of the continent of Australasia. It turned out to be a bright modern town of concrete, bricks, steel and glass, whose inhabitants catered for the swarms of rich Japanese tourists as well as unbelievable numbers of backpackers. There wasn't really that much to the town that interested Al apart from the museum and gallery which was a pleasant surprise to find. The shops were the same as they were in any other town and it was wrong of him to think that somehow Alice Springs was cut off from the rest of the country, not now, not in this age of jet aircraft and satellite television. It was less cut off than many parts of Britain were.

He spent many hours sitting in the sun on Anzac Hill. There was little else that he wanted to do and at this moment in time he was happy to stay put for a while. So there he sat, soaking up the sun. His face, neck, arms and legs were well oiled with sunscreen and his olive skin shone under that oil in the bright light. It felt good. He felt good.

"Oh it's a hard life sometimes, but someone has to sit in the sun and notice life as it passes by." He watched the flowers and shrubs, the butterflies and birds, but most of all he watched the people who came and went. It was amusing to watch the tourists arrive and to watch them as they went through typical tourist routines while they spent some time on the hill overlooking Alice Springs and although they all did the same basic things, it was the way in which they went about these tasks that amused Al. He studied them as David Attenborough studied any other animal, watching facial expressions, courtship displays, leadership struggles and the like. He discovered that there were four groups of tourist into which all the visitors fitted with stereotypical uncannyness. Al watched; invisible to them, as they went about their business as he sat in the sun.

Observations on Anzac Hill, Alice Springs, Australia, May 1989 by Arif Kemal; an East Anglian abroad.

The first group that I'd like to introduce to you are my favourite of all the four sub-species. They are by far the most entertaining of the four groups that have evolved in the short space of time that has elapsed since the advent of the jet engine and mass travel; they are the Japanese sub-species, Touristii anzacii japanii and are by far the most gregarious and active of all the visitors to this small hill in the centre of Australia, which so obviously holds some deep religious meaning to all Touristii. So sacred is this hill that it draws them from all corners of the globe in mass migration and at times there can be as many as sixty individuals on the hill. There appears to be no one particular season for the visits, so it still has yet to be fully understood what the reason is for them coming here. These Touristii normally arrive by coach and in groups of up to thirty or so individuals. As soon as the coach door opens they rush about, pointing in all directions, talking with great enthusiasm and laughing a lot. This is accompanied by a constant click-click of the very expensive cameras which they all carry and this may also be of tribal, religious, or sexual significance, but once again it is not fully understood by experts. The frenzy of activity continues for the whole time that they are allowed to run about on this sacred hill. There is almost a kind of demented ferment in their eyes and smiles and one gets the impression of a mixture of extreme excitement and amazement in the minds of this most interesting animal. Towards their final moments on the hill the Touristii anzacii japanii display a behavioural trait which is almost unique to this sub-species. This is the time for the group photographs and during this time these creatures line themselves in neat little rows and smile as if their lives depend upon it. They take it in turns to take a photograph and by the time they leave all members of the herd with have their own record of the holy visit.

In contrast the second of our sub-species to make the sacred pilgrimage are very sedate. These are the Touristii anzacii germanii and come from central and northern Europe. They often arrive in pairs and prefer to walk up the hill rather than drive. Their striking features; slim, well-tanned faces with blond or light brown hair make them stand out; and as David Attenborough was sat on by a mountain gorilla, I would not mind at all if one of these creatures were to sit on me (providing it was male and of the blond strain!). Their conversations are very quiet and they appear to be deep in prayer or thought and of all the Touristii, they stay the longest on the hill. Although they were the least active, because of their stunning looks, they were the most pleasant to watch. After a stay which lasts for at least fifteen minutes they depart as quietly as they came.

In contrast to the germanii, the third herd to visit the hill were the least attractive in all ways. These were the Touristii anzacii olduswrinklii and could be further split into roughly equal numbers into American and Australian types; the only way of telling the difference was to listen carefully to their raucous cawing and squawking, the Australian, having a slightly higher pitch whine to the more drawn out tone of the American type. One had to feel a little sad for these creatures as they were generally over-weight and coming to the end of their years. They did not really have a lot going for them and could become extinct at any moment without warning. The oldus-wrinklii appeared to have a wealth far in excess of their worth and always drove up the hill in large cars, or occasionally in a small coach. They were a very noisy collection of individuals and could easily be likened to the North American turkey, or to the Australian galah as they gabbled and squawked incessantly during their visit and most of the gabbling was about previous places that they had visited, or about friends and family; generally anything which was totally unrelated to their present situation, but obviously they still felt some deep and holy feeling for this sacred hill in order to spare the time to visit it.

The fourth group were almost as noisy and sadly not the most intelligent of creatures to walk upon the planet. They were very young and a forty/sixty mix of Australian and British sub-cultures. Yes, they are the easily recognisable Touristii anzacii slobii. They tend to arrive in groups of between two and six and walk up the hill on three of their four limbs, the fourth paw gripping onto a stubby; a stubby being a small metal container of alcohol, which this sub-species seems unable to survive without for more than a few minutes. They are loud and tend to say totally uninteresting things, usually swearing a lot and eager to leave in order to hunt down a new source of alcohol.

There is a fifth sub-species, but they are so rare and secretive and seldom seen or heard that little is known about their true behaviour. These are the Touristii anzacii wanderus-reluctii.

Al had sat in the sun for a few hours, his body hot and golden-bronze in colour. He grew restless and felt that he had to leave, which was stupid as he had nowhere to go and nothing to do. He felt hungry, but not for food and not for anything that made any sense. He couldn't understand why he should feel as if he had to be somewhere else now. He ignored his feelings and continued to observe the world; or at least a small part of it, as it passed him by. He was feeling extremely lonely, but wouldn't admit it to himself; watching all the other tourists come and go. Everyone had someone to talk to, except for himself.

He started down the hill, without reason, without understanding. Speedily he descended the small hill and crossed the road without looking for traffic. It was a hunger, he was after something, but what he didn't know. Al felt silly, he felt that he wasn't in control of his own body, as if he was being drawn forward, a cart pulled by horses and he the cart with no power over the horses. The feeling stopped as quickly as it had started. He sighed deeply.

"Now I know that I'm going mad. I talk to myself, I imagine that I've spoken to... and now this?"

Surrounded by tarmac, concrete and buildings it was hotter than it had been up on the hill. Al needed shade. He needed to retreat from the mid-afternoon heat. He was close to a church, but was reluctant to go in.

"Don't be stupid Al. There isn't anything in there that can hurt you. Or do you think Coober Pedy was real?"

"Of course I don't believe it was real. What do you think I am?"

"It will be cool in there; and empty."

The voice of temptation got the better of him and if he didn't believe in Coober Pedy then what was the harm? He walked into the church and out of the blazing sun and heat. He stood motionless for a few minutes until his eyes adjusted to the dim light. Inside the building it was silent, from outside came the sound of a passing motor car and the call of the Australian magpies.

He walked along the aisle with a feeling of defiance and sat down in the second row.

"Was it really you?" Al whispered. "Well, are you real or not?" There was no answer, not that he really expected one.

"Well if you are real you ought to know that all you've succeeded in doing is screwing my head up well and good!" Still no answer. Al took heart from this as it just served to confirm that he had imagined everything at Coober Pedy.

"I find it more than a little inconsiderate of you to behave in this manner, don't you?"

Al, now bored with this game, looked around at the modern building, not totally unimpressed by it. There was a stained-glass window with the image of Jesus in it. Al smirked and thought that it didn't look very much like Robert Powell.

"You're a selfish prick you know, but I guess that you don't know that because you're not real."

Al stood up ready to leave, but a blinding shaft of light burst through the window and down to the floor in front of him. It was so intense that he had to raise his hand to cover his eyes and it forced him backwards making him sit down again. The light hurt him, but gradually began to fade and he was able to remove his hand from his eyes. In the centre of the shaft of light Al thought that he could see the figure of a man who was a little older than himself who wore a white robe. His arms outstretched, his eyes filled with kindness.

"Oh my God! Now I know that I'm going mad. This can't be real because it looks too much like a tacky Hollywood movie; and besides there aren't any holes in his hands and no blood!"

The figure's face wore a huge grin and seemed to be laughing with Al, his thoughts and conversation.

"Yes I am real Arif and yes it does look like a tacky Hollywood movie, because you would recognise who I am like this. If I had just walked up to you in the street you would not believe who I am. You would think that I was just trying to pick you up! And why should I have blood pouring from my hands? I am alive and well."

Al sat rigidly on the bench, looking for any sign that would show him that this was purely a trick of his own imagination.

"I always thought that seeing was believing, but now I'm not so sure. You can't be real." Not one word passed Al's lips, but he knew that he was heard.

"So why the fuck didn't you show yourself at Coober Pedy? You knew that I wasn't sure if it was real, or just my mind playing tricks with me."

"You were not ready then. You still would have found reason to doubt, to be afraid. Why are you so frightened to believe what your eyes and ears and heart tell you to be true? You are so frightened by the thought that this is real. By the thought that I am real. Don't be."

"Well if you are real..."

"I am."

"If you are," Al emphasised the if. "Then you can change what has happened."

"No Arif, I can't. You know that I cannot bring back time that has since passed. What has come to pass will one day be in your past and you will be richer for it. There will be a day when you no longer feel the pain that you carry. No pain is carried forever. Have patience my friend and you will one day be free. I know that you think that you want to be free of this Earth and that day will come soon enough, but so much needs to be done before you can leave. You have much work ahead of you and certain events must come to pass before you can be free. You are a special person Arif."

"I don't understand a fucking word that you're saying. What do you mean? And don't keep calling me Arif!"

"I know that you don't understand. Listen Al, you will stay in Australia until you are ready to go back, but don't assume what the word ready means. Everything has a reason and often a great deal of time passes before all is fully understood. You have to be strong enough for your life's journey and it will not be easy. You will be tested along the way by events which are not under my control, not of my doing. You must remember that you can change the results of these events by the way that you deal with them. You will have help. I will guide you to people who will be your friends in times of need, as I have already done. Do not look for these people for you will not find them by looking and do not trust all who appear to be trustworthy."

"I still don't understand what you mean."

"You need to have faith. You need trust. Fast on bread and water each Friday from dawn to dusk. It will give you strength and help you focus clearly on what really counts. I will be there when you think that I have deserted you, but I cannot change what will come. I can only guide you."

Al looked at the man stood in front of him. It was as if he had always been close by. It did not seem strange or unnatural that they were here together.

"Please let me go home. Give me another chance."

"I do not make good or bad things happen. I do not punish or reward as some people would have you believe, but you have known that for many years." He smiled at Al as if he had just told an in joke. He made Al feel like an old friend.

"I know. I actually had something right didn't I." Al laughed half-heartedly. "Are Sarah and Christopher alright?"

"Yes, they are well. You have no need to worry about them. They worry for you though and you owe it to them and yourself to be strong."

"They are such good friends."

"Yes they are and you deserve them. Do not worry, for you will see much more of them."

Al was glad to hear that and he looked for his pocket, for a tissue to wipe his eyes.

"I'm looking forward to seeing them again," he said. But there was no one with him now and he stood up and breathed deeply. He was alone.

Al walked back along the aisle, turning one last time to look at the empty building.

"No one would believe this would they..." He looked up to the window through which the light had come. It was still bright outside, but the sun was not coming directly in, how could it, it was directly overhead and that stained-glass wasn't even stained-glass, just a plain window high up in the wall. "...How can my eyes be so easily fooled?"

He had stayed in Alice Springs for five nights and was now restless. His surroundings were too familiar, but still they held no comfort for him. It had been a long time since he had left Perth and it seemed just as long since he had last seen Tony. He packed his tent and set off for Ayers Rock, easily getting a lift as far as the airport without delay, but then found himself waiting on a broad dusty strip of land at the side of the highway. Flies buzzed around him as he hit at them with his map. Was there never an end to the flies? A camper van stopped and he walked eagerly towards it.

"We're not picking up, just dropping off." A woman said to him.

He returned to where he had been standing with a sinking feeling in his stomach and he watched as a young girl emerged from the van and carried her pack clear of the road. Al decided; rather bravely for him, to go over and chat to her. Grete was Austrian. Al had thought that she was either Dutch or German, so he wasn't too far off the mark. As he stood talking with her he was conscious of how few people he had met since arriving in Australia, other than those people who had stopped to give him a lift.

He soon found that Grete was definitely Germanic in her approach with people. She wanted to know all about Al's travels to date, where he was going and why? Then she wanted to know why it was he was in Australia at all? He wasn't typical of the travellers that she had met and she dug deeper and deeper into his reasons and Al felt vulnerable with her and no matter what he answered she would not be satisfied. He was relieved when two boys arrived near them, it diverted her attention from him. He didn't think for one moment that Grete's interest in him was purely physical, why should he?

"Germans," she said disapprovingly. "I saw them coming out of the bush a little way back."

"This isn't going to make things any easier here." Al answered.

The two German boys stood talking to Grete for a few minutes, occasionally speaking to Al. He found it strange that they spoke to her in English instead of their native language. Were they just being polite because he was there? Or was it typical of Europeans to use their language skills, maybe English was the international language of travellers and he just didn't know?

"My God, they stink bad." Grete said when the Germans walked away.

"Yes, they could have made an effort to smell a bit sweeter." Al answered. "I better move away and be ready for a lift."

"You'll like Ayers Rock," she called out to him. "Maybe I'll see you in Innsbruck one day?"

"That would be nice. Hope you get to Adelaide O.K."

Al, Grete and the two German boys sat on their packs waiting for the chance of a lift south. Between each of them lay some twenty metres or so of red dusty sand and in the air flew swarms of flies. Above them the sun beat down, still raining on Al. It was going to be a long wait, each of them knew that. Every time a car approached they jumped to their feet, held out their signs and smiled innocently. No one stopped. Al had been here for three hours and he still believed that he would get somewhere, but the thought of arriving at Yulara in the dark loomed up at him as reality.

"I won't panic. The whole town is only there to serve tourists and it would be the easiest place on the planet to arrive in at any time, day or night." He wasn't convinced.

The German boys gave up jumping to their feet, they just sat there dejected, praying for a lift.

"No wonder you lost the war!" Al shouted.

They were not amused and did not answer.

"Ooh get you, very touchy!" Al said in a Frankie Howard voice.

Al sat waiting, unaware that Grete was studying his face and body as she waited for her lift. She thought about going to Ayers Rock again so she could be with Al, but she had been there a week ago and didn't really want to go back. Five hours after arriving at the dust strip Al had a lift. He waved goodbye to Grete and she sighed with relief at the knowledge that at least one of them was on their way and with sadness that this sweet young boy had left and she would never see him again.

Richard was not going all the way to Yulara, but could at least take Al more than half way. Al was offered a beer, he declined. They talked and Al was surprised at how easy he found it to talk to this stranger. He soon realised that his ease only came from the fact that Richard reminded him of Christopher. How trusting he was of Richard only because his eyes were almost identical to Christopher's; as was his nose, small and sweet, a perfect shape, so unlike his own. And there was that smile, oh how it reminded Al of his brother so many miles away.

Richard was going to see friends on a ranch for the weekend. Al wanted to go with him and was hoping to witness some Australian hospitality that he had heard so much of on the television back home. He wanted to spend some time with this man who remind him of someone he missed, but there was no offer to stay on the ranch and there was no chance of spending some time with him and in two hours Al found himself once again in the heat and flies of central Australia in the tiny settlement of Mt. Ebenezer.

Under his feet the bitumen was soft. Across the road Aboriginal children played in the wreck of an old Holden under a clump of trees and a dog was pushed out through the open window, then tried to get back in again, much to the annoyance of a little girl. She cried. Al watched for a short time, scanning the area which was strewn with litter and pieces of old broken vehicles. It felt like the end of civilisation. A few feet from Al a young white boy was trying to fix his motorbike. He was the only other white face in this place, which could not even be described as a shanty town. Al was uncomfortable with the thought that he stood out so much. The Aborigines didn't give him a second glance, but Al felt vulnerable, he needed to blend into the crowd; another face in a sea of faces. He needed his anonymity.

An old man sat on a chair on the veranda of the café and a cock crowed from somewhere behind the building which was in a desperate state of disrepair. Paint flaked from wood and time drifted only slowly, lingering in this place, itself unsure of what to do. This place worked at its own pace and not even time had an effect upon it.

A few small trees and shrubs afforded a little shade, though it was no longer so hot that it was totally unbearable. Al stepped back from the road and stood in the shade of a wattle and looked in silence at the young lad as he got his hands greasy with oil.

"Yuck!" Al thought.

A car passed, but did not stop. Al wondered if he would get a lift out of here and on to Yulara today? He knew that there wasn't anything that he could do about it, but nonetheless he didn't want to stay here. Was it racism on his part? Probably; but more than that it was the feeling of being noticeable, uncomfortable, unsure of his surroundings. He looked over to the white boy again, he had his back to Al as he carried on with his work. Al walked towards him.

"Hi, is it anything serious?"

"No, I can fix it. I just need to get back as far as the main road and I'll put it on a trailer back to Adelaide." Al was pleasantly surprised to find a Welsh boy out here, for a while he felt less alone.

"What part of Wales are you from?" Al asked with real interest.

"Do you know Wales?"

"Yes, quite well."

"Gelligaer?" He answered in a questioning tone which told Al that he assumed that Al would not know where it was.

"Oh yes." Al was surprised, but he wasn't sure why he should be so, probably pleased that he did know where it was.

"You know where it is do you?"

"Yes," Al answered, slightly irritated that his knowledge should be called into question. "Between Merthyr and Cardiff. There was a Roman Fort there."

The boy looked at Al, yes he knew Wales.

"It must be good to travel around by bike?" Al half asked, half stated.

"Yeah, it's better than these people who travel around in buses all the time. How do you get around?"

"Hitching and an awful lot of walking."

He nodded his head. Al wondered if he was being dismissed or getting a nod of approval.

Another car passed and Al knew that he did not want to stay here over night. A truck stopped on the other side of the road and Al went over and asked if he could have a lift back to Erldunda. The man said yes.

The journey back to the main road was short and cold in the back of the open truck, but at least it was fly free and that could not be bad. It was difficult to talk and hear as they moved along and all Al could get out of the boy he sat with was the fact that he was Israeli and could earn more in a month in Australia on the gold mines than he could in a year in Israel.

On arriving at Erldunda Al noticed that there was a job vacancy in the kitchen here at the roadhouse. He had heard that the money was good in these places and because there was nothing to spend it on it made saving extremely easy. He still had a lot of money, though he knew that it wasn't going to be enough to last, but more than that was the thought that he would be able to stop travelling and stay in one place and that he would have something to do. He filled in an application form and had a very nervous interview. It was so obvious to him that had he had a pair of tits he would have been given the job there and then. He gave up on the hope of work and went to pay for a tent site for the night. It was almost dark and he wanted to be pitched and have dinner cooking before nightfall, but the receptionist began to lecture him on how rude English people are. Al said nothing as he gathered his thoughts. What had he said that justified her outburst? All that he wanted was somewhere to stay for the night. The high pitch squeal of the Australian woman's voice grated on his hearing. He stood there and listened to what she had to say. Minute after minute she continued her attack on English people, on him, on anyone she didn't like. Al stood and listened, halfway between outrage and hilarity and then she stopped. Quick as a flash Al was on the attack, unpleasant words, delivered with a polite voice.

"Firstly, one is obliged to say that I am an East Anglian, not

English. Secondly, I would suggest that one might stop engaging one's mouth and think a little more about what one wants to say. Finally, would one be correct in thinking that you have been hurt by an Englishman? Yes I thought so. I think he fucked you and then fucked off." With that Al turned and left the building. The air silent behind him, the woman, mouth open, stood silent and bemused.

It was a good feeling to be up with the dawn and Al rarely stayed in his tent for long. It always got too hot, too quickly and that was unpleasant. He had his breakfast, crackers, jam and instant coffee. It wasn't bad, but it had taken him a little while to get used to it. He still longed for muesli, croissants and freshly filtered Van Nelle. He looked up at the sky, the blue sky unbroken for as far as he could see. The sun had not yet risen high enough for him to see it, no dazzling sunlight, just a warm clear blue against grey-green and ochre. He packed and walked to the road and while he waited for his lift; which he had already decided would not be long in coming, he watched the hawks soaring high in the sky above him in giant circles; dark silhouettes against a blue background, moving without the slightest effort.

"The nearest I've ever come to that was gliding in a K21. I'd love to be up there now."

Lost in his dreams of flying, time ticked past slowly and a combi-van stopped for him. He was right to feel so confident about this day. A German woman got out and put Al's pack in the side of the vehicle and then sat him between her and the driver. Ursula was from Hamburg and was staying in Australia for a few months. Stan was from Melbourne and was an artist. They drove towards Ayers Rock and Stan answered every question that he was asked about Aborigines, their history and culture and the native flora and fauna of Australia. Stan was happy to share his knowledge with Al and was pleasantly surprised how much Al already knew, though Al thought that he knew so little, but accepted Stan's compliment with slight embarrassment. They stopped an hour and a half later at a viewpoint for Mount Conner. Ursula and Al ran off up a hill for a better look, while Stan made them both a cup of tea. As they climbed the hill they realised that the undulations in the landscape were massive sand dunes which were covered in scrubby plant growth and spinifex grass. Al always thought of the Saharan and Arabian deserts when he thought of sand dunes, not scenes like this with plants everywhere. Mount Conner stood tall and proud against the vast backdrop of the plain. It stood flat topped and lonely and Al thought that he had seen it many, many times before because it looked like the flat topped mountains on American western movies. From its summit fell a sheer drop, a cliff face that Al could not even begin to guess the scale of. From the base of the cliff to the plain below a steep slope flowed and looked as if it might have been scree that had fallen off over the past few hundred centuries. Al turned to look behind where a huge lake stretched off into the unknown. There was so much water in this so-called desert.

Ursula called him, his tea as ready. He bounced happily down the dune, glad to be seeing these amazing sights and to have someone to talk to. He began to think that it was a pity that it wasn't Steven who he was sharing this with, but that thought stopped when he tasted his tea.

"You'll get use to the salty water. Ursula smiled. She knew what he was thinking.

Al looked at her. This was the first cup of tea that he had had in over three weeks and all that he could taste was salt. How could he get used to this?

It was nearly midday when Al got his first glimpse of Ayers Rock. It lay on the plain like some prehistoric beast asleep in the burning sun. He felt like he wanted to grab hold of Steven's hand and say, "look Steven, look, that's Ayers Rock, we're here." His thought detracted from the experience of this moment, though it was still an amazing sight.

"I can't believe this. I've seen it more times on the television and in books than I can possibly recall and it's so familiar, but still so alien to my eyes. It's beyond my comprehension that it is one giant rock and not a mountain!"

"It is impressive isn't it. Every time I come up here I still feel the same as you do." Stan answered.

They dropped Al in the town centre and pointed him in the right direction for the camp site. He set off through the large central reservation.

Yulara was a purpose built tourist town which has sprung up along a large circular road. Al was taking the short cut across, but he found it hard work walking in soft sand with the weight of his backpack pushing him deeper into the tiny grains of quartzite. To his right, Ayers Rock would rise and fall between sand dunes which were clothed in flowers of every colour. Desert oaks shot up straight into the air with arrow-like form. They had no side branches, but where covered in a mass of long grey-green hair-like leaves, Al thought of Ken Dodd and the Diddymen as they made him think of feather dusters. What he had always thought of as desert turned out to be nothing of the kind. Nowhere was there a square metre of sand without plant cover, unless it was made that way by man.

An hour later he returned to the town centre and fell in love with the ultra modern design. Al was a bit of a traditionalist when it came to architecture, but this worked. It was interesting and sympathetic to its surroundings. So much concrete had been used, but used well, textured and painted in dark ochre and contrasted subtly against the pale orange-pink of the sail-like structures over the main square. Piped out into the afternoon air; probably all day, every day for all Al knew, was a wonderful soft melodic tune which was designed to relax. It relaxed Al, but he suspected that it would have driven some people to distraction. He walked around, looking at the small town; it was much smaller than he had imagined, but he liked just about everything he saw. It was the sort of place that he could be happy living in for a while if he had a job.

It was late afternoon by the time he entered the information centre and wandered around the displays of the region's flora and fauna. He wondered when he was going to see some of this world famous Australian fauna; up until now all he had seen were a half dozen species of birds and countless millions of flies, not quite what he had expected! He absorbed as much information as he could, like a sponge sucking up water. He remembered how Steven would liken him to a sponge; sucking up as much love as he could get.

"Why can't you be here with me Steven. I've seen Ayers Rock for the first time today and the first thing that I thought of was you. Why aren't you here with me? I couldn't have been that bad, could I? It's not right that I should be here alone."

"Hey, Al!"

He turned around, surprised that anyone knew his name, but there was Grete.

"I thought you were going to Adelaide?" He asked, both surprised and glad to see her.

"I was, but a little while after you left, I got a lift here. I looked for you yesterday." She didn't tell Al that she had a chance of going south to Adelaide, but chose to come back to Yulara because she knew that he was going to be here. She didn't say that she had searched the camp site for his green tent. None of that mattered now, she had found him and was glad that she had returned this way. Al was so cute. Quiet and nervous, so dark, slim and handsome, jet black hair and deep brown eyes.

"I didn't get here until today..."

They sat talking for a long time as if they were old friends, not two people who had only met yesterday at the side of the road for the first time. Al did not notice the way in which Grete was looking at him. He would never expect a woman to look at him in such a way, it had never happened before and he had certainly never courted such advances.

"Hello Al."

Al turned around at the sound of his name being used again. He didn't recognise the voice, though he felt sure that he had heard it before, he obviously had, but where?

"David!" Al was surprised and a little disappointed that it was him and not one of the many other people with whom he had hitched a lift.

Al introduced David to Grete and they talked for a while before Al and Grete left to hitch out to the sunset strip at Ayers Rock.

"I don't think you really wanted to see David?" Grete interrogated in her typical Germanic manner.

"No, not really. Oh he's alright, but I travelled with him for four days and we had nothing in common. He wouldn't even stop to look at things, apart from the sea! I regret not crossing from Perth with my friend Tony. He's a good friend and it would have meant something with him. I guess it has worked out well that we didn't, because he might have become really bored with my behaviour."

"What do you mean by that?" Grete quickly asked.

"Oh, nothing really, I just haven't been good company for the past few months."

She let the subject drop, she could understand that he had been hurt and she knew that she wouldn't get too many answers out of Al. But Grete thought that Al was ready for a pretty blue-eyed blond like herself.

"I want to get something to eat before we go out there Al." Al agreed, it was going to be a few hours before he would have a real meal.

They looked around the supermarket where the prices were so highly inflated, both being drawn to a packet of chocolate marshmallow snowballs which they could not resist. They walked through the town stuffing them into their mouths, but the look on Grete's face showed Al that it was not just he who was disappointed with their acquisition.

"I eat so many of these in Austria, but they are much nicer at home." Grete said as she pulled the sticky remains of one out from her mouth.

"Yes, I now what you mean. Even in Britain they are better than this."

Walking along the road out to the rock they tried to hitch as each car came past. Within minutes they had a lift out to the Olgas, which both Al and Grete were pleased with as it would have been more difficult to get there normally because the road was not tarred. They sat in the back of the four-wheel drive, on wooden benches which ran along the length of the vehicle. The road was nothing more than an uneven dirt track and was well rutted. Their driver was a young chap, who was intent on getting there as quickly as he could and gave them a ride to remember as they bounced up and down and side to side for over twenty kilometres. Even before they were halfway their backsides were becoming more than a little sore.

As Al caught his first glimpse of the Olgas he couldn't believe what he was seeing. This strange collection of lumps so close to Ayers Rock was far more impressive and totally unknown to him. He tried to take in what he was seeing, trying to describe it to himself, but for once words failed him. The tall rounded lumps stood proud from the surrounding desert, sensuous and secretive. They continued past them and parked. Grete and Al got out of the jeep and headed off up a gorge with the driver and his girlfriend. They had an hour before sunset in which they could take a closer look. A stream of crystal clear water ran swiftly from it and Grete searched for the fresh water shrimps that live here and Al remembered the tiny fresh water shrimps that they would catch in the stream at Great Cornard when they were kids. She searched with Al for a while and then gave up and went running off over the fallen lumps of dark red ochre rock.

"Come on Al!" She shouted.

Al stood up and watched her go, thought, "what the hell," and followed, running after her like they were two kids in a giant playground, as if they were twenty years younger and had known each other for as long as they could remember. Grete was as nimble as Al and looked around to see if he was still chasing. Al had no idea that this game was foreplay in Grete's mind. Here and there bright flowers were in bloom and everything was a spectacle to behold. She slowed a little to make sure that Al would catch up to her soon, but the man who had given them a lift called out and told them that it would soon be time for the sunset. Al stopped a couple of metres short of Grete and turned back towards the car park. Playtime was over for Al and Grete felt annoyed that he should be more interested in the sunset than in her. She followed him back, running to catch up with him. They walked together and talked and Al held back branches of shrubs which blocked their way as a gentleman should do for a lady and when Grete said, "thank you." Al answered, "my pleasure."

"Maybe this was how the English behaved? All was not lost," she thought.

They had been joined by five other vehicles and the small crowd waited in anticipation.

Al stood listening to the people talking around him. He had nothing to say, so said nothing. He didn't feel too comfortable being with such a crowd of people, but wasn't sure if he would have rather been here alone, he would have only thought of Steven if he had been. The sun fell lower in the sky and the shadows cast by the trees and rocks grew longer and longer. The bright colours of the outback began to fade into various shades of grey and brown, but held their new colour for only a few seconds before changing their shade and guise once again. The bright red rock of the Olgas grew more and more intense, it became a much more vivid orange red and stood out even more as its greying background became even less bright. The rocks slowly changed into a reddish brown and then took on a deep purple hue and then changed again into dark brown before finally turning grey as the last rays of sunlight fell beyond the horizon at the edge of the massive flat plain.

In words the imagery is only words, but in life the imagery is a physical mysticism which falls deep within one's body and soul. A mysticism which lasts for but a few minutes, but lasts forever. A mysticism dramatically emphasised by the rapid and extreme drop in temperature that accompanies the setting sun.

Al sat with Grete in the information centre for a while after returning to town. He liked the idea of hitching a return lift, it was just a pity that it didn't happen very often.

"I'm going to go and eat now." Al said, he was getting hungry.

"O.K. Al. I probably won't see you again," she said, somewhat disappointed that Al hadn't realised that she liked him.

"Are you staying in the hostel again?"

"I don't know yet... It depends on whether I can sneak in, as I did last night."

"What if you can't?" Al sounded concerned. He was being naive again. All Grete had to do was to walk in, her pack was already inside. He thought about asking her if she wanted to share his tent, but decided not to in case she got the wrong idea about the offer. He couldn't see what was in front of him. She wanted him to make that offer. She wanted him. Al didn't wait for an answer to his question, he left. Grete watched Al leave and kicked herself for not asking to share his tent, once inside it would have been easy to make it clear what she wanted. She couldn't believe how sweet and innocent Al was, quiet and thoughtful and totally oblivious to the subtle looks that she had been giving him. It never once occurred to her that he was homosexual. He didn't look the type.

Al had just settled down for the night when a mouse decided to use his tent as a climbing frame. He spent the next ten minutes trying to scare it away, he didn't want to wake up and find mouse holes and droppings in his tent in the morning.

"At least the mice aren't on an Australian scale!" He laughed to himself.

As Al chased away the mouse that was searching for food, Grete was searching the camp ground for Al. She would find him and say that she had nowhere to stay and he would have to let her sleep with him, but as she searched for Al, dark clouds began to gather above her and Al had placed his tent in a clump of bushes which hid it from three sides and in the darkness his tent merged as one with the shrubs. It began to rain and Al was asleep before Grete was in earshot calling his name. Soaked, she gave up and returned to the hostel.

Later that night Al was woken by the storm. The rain had become heavy and the atmosphere was charged with a massive electrical energy which frightened him as it began to release itself onto the

Earth and he didn't like this while he was in a place that did not allow him to watch what was going on.

* * * * *

It had been a hot day, much like everyday of the holiday so far and they had spent the evening watching the storm lighting up the sky several miles away. It had threatened to come their way, but until they had crawled into their sleeping bag it had stayed dry.

They had picked a pleasant camp site. Halfway between Morez and St. Claude, close to the edge of a steep hill at the bottom of which a river raced. Al was irritated by the huge numbers of Dutch who sat around a camp fire until the rain started; about one in the morning, singing loudly in Dutch and playing their accordions even louder. Steven knew how irritated and intolerant Al was and this made him fed up with Al.

"Why did we even bother with this holiday?" Steven thought, though it had been very good up until now and he had been glad to be with Al.

The storm arrived in earnest about two-thirty and woke everyone on the camp site with the first crash of thunder which burst immediately overhead. The camp site was over a thousand metres above sea level and the storm was not much higher. The ground shook and made Al imagine it was a Earthquake. He grabbed onto Steven; not that he was that scared, it was just a good excuse to hug him without Steven getting irritable. Outside the tent a dozen car alarms sounded as the vibrations triggered them off and Al was annoyed by the Dutch once again and then once more when they took their time in switching them off.

"Serve themselves right that they'll all get soaked switching them off!"

Steven and Al lay awake throughout the storm, as did everyone else on the camp site. Al didn't mind the storm, or the fact that he was losing sleep, not when it meant that he could be touching Steven. He loved touching Steven.

* * * * *

Steven was not here to lay next to and losing sleep did not hold the same attraction now. The thought of Steven so far away weighed heavier on him now than it had done for a long time. He stared up at the roof of the tent and watched it light up with each flash of lightning. He closed his eyes and saw Steven as clear as daylight.

"This is the first rain that there has been in the month that I've been here," he said aloud, trying to occupy his mind. "Good grief, I've been here a month already! What have I done with all that time?"

By the early morning the rain had stopped and any puddles that there had been in Yulara had now gone. The sky was blue and it was warm. Al had breakfast in the opening of his tent and watched for any life. No other person was out, but he was joined by a pair of crested pigeons. They scratched around for food and Al shared his bread with them. He felt good with birds around, he preferred wild creatures to people.

Reluctantly he accepted that he could not sit there all day and if he was planning to go to Ayers Rock he had to go and wash some clothes first. He walked silently across the wet red sand, leaving the faintest of impressions where he had stepped.

After a shower and having done his washing he could see David in another part of the camp site.

"He's up early." Al said to himself as he hung his clothes on the line. He watched for a while and considered going over to talk to him, but he really did not want to do that, instead returning to his tent for his bag and set off for the Rock.

There were few people around as he walked across the sand. The flowers still and silent, looking up to the sky above. A bird called from the undergrowth, but it was hidden from view and Al went about his journey as he might have done if he had done it everyday for years. He was quite prepared to walk all the way to Ayers Rock, but that wasn't necessary when a large car stopped and picked him up, despite there already being six people inside. They chatted with Al and made him feel that they had all known each other for quite some time. There was a husband and wife with a small son and daughter, they were Germans and lived in Darwin. The other two were from Germany, one was their nephew and the other was his friend and were both about Al's age. They arrived at the Rock. Al looked at it, not quite believing that he was really here. It loomed up massively beside him. He had never thought that he would ever get to see this amazing sight; not even in his wildest dreams. They got out of the car and Eric, Johann and the girl were going to climb with Al; they assumed that he would want to stay with them as he was on his own. Al quite liked the idea, but would have preferred the little girl to stay behind as it looked like a hard climb.

"O.K. We'll see you in a few hours," the mother of the girl said, she still had a German accent even though she had lived in Australia most of her life.

On the rock were fixed five small plaques, one for each person who had died trying to climb to the summit. Al touched the stone. It felt like stone and he was disappointed by that. He had this strange notion that Ayers Rock would feel special, different to anything that he had ever felt, but it wasn't. He felt like he should have said a little prayer, but that was silly; he wasn't Aborigine so why should he pray to it? They began to climb, taking it slowly, which was the most sensible thing to do. It was not quite nine, but already was hot.

Beneath their feet the ochre rock was solid, no pieces of scree to stumble over, just a smooth surface to ascend. Because it was so steep it didn't take long before they were high up the side of it and progress was slow. Katie was becoming more and more distressed each time she looked back and Eric and Johann decided to take her back down.

"Are you coming back up?" Al asked. After starting the day feeling that he wanted to be alone, now he wanted the company of these two boys.

"No, I don't think so," Eric answered. "I don't think that we should because the others would have to wait for us." Al was disappointed by his answer. Johann looked at Al silently; he spoke no English, he too was disappointed. Al sat on the side of the rock and watched them descend as he had a drink of water.

"I wish that I had someone to travel with. I guess Tony and me would not have got on so well, not if he wanted the bright lights and bars. There must be someone out there who I can travel with for a while."

Upon reaching the summit Al was surprised to find over a hundred names in the visitor's book for this day which had only just begun and like all good tourists he signed in and left a record of his presence, feeling glad that he didn't make this journey on a day that was busy with tourists, though he couldn't imagine it busier than today.

He walked away from the summit and sat alone nearer the edge. He had expected the Rock to have been flat on top, but it wasn't. The walk across the top was crossed by deep troughs which were steep and Al thought that the Olgas must have begun in the same way. He ate some chocolate, fruit and drank some water as he stared out to the horizon. Around him there were thousands of square miles of seemingly flat bushland with millions of yellow, purple and white flowers which stretched in an ocean as far as he could see. Yulara was out of sight, cleverly hidden by a series of sand dunes and in the distance a mountain range looked like a row of ant hills. Thirty Ks away the Olgas seemed to swell up from the Earth itself like some sacrificial offering to the Sky Gods. In the opposite direction Mount Conner stood alone and silent; it looked sad and lifeless.

"Steven my love, you should be here to see this with me."

The climb down was better than the climb up, even thought it was harder on the knees. Al met up with a young and extremely beautiful Swede; even if she was a girl! They seemed to get on well together and sat talking for half an hour once they were down, while she awaited her bus. Al was embarrassed by the standard of her English, even if it was American not British; and she was aware that it was American and apologised. Al said that so she should be sorry and they had a laugh at his cheek. Who was he to talk? Armed only with C.S.E. French, which was poor at the best of times. Maria left and Al strolled around to Maggie Springs where he found a crush of tourists looking at the waterfall. There were only five other people there, but that constituted a crush of people to Al.

"It's really strange to think that there's a waterfall on Ayers Rock. I wonder where it all comes from?" Asked a married woman turning to Al.

Al looked at her and pondered her question. He found it strange that she should want to talk to him when she was with her husband and with there being three other people of her own age to talk to. Still, it might have had something to do with the way he pushed his way past all of them so he had the best view.

"Yes, it is strange isn't it," he answered in polite agreement.

She smiled to Al then said, "and I wonder why it's called Maggie Springs, I mean it's not very Aboriginal is it?"

"Umm, it was nice of them to name it after Queen Maggie, though

I did think that the Rock predated her by a year or two." Al smiled, then grinned.

The group of people around Al laughed at his suggestion of it being named after the Iron Lady and the thought of her as Queen.

"I don't know why you're laughing, who else do you think it's named after?" He mocked.

"I'm glad it's not crowded here. I thought that there would be so many people it would ruin the visit," the woman said when she stopped laughing.

"What do you mean? There's far too many people here. Look there's six of us here!"

"If that's busy, what would you like to see?"

"Well the whole bloody rock to myself would be quite nice for a start!"

"What?" She exclaimed. "Don't you like people or something?"

"I travel alone, eat alone, sleep alone, visit alone..." Al answered matter-of-fact.

"How awful." She said full of concern.

"Why's that?" Al answered, getting on the defensive, looking back to the waterfall.

"Well I couldn't cope with that." The other people nodded in agreement.

"It's lucky that we're not all the same and doing the same things then. Isn't it?"

The group didn't answer Al and left him alone with the waterfall.

"At last, no people."

Later that evening, after tea, he tried to work out how many photographs he had taken since arriving in Australia. Surely in four weeks he had taken thirty six frames? His fears were confirmed when he opened the camera and found that the film wasn't winding on.

"You stupid pillock!"

Thoroughly pissed off by his stupidity he headed into town to the information centre. After arriving back from Ayers Rock he had noticed a sign advertising a FREE star talk with a ranger. He liked the sound of anything that was free of charge. The ranger marched a group of twenty people out to the central reservation and the group followed sheepishly up to the top of a sand dune. Al knew a little about the stars and could also recognise Mars, Venus and Jupiter when they were visible and he watched his star sign, Scorpio, being swallowed by a rising full moon. The ranger pointed out a few constellations and gave some information about the heavens and at the end of the hour Al concluded that it was all very good value for money, even if he did feel cold after standing out in the night for so long.

"Not everything that is free was necessarily good value, but as you quite rightly say, this was." Al said to a woman who had turned to him saying how good it was.

There were still another two hours before the information centre closed and he went to watch whatever video was being screened, as he had last evening with Grete and as he would for the next two evenings. It was an easy way of learning about the country and free entertainment, which was not to be knocked.

Early the next morning he set off for the Olgas. He didn't think it likely that he would get a lift and thirty kilometres was going to be a long way to walk. He needn't have concerned himself about that, within half an hour of setting off he was picked up by two boys a little younger than himself, one was a New Zealander, the other a Canadian. Al tagged along with them as they climbed to the view point. It was strange to be with people his own age and sex and he almost liked it, but these two boys were a bit immature and silly and Al thought about the two Germans he met yesterday. He still wanted to pass some time with people like them, but he didn't know anyone here and he could not pick and choose who could be bothered to talk to him. He didn't feel like a kindred spirit with these two and it felt a bit like company for the sake of company, so he left them halfway down and headed off to the far side of the Olgas. Alone, he headed through a gorge to find a valley where parakeets and finches flew wild and free. He recognised them; he used to keep these birds back home in East Anglia many years ago, in days long lost when he was young. They had occupied his time and mind when there was no one to talk to, no one to turn to and it gave him an excuse not to do the things that 'normal' boys did. It wasn't healthy for young boys not to have an interest, so he created his own interests in aviculture and East Anglia.

Everywhere was damp; but a stream had begun to dry and split into separate pools, cut off from one another. In the pools were hundreds of giant tadpoles. They wriggled their way around looking for food and deeper water in the shrinking pools. Al grabbed a handful that were in a pool which was more tadpole than water and moved them into a much larger and deep one which still had some water running into it.

"Now they can become bigger and they'll be more meat for some other animal to eat... but what if I've created an imbalance and created too much competition for the available food? Now less might survive." He sat watching the pool wriggling with life as he ate a sandwich. He threw some bread into the water and decided that he could redress any imbalance like that. He wasn't totally convinced, but they seemed to like wholemeal bread.

He had wandered around for more than five hours and figured that he should start to head back to the road. He was disappointed that he still had not seen any kangaroos or wallabies, no snakes or lizards, not even a rabbit which were supposed to be so common! At least there were thousands of flowers and he even found a bush which had but one perfectly formed Sturt's desert rose on it. All the other flowers had long since shrivelled and turned brown and he examined its perfect form.

"Oh Steven, you should be here with me, seeing all this with me."

Everything he saw, everything he did led back to the same thoughts of Steven and how he might react to the things that Al was seeing. Al had become an emotional cripple and he couldn't see it. He had passed the hate stage, but that had just allowed him to love again. How could one person love another to the extent that they became dependent on them? What could he do to change it?

Al allowed the rest of the day to drift away. He did the same with the following day as he walked around Ayers Rock. Few people walked around it, it was too far for most, so they drove around. He was able to be alone as he wandered about and a rustling sound in the bush made him think of dingoes, but he could not be bothered to panic, he just thought of Steven. He saw Stan painting, he could see his picture and he liked it, but said nothing as he walked past. He watched a sunset on Ayers Rock, alone amongst thousands of other tourists. It was a beautiful sight, it was awful.

He packed and left early. Still a little numb from the previous two days, but thinking that he should make an early start because there might be a lot of hitch-hikers trying to get out.

He waited and then two girls and a boy came and waited for lifts further along the road. Al watched them as they passed by. He was annoyed when he saw the girls get a lift within half an hour and furious when the boy went after an hour. He stood there in the heat and flies, angry.

"Why the fuck do I bother?"

Fifteen minutes later a man stopped and helped Al put his pack into the boot of the car and he was on his way.

A DREAM, ONCE DREAMT, IS FOREVER LOST

Yulara, 22nd May 1989

In almost a month, Al had travelled more than three thousand miles. A distance that he could not even begin to imagine, but somehow he had traversed it. It had been a long journey since he left Perth, as much in statue miles as in his mind, but maybe three thousand miles wasn't so far after all? It certainly was hard to imagine that all his travelling had been done within just one country and just a small part of it at that. However, not a day had passed when he did not think of East Anglia, home, friends. It was hard to accept that he was missing out on the summer. He felt cheated after living through the winter and now missing out on the rewards, not that it had been unpleasant here. The only rain that had fallen had fallen at night and did not affect his time at all. In spite of the good weather, his heart was dark. Hourly he thought of Steven. Hourly he missed him, longed for him. A dark cloud indeed, it saddened him. He treated each day by whatever mood he was in at the time. He didn't make plans, instead drifting in and out of each day as it came, unable to think about what he was doing wandering about Australia alone. He was no tourist and did not want to see the sights and although he could appreciate the beauty of places like Ayers Rock and Mt. Olga, it was the wild unspoiled bush which impressed him the most. The vastness of it was somewhere harsh in which he could hide from the world and from himself. Here, he could feel a strange sense of security in the isolation of the outback.

He looked out from the car as it raced along at over one hundred miles an hour. Outside, the burning heat and dry air and hoards of flies. Inside, cool air circulated around his face and feet, comfort that he relished. He sank deep into the soft seat and relaxed. Red sand stretched endlessly along each side of the road. Scrub and low bushes sprouted dry and dead-like from it. An occasional desert oak stood tall above everything else. He turned to look at David as he answered a question, the conversation stopped and restarted intermittently. Al looked at his profile. He was a good looking man, mid-thirties, and he seemed a likeable sort of person. Al wondered why he had stopped to pick him up when so many other people had continued past? Was he just a much more pleasant type of person? Did he really just want company for part of his journey to Alice Springs? Maybe he wanted something? No, Al didn't think he was after anything. He had been in the car for an hour and he hadn't been given any reason to question his motives, but still Al was sceptical about the reasons behind his kindness. So what would Al do if he was after something? And Al knew that his something was a less unpleasant way of saying S E X. He knew that he would not demand David should stop the car and let him out in the middle of nowhere, not that being in the middle of nowhere bothered him. It's just that he knew he would not do it. He wasn't confident enough to demand anything. Al's eyes ran over the outline of David's face. Did he want to have sex with him? A quick NO! flew back at this thought, but Al was aware of the way that he was looking at David which told him that although he wasn't lusting after him, although he didn't want he have sex with him, he did want to touch him! He did want to feel closer to him than sitting in the passenger seat allowed. Al didn't realise that what he desperately wanted was someone to feel close to. Someone to be a friend. Someone to hug and yes, maybe even sleep with. To sleep with someone, to feel the warmth from another naked body. To wake up one morning in a real bed, entwined with someone, but without the sex. He didn't want or need the sex, just the comfort. Just love and some kindness in the darkness instead of being alone, crying himself to sleep because he was so far away from Steven.

* * * * *

Al looked at Steven's naked body as he knelt by him, unsure of what he could do. There was so much pain in Steven's eyes that Al had never seen before. What had he done to him?

"I am sorry Al..." His words faded into silence and despair.

Al reached up and put a hand on the back of Steven's head, gently running his fingers through his short hair. He rose to his knees and pulled Steven slowly towards him, embracing him with pure love. Steven's body was so warm and Al, who was cold, never wanted to let go. He buried his head in Steven's chest and cried, shaking as he held his arms firmly around Steven. Steven was nervous, unsure of what to do. He feared that Al might lash out at him at any moment, but he held Al in his arms and rested his face, also wet with tears against Al's head. The clock ticked slowly past midnight, time meant little as they hugged each other in fear of losing something, something which neither could admit to already having lost. Al lifted his head and gazed into Steven's eyes, he stroked his face softly and wanted to tell him that he knew that it was also difficult for him. No words came from Al's lips, but Steven could feel Al's silent pleas and understanding. He was silent as Al's fingers ran slowly along the tear lines on his face as Al's eyes screamed I'm sorry to him. The room, although lit by a spot light by the bed, felt dark and full of despair.

"Al," Steven whispered, "it's getting really late and we're not doing ourselves any good like this. Please come to bed and try to get some sleep."

Al was a physical and emotional wreck and he could no longer argue even if he had wanted to. Steven carefully helped him up from the floor.

"Come on Al, you're so cold." Al looked at him in tacit agreement.

Al began to remove the remaining clothes he was wearing, though it was a real effort. Steven got back into bed and waited for Al to lie down beside him, making sure he was covered by the duvet when he did get into bed. Al had his back to Steven, staring at the door. Steven was still, looking at Al, feeling as low as he could for doing this to his little friend, his happy, smiling, dancing, ever present, reliable little friend.

"I am sorry Al." Steven said painfully. Never had those words carried a more honest and heart-felt meaning, but they drifted around Al's head and unable to find a place to rest they faded into the deepest recesses of his mind, the places where things go, when although Al knew they were important he forgot them until it was too late to remember. He had never felt so lost or alone, but how could he be alone when he was lying in bed next to the person who was at the centre of his life? He turned to Steven, the light bright behind him, he looked deeply into his eyes. Steven could read HELP! in Al's dark and reddened eyes, but was helpless. Reaching out his arm, Al rested it on Steven's chest with such tenderness and love that it caused Steven real pain. They were both exhausted, but neither wanted to fall asleep first. Neither wanted to switch the light off. They needed to see each other, they agreed on that without speaking a word. In silence they looked at each other and found some comfort in the silence which they were sharing together, even though it carried so much pain. Steven's chest was warm to Al's touch, his skin was soft and his body smelled good. it was familiar.

"I want to make love to you Steven," he whispered without any expression on his face.

"Why?" Steven was confused by such a request.

"Because I love you." Al answered in a way that conveyed the proclamation that it was the most natural thing to ask of him and a little surprised that Steven needed to question him.

"I don't think that it would be a good idea Al." Steven was off his guard. It seemed to him a very strange thing for Al to want, but he could not give him an outright no. Al looked intensely into his blue eyes.

"Please Steven, I love you and right now I need to feel close to you." Silent tears ran freely from his eyes carrying so much pain, so much confusion and betrayal. Looking at Al, Steven knew that whatever he felt about Al's desire to make love he should not show it to him. Steven did not want to have sex and he couldn't begin to imagine why Al should want to, but he agreed, reluctantly and silently.

It was not love; not by a long way and Al knew it, when he orgasmed inside Steven. It was only a physical release for someone who was so confused and terrified that he was losing something very special to him. He was losing the very person he loved. The person with whom he was now sharing such an intimate physical act, but one that felt less than satisfying. Did it need to be satisfying? It made no sense, but Al was not looking for sense, only comfort. Steven felt nothing. He tried to think of the young lad who had charmed and excited him so many years ago, with whom he had fallen in love with and now felt like a stranger in his bed. He tried to remember happier times as he felt Al's tears on his back. What was happening now confused him and he blanked it out of his thoughts. He hated the pain and confusion which he was sharing with Al at this time.

* * * * *

Ayers Rock had long since disappeared behind him, so too had Mt. Conner, banished to the realms of memory and the been there, done that! It was just a few kilometres to Erldunda and Al thought carefully about whether he should say that he would go north, back to Alice Springs? Was it just the fact that he did not want to get out of the air conditioned car yet, or was he placing too much emphasis on the fact that David had told him that he was unmarried and would be stopping in Alice overnight in a motel before returning to Yulara? There was no body language, or any look which asked Al to stay in the car and travel to Alice with him, as they stopped at the roadhouse and Al reluctantly got out of the car and into the heat and flies. He lifted his pack and bag from the boot, shook David's hand and said goodbye.

"So much for the thought of comfort and a warm bed." He watched as David fell from sight and he looked around feeling a little lost in a place he had been to three times before. It wasn't being in the centre of Australia that made him feel lost. It was a burning passion, screaming inside of him, begging himself not to be alone any more. He wanted to be with someone who he felt close to for a while. He wanted and needed a friend.

Across the road, on the road south towards Adelaide, he could see the two girls from Yulara. He felt a little nervous as he walked towards them. He had never hitched where there were already other people, even if they had taken his lift.

"Hi," the dark haired girl said as Al came nearer. "Was Darryl still there when you left?"

"No, he got a lift not long after you."

"We felt a little bad that we got a lift before you, but the driver said he never picked up blokes."

"Yeah," Al sighed. "As if I'm going to cause anyone any trouble! I figured it was something like that. I just thought it was a bit much that all three of you were gone half an hour before me after I made sure that I was up early and out on the road before anyone else!" Al laughed at the way all his effort amounted to nothing. Or did it? At least he had got a good lift, with a driver that he felt comfortable with, even if he didn't offer Al a free meal and bed in Alice Springs without any pressure of sex. Had he really wanted that? He didn't rightly know. He was just so lonely and so bloody confused.

"You must have got a fast lift."

"Yes, just over an hour from Yulara."

Al stood talking to the two girls, who were Dutch, Nina and Anna. They had been travelling through the far east together and their friend

Darryl was American. They had met him in Indonesia a few weeks earlier and were now travelling together through the centre to Melbourne. Darryl arrived after a few minutes.

They positioned themselves along the road and waited in the heat for a lift. Hour after hour. Fly after fly. Each time a car approached their hopes were raised, only to be dashed as it went racing past. Mid morning saw a change in the weather, a cool breeze got up and although it was probably just a little below twenty degrees it felt cold after weeks in the high twenties.

They stood waiting all day and as darkness fell they gave up and went into the roadhouse to get some food. Al was feeling very comfortable with his new companions and by the time that eleven o'clock came around and the roadhouse closed he was quite pleased with the situation. Dare he hope that he had found some friends?

Darryl suggested that they pitch their tents on the grass outside the building and although Al would not have dreamed of doing this had he been alone, he went along with the idea. There were four people and only two tents. Darryl's was a very small two person tent and Al felt compelled to offer a space in his, which was bigger. His offer wasn't the most natural statement he had ever made and he was a little uncomfortable in what was a new situation for him.

"It's silly for you all to squeeze into your tent, if one of you don't mind sharing with me, there is obviously room."

"Yes, that would be better Al. What do you think Nina?" Anna said, making it obvious that it would be Nina who would have to share with Al. Anna and Darryl wanted some privacy.

"Yes, that's alright." Nina answered. She looked at Anna, in an almost apprehensive way.

"So Al. Is it alright if Nina shares with you?"

Al said that he had no problems with that. No more problems with Nina than he would have had with any one of them. For his three new friends this was no big deal, they were well travelled and not narrow-minded like Al, who, despite being homosexual, had led a quite sheltered and shy life. The only time he had spent the night with anyone was one night in a van with Tony and he had known Tony for years.

It was cold and dark as they crawled inside the tents and Al was glad that he had a lamp which very soon warmed things up.

"Now just you remember not to try anything, because I've got this mallet so I can defend myself!" Al waved his oversized mallet around and they both laughed. It made them feel a little more relaxed.

"I don't think I snore, at least I hope that I don't. Well, if I do, just give me a thump and I'll do something about it, though what I don't know?"

Al didn't think anymore about being in his tent with another person. He was so tired that he slept almost as soon as he crawled into his sleeping bag, fully dressed. He hadn't been sure about stripping off in front of Nina and as she did not take any of her clothes off, Al thought that it must be the norm under these circumstances. He had no idea what was, or what wasn't acceptable behaviour.

He was awake before the sun rose and lay quiet and still until Nina woke.

"Did you sleep alright?" The silence was broken.

"Yes."

"Did I snore?"

"No, well if you did then I didn't hear you."

Al got out of his sleeping bag and left the tent, he stood in the quiet of the morning air which was crisp and fresh. The grass under his feet was wet with the morning dew which hung from the blades of grass like tiny gems. Anna and Darryl were still asleep in their tent as Al soaked up the feeling of the new day. He was at his best in the early morning when most people were not awake, and therefore not able to intrude into his life.

It was a good morning. The sky was clear and it would soon be warm. There was something special about the morning light which made Al feel like he belonged to the sunrise. Something in the quality of the pastel shades in which everything is painted for those few precious moments before the night finally retreats and the gaudy colours of the day enter the stage and take a firm grip of the scene. The sun, she looks so far away on the horizon and it's as if she is touching the very edge of the Earth, before climbing higher into the sky and out of reach. The silence of the morning broken only by a few birds, their sounds adding to the mystery of the new day. Their calls never intruding into the motionless world, never out of place and only adding a new dimension to the stillness of the moment which is so restful to one's soul. The sun she climbs higher and takes command of all the creatures of the land, life bursts into a new day and a joy of life fills the scented air. Birds take to the sky, higher and higher they soar. Insects begin to move their tiny bodies as they receive the sun's gift of warmth; and flowers unfold their sepals and petals to paint a brand new day in colours not found on any artist's canvas. Each one a world in miniature. Each one a new dream. Each one perfection. This Earth is surely paradise.

"Oh it's so cold out here." Nina said as she climbed out of the tent and entered Al's thoughts and feelings.

"Yes, but it's so beautiful." Al replied, lost in his own world. Nina was too cold to agree.

Within a short time they had the tent packed up and finally Anna and Darryl got up.

"If you and Al try and get a lift together and Darryl and I will do the same and then we will only need two lifts."

Anna organised things and Darryl wrote the address of a backpackers hostel in Adelaide where they would all meet up again sometime in the next few days. It was a long way south, at least 1300 kilometres and a good lift would still take a full day and no one was expecting to get a good lift after yesterday.

They waited along the highway and another car dropped off two girls, who walked towards Nina and Al.

"Hi. How long have you been waiting?" One of the German girls asked.

"Twenty three hours and thirty minutes," Al smiled. They looked at each other in abject horror.

"Oh well, we had better walk up there and make ourselves comfortable."

With that they continued along the road, stopping to talk to Anna and Darryl on the way, before sitting down at the far end of the slope, some two hundred metres further along.

"Here comes a road train. Hold onto everything." Nina said and Al looked around as he grabbed his pack and held out his sign. The ground shook as the monstrous vehicle thundered towards them.

"He's going to stop!" Nina shouted with excitement. "That will be a lift for Anna and Darryl."

The road train was indeed going to stop, but it rushed past Al and Nina in a hurricane of cold air, dust and plant debris. They looked behind and saw a row of red lights across the back of the machine.

"It's not going to stop!" Al shouted in disbelief.

The truck was beginning to swerve about as it tried to slow down. Anna and Darryl gripped onto their packs and onto each other as it raced along the road and past them. Still it was slowing down. The German girls stood up as they saw it coming, held onto everything as it passed and watched as it came to a halt some two hundred metres further along the road. They turned to look at Anna and Darryl, who watched and did not move. It was too far to run after and they watched as die Fraulein half ran, half walked along the road towards it.

"I don't believe this! We've been here five minutes short of twenty four hours and they just have time to sit their fat Kraut arses down and they take our lift! Who won the fucking war anyway!" Al shouted along the road.

So there they were at the side of the road in central Australia, waiting. Al thought of Steven, but stopped himself again by talking to Nina. He was so glad to have met these people, who unlike most of the British tourists he had come across seemed like a non-intrusive group to spend some time with. For a little while he enjoyed their company and the stability it afforded him. He was in no hurry to get anywhere, indeed he didn't know where exactly it was he was heading for. Adelaide? Yes, or at least at the moment. He might go and change his mind tomorrow, swept along on another whim, another moment of panic or fear. The sun had now risen high into the clear blue sky, but the promise of warmth was not fulfilled. A cold desert wind blew and jackets were needed to keep bodies warm. Flies, it seemed, did not mind the drop in temperature from a few days ago, nor did they mind the wind and they continued to pester the travellers as they waited hour after hour at the side of the road on the red dusty verge. Nina sat on her pack and wrote a letter. Al walked over to the roadhouse, he needed a moment alone and some distraction from the realities of waiting at the side of the road hour after hour. After a little while he came back with two large packets of crisps. He had a craving, a need for some junk food, so he bought some which he would enjoy, he was determined to enjoy it.

"Don't eat them all before I get back," he smiled to Nina as he gave her a packet and walked along the highway towards Anna and Darryl. As he walked he noticed the stones which lay everywhere, dry grasses and pieces of wood. He looked to the horizon and the unchanging land between him and it. All so different from East Anglia, yet here he was and something inside him said that he belonged here. Something stirred inside him and told him he had a freedom which he should make the most of because it would not last forever. He held onto the moment. He feared that it would be gone all too soon. In his calmness he wanted to stay here for a while, but he also wanted to be with these people. Yes, he enjoyed his isolation, at times, but he also enjoyed this company and wanted to hang on to it, onto every moment while he could. He knew that the time would come when these people would leave him and he would be alone once again, whether he was ready for it or not.

"I don't want to be alone yet."

A car passed, without stopping. It was no surprise to them. He reached Anna and Darryl, it had taken a minute or two to reach them.

"Do you believe what happened?" Al asked, referring to the two German girls and the road train.

"I know! I bet Nina was swearing down there with you!" Exclaimed Anna.

"Believe me, you don't want to know what was said!"

As Al had expected; and half hoped, they did not get a lift and although at times it felt that time stood still, it was in fact a short day. About five o'clock Al wandered off to find some wood with which to make a fire, if they were going to be camping at the side of the road for another night he wanted a little more heat. He found a dead tree and strangely enough two railway sleepers, which were miles and miles from the nearest track. Darryl and he carried them over to where they would make camp and Al made the fire and then they decided that they should eat.

"What food have you got?" Anna asked.

"Not much, jam, crackers, coffee and noodles," Al answered.

"We've only got coffee, you're better prepared than us."

Needing something else that would make a meal Al went to the roadhouse and returned with a tin of tuna and creamed sweat corn. Added to the noodles it made a nutritious and quite appetising meal... given the circumstances. Anna, Nina and Darryl were amused by the contents of Al's backpack.

"A non-stick pan?" Anna queried.

"An essential to life!" Al rebuffed.

"Saucepan? Stove? Lamp?"

"I need both a stove and a lamp so that I can cook meat or fish, rice, pasta or noodles and two veg."

"You need a lot of things don't you?"

"One must maintain certain standards. I am an East Anglian after all and I wouldn't want people to think that we still went around in chariots, slaughtering people and torching cities... though that might be something worth reviving - a route to independence!"

"Al, I think you are a little mad?" Anna laughed.

"Oh yes, quite possibly," he replied with a smile.

They ate and talked. Nina, Anna and Darryl tried to get to know something about this strange East Anglian. They tried to work out what was so odd about him? He was giving so little away, but there was something not quite right. Al was enjoying himself and as the evening progressed and he relaxed a little more, though not enough to let his barriers down and open up to these people. Darryl told them some riddles while they sat around the fire; which raged as the tree and a railway sleeper burned, drinking coffee and being at one with the situation in which they found themselves. Al wasn't normally good at solving riddles, but for some reason unknown to him he solved each one within a few seconds, without thought or effort. Darryl, Anna and Nina were all impressed by this and so too was Al, for he had no idea how he managed to do it.

They sat around the fire until midnight. Al felt like he could have stayed there forever. The flames rose up into the night's sky and must have been seen for miles around, by anyone who might have been in the bush. Above them a million stars shone and the light from the first quarter; or was it the last quarter? Al could never remember the order of the phases of the moon; but whether first or last, it cast enough brightness to show the outline of the trees and bushes in a pale grey hue. The fire began to lose its flames as the wood was all but burnt. A huge pile of embers glowed orange and heat poured out towards them and kept the freezing air of the desert night in check behind them. They crawled into their tents and Al lay awake far into the night, listening to the fire as every now and then it would burst into life as a breeze passed over it. The noise of the last pieces of wood crackling made him worry about the flysheet melting as a wayward spark landed an it. The night advanced and gradually he drifted into a deep and restful sleep. Smug in the knowledge that he would wake up to a second morning and know that he was not alone, but with people whom he liked and even dared, at this early stage, to think of them as friends.

    Al's favourite time of the day was not long in coming. A beautiful bright sun burst over the horizon as he crawled out of the tent. The fire was still giving off heat and he put on some water and made himself a coffee. The chilly air was a little too fresh and he pushed some wood onto the remains of last night's fire. It flared up and chased the chill away.
    "This is so civilised. What is the point of a twenty five year mortgage and two weeks in Spain or Florida every year? Who really needs more than enough?" He shuddered to think of all the things which he had once thought of as necessities and which he now saw as part of the falseness of modern life, but it is easy to see such things when you don't have them any longer.
    This was their third day at Erldunda, standing at the side of the road, waiting, hoping for a lift which would take them south. It turned out to be another cool day, they all wore light jackets or jumpers, no more bare arms and legs in sight. Minutes and hours passed and it turned out to be a repeat of the previous two lifeless days and by five o'clock they found themselves once again sitting around the fire.
    "What do you think about getting the bus down to Port Augusta?" Anna asked Al.
    "I think it may be the only way out of here." Al answered, half regretting not going to Alice Springs with David three days ago, but then he would have missed out on meeting these people. It was no good regretting a decision made, he hadn't done too badly so far, much to his surprise. He had quickly forgotten how lonely he had been feeling. Yes, it was so easy to forget in the company of these people.
    "We might be able to get the bus drivers to do a deal for us. Maybe fifty dollars each and it can go straight into his pocket." Darryl said, sounding as if he knew something about free enterprise in Australia that Al hadn't heard of. Just before eight o'clock the buses started to arrive. Al approached a bus driver and gave a sob story of how he and his friends had been stuck here for three days and had very little money left and asked how much would it cost to get to Port

Augusta? Al was nervous of doing this and combined with his inherent fear of talking to strangers, he came across as quite genuine, not that it got him anywhere. Each bus driver gave a similar price and at eight thirty they found themselves sitting on a bus heading south and out of the red centre. They watched, a little sadly, as the bus passed their camp at the side of the road. A faint glow could still be seen from the fire. They looked to each other and then out of the windows and into the darkness outside. No one felt like speaking. Al thought that it was strange to be travelling with people whom he had come to know purely through trying to hitch-hike and not being able to get a lift. He hadn't asked to go south with them and they had not asked him. It just felt like that was what had been agreed many months ago, as if they had planned to meet up and spend this time together.

After an uncomfortable twelve hour journey during which Al slept fitfully; waking at Marla, Coober Pedy and a couple of places in between with nothing to see, they got out of the coach at the service station beside the camp site in which Al had stayed. It was just over two weeks since he had left here and gone north. It could have been years since he had said goodbye to Tony.
"Where was he now? He should be working and having quite a good time in Sydney, drinking and..." Al stopped himself from thinking any further. Wasn't he judging Tony? He did not want to, though it sounded like it to him. No, it wasn't a judgmental thought, purely a hope that he would change his ways and find out what it was that he needed and wanted. A hope that he could be happy.
"Let's get a coffee and something to eat before we head on to Adelaide," Anna said, leading them all into the cafeteria.
"It's a long walk to get through town. We're out on the northern edge and you know what these Australian towns are like, they go on forever," Al informed his friends. "I doubt that we'll get a lift until we're many miles south of here."
Unfortunately Al was right. After a rest, a coffee and something to eat they walked and tried to get a lift as they went, but with no luck. They split into pairs again and it had been over an hour since Nina and Al had seen Anna and Darryl, they hoped that they had got a lift already. It wasn't so. Anna and Darryl were still walking and only a kilometre in front of them. Two hours passed and then three, then four and then five. Al and Nina had reached the south of the

town and were waiting on an exposed flat area. Here, the dual carriageway crossed some tidal mudflats and the wind was cold as it whipped across at them. It was bitter.

"Let's go and get a coffee across the road. Warm up a little," Al said to Nina, she didn't need convincing.

"That's the best thing I've heard you say in the past four days," she said and managed a smile.

They took a little while in crossing the road, the traffic rushing past at such high speeds and their packs were too heavy to allow them to dash out between cars, so they had to be patient. Besides, after a night journey and all morning trying to get a lift, the walking and the cold, they didn't have the energy to run. When they made it across they peered into the windows of the ye olde worlde tea rooms. If it hadn't looked so tacky it might have appeared quaint.

"Americans love this sort of nonsense!" Al said disapprovingly.

Nina said nothing and they went inside where it was even worse.

"I think we should have a home made biscuit, yes?" She asked, but her hand was already inside the jar and pulling out one each.

Al nodded and smiled. They took their biscuits and sat down, waiting for their coffee to arrive.

"Oh God! Look at this really awful table cloth! I have never seen anything so horrible. We have such nice ones in Holland."

"This is the worst of the worst of Englishness." Al said as he looked around, "tack, tack, tack! It's all junk. It's all what traditional Britain is supposed to be and never was." The coffee arrived and they stopped moaning about the surroundings for a while. They were so grateful to be having something hot to drink. Nina bit into her so-called home made biscuit and Al read the look of disappointment on her face and expected nothing from his as his teeth sank into it. She was right to be disappointed. It was hard and full of oats; and the chocolate colour was nothing more than that; colouring!

"It's never seen a cocoa pod that's for sure." Al snapped as he looked around the tawdry room.

For both of them it was a much needed distraction from the realities of standing at the side of the road in the bitter cold. For half an hour they sat in the warmth. There were no other customers and they lowered their conversation to a whisper as they suddenly realised how loud they sounded in the empty shell of the café. Outside of the window, cars continued to speed past in both directions. Nina's face was full of disappointment and dread of returning to the act of trying to get a lift. She hated the waiting, she hated the cold.

"We had better go and try again." She said with as much enthusiasm as a pig in a bacon factory.

"Oh come on Nina! We'll walk across the road and get a lift within one minute." Al tried; vainly, to lighten her mood.

"Ha!" She snapped.

Their first problem was to get across the road. With the speed of the cars, having two lanes to cross in both directions, heavy packs on their backs and against a strong wind, this proved less than easy.

"We'll get a lift within one minute will we? It will take an hour just to cross the road!"

Al said nothing as they made a mad dash across the road, through a gap in the traffic which they hoped was long enough. A car sped towards them, not slowing at all. The sound of its horn blasted out at them, coming nearer and nearer, then past.

"Fucking Aussie wanker!" Al shouted. "Too much trouble to slow down just a little. Dick-head!"

They prepared themselves to cross the next carriageway, which was not so busy, it wouldn't be, it was the way in which they wanted to go. They crossed.

"You know Nina, I have the strangest feeling that we've been here before," Al said as he put his pack down.

"Yes, maybe in another lifetime?" Nina said, almost smiling.

Al held out his sign as another car passed.

"Al, look!" Nina shouted. Behind them a car had stopped and was waiting for them.

"See Nina," Al said as they ran towards the waiting vehicle.

"I told you that we'd get a lift within a minute. You just need faith."

"Luck is the word I think you want," she said as they pushed their packs into the car.

Things weren't so bad after all. They had a lift through to the centre of Adelaide and in a few hours they would be there. Both imagined that Anna and Darryl had been there for hours, but they were only three hours ahead of them, approaching the northern edge of the city, from where they would try and get a lift, or take a bus into the centre, which ever came first. It turned out that it was an hour that they waited with no offer of a lift and then a bus came, another hour later they were at the hostel where the four travellers had planned to meet.

Dusk began to fall before Al and Nina reached the edge of the city. To the horizon and beyond, the sky was full with what seemed like millions of orange and white lights; like a galaxy of stars; like a dream. They watched for road signs as they drove through the urban sprawl, they were still some distance from the centre.

Eventually they were in the main shopping area and here they got out and found their way easily to the hostel. After some confusion as to how to get in; the front door was locked and had not been opened for some time, they walked down an alley at the back of the hostel.

"The girl is Dutch and she's with an English boy." They heard Anna saying as they walked towards the building.

"East Anglian. Not English!" Al shouted as they approached.

A look of surprise flashed across Anna's face as her two weary friends appeared from around the corner.

"Oh great, you've made it!" She was so happy to see them both arrive. "Darryl and I are going to have a look for somewhere cheap to eat. Do you want to come with us, or get cleaned up first?"

"I want to have a shower, come back for us Anna." Nina said lethargically.

"Yes, I need a shower before I even think about anything else." Al answered. The thought of hot water and soap sounded almost magical to him; it was four days since his last shower and he was feeling somewhat more than just a little grubby.

Nina and Al were not in the main hostel, but were put into a little cottage which stood behind it. At some time in the past it would probably have been servants quarters for the main house; it could have been a barn, but Al didn't think that it showed signs of barn or stable conversion. They walked in, Al not having any idea of what to expect and was nervous about being in yet another situation which was totally alien to him. The little cottage had a basic lounge and a kitchen, from which a flight of stairs rose around three walls and up to one large bedroom in which there were only five beds. He was surprised by the lack of bunk-beds and he dropped his pack onto the bed by the window which stood alone. Nina took the end bed, the one next to her stood empty and the other two were obviously taken; they were unmade and strewn with luggage. At the end of the room a door led through to a little bathroom, which was only for their use.

"This is alright Nina," Al said with a note of surprise and relief in his voice.

"Yes, it is Al. Not at all bad for a hostel." She was as surprised as Al.

"Do you want to take the first shower?"

"No. You go first and I can unpack and sort out my things, but don't use all the hot water!"

"I'll try not to. I'll even have a shave. How about that!" He smiled, he felt good.

He disappeared through into the bathroom and scraped the razor through four day's growth which adorned him. It tugged, it pulled, but slowly it came off leaving a smooth and soft face. The water was hot and the dirt from days of travelling and sitting at the side of the road washed away and he felt positively human again. Out in the middle of nowhere, where there was no running water it hadn't bothered him to be dirty; not that he enjoyed it, just that he wasn't going to let it bother him. After all, the Aborigines had survived for forty thousand years with not washing! Nina listened to Al singing in the shower as she sorted out what clothes were clean and suitable for wearing to a restaurant, pushing everything dirty to the bottom of her pack, where it would stay until she got to a launderette.

The bathroom door opened and Al emerged clean and happy.

"Oh Nina. I could have stayed in there all night. It was wonderful. My skin feels like I've been soaking in baby oil for a week."

"That may be so and in that case I am very pleased for you, but I'm glad you didn't stay in all night and I hope you have left enough hot water for me!" With that she went into the bathroom and washed.

Al sat on his bed and looked around the room. He thought about sharing a room with three other people, two of whom he hadn't even met. Not too long ago this would have been a totally outrageous thing to even think about. He had changed in the past few weeks and he could see just how much in situations like this. If anyone had told him to sleep in a hostel a few weeks ago he would have been horrified at the suggestion, but here he was now, about to do just that and what made that possible was his new found friends with whom he was so happy to be here with; an oasis of stability in his troubled mind, a calmness in the stormy sea of his life.

"I wish Steven was here. He should be sharing this with me."

The pain which he had been suppressing so well in the past few days came a little closer to the surface as the knife twisted a little more in his mind. He knew that it was only a matter of time until he did something else that was stupid. Yes, it was only a matter of time; though how long he did not know, until he could no longer keep a grip on his situation. He didn't know when, where or why? The only certainty was that it would happen and he dreaded even the thought of that time. His mind drifted and drifted, he began to sink deeply into the abyss from which it seemed he would never escape; lying on his bed, lost, until Nina came out of the bathroom and interrupted his thoughts of his past. He had drifted into memories of holidays in Wales. The Brecon Beacons, Snowdonia and even an argument in Pembrokeshire one sunny afternoon; hell in such happiness.

Anna and Darryl had arrived back from the centre and their hunt for a pleasant, but cheap restaurant;

"Welcome to our humble abode," Al said upon their entrance into the bedroom. He sat up, Nina brushed her hair.

"Oh it's so nice up here, much better than where we are. We're in the basement with six other people," Anna said.

"Oh please! One must maintain certain standards. We couldn't possibly sleep in a basement. Could we Nina?"

"No, that would be beneath us," she answered.

"What a terrible pun Nina," Darryl said, he wasn't impressed.

"I thought it was pretty good myself," Al said in her support.

"Well, if we can leave the basement for a moment I'll tell you that we have found a cheap Italian restaurant which looks quite nice. Do you like Italian Al?" Anna asked.

Al was again aware how strange, but how natural it felt to feel close to these people, they were really a group of strangers to him, who didn't even know what his likes were. He had no dislikes when it came to food; except Brussel sprouts. These people might not have even given him the time of day had they not all been stuck in the middle of Australia a few days earlier, but he didn't want to think about that.

"Anna, my dear girl. If it's food just lead my face to it and the rest is automatic! Come on, what are we waiting for. My stomach says that it is time to eat!"

It was just a short walk into the city centre, in fact just two streets away. The evening was cool, a cloudless sky opened up onto a collection of stars which did not shine brightly against all the city lights. They filed into the restaurant. A small and quite plain affair and rather crowded. It was a shame that they had to spend nearly ninety dollars on the bus fare as that could have allowed them a freer hand in choosing somewhere to eat. Still, the four travellers were happy to be in this humble eating house, happy to be in Adelaide and happy to be showered. They were shown to a table, well away from the door, so they were out of the cold draft which would trouble those people sitting near to the exit. They sat and browsed the menu.

"Have you decided yet Al?" Anna said, not really giving him much time. She went out of her way to include Al in everything they said and did. Al appreciated this, it made him feel like he should be with them and less like someone who was just tagging along, unwanted, unnecessary. Despite not having been giving long to study the menu, Al had in fact not wasted a second and had indeed chosen.

"Lobster cocktail; followed by veal, petit pois, French beans, sweet corn and rice. Then either chocolate cake or cheesecake, depending on the menu."

"You don't waste much time do you!" Darryl answered for all of them.

"There is an old saying in East Anglia by a very wise person, who once said: He who wastes time choosing his food often leaves the table hungry."

"Who said that?"

"Me!"

They laughed and Al still had to wait while they decided what to eat; he looked around the room, through the sea of faces; faces of strangers in a strange town and country. Why did it not feel odd to be in this city? It could have been the next town along the A12 from Ipswich for all he knew, felt, or for that matter, cared! He had no worries at the moment and allowed himself the luxury of smugness in the knowledge that for a little while longer he was not alone.

Smoke rose from the table behind Anna, it drifted up almost three feet before coming to a halt as it hit a barrier of warm air. A waiter carried food to a table, past Al. He sighed at the smell of such good food. It had been a while since any of them had eaten as well as they now would.

"Well I've decided now. How about you two?" Anna asked

Darryl and Nina. They had and Anna called a waiter to take the order.

"Why couldn't she call that other waiter? He's much better looking than this one." Al thought, then he thought that he wasn't particularly good looking anyway. No one was good looking compared to Steven. "I wonder how he is now? It's nearly lunch time in Suffolk. He'll be looking forward to a break from teaching those little shits in the third year. The end of May is usually a good time, warm and dry, the evenings really becoming noticeably longer now."

It would have been a good evening out, even with Al's thoughts of Steven, but the atmosphere hung over the table like a lead balloon after a very heated discussion about an E.E.C. ban on American beef imports because of the hormones that the cattle were reared on. The three Europeans defended the ban on the grounds of the less hormones and chemicals used in food production the better it was for everyone. Darryl saw it as blatant protectionism. Anything which reduced the American influence in Europe was a good thing in Al's eyes. He, like many of his fellow East Anglians, held a deep resentment of America and what it stood for and since the bombing of Libya from East Anglia the anti-American feeling had been heightened. The so-called special relationship between America and Britain only existed at a Government level and not with the citizens of the British Isles. How can there be friendship between peoples when so much money from America goes to buy weapons for terrorists who kill people in Britain? With friends like that who needed enemies?

* * * * *

Tony had not found more than a few hours work in Sydney, though for most of the time he was not sober enough to look, let alone do any. For almost a week, in fact within a couple of days of arriving in the city, he had been seeing a girl he had picked up in the Hard Rock one night. Seeing? For almost a week he had been having sex with a girl he had picked up, or was it he that had been picked up? For days he could not remember her name. For days he called her by the name of his girlfriend in East Anglia. He missed Diane, longed for her, but while he had been with her he ran from the thought and possibility of a long term relationship, with long term commitments and the trappings that went with it. Jenny was nothing more for Tony than a companion to help him through the long and lonely nights in Sydney. Ten thousand miles from where he wanted to be, but too drunk to realise the realities of what it was that he wanted; who it was he was longing for. Jenny lived on the streets of Sydney; though Tony didn't know that at the time, she told him that she didn't get on with her parents and that she couldn't tell him her address in case he came around when her father was in. She explained the bruises and cuts as her father's work when he came home drunk. In reality they were from a succession of casual affairs with whomever was available, mainly from fellow street walkers and clients. Tony and Jenny spent their nights in his hostel, she would sneak in when it was safe to do so. They would have drunken sex, disregarding anyone else who might have been in the room, awake or asleep, then slept. During the day they didn't see each other. Jenny would be gone before Tony got up. A few times he woke as she got dressed, but he just turned over and went back to sleep, in part with the feeling of smug satisfaction in having had sex, partly in disgust with himself. For a week this went on and Tony had got into a habit of late mornings; sometimes afternoons; and drunken evenings followed by nights filled with the scents of sex.

The last time that he saw Jenny was late in the evening after she hadn't turned up at the pub as arranged. Tony was puzzled by the feeling he had; he actually missed her. Not that he missed her as a person who he looked forward to seeing. He didn't miss her as a person at all. It was just that he had grown accustomed to her, it seemed like she was always there and now she wasn't. Like an alcoholic without a drink, he missed her. He spent the evening alone, drinking, looking at the door each time someone came into the pub. He was drunk by the time he left the noisy pub and entered the dark King's Cross streets. He left the safety of the busy and well lit areas and headed down the hill towards the naval docks at Woolamooloo. He was aware that he was going there because Jenny had once mentioned something about the area, though what it was he couldn't remember or reason. He was convinced that he would find her even if he didn't know where to look.

He did find her, he found her with three men and although he was drunk, he approached cautiously, he didn't like the look of what he was seeing; or thought he was seeing in the dank tourist free streets of Sydney.

The four were startled by his approach and before Tony could say anything, two of the men; both bigger than Tony, were on him, thumping and kicking. The third man, slower and fatter, joined in the kicking.

"See if he's got any money," one of the men said to the fat man who proceeded to finger around in Tony's pockets as Tony lay bent double on the floor, in too much pain to move, scream or cry. The fat man found several dollars in coins and over a hundred dollars in Tony's wallet.

"I know him!" Jenny shouted as she came to have a look.

"Shut up you stupid bitch!" The tallest of the three shouted at her as he slapped her hard across the face.

"Come on!"

Jenny stood there looking at Tony, she wanted to help him, but was scared.

"Come on you bitch, or I'll fix you!" He grabbed her arm and pulled her. They ran into the early morning darkness and were gone, leaving Tony in agony in a side street.

It was nearly half an hour that Tony lay there doubled over himself, in pain, unable to move. The blood from his nose, mouth and cheek had stopped flowing and he had begun to breathe instead of gasp for air. His stomach, back and testicles hurt more than anything had ever hurt him before. He slowly, very slowly and painfully pulled himself towards a building which he was able to rest against. The stone was cold against his back and he opened his jacket, shirt and trousers to check if he was bleeding, he wasn't. He gritted his teeth and closed his eyes at the pain, his flesh tender beneath the gentle touch of his own hand.

In the distance there was always the sound of traffic on wet roads, but not once did he hear any sound come in his direction. Near him, the night was silent and left him alone in his pain. An hour passed. He sat in the cold damp street, against the building, old and redundant. An empty can rolled along the street for twenty or thirty centimetres as a light breeze caught it, hitting the kerb and falling silent again. A second hour passed and Tony tried to stand, but it was too painful to move and he sat back against the cold, but soothing stone.

Distant, far out over the Pacific, the sun began to rise from behind the low cloud cover. The sound of the traffic grew to a more persistent rumble as the morning rush hour began. Tony, still in so much pain even after so many hours, so very cold and tired, got to his knees and eventually stood, though not without the support of the wall. He waited for almost quarter of an hour before he even thought about moving. His eyes looked at his dried blood on the tarmac and now it was dawn he could see evidence of what he had suspected. A needle, discarded on the path not two metres away. Last night's needle. One, shared by four.

"AIDS!" An alarm bell rang loudly in his head, but the immediate problem of the pain he was in pushed that thought to the back of his mind. Taking slow and careful steps he made his way back to the hostel. The streets were busy by the time he came close to where he was staying and although people stared, he couldn't care less, he cared so little that he couldn't even be bothered to give them any abusive language in return. It wasn't easy getting up the two flights of stairs to his room and he was quite pleased that he didn't see any other backpackers. The early ones had long since gone out and the late ones were still asleep. Tony crept into his dorm and took his shoes off with an amazing amount of difficulty before lying down and drifting into a fitful and painful sleep.

* * * * *

Anna and Darryl had decided that it would be better for the four of them to rent a caravan rather than stay in the hostel. They assumed that Al would still want to stay with them, though no one asked him and he did not question their decision. Leaving the hostel in the late morning, first waiting for the rain to subside a little, then going for a bus. It was not far to the caravan park and they could have walked, but with the threat of more rain they were forced into the decision of being lazy. Al had not used a normal city bus while carrying his backpack and whether he wore it, or carried it, it was still difficult and totally inconvenient. He was, as they all were, relieved when ten minutes later the four of them spilled forth from the bus, bodies and packs out onto the footpath.

"Anna and I will go and check in and when it's all clear one of us will come back for you." Darryl said. Al hadn't heard about any of this before now and wondered why not? There was obviously prior planning and discussion and he had been excluded from it, but at the same time, included.

So it was that Darryl and Anna went into the caravan park and checked in, while Nina and Al waited outside in the street. Al hadn't done anything like this before and was nervous about sneaking in. It seemed to Al that so many of the things that he had done in the past few weeks were new to him. What had he done with his life? He liked the idea of being able to save a little money, but he was still unsure of this. Above them the sky darkened again and within seconds it began to rain heavily. Al looked at Nina and Nina looked at Al. Neither said anything, neither had to, they knew each other's thoughts. The rain fell increasingly heavily. A wall of water in front of them in every direction they looked.

"Oh, please hurry Anna, please." Nina pleaded, as her pack began to soak up water.

It seemed like hours that they stood in the rain, in the cold, then finally Anna appeared from around the corner.

"Oh no!" She looked at the two of them, dripping wet. For a moment she could only stand there and stare, unable to speak.

"We're in number eight, four back, three across, near the shower block. Give me a minute and then come in." She said leaving as quickly as she could.

Nina looked at Al, unable to say anything as she watched a rivulet of water running down him and into a lake at his feet which met with the flow of water from herself.

"I'm not looking forward to this," he said.

"No, neither am I. Shall we get it over and done with?"

"Well, I am as ready as I'll ever be. Let's go."

The two marched in as bold as brass, both dripping wet and attracting the total attention of anyone who glanced in their direction. Al adopted his 'if you look as if you own the place, you'll be alright' approach. They strode, outwardly confident, inwardly nervous, towards the first caravan. It seemed like a long hike across a wide open expanse of flat and vulnerable ground, which surely had snipers hidden in the bushes on either side. They were sitting targets, but they had to cross this area if they had any chance at survival. They reached the first caravan and out of the corner of his eye Al could see someone coming out of the office.

"Walk faster, someone's coming."

Panic, nervous panic pulsed through their veins as they tried to walk faster than their pursuer, which was not easy with the weight of their packs and wet clothes. Thump, thump, thump, the sound of their hearts as they worked hard pumping oxygen around bodies which were struggling to move their mass forward at an unacceptable speed. Both Nina and Al thought that they could not only hear their own heart beats, but also feel the vibrations from each other's. A new cloud burst open above them, it mattered not, neither could get any wetter. The woman was still coming after them as they zigzagged between the caravans.

"She's still coming. Now I know what it's like to be a fox that's being chased by a pack of hounds. She's probably foaming at the mouth ready for the kill," Al said as he half ran, half walked. Nina was too out of breath to respond.

"Hey you stop!" the woman barked behind them.

"I didn't hear that, keep going Nina."

They were nearly there. The caravan door swung open as they approached, making one last dash and diving into the caravan, pulling the door shut behind themselves.

"We've been followed."

A silence, heavy with fear, fell over the four as they stood in the caravan waiting for the inevitable to happen. Nina and Al tried to breath silently, though they were both gasping for breathe. A few seconds of silence which felt more like hours of torture. Bang! Bang! Bang! They all jumped as the caravan reverberated to the sound of the thumping on the door. Reluctantly, Al, who was nearest the door, pushed it open, no one else wanted to move. A puddle of incriminating water lay at his feet, Nina standing protected behind him.

"Are you staying here?" She snarled at him.

Al looked at her, hound-like she was. Rain water flowing down her face, or was it saliva in the corners of her mouth? Maybe she had mistaken him for a fox and was about to rip into him! All four friends stood in silence as they searched their minds for something to say, but what could they say in order to make things right?

"You should check in at the office before you move in!"

"Yes, we are sorry. They will come over to the office in just a minute," Anna quickly said, trying to diffuse the situation.

It seemed to satisfy the old hound and she stormed off, obviously very pleased with the fact that she had caught them, even if she was now soaking wet.

Al pulled the door shut and looked at the others, Anna and Darryl at the end of the caravan, dry and warm, while Nina stood beside himself, dripping wet. They laughed at the absurdity of the scene.

"The only thing we're sorry about is the fact that we got caught."

"I guess that we should go over and pay, while we're still wet." Nina said lethargically and tragically.

The two wet travellers walked sheepishly into the office and quietly paid, but before the hound could say anything about their behaviour Darryl came rushing into the office and put on an amazing display of grovelling.

"I'm very sorry, I'm very very sorry. It was all my fault and I know it was very wrong and I'm very sorry. I know it was bad and I am very very very sorry. It was naughty and I'm sorry..."

Nina looked at Al, who was looking at her, both with as much surprise as was displayed on the hound's face. Darryl was so insincere and so obvious that no one else dared to speak and interrupt him. Al glanced at the door and Nina took the hint and they were both outside before the hound noticed, she was still bemused by Darryl who quickly followed them, leaving the hound open mouthed behind the desk.

Back at the caravan Al emptied his pack. Everything was wet, including his last set of clean clothes. He went for a long hot shower and then did some washing. It was a relief to know that once again he had a pack full of clean clothes. The need to wear the same set of clothes for more than one day was over.

None of Al's travel companions had said anything about how long they would stay in the caravan, or indeed how long they would stay in Adelaide and Al didn't really want to know in case the answer was a much shorter period of time than he could deal with. Yes, by now he was so used to being with these people and he knew that it would not be such a long time before he would have to say goodbye. That thought scared him. Right now he felt as if he had always known these people. He enjoyed their company and almost relaxed with them, but beneath his initial reaction to them he was still guarded. He was still secretive. He was still alone. His mind was as troubled as it ever was and they could sense that he had his problems to deal with. They knew that something was wrong and often wondered what it was that made him seem so unhappy, deeply unhappy. Even when he laughed and joked with them they could see that it was not a total commitment to the here and now. Part of him was trapped in some horror in his past. A horror that he could not share with them, though he did want to talk to someone, but couldn't. Here, he may have been with new friends, good people, but here he was just as alone as he ever was. More alone than he been in the bush in Western Australia all those weeks ago.

Cities and people; especially people you come to like and trust, can make you feel at a most isolated and vulnerable low.

It had stopped raining by the afternoon and the sun had even made an appearance, although it was a weak and watery sunshine. They walked through the park towards the city and talked and enjoyed being in Adelaide. The city gave off a good friendly feeling and it relaxed them all.

The lawns over which they walked spread out, leaf littered between large trees. Autumn had passed and winter was here. It was cold. Nina went off to look at the city on her own. Anna and Darryl went off together and Al headed off in another direction, alone. He wandered about and came across a foreign language bookshop and he remembered how embarrassed he had felt at Ayers Rock by the many Europeans who could speak English when all he could manage was a few sentences of French. He went in to browse through the shelves of books and quickly, impulsively, decided to learn a language while he was in Australia.

"It will give me something to do with my time here. Make me use my brain a little, but what the hell do I want to learn?" He looked and thought. "Welsh would be good," he flicked through a book and was reminded of his holidays with Steven, putting the book back again. "Turkish?... Make my father proud of me. Swedish? Too difficult. It's got to be useful and not too difficult and not French. That leaves German, Russian and Japanese, but aren't Russian and Japanese difficult?" He looked at some of the courses and quickly decided on German, mainly because in many ways it looked a lot like English and therefore could not be too difficult. He found a course which consisted of a book and four tapes which cost eighty dollars and was ready to buy it, but thought that it might be wise to see how much a tape player would cost.

He found a tape player for thirty dollars and unlike him, he bought it without second thought or doubt. Normally he would think about something like this for days, if not weeks, especially if he knew that he didn't have money coming in to replace the amount he was spending. Returning to the bookshop he bought the audio language course then crossed the road to the botanic gardens and sat reading the instructions leaflet. The first tape began as he walked through the gardens; it was far too cold to sit and listen, besides he enjoyed looking at the collection of trees and shrubs which he found quite impressive for such a young city and although the gardens were small, he ranked it third after Kew and Geneva which were his favourite two.

"Ich bin, du bist, er ist, sie ist..."
"Oh my God, verb tables. I hate verb tables!"

The tape played in his ears and once or twice he tried to repeat the sounds that he heard, though without much success. The harsh sounds of German were more difficult to imitate than the owner of a soft East Anglian voice had at first imagined.

It was beginning to get dark by the time he returned to the caravan. Nina was still in town, but Darryl and Anna were there and Al sensed that they had not long had an argument, so he was glad that he had not arrived back any earlier.

"Sieg Heil possums!" He said as he entered into the tense atmosphere with a huge, but false, grin on his face.

"What?"

"I'm going to learn German. Itch bin, dew beest, air eest, see eest and all that!"

Anna cringed at his pronunciation; she spoke Dutch, English, German and some French and she could see that Al was in for a hard time with most of the German sounds, but she was impressed that he was willing to try and learn, unlike most of the British tourists she had met.

* * * * *

Tony woke from a painful sleep. His face, back, stomach, testicles and legs still hurt. He had sobered up and was hungry, but food was not the most important thing on his mind at the moment. He eased himself up from his bed, grabbed his towel and some clothes from his pack and walked to the showers.

He stood looking into a mirror above a hand basin, holding onto it, he still felt that he needed support. His face was cut, but no black eyes and anyway the cuts would quickly heal. He went into a shower and peeled off last night's clothing. It hurt to stretch, it hurt to bend. Standing beneath the hot water he lost all sense of time and reality. Slowly he lathered up some soap and very gently began to wash away the dry blood from his face, tenderly massaging his body. Several bruises showed and who knew what damage there could be internally? Soapy water mixed with urine as it swirled down the drain.

"Why?" he asked himself, but he wouldn't ask the full question of why did he drink so much? The hot water poured over his head and down his back, it almost felt good.

"Jenny shared her needles with those others. How long had she been doing that? Fuck that! I've been fucking that bitch and she could have AIDS." Again the question of why? Tony thought of Diane; how this could affect her, he was worried more than he had ever been worried before. Why?

The water began to cool, so he dried himself, partly dressed and made his way slowly to his bed and lay awake with the thought of the risk he had so easily, so willingly, exposed himself to. He hated Sydney, he wanted to leave, but it hurt to move now.

"I have to get out of here, get a job and not drink. I have to. Oh God, Al, where the hell are you. I think I need a friend now and I bet you still need a friend to turn to. I should never have left you in Port Augusta once we had met up again. I wouldn't be in this mess now. I'm going to Canberra tomorrow Al. Are you going to be there?"

He slept for the main part of the evening and night, still sore, still in pain. Physical pain from being beaten up and mental pain from the fear of the unknown and the loss of Diane, so many miles away. He dreamed much that night. Nightmares would be a better description; as he saw himself drunken, old and frail, but he wasn't old, no, he was ill, wasting away. Alone, not one friend around to be with him. He hadn't told anyone and no one asked and alone he wasted away. A twenty two year old in the malnourished form of an eighty year old. Too ill to sit up by himself, too frail to move. Propped up in a high-sided chair, dying. Al? Where was Al? Was he alright? He would have been here with him had he known, but Al was out there somewhere. He also was alone and still running from himself. Maybe Al was in the same boat as himself? Steven could have easily given Al AIDS. Easily. Poor Al, out there on his own, dying because he loved someone.

And so Tony's night went on, almost without end, without rest. But the night did end and he packed his things as best he could and he tried to ignore the pain; which although was not anywhere near as bad as yesterday had been, it was still bad. It had been a long time since he had last been up so early in the morning; unless he hadn't been to bed the previous night. He made his way towards a bus terminal and bought a ticket on the first bus and some food to take with him. Within half an hour he was being shaken about uncomfortably on his way to Canberra; still scared, worried for himself, Diane and for his crazy friend Al.

* * * * *

Nina had not arrived back until an hour or more after Al. She didn't say where she had been, or what she had done, in fact she said very little at all. The atmosphere that had been so noticeable when Al returned had cleared, Al had a way of distracting people even if he couldn't find a way of distracting himself from his problems. Anna and Nina got on with preparing the evening meal, after which they sat down and played cards. The evening was passing by, but still there was such obvious tension and Al got up to leave.

"I'm going out for a walk." He couldn't cope with the strain of whatever these three people had said to one another and he needed some time to be alone. His preoccupation with Steven was looming ever larger in his mind.

He stepped out into the cool and dark of inner suburban Adelaide and before he had got too far it had started to rain. He could not be bothered to worry about it. He was suffering under the pressure of being homosexual in a heterosexual world. He didn't feel that he should have to make an issue of his sexuality, but once again he felt that he was being deceitful by not saying something. He hated the way he felt, that he always had to pretend, he lived a lie, a lie that he was forced into by society. The rain fell, not too heavily at first, but then heavier. He remembered seeing a notice at the hostel, there was a list of gay pubs in the city. He wanted to go to one. He wanted to go somewhere that he could just relax and be himself and not have to worry about putting on a front, or having to explain himself to anyone. In a gay pub it would not matter, he would be surrounded by people who were like himself, people with similar feelings and fears. He wouldn't feel like some sort of outcast freak, an outcast from a society that could tolerate many outrageous things, many hideous crimes, but not homosexuality. But what would be the point in going there? He always felt just as out of place in a gay pub as he did in mainstream society. He felt that it was almost impossible to be treated as a person and not just seen as an easy target for a lay. He hated the thought that someone might try and pick him up. He hated the thought of those cock-happy queers who see anyone as fair game. He was no more a part of that scene than he was part of the straight world; he didn't belong anywhere.

As the rain began to soak through his jacket he could picture in his mind's eye a pub full of camp panel-beaters called Lily and macho-man store managers with the stereotypical dead cat on their upper lip, it made his skin crawl. Slimy over-the-hill civil servants who hunt out young boys, who leer at anything young as if dinner had just arrived and worst of all, those highly respectable doctors, solicitors, priests and teachers, who you would swear were 'normal', but turn out to be as bad as the rest. No, worse than the rest, because you expect far more from them. You expect to be able to trust them, or at least Al expected to be able to trust them. He wanted to be able to trust someone.

"No, I don't need any of that!" He cried into the rain and darkness as he walked in streets he did not recognise.

He had walked for over an hour and covered quite some distance before making a large circular route and arriving back at the caravan from another direction. The atmosphere hadn't changed since he had left.

"Oh no, you're soaked again." Anna said sadly.

"That's life I guess," he answered. He would have been quite happy if the weather was the only thing on his mind to be a problem for him.

They sat playing cards until quite late into the evening. They relaxed a little and had a few glasses of wine, which helped to lighten the mood of all of them.

"I'm going to bed now," Al said as he stood and made his way onto the top bunk. It was cold up there and it hadn't been his imagination that the caravan had been losing its heat for some time.

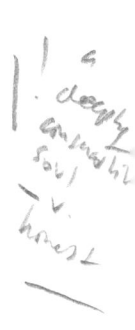

Al recalled that the only other time that he had been in a caravan was on holiday in the west of Scotland with Steven, Jonathan and Mrs Brown. He tried to only remember the good times from those four days and chose to forget the afternoon he walked the five miles into Oban after an argument. He almost got on the train to Glasgow without telling the others that he was heading back to Suffolk. That was another example of him failing to fulfil his desire and need to feel and to be special. Why did he need so much love from Steven? Why did he need to be shown it in the most obvious ways? Steven had so much to put up with and he could not deal with it because he did not understand the reasons behind Al's needs and insecurities.

They stayed in Adelaide for another two nights before Anna, Nina and Darryl left to get the overnight bus to Melbourne. Al thought that it would be wise to stay behind in a city that he was beginning to know and in which he felt comfortable. He packed his things and left to find a camp site; he didn't want to stay in a hostel, but every site he phoned charged the same price for a single person as they did for two, which was a lot more expensive than a hostel. He was a little rattled by the thought that single people always drew the short straw and incensed by the thought that if he stayed in Adelaide it would cost him twice his normally daily living allowance. He had to get work, but his money would not last long here. He mulled over the options that presented themselves to him. He thought about his friends leaving on the next bus to Melbourne and he wished that they were not going. So quickly, what seemed like an easy task to find a new place to stay, one where he could be alone as much as possible, became an insurmountable problem. He marched to the bus station, meeting his friends on their way back into the city for the few hours they had left.
"I'm coming with you."
"Are you! Why?"
"I've changed my mind about staying here."
They waited for him as he pushed his way to the front of the counter and bought a ticket for himself. He knew that he was just delaying his inevitable departure from his friends, but that didn't matter. He would have a few more hours with them before leaving them upon their arriving in Melbourne. They were pleased that he was coming with them, they were only too aware that he wanted to stay with them and didn't understand why he felt that he had to leave.

There was no reason why he couldn't stay with them for the next couple of weeks while Anna and Nina stayed put to do some work, but that was his decision and they were not going to push for reasons.

The evening sky had cleared into a cool and dry darkness. The city lights lit up orange beneath the blackness and stars. Al met with Anna and Darryl in a pub an hour before the bus was due to leave and it didn't take Al long to drink a few gin and tonics; and even less time to savour the taste once again. It had been a long time since he had last tasted that taste; the pleasures of juniper.

At the bus station they watched Coronation Street while they waited to board. Al found it so strange to hear the northern British accents after so many weeks of Australian sounds. Indeed it was strange to see a television programme, it had been a long time since he had last sat and vegetated in front of an idiot box.

All so quickly they were sat on the bus as it climbed the hills into the Mt. Lofty range. Adelaide sprawled out below them.

"I hope we don't have that stupid Fame video again!" Nina said. Al laughed at her, then returned to staring out of the window. In twelve hours they would arrive in a new city and Al was well aware that the hours passing by were his last hours with these people. He slept a little, though it isn't very comfortable sleeping on a bus seat, not even for a short person such as himself.

The bus rambled through the darkness. Outside, an old Eucalyptus was lit up, first by the headlights, then by the light inside the coach. It stood old and alone, dead or diseased, leafless. Al stared for hours out of the window and often at little more than his own reflection.

"I wonder what would have happened if I had not come to Australia? I doubt if I would still be living... And dear Christopher, so patience so loving, always a support. It seems like a life time since we said goodbye and didn't I then know that we would never be together again? Still it seems impossible that I will ever see my brother again. My brother? He is such a good friend to let me call him brother, to be able to love me and not worry about what I am.

* * * * *

"I just don't understand why you can't tell me Al? Christopher said, he was hurt because he was being kept in the dark about something by his friend. He looked at Al; both confused, Al's fear,

Christopher's concern.

Al returned his look. He could see that this was no idle curiosity. He could see that Christopher wanted to be able to help, but how could he if he didn't know what was going on? Al didn't want to have any secrets from his friend. He wanted to tell Christopher everything that there was to tell. He loved Christopher, but that only made it harder, not easier. The air was tense, with fear and pain and Christopher's blue eyes conveyed the pain he was feeling at being excluded. There was no use in prolonging this. It was time.

Sat next to Al on the bench; it was lunch break, was Linda. She had known for nearly a week and she understood how difficult this was for Al. She understood how he was being torn between being honest with his brother and the very real horror and fear that he might lose his friendship. It was not a risk that he wanted to take, but he had no choice now.

"Well Al?" Pleaded Christopher.

Tears formed in Al's eyes as he looked at Christopher.

"O.K. Christopher. I can't not tell you any longer. Can we go outside?"

"Yeah, sure. If that's what you want." At last he was going to be told what was going on. Whatever it was, it was obviously weighing heavily on Al's mind and he knew that this was not easy for him, though he had no idea why? Al stood up next to Christopher, he looked at Linda, she smiled vaguely.

"It will be alright Al. I'm sure it will."

It was nearly quarter past one. Al and Christopher made their way between the machines and through the noise. It was always noisy there, even at lunch time when only a few people were working; these were the days before the continental shift system. Al felt ill, he imagined all his worst nightmares were about to come true in the next few minutes, the worst one of all, that Christopher would no longer want anything to do with him. It was a real horror in his mind.

They walked out of the factory and into the sunlight, it was so bright outside, and warm. It was turning out to be a good summer, at least as far as the weather was concerned. Not so, for Al's personal life. The source of his happiness in recent weeks was like a drink from a magical chalice, one tasting of sweetness and joy, but with that drink a bitter and unhappy after-taste, which was reality and reaction. Soon he would run from reality, even if it was only for a two week holiday.

"We'll walk down here, so we're ready to clock in when the bell goes," Christopher suggested, knocking Al on the shoulder and nudging him along, smiling.

They walked along together, the distance left to walk reducing rapidly. Time was running out.

"How the hell am I going to tell him." Al tried to think of an easy way for him to say what he had to say and one which would be easy for Christopher to cope with. There wasn't one.

"I can't imagine why there is such a problem, Al? Why is this so difficult for you? I am your friend after all."

"I know Christopher. I should be able to tell you everything, anything, but..." he paused, but what? "I'm scared."

"But what have you got to be scared about?"

"I think the world of you, you're the brother that I always wanted. I look up to you and I don't want to risk our friendship."

"Well right now I don't feel much like a brother. Why can't you just tell me her name?"

Life in a small East Anglian market town in the mid nineteen eighties had not really progressed very far along the path to liberation or tolerance. Some things, homosexuality, still did not happen there, or if they did it was one or two weird people out of the tens of thousands in the town and surrounding villages.

To grow up almost totally alone in a society which doesn't just not accept you, but also hates you, despises you, is something that is hard to imagine, really imagine, unless you experience it first hand. Sympathetic people can be understanding, but they can never know the torment inflicted by the so-called normality which swamps and suffocates anything, or anyone who will not, or can not, conform. Al was more than a little frightened. He had been secretive for so many years and now that he had met Steven he had found happiness. A happiness which he thought he could never find. A liberating freedom. A huge weight lifted; once so burdensome, from his shoulders. Not that it was that easy. Mixed with all the joys of having someone to talk to, someone who was the same, someone to sleep with, plan with, laugh with, have sex with; along with the joys came yet more secrets, the need to be even more careful. Yes, along with that joy came yet more unhappiness; to be more secretive, or to face the world. Al chose to confront the world, his world, the people in it. It was not going to be easy, it was not easy. Less than a week ago he had finally plucked up the courage to tell Linda, that wasn't easy, but he was glad that she knew; one less person to deceive, one less person to pretend to. Now it was Christopher.

"What's the matter Al? Is she black? Do you think that I'm going to mind if she's black?"

Al looked at Christopher. He wanted to say yes she's black, it would be less hard and Christopher could accept that. Why couldn't he have fallen in love with a black girl? It was a natural assumption for Christopher to make as Ipswich had a large population of black people compared to many East Anglian towns, especially here in the eastern parts. Al was so aware that Christopher was totally unprepared for what he had to tell him.

"No Christopher, she's not black," he emphasised the word she with a sense of loss. He stopped pretending to be heterosexual after six years of unhappiness.

They stopped walking and looked at each other. Christopher searched his mind for anything to say that might help Al, make it easier for him.

"Well Al?" He asked softly, compassionately.

Al sighed heavily and sat down in the gravel, resting against the factory wall. He tried to talk; which was not normally a problem for him, but no words came out.

"Al?"

"I have tried to tell you Christopher, I really have." His eyes wet with the tears which he fought hard against as best he could.

"Tell me now Al; please." Christopher stood close to him and waited for Al to begin.

"You're not going to like this, you're probably going to hate it; and me."

"I'm not going to hate you Al, we're friends, but if you don't tell me soon I might think about that!"

The minutes ticked away. There wasn't much time left before the afternoon bell would sound and they would have to go back to work.

"This isn't the place for this, but nowhere is the place for this," he took a deep breath. "His name is Steven."

He had said it, it was out in the open. Forced out of his mouth quickly and without any real pain, but following his statement; as far as it was a statement, there was a pause and a terrible silence.

"Who's name is Steven? What is he on about some bloke called Steven for?" Christopher asked himself as he tried to make sense of what Al had said. Then he realised.

"Oh no Al. No," he said as he dropped his head and shook it in disbelief, in amazement, in pity, in horror and in loss. Al was horrified by the sound of Christopher's voice and the look of abject disappointment on his face.

"How could he be a poof?" Christopher thought, looking at his friend who sat in silence, in almost mortal fear on the ground. "He doesn't look like a poof. Why didn't I realise? What can I say to him? How can I help him?" Christopher didn't know what he could say anymore than Al did, so for a while neither said a word.

Eventually it was Al who broke the silence.

"I'm so sorry Christopher. I've been trying to find a way to tell you for the past two years. I hated you not knowing the truth, but I was too scared to say anything. I didn't want to lose your friendship."

Christopher didn't answer, he stood in silence trying to digest Al's words. He didn't blame Al for not telling him sooner, he couldn't even begin to imagine what it must be like to be homosexual; and in Sudbury of all places. He had never met anyone that he knew to be homosexual and Al wasn't what he expected at all. Al seemed quite normal, except for the dyed hair and make-up whenever he went to Gary Numan concerts and discos, but that was fashion, that wasn't Al.

"It must have been so difficult for him to say that and I have to tell him that it doesn't matter, he's my friend." Christopher tried to form a sentence, but he was still stunned by what he had heard. "I felt sure that he was going to say a black girl, not a white boy. God, I wish I hadn't mentioned a black anything, that must have made it harder for him."

Al looked up to Christopher, he was still there.

"No wonder you couldn't just tell me," he finally said, once he had gathered his thoughts. "Does Linda know?"

"Yes," Al was relieved that they were talking. "I told her on Monday. I had to because of her wedding."

"So why aren't you going to the wedding?"

"Steven doesn't think that it would be a good idea if he went and I don't want to go without him. I love him Christopher and I shouldn't have to pretend about that. It's not fair, either way I lose."

"Why wouldn't it be a good idea if he went to the wedding? Sarah will be coming with me."

"If Steven came with me it would be pretty obvious to everyone that I'm homosexual and it would be all over the factory by tea-break on Monday and all over the town by Tuesday. It might prove difficult with my dad working here."

"I can understand that." But still he couldn't understand how Al could be a poof. He wanted to ask why? How? But didn't. Homosexuality was something that happened in London, not in Sudbury and not to people Christopher knew.

"How can he say that he loves a man and mean it like I love Sarah?" There was another short and uncomfortable silence. Across the road in the beech hedge a pair of blackbirds flew to and from their nest; a second brood, or replacement clutch, the normality of the boy/girl world, babies everywhere.

"I can't help what I am. I didn't wake up one morning and say to myself I'm going to be a poof now." Al explained. Christopher said nothing and factory workers began returning lethargically from town ready for the afternoon shift. "I didn't mean to hurt you Christopher. I think a lot of you."

"I know Al, I know."

The factory bell began to ring. It was half past one and time to go back to work.

"We had better go back into the funny farm." Christopher said trying to lighten the atmosphere.

Al nodded in agreement and they made their way into the dark and noisy factory; the stench of the oil was sickeningly thick in the air that they breathed. Christopher pulled out his clock card from the rack and punched it on the clocking machine. 1.30pm. Al searched for his, the clock ticked on. 1.31pm.

"You're late Al!" Christopher said with a smile as he waited for him.

Al tried to return Christopher's normally infectious smile, but couldn't. Time was the least of his worries at the moment.

"Cheer up Al. It's not the end of the world you know."

"You've never had to tell your best friend what I've just told you."

"It really doesn't make a difference; not really. It just came as a bit of a shock," he smiled again, still no response.

"It's not everyday that your friend tells you that he's a.... something like that." Christopher blushed, Al understood, or at least

he thought he understood that this was also difficult for his friend.
"I didn't expect you to react like this."
"What did you think I'd do? Throw a wobbly?" He grinned broadly at the suggestion. Al was his friend, why should he have reacted in such a way?
"I thought that you would at least hit me and then not want to have anything more to do with me."
Christopher felt so bad upon hearing that, he began to realise just how hard it must have been for Al. He couldn't imagine what it must have been like growing up homosexual and alone. He remembered all the schoolboy remarks about queers, poofs, fags, benders; Al must have had to put up with all that at his school, it must have been hell. Now, years later he was having to risk the reaction of friends, family and workmates. He knew that attitudes had not changed much, even if it was 1984.
"No matter what you are, you'll always be my friend and nothing is going to change that," Christopher said with conviction. "And of course I wouldn't hit you! It was a bloody shock though!"
Christopher turned into a separate gangway, time was passing and both were late starting work.
"I'll see you later," he said to Al as he went.
"Yes," answered Al. "I hope so Christopher, but how can our friendship be the same as it was. I saw the disappointment on your face."

* * * * *

"Oh my God, it's freezing!" Anna said and spoke for all of them upon their arrival in Melbourne.
It was a mere one degree Celsius as they waited, shivering, for their luggage. Their first impressions of this city were not good. It seemed dirty and noisy and could have been any one of a dozen European cities, or even American cities. Al knew that it was time for him to say goodbye, he had delayed this for a day and now the time was right to make the break; for better, for worse. He had no logical reason for having to leave. His friends didn't want him to go, he did not want to go, but he longed for something and thought that he was after isolation.
After a quick goodbye; kisses from Anna and Nina and a firm

handshake from Darryl, Al crossed the road and headed towards the city centre. He had made the break.

The noise and smell screamed big city rush hour. The last time Al had experienced this was the day Tony and he had gone into London to get their visas. He thought of Tony as he ran across the road and wondered where in this country Tony was? Totally unaware that Tony was himself just arriving in Melbourne at the bus station that Al had just left.

People rushed and pushed in a frenzy of having to be somewhere; and getting there before they had even left the place that they had come from if they could possibly manage it. Exhaust fumes from cars spewed into the air and the clatter and clanging of trams could be heard everywhere. The sky was filled with noises, painful sounds. In the crush of people and noise all the streets looked the same and Al became disorientated. He was knocked around by the masses and the thought that he had actually chosen to leave the safety of his friends.

He found the tourist bureau, it was closed and would remain so for another two hours. It was too cold to stand around and wait, so he went for a walk, both to keep his body warm and to keep his mind occupied. Al was unimpressed with the city, the noise, the density of people and most of all his own reaction to the situation that he had put himself in.

The seconds ticked past, minutes, he became agitated; less and less able to deal with the day ahead. Where was he going to get work? He didn't have a visa to work. Surely he would get caught?

"You should be in East Anglia, not here in Australia. You don't belong here... Why the hell is it so bloody cold? It never looks cold on Neighbours!"

The never ending tide of people swept past him in all directions. Grey people, grey thoughts, grey expressions; heading to offices to do the day's work, like the day before, like the day before that. Routine. Responsibilities. A home, friends, belongings and belonging. Al had none of them. He envied them for their boring jobs; and securities; and for being surrounded by familiar things. Panic had firmly set in and he walked back to the bus station, fighting his way against the flow of people who kept knocking into him. No matter which way he went, he always seemed to go against the crowd.

"Story of my life!" He scoffed. "Never have fitted in and never will. Queer in every sense of the fucking word!" Despite all the roads looking similar, his good sense of direction didn't fail him and within ten minutes he was at the bus station.

"Can I help you?" A girl of about Al's age asked, deep brown eyes looking hard and bored at him. She wanted to be on a bus to somewhere instead of being stuck in one place watching other people leaving, day in, day out.

"Yes, I want a seat on the next bus out of here." He answered in a less than friendly way, though he had no reason to be rude to her.

"Where do you want to go?" The girl was amused by his vagueness.

"I don't really care. I just want to be on the next bus out."

She gave Al a strange look, she had probably had requests like his before; infrequently, but it did happen.

"Nine thirty to Brisbane." She said calmly, matter-of-fact, as she looked at the departure sheet.

"That will do. I'll have a ticket on that. Here's my luggage."

* * * * *

Tony had not found work in Canberra, though he had tried to get some. Maybe he would have tried a little harder if he hadn't still been feeling so sore and frightened. He had however, managed to remain sober for the two days that he was there. He hadn't even wanted to have a drink. For two days he sat in a hostel after job hunting, not speaking to anyone other than hi or bye. He wanted to be alone. He wanted to be free of his fears which were very real inside his head. For two days he shut himself inside himself, shutting the world out as he watched the other backpackers, listened to them. They all seemed so shallow; so unaware of real life. Many were travelling around on daddy's credit card, or had come straight out of college, university, or even school on a round the world ticket; otherwise known as an excuse to see six or seven countries; or to be more precise, six or seven cities and as many pubs as possible. He was aware that he was being cynical and bitter; an escape from his situation. A distraction from what he had been doing, an alternative to the reality of facing his own fears. Had he not been feeling this way, had he not been isolated from the people around him, would he not be spending time with these types of people? The types who he had laughed and joked with and been drinking with far too much since he started to travel across

Australia. Had he not been feeling the way he was, he would have stayed in Canberra, but he didn't like what he saw when he watched them. So he left on the night bus to Melbourne. Unplanned and unthought out.

So it was that Tony arrived in Melbourne on the same morning that Al had arrived from Adelaide. They should have been able to see each other once again, something that they both wanted, but the bus from Canberra was half an hour late and as Tony's bus was coming to a halt Al was walking out of the bus station and preparing for leaving his friends behind. It should have been a chance meeting that would have been good for both of them, both needed an old friend to trust, to talk to, to rely on. They both needed that support. They both wanted love. Tony was not the sort of person to panic easily, but these were trying times for him; he had not felt this emotionally vulnerable since he was a child, it was an alien feeling to him and liked it less than Al did. Now he was in Melbourne and he was clear in his mind what was going to happen here. First, collect his luggage. Second, find a hostel and food. Third, find himself a job and have a blood test.

Tony had missed Al by minutes when he arrived and now as he walked along the road and turned right; in the direction that Anna, Nina and Darryl had taken, Al arrived at the same junction just minutes after Tony had left. But it was not only twice that they managed to miss each other, but three times. Tony decided to get some food before finding a hostel. He went into the Victoria Markets, which was where Al headed for as soon as he had bought his ticket to Brisbane. Only metres away from each other; a cruel fate indeed that neither turned right instead of left between the stalls; that neither turned to look in the other direction at an opportune moment when they would have seen each other. A dark fate indeed was at work that day, for only dark fate would keep two friends apart when they needed one another.

* * * * *

Al was calmer now, safe in the knowledge that the next twenty four hours were taken care of with a bus journey to the north; where it would be warm and sunny, but wondered if his panic was going to be repeated upon his arrival in Brisbane?

"More money gone. I've got to get a job soon. Why the hell

didn't I just get the bus to the edge of the city. Somewhere close enough to be able to travel in to look for a job? I can't believe I'm so stupid, I've got no idea what the hell I'm doing, do I?"

It was a long and tiring journey. Al sat near the rear of the bus, which was only half full. Behind him an Australian man sat talking to a young lad on the adjacent seat, talking about alcohol, Brisbane, more alcohol. Al listened to their conversation, he wanted to talk to someone, but not to these people, not their conversation. He didn't want conversation for the sake of conversation, he wasn't that desperate, not that mindless.

He had two seats to himself and that was something that he was glad of, having extra space to stretch out made it a little easier to have a sleep, maybe catch up on last night. He wondered what Anna, Nina and Darryl were doing in Melbourne. Had they settled in? Were they already looking for work?

Hour after hour he read and repeated his first, second and third German lessons. He was glad he had bought the course, it gave him something to do and he was actually enjoying it; and anyway there was little else to do except look out of the window at a mundane and almost never ending unchanging vista; brown-yellow and empty, despite the rain. He had seen all this before; red soil and emptiness to the horizon, seen it far too much in the past few weeks to still be impressed by it. He slept.

Brisbane awaited him; waited for him to panic, or to make a go of this new place, the choice was his. He wanted to be alone and decided that he would cope better if he could be in his little tent again; that way he could avoid talking to anyone unless he wanted to talk; that way he need not see people around him who would make him feel lonely; that way he didn't have to pretend.

Al phoned around a few camp sites, they were a long way out of the city and would only take tents short term; positive thinking... they were no good as he couldn't stay there if he found a job. He resigned himself to the idea of a hostel, he knew what to expect now and it wasn't too bad at all and if he wanted to be near the centre of the city he didn't have a lot of choice. He found out where the nearest hostels were and headed off in search of one. He would book in for one night and see what tomorrow would bring; what mood he was in.

He was tired after the journey; exhausted after the torments of needing love; still needing to feel special; needing Steven, but to his surprise he was coping quite well with being in this new place. It helped that it was sunny and mild, if not warm. Sunshine could lift depression as clouds drifted on a summer breeze. He climbed the hill and headed into Chinatown and managed to get himself lost for a while. He hated using maps which were not clear; hand drawn, photocopied efforts pissed him right off! Eventually he found the place that he had been searching for. It looked a bit of a wreak; a small wooden construction, paint peeling, tin roof, overgrown garden with a view of the Storey bridge. No, he didn't like the look of it, but he was tired. It wasn't that close to the city centre, but he went in; almost unworried; almost confident, almost.

He checked in for the night and returned to the city; he needed the anonymity of the faceless city streets. He walked around doing nothing in particular, looking, walking, thinking.

"Steven, why?" Thoughts like these were too much for him. Al didn't realise that he had been storing up the pain while he spent time with his friends and now it began to get to him, he knew he was alone again.

It felt like weeks; it was weeks, since he had last seen Steven, nearly ten weeks. Time went too fast and yet never fast enough.

There are times when you are the last person to know something about yourself; usually when the rest of the world has known it for some time and that was how Al felt when he acknowledged the state in which he now found himself, when hanging onto a telephone receiver; not for the first time, in a city side street between two towering office blocks; hemmed in by concrete and glass; trying desperately to get the telephone to accept his credit card; trying desperately to get a line to East Anglia, to Steven. He had descended into the depths of confusion and despair so fast that he didn't even have time to notice. Card unacceptable flashed on the display and he asked it why? He swore at it. He hit it. He could have asked the operator to connect a reverse charge call, but Steven would not have liked that; not that he would have refused. No, he could not refuse that.

Eventually he gave up trying to get the telephone to do what he wanted and headed off towards the airport. He would buy a new ticket and fly back home...

"Wait a minute! What the fuck am I doing? What's going to happen when I get home? Do I really think that he's going to let me move back in and life is going to carry on where we left off as if nothing has happened? And what is so bad about this place that I can't cope with?" He scolded himself. For a moment a harder, more logical side of him spoke and made some sense and more than that, he listened.

He sat in the botanic gardens, in a patch of sunlight that gave him warmth, which gave him a calmness and sense of hope, or maybe it was relief. From somewhere close by, though he couldn't see where, he heard a radio playing. The presenter announced that the weekend was going to be dry and that it was the first dry weekend of the year. Al thought about his statement, it drifted around his mind like something that could not be comprehended due to drunkenness.

"But this is June? Brisbane has had six months of wet weekends?"

Around the gardens were a wide range of massive Ficus. They stood firmly in the ground, heavy, solid, permanent; huge buttresses and boles with roots spreading over the ground about the trunk, growing on top of the soil. Al looked at them, they were no more permanent than he was in his life with Steven; no more than he would be a permanent part of life on this planet; nothing was actually what it seemed. Everything was changing, a series of beginnings and endings, over and over again. A circle, a system, life and ultimately death. What did it all mean? Did it mean anything? Lost in the less than acute thoughts that he had he walked slowly back to the hostel; calm now, showered, then slept.

Sunday morning arrived; brightness coming in through the window into the six bed dorm. The radio was right, it was to be a dry weekend, but even better than that, it was warm and sunny and things always look and feel better in sunshine. Al sat on the veranda with a sandwich and coffee, reading through his German lessons. These hours of trying to learn a new language were becoming a major source of stability and comfort for him. They gave him a routine, a task to achieve, something that would not change from day to day, even while he was running around Australia. He disciplined himself and studied a few hours each day, sometimes he would come to spend half a day, and sometimes more, trying to learn; if not master this thing that he had set himself to achieve. He sat alone for an hour; almost happy to be alone, well, if not quite happy, then certainly contentment in his own company.

A German girl came had sat beside him, she was interested to find someone who was travelling, actually trying to learn a language which bore no relevance to the country in which they were in.

"But it does not make sense that you learn German when most Germans can speak English. There are people here from all over Europe and Japan and they all speak English together."

"Yes I know, but that does not excuse the need to speak another language. That just makes it harder for native English speakers to bother to learn."

They sat talking about the merits of learning, or not learning a foreign language as the hostel began to come alive, slowly. A young blond boy came running out to a waiting taxi and was gone.

"Swedish," Al thought. "He's got money for a taxi!"

A few more hungover travellers emerged and Al decided that it was time to head into town where he stayed until late afternoon, doing nothing in particular. He couldn't stay with all those travellers; what if someone else spoke to him?

The sun began to sink in the western sky, behind the trees and the steel framework of the bridge; leaves and branches dark against its brightness. In the air a heavy and enticing scent hung around the wooden building; large exotic blooms, late flowers from last summer, grand and white, though few. Birds sang and insects buzzed around the sweet winter flowers; one last feed before night. Al relaxed in the rich sounds, scents and warmth of the evening as he wrote a letter to Christopher. Despite panicking so badly the previous day he had settled down and relaxed now. He felt close to Christopher whenever he wrote; and therefore safe. At the next table other tourists gathered and talked. Al wanted to join in, but as usual he felt more comfortable not saying anything than if he had spoken. He read a little more German; ich kann, du kannst, er kann, sie kann.... as he listened to the conversation next to him. A conversation which was in English, though not one of the people sat at the table were English. Al picked out by the accents that two were French, one German, a Swiss girl and two Norwegians; not Swedes, as he had assumed earlier. The conversation drifted as the light faded, eventually coming to God, black magic, clairvoyancy. All through the conversation Al had kept silent, but was part of the group, even if he sat alone at the next table. One by one the travellers retired for the night and by midnight Al found himself alone with Stefan; the boy whom he had seen running to the taxi in the morning. Turning to Al, he looked deeply into his eyes. Al went cold, no one looks that intensely into the eyes of a stranger. For a moment neither said anything. Al was aware that Stefan was extremely good looking and that frightened him. Had he given off some sign that he was homosexual? Had Stefan guessed that Al was homosexual? His eyes continued the fixed look on Al; deeper, more deeper than deep, as if reading him like a book; reading his soul and his most protected thoughts.

"Tell me what it is you have experienced?" Stefan asked, almost as if he already knew the answer.

Al was scared, but also comforted by his gaze. Frozen; though not unpleasantly, by his bright Scandinavian eyes. He felt that he had been here before. He felt like he already knew Stefan.

"We'll go downstairs to the lounge. We can be alone together and we will not disturb anyone." Stefan said leading Al like a lamb, who followed willingly, but did not know why. He went for safety and comfort in the presence of this stranger who guided him through the darkness, down the stairs, into the garden, to the lounge.

Over the next seven hours Al proceeded to tell Stefan everything that had happened during the previous five months, leaving no detail missing. Stefan listened attentively to all he had to say. He understood and shared Al's pain with him. Al spoke, his voice was filled with distress and with pain; and heavily burdened with loss and isolation. Tears were fought back as he spoke; not just in Al's eyes, but also in Stefan's.

On the floor a body; that neither of them had noticed, rolled over. A head lifted itself from the floor and looked around the room before lying down again. Stefan and Al laughed together, then ignored it. Reaching out to Al's tightly clasped hands, Stefan took Al's hands and held them firmly in his. He could feel the pain that Al was feeling, he could help, he was helping.

It was still dark, when at six o'clock Stefan's friend came in to say that he was leaving for Cairns. Stefan was following on the evening bus, but right now he was preoccupied with Al for anything more than a few words in Norwegian with his friend.

As the sun began to rise, Stefan; who was by now more than a little emotionally drained, left Al and went to bed. He would see Al in the afternoon when they would have a little more time together before he left. Al, who now felt less troubled, walked into the city and spent the day doing what he enjoyed doing best, sitting in the botanic gardens, in the sunshine. He thought of nothing and yet everything. He felt a strength that he had not realised he had; a feeling of no matter how bad things might get there was always someone who he could turn to, even if he didn't yet know them. Of course God was always there, but Al wasn't going to become an emotional cripple reliant on God for strength. He still found it hard to separate all his preconceived ideas about the God of religions and all he had been told by followers of such Gods and religions from what he had experienced. He had experienced something special, though he had tried to deny it. He knew that what had happened would always be there and that he would never fully understand it, but more than that was the knowledge; he thought of it as knowledge, that it did not matter that he understood so little. It did not matter that he had doubt. It did dot matter that he questioned everything with suspicion in search of the truth. He recalled being told that there would always be people to turn to when he needed someone. Here, there was Stefan, an old friend, yet a stranger. Nina, Anna and Darryl. Grete, yes Grete. He needed her far more than he realised at the time, but now he could see that and he was glad of her company. Yes, he felt a kind of comfort when he thought that no matter how alone he felt there was always going to be someone to offer a hand in friendship. He had to learn to trust a little more and judge a little less. The world must have so many people like Stefan and Christopher. So many.

Stefan woke at three and found Al sitting on the veranda with his head in his German book once again. He stood in the doorway of his room looking over to Al and smiled; smiled as someone who had shared an intimate experience with another human being would smile. Like the most intimate of lovers; though they were not lovers, but loved they were and love they did. A lifetime of intimate friendship condensed into one night of honest and almost, no, a totally passionate exchange of spirits and minds. No sex, indeed Stefan was not anything other than heterosexual. Though they touched, holding hands for hours and it was not Al who initiated that, but Stefan. He stood there in silence, in a happy contentment of friendship and it was a while before Al realised that he was there.

Stefan said nothing when Al finally noticed him, their eyes met and entered into silent conversation then he left Al and went for a shower. Al watched him go, as he would have to watch Stefan go in a few hours when he boarded his bus to Cairns. He watched in love, in friendship, in sadness. He thought for a moment about the possibility of going north with Stefan, but dismissed it out of hand as unwise. Their time together was short and was meant to be that way. Al did not like the knowledge of losing such a friend so soon, but his path lay in another direction and it was for him to make the best of it. Path? That sounded organised and logical. No, he was still running and still Steven filled his heart and mind with pain, but that felt different now. His path was to find some work before he managed to spend all his money and to use the next five months to learn German, beyond that he had no idea. He could not think that far. Would he ever go back to East Anglia? That was something that he could never imagine, that was something which he both longed for and feared.

Stefan returned from his shower. His hair standing up on end, a towel around his waist and his skin still pale, despite spending so long in south east Asia on his way to Australia.

"I'll just get dressed and then we'll go into town," he said.

Al smiled, but said nothing. Stefan knew that Al wasn't ready for his departure, but also knew that Al accepted things were as they had to be today.

Three hours; when waiting for something to happen can drag on and become an almost unending period. Likewise, three hours, can be so short a time when something you never want to lose, drifts away beyond your reach and nothing, absolutely nothing you can do will change the events unfolding around you. So it was that Al and Stefan spent their last three hours together, enjoying every minute to the full in the presence of each other and yet at the same time looking at their watches in horror as the minutes raced away from them. Stefan's love enveloped Al and carried him along that afternoon and showed him that there would be moments; other than the times that he had cherished with Steven, that would be important, so important that he would never want to forget and never would forget.

They walked together, they talked, they gazed into each others eyes and saw things that no one else could guess. A love so pure, a love of hope and joy and trust. Stefan did not judge Al for what he was, all he would do was help him in the only way he knew how, by giving himself. They walked across the city towards the bus station. A tramp stopped them in the square and asked for money. Al felt uncomfortable, but watched Stefan as he talked to this man, who, for whatever reason was now homeless and alone. Living on the city streets, begging for money. Stefan broke the pie he had bought into two pieces and gave the largest part to the tramp. Al watched in awe of his new friend, he watched in love and admiration. He watched in silence. Stefan dug into his pocket and gave the tramp fifty cents, then they left him and headed to the bus station.

"I'm amazed by what you did, Stefan. I am ashamed to say that I would have ignored him and walked on."

"Maybe, but that would not be what you wanted to do, only your reaction and embarrassment because you don't know how to deal with these people. We all need help in this life," he looked at Al who was looking dejected.

"Yes, I know. I know only too well that some of us need help..."

"And what did I do? Gave him a little food and a small amount of money."

"But he'll buy alcohol with the money he gets and that isn't going to help him is it?"

"No it won't, but at least he has had something to eat now; and who is going to give him the time to help him, really help him? Not I, I will leave for Cairns in an hour. If getting drunk is his way of dealing with his problems then who am I to judge if I am not prepared to help? It is not the answer, but it is his way, as coming to Australia was your escape. You are trying to deal with your life in a crazy way, just as he is. I know you will be more successful than he."

Al looked at Stefan silently, as a child scolded for some misdemeanour. He loved him and felt so loved.

"You have more faith in me than I do."

"I know you Al. I know your heart. Trust me as I love you." He reached to Al and rested his hand on Al's shoulder. Al was both happy and sad. He wanted to laugh with joy and cry in pain.

"Would you like a cup of tea and something to eat before your journey?" Al asked.

"Yes. I would like that. A nice British way of spending our last minutes together." Stefan said.

They sat in the canteen at the bus station sipping tea and eating a piece of cake. Al felt guilty at being able to do this when the tramp they saw was begging for food.

"You can't change the world Al." Stefan said, reading his thoughts. "You've got to sort yourself out first!" He smiled to Al and Al smiled back. Stefan had a way of making everything seem possible, there was always hope with him. Time was racing past and Al found it unfair. He felt cheated, as he did at Port Augusta when he had such a short time with Tony.

"You are a very special person Al. You must remember that."

"Why do you say that Stefan?" Al questioned the tone in which he said it.

"Because you are, though I know that you do not believe it."

"But why do you say it? I feel that you know me better than I know myself. I feel as if you know something that I should know about myself, but what it is I have no idea?"

Stefan smiled and did not answer Al's question. He could not say anything that Al would understand or believe, so it was better to say nothing.

"I have to go for my bus now. It leaves in ten minutes."

They took a stroll to the departure bay and Stefan spoke words of friendship and hope to Al, then held Al close in a long and firm embrace. Al felt so safe and he didn't want Stefan to let go. He felt the same pain as on that afternoon when he last saw Sarah and Christopher. He held back his tears as bravely as he could. Stefan released his hug, but held Al's arms.

"You'll be alright Al. Trust me and learn to trust yourself and God."

"Thanks Stefan. I will miss you."

"Bye Al. Come and see me in Bergen one day."

"I will."

Stefan boarded the bus and the door closed behind him. For a few minutes longer the bus did not move and Al wished that it would go. He wanted it to disappear from his sight and eventually it would. Stefan stood and waved, Al returned the wave and once the bus had gone a tear formed a perfect droplet and ran slowly down his face.

Calmly, he stood staring after the bus which was well gone, he thought about his next move. He didn't want to stay in Brisbane any longer. He thought that it would be a good idea to head towards Sydney and look for work and maybe find Tony. Deciding to take the bus to the New South Wales border; because he had found out that it was illegal to hitch-hike in Queensland and if half of the things he had

heard about the Queensland police were true then he did not want to
have anything to do with the police here. He booked a seat on the
morning bus and returned to the hostel for a last night, through which
he slept soundly after so many hours without sleep and strong in the
knowledge of the love Stefan had shown him.

* * * * *

Tony had been without alcohol for almost a week. He had avoided
conversation for almost a week, except for when it was necessary to
indulge in the company of others. He was living through a mentally
torturous time. A time when he felt that he understood more about Al
than he had previously realised, now that he was also suffering an
emotional crisis. He longed to see Al again, he wanted only for the
company of a close and trusted friend. He did not want to be alone in
the sea of tourists; changing faces as they came and went like the tide,
continuously and unending. He had looked for work in the city, but
with no luck so far. It was getting him down. He needed the
distraction of a job and he certainly needed to earn some money
before he spent the last of his. But no matter how low he got on
money, his mind was not wholly on finding a job. He was distracted
by his fear of what might be inside his body after the events; and
after his behaviour in Sydney. Every time he thought about it he
broke out in a cold sweat. Each time his mind drifted into that darkest
of tunnels, he panicked at the thought of what might be.

Resolutely, he headed towards the hospital early one morning. He
had to know one way or the other. But what would he do if it was
positive? He couldn't think about it. It was too horrific. He sat in the
waiting room. There was only one other person there. Tony looked
nervously towards him.

"Gay," he thought, "the gay plague? Al isn't like that. Al hasn't
done anything to deserve getting AIDS, but he hasn't had the test.
Shit! What if he has it?" Tony thought about that and told himself that
it would be so unfair if Al had the disease when he hadn't slept
around; and although Tony prayed that he himself didn't have it he
decided that if he did, then it would be his own fault.

"Davis?"

He was called by a councillor, by his pseudonym. He stood up
and was horribly cold and sticky. Guilt. Shame. Embarrassment.

Stupidity. Feelings which ran through his mind as he walked across the waiting room. It was a long way. He felt the eyes of the other man on him. He felt so dirty.

"I know where you're going." Tony assumed that that was what the man was thinking; and he probably was. Wasn't he here for the same reason?

He entered the small room. Three chairs, two to his left and one straight ahead, a small round table between with leaflets about a dozen diseases and safe sex.

"Sit down." The young woman said.

He nervously sat down and thus began a long talk about HIV and AIDS. Following this were a whole series of questions. Had he had sex with men or just women? He answered, but felt sure that she didn't believe him. When did he last have sex? How many partners he had had in the past six months? What sort of sex did he have? Had he used condoms? Had he injected drugs? Shared needles? He answered a bombardment of questions, never once did he feel that he was believed. Had he ever felt this nervous before?

After an hour of interrogation he was asked to return to the waiting room, he would be called for his blood test. There were more people waiting, nervously, trying to look calm and nonplussed, heads in magazines; vogue, gay news, motor racing. All looking up to see the face as he returned and sat heavily in a squeaky and uncomfortable chair. The wait to be called was long and he was both relieved and terrified when the needle was in his arm and his blood was taken. He left the hospital as quickly as he could and returned to the anonymity of the hostel. He could look for work, but he couldn't face that now, instead he accepted the offer of a beer from a couple of English boys who had just arrived. Tony drank it like beer was going out of fashion and so started the beginning of a week of drinking while he waited in Melbourne for the result of his blood test, one that he was convinced would come back positive.

* * * * *

The rain fell heavily on the tin roof just above Al's head, it woke him ten minutes earlier than he had set his alarm for.

"So much for the first dry weekend in six months, it was only just a whole weekend."

He packed and phoned for a taxi, he couldn't see the sense in walking for forty minutes to the bus station, he'd be soaked and would stay soaked for the rest of the day and he didn't want that. He was pissed off that the taxi fare was just two dollars cheaper than a two and a half hour bus journey and begrudged paying the fare.

He was early for the bus and sat in the waiting room and scribbled a letter to Stefan, he felt good and wanted Stefan to know it. He sent it to the G.P.O. in Los Angeles, Stefan would be there in three weeks and said that he would call to see if he had any letters from home. The bus left and Al was glad that things had seemed so bad for him in Melbourne and that he had been led to Brisbane. He was certain that it was not coincidence that he ran here, where he found Stefan waiting for him.

Looking out from the window he was happy not to be stopping on the Gold Coast. It was how he imagined many of Spain's coastal resorts; horrible concrete blocks, congested roads and swarms of people on the beaches. He could not think of a worse place to come for a holiday.

The bus made a stop, some people got off, others got on. By the time he arrived at Tweed Heads it had stopped raining, much to his relief, he had not fancied his chances of getting a lift if he was wet through. He decided to take a short stop to get some food and a drink, as if previous experiences were anything to go by, it might prove to be a long time before he would get another chance as he would have to spend so long standing at the side of the road. He was wrong. Within half an hour he had a lift and the journey south began, passing first through sugar cane and then through banana plantations. He had never seen anything like it before, it was so tropical. The greenness struck Al as something quite odd, almost unusual, quite unlike any other parts of Australia that he had yet seen. Plants grew lush and tall and looked like healthy plants should look. There was no red sand to be seen, no desert oaks or scrubby vegetation. It all looked so alive. Feeling rather good with himself after his time with Stefan and now with a lift; an easy lift at that, he looked forward to getting to Coffs Harbour. He sat looking out of the car window as the scenery passed by. His driver was a young man, maybe his own age and was heading south for the winter, for the ski season.

"Skiing in Australia?" Al queried disbelievingly.

"Yeah. We got a lot of snow here. It does get cold you know."

"Yes I know. It was one degree in Melbourne when I was there, but snow? Skiing?"

The instructor proceeded to tell Al all about the Australian ski fields and how he would be able to get a different girl every night, Al thought that that was quite possible as he was slim, dark, tall and had a very handsome facial structure. Yes, Al could believe that he would be able to lay a lot of girls in the season, but then he went and ruined his image and Al's first impressions of him, when he took off his dark ski glasses to reveal a pair of beady eyes which were far to close together. Al thought that it would be more of a case that the girls would find their way into his bed because they were slack and easy tarts and it would have nothing to do with his looks.

Once at Coffs Harbour he got himself sorted out at a camp site and proceeded to walk along the main road and town centre, going in and out of every shop, hotel, garage and even, much to his surprise, McDonalds! If he wanted work he would have to do quite a lot of walking and searching. For three days he searched. For three days he felt guilty that he was going to break the terms of his entry into this country and try and earn some money. He did not have much choice if he wanted to be able to eat and have access to hot showers. He had no luck. It was the wrong time of the year. A few months earlier, or a few months later when the main tourist season was on, but not now.

At the camp site were four men from Sydney. They were on the dole and having a holiday, courtesy of the tax payer. Each night they drank, each day they drank and there was always bacon and eggs for breakfast. They asked Al why he was looking for work when he could just sign on the dole instead. They told him that working was for other people and not for them. It was far better having a free life and a free lunch. This incensed Al, here he was, quite prepared to work to get some money and native Australians were encouraging him to rip the system off!

"Maybe in Britain where I have paid taxes, but not in some other person's country. I guess I shouldn't be feeling guilty about needing to work, at least I'd be helping this country and not sponging from it." He wasn't quite convinced that his conclusions were valid, but it helped him feel better about looking for work and the problem of guilt would only really arise if he actually found a job.

He spent another two days in Coffs Harbour, but looked no longer for work. He spent his time at the coast looking out to sea; looking to the horizon in the hope of seeing a humpback whale or two, it was at this time of year that they passed the coast in the area. There were no whales and he just sat on the rocks and lost himself in the waves as they crashed against the base rocks at his feet.

"Steven would love this," he said to the waters as they came and went. He sighed in the sunshine. It was twenty one degrees and it felt extremely pleasant. He recalled how wonderful East Anglia would be at that temperature. It was Whitsun holiday at home.

"Where would Steven be now? Scotland? Who would he be with?" A large wave smashed on the rocks and broke his thread of thought. "I'm not going back now. I'll sell my ticket and go to New Zealand."

The Pacific Ocean lay at his feet. Somewhere out there, to the south east, was New Zealand. The vast expanse of blue stretched as far as he could see and beyond. The world, for Al, was once a big place, but now it was only a small prison. He could only be in one place at one time and therefore the world was only as far as he could see and certainly it could not be any bigger than he could perceive.

"How did you pretend for so long Steven? How did you look me in the eyes each day? You knew what you were doing and yet you still did it. Why? How?"

The ocean rolled endlessly towards him, but with it came no answers to his questions.

These two days were spent half in dreams of what were never going to be and half in the knowledge of what was. Al recorded his thoughts, as he had since his arrival on this strange island and then wrote no more. He had reached a turning point, a point where he was sure that he would never return to his home, never to see his brother again, always to be alone and on the move. His friends had given him strength, which, though it was not infallible, it helped him get through each day a little more easily than he could manage alone. He still had a long way to go before he could understand what had happened, maybe he never would. He did not believe for one minute that he would ever be free of the pain that he was carrying; it felt a heavy burden to shift. It weighed on him.

Writing to Steven, he sent all the thoughts that he had written since arriving in Australia, though he wasn't totally sure why he did this. Was it to hurt the person he loved? His words would certainly cause distress, they were so honest and heart-felt. No, Al wanted not to hurt Steven, though at times he thought that he did. Inside, he hated the thought of Steven feeling anything like the pain he was himself feeling. He couldn't bear the thought of the man he loved being in pain while he was too far away to be of help. Al almost didn't send the letters that he desperately needed to send, but then decided that he should not worry about Steven's reaction to his words, surely he would know that he was not out for revenge, he loved him far too much for that. To make sure of this Al wrote a note explaining his feeling and moods, clarifying them, trying to remove anything which might be seen as hate, so Steven would not misunderstand his motives for sharing them with him. Yes, sharing his thoughts and words, it was the most natural thing for him to do. He had spent years sharing with Steven, so why should it not be right now? They might be apart now and not just because of geographical distance, but Steven was always there with him. Always. Al's memories of him would flood back in the most subtle of ways. The shape of a rock, colour of water, size of a cloud. The cruellest of things would be the sound of a piece of music. It always struck where there were other people and always without warning. How many times in the past few weeks had he heard Leonard Cohen or Fleetwood Mac? How many pictures played in his mind of their holiday in La Jura and Switzerland? Cruel, so cruel. A line of a song could evoke the smell of food, the scent of a plant, a conversation, a view. Hideously cruel was the sound of music. Yes, Steven was always close by.

As his letters to Steven fell into the post box Al felt it was time to move. He didn't want to stay somewhere where he had felt so close to Steven. In the morning he would leave and head further south. He decided not to go to Sydney, even though the hope and chance of meeting with Tony was so very tempting. No, he didn't want to face another big Australian city. He had not coped with Melbourne, or even Brisbane until Stefan came along to help him.

It was with conviction and a resolute faith in his friend Stefan; faith that things would go well for him, he packed and walked through the banana town trying to get a lift as he went. Several hours later he was glad of a short ride to Nambucca Heads where he started the waiting game once more. He put his pack down and gazed at the river, which, it seemed, was not too dissimilar to the River Stour. It was much larger, but there was something very familiar about it.

There were trees and reeds along its banks and as it meandered its way slowly to the sea pelicans replaced the mute swans of home and swam gracefully along. It was a world away from Erldunda where everything seemed to anticipate death at any moment. Here, plants and animals took life leisurely and grew as they would with so much water around. Erldunda had been a fight for survival.

A panel van stopped and Al pushed his luggage into the back. He climbed into the front and looked at the young man whose eyes were shinning like eyes rarely do, his face covered in an orange-brown bearded growth.

Once again he was moving and though he was glad, he wasn't really too bothered if he got anywhere or not. South and further south. Lush, rich greens gradually gave way to the dry bush that Al had grown used to and come to love. Yes, he had grown used to it, it was familiar and in things which are familiar one can find comfort; once accustomed to isolation one finds company in it. Al was becoming more and more isolated and though he longed for company, it was only the company of friends that he wanted and not company for the sake of company, but the problem with the friends he had met and shared some time with was that cutting edge which was when they said goodbye and there was always the goodbye to be said.

Gary and Al chatted away. Al found him to be good company, though for Al, Gary had a little too much energy. He seemed almost hyperactive, or was it true that Al was becoming very lethargic with all this time on his hands? All day to do nothing or everything, or something in between, whatever took his fancy.

The Pacific highway was unlike any other Australian road Al had travelled on, it was neither flat, nor straight.

"They call this the race track." Gary said to Al as they started down a series of tight bends on a steep section of road.

Al went white as the van barely managed to take each bend, but he also thought that it was quite good fun. It was something he would never have done; being too sensible and boring. Gary laughed, he was getting a buzz out of Al's reaction as well as the driving.

"You can wipe the sweat from your hands now." Gary laughed as they reached the bottom of the hill.

"I think you should have gone a little faster," Al said to his surprise. "If you're going to kill yourself you may as well go out in style!"

Gary looked at his passenger strangely. Al's voice was without emotion, as if it did not really matter if he had killed them both. Gary reduced his speed and continued the rest of the journey within the permitted speed limit, feeling a little ashamed about what could have so easily have happened.

It had been a long day. It always was a long day when so many hours were spent standing at the side of the road, waiting. Al seemed to always be waiting to get somewhere, waiting to get from somewheres, or waiting between somewhere. It seemed to him that he had not been to, or come from any place in particular; just been there and then gone again. Alone usually, but occasionally he was lucky enough to have friends, lucky enough to have been able to share with friends. Share his food, his time, his self. They were the good times that he tried hard to remember, tried hard to hold onto for fear that they might slip away and the darker side of life would creep back and cloud his days with the spectre of isolation and memory. Yes, there had been good times, but that was not the whole picture.

So now as he headed south with a new travelling companion. Day turned into evening and evening into night and the feeling of panic began to grow, like a seed swelling upon imbibition.

"I'm not actually going into Newcastle," Gary said.

The worry about finding a hostel or camp site in the city need not have bothered Al, it seemed that he would not get there today. He wasn't about to hitch in the dark, so he would just have to hope that he could find a stand of trees to hide his tent in overnight.

"I figure you have two options. One, I could drop you off at my turning and you could try and get a lift the rest of the way, or two, you can come with me and stay at my place tonight. You could give me a hand with some plaster board that I have to put up."

Al felt a rush of blood to his brain.

"What was he after? Isn't everyone on the take? No, not everyone. Not by a long way." Al was frightened that Gary might not be the person who he appeared to be. Stefan might not have been the person he appeared to be, but he was. The problems in Al's head grew larger and larger. What did he want in return for his hospitality? What would Al be letting himself in for if he accepted?

The darkness outside grew darker. It wasn't so late, but the dark evenings of winter always made it seem much later than it was. Al thought about Gary's offer, he thought about the problems which had manifested themselves in his head and decided that that was all they were, problems which did not really exist apart from inside his head.

"Thanks Gary, I would like to stay at your house. It's really kind of you to offer," he answered, quite happy now that he had made a decision and one which he felt sure was the right one.

They stopped for an hour or so at Gary's brother-in-law's house, where they were given a large and very filling meal. Al found it strange and somewhat uncomfortable to walk into the home of someone whom he had never met and find that he was treated as if he was not only expected, but also welcomed. It was so unlike any situation he had ever found himself in before. Al had never been able to invite the one or two friends he had at middle school around to his parents house and because no one ever called for him he did not begin to learn how to relate to people until he had moved to Ipswich to be with Steven.

They left on the twenty minute journey to Gary's house.

"Have I been picked up or picked up?" Al thought, now the doubt of motives raised itself again. He wanted to believe that he had met another person like Stefan. He hoped for it. They drove into the village. It was cold outside and also inside the van as the heating was not working and there were draughts coming in from all directions. The air was heavy with a drizzle which couldn't make up its mind whether it was precipitating as rainfall or hanging around as a dank mist. The buildings were dark, shrouded by vapour.

"That's the house that the Chamberlains used to live in," Gary said as he pointed out into the mist.

Al looked, he saw the outline of a wooden house, dark in the gloomy night's sky.

"You've heard of the baby that was taken by a dingo at Ayers Rock have you?"

Al searched his mind and recalled many times when the story had been featured on the national news at home. He remembered that most of the people who had mentioned the case believed the baby was killed by the parents and not by a dingo.

"Yes. We heard quite a lot about it on the television. I wonder if it was a dingo?"

"Of course it was," Gary snapped. "There was so much false evidence given at the trial. She was locked up because of public opinion that's all."

Al let the subject drop. He had touched a raw nerve here and who was he to judge when his only knowledge of the case was what he had been told via television. Gary knew the people and was in a far better position to judge. Though only those who were there could ever be sure of the truth. They turned off the road and into the drive of a house.

"This is it," he said as they walked around to the back garden.

Gary was expecting the door to be unlocked, it wasn't. He forced a window and climbed through. Al stood outside in the damp and cold and waited for him to open the door. Once inside they began fixing the sheets of plaster board and Al felt that he wasn't really much help, he just held the board still while Gary fixed them in position, still, he was better than no help at all. They talked as they worked and gradually Gary got Al to talk about his reasons for being in Australia. Slowly; and without intention on Al's part, he started to break down the barriers that Al had put up to hide his past. Gary had a way of asking the right question in the right way which made it difficult for Al to avoid answering. The statements he made were; so it seemed to Al, designed to get at the heart of what was bothering Al, both with his failed love affair and with what he had experienced at Coober Pedy and Alice Springs. It was as if Gary already knew what was in Al's head, as if he had already been told. Just like Stefan, who seemed to know far more than he let on. Al was baffled by this as it could not be so, he couldn't see how it could be so and therefore it wasn't. They spoke together as if they had been friends for some time, just as Al had with Stefan. Al would not mention Steven's name and just as a friend would do, when Al was obviously getting uncomfortable about the questions being asked, Gary did not push for an answer. He showed Al compassion and a gentle wisdom that is so rare, but in such a short time Al had met two such people. How could this be so?

It was late by the time they had finished the work in the laundry, the last of the work for the new owners. The house was empty of all furniture and now, as they went through to the kitchen to wash Al could see how big it was.

"I'd kill for a kitchen like this!" He said as he looked around at a huge room, in the centre of which was a large work bench and stove. Around this were cupboard after cupboard. So much space, just enough to be Al's ideal. Down three steps from the kitchen on the opposite side from which they had entered, there was no wall. The kitchen opened onto the lounge/dining room, which was also larger than life. Al was amazed. Gary was obviously not wealthy, but here was this house which suggested otherwise. They collected their sleeping bags from the van and unpacked ready for the night. Al's sleeping bag was cold to the touch and he knew it was going to get much colder in a room as large as this in which there was no heating.

Through the skylights above, Al could see no moon, tiny water droplets covered the glass. Strangely, it was not dark, though it was almost midnight and he could not work out where the light was coming from. They settled down, two metres of floor between them, chatted for a short while longer before Gary disappeared beneath a mountain of blankets.

Al lay awake for an hour or so. Gary was asleep. He wondered why Gary had brought him back to his house if he wasn't after sex?

"How can I have become so trusting? Why have I become so trusting? Is it the isolation from my friends at home which made me like this? Or is it the pain from not being with Steven?" His behaviour was so totally out of character and the strangest thing of all was the feeling he had that he wanted to hug Gary, as he had hugged Stefan at the bus station when they said goodbye. He wanted to feel the warmth from the body of another human being, but most of all he wanted to feel that warmth from Steven and he wanted it now. He longed for it, he yearned for it.

The morning came early; and it came cold. Al lay awake and listened to the silence. Staring up through the skylight at the grey sky. The weather was still the same, the sort of weather that makes you feel like you want to stay in bed all day and cuddle up to someone whom you dearly love. Staring up at the view of nothing much in particular, he waited for Gary to wake. It was warm inside his sleeping bag and he was happy not to move out of it, but then Gary awoke and they got up and cleared the laundry of the debris of last night's work before going to buy, what Al took to be good Aussie tucker. They returned to the house and sat in the kitchen together and talked. Gary was still fishing around after the things which were making Al hurt so much. It was so obvious to everyone except Al. Everyone who met him realised that inside he was tormented by his emotions and all Al could do was try and kid himself that he was doing a great job at hiding them from everyone he met. Only Al thought that, the rest of the world could see the strain on his face, hear the pain in his voice, feel the silent and yet very audible scream for help which always seemed to surround him. Al looked at the spring rolls in a rather suspect manner, but tried one.

"Well?" asked Gary.

"Yes. Not as bad as it sounds or looks," he said, somewhat surprised. "Though I can't think of an adjective which fully describes it. Chips, I can cope with, even if it is for breakfast, but chocolate flavoured milk? Hot chocolate, yes. Cold milk, yes, but what kind of society was this that had cold milk which was flavoured with chocolate?"

Gary laughed at this very strange person whom he had picked up. What kind of place was this East Anglia of his?

Mid afternoon came and Gary left for Sydney. He was meeting his wife at the airport upon her return from New Zealand.

"I've put the hot water on Al, so help yourself to the shower. Stay here as long as you like, but make sure the house is locked up when you leave."

Al was surprised that he, a stranger, should be left in Gary's house, even if there was no furniture in it. Al stood in the doorway and watched Gary leaving. The van, dirty white in colour, merged with the mist, or drizzle, or both. Sighing heavily and in contentment in the knowledge that he had not misjudged Gary's motives he returned inside the house, closed the door behind himself and felt a little sad. Why? He didn't know the answer to that, maybe he did not want to see Gary leave just yet. Maybe because he missed Steven or Christopher. Maybe it was just because he was alone again and hated the thought of being alone. Desperately he wanted to hug someone. Where was Tony? Was he alright? Why couldn't they be together for a while? Why? Why? Why?

* * * * *

The weather in Melbourne was no better than the weather in Cooranbong, where Al was. In fact it was teeming with rain. Tony was totally pissed off with it, he hadn't seen rain like this since he had been to the north of Thailand two years ago. He sat on the tram as it trundled through the streets of Melbourne. He should have got off two stops ago, but he just sat there staring out at the street scene, at a thousand faceless people as they went about their everyday business. Nothing of the view was taken in and it was a good twenty minutes before the tram stopped at the end of the line and waited for ten minutes before starting the return journey to the city centre. This time he got off at his halt. His halt? The hospital. He was returning for the result of his HIV test. He had never felt so nervous before. So nervous that he felt sick. He had had to force himself to return for this result, for he did not want to know the answer in case it was not the answer that he wanted to hear, but instead the answer that he dreaded. He walked into the hospital, guilt, shame, embarrassment. At the desk he spoke quietly to the receptionist. He was told to take a seat, he would be called. He sat, he waited. He looked at the clock on the wall. Time was able to travel so slowly when it wanted to. He picked up a magazine, something, anything to hide behind. To hide from the glances of other eyes which waited for their tests, their results, their treatments. He opened the magazine, randomly. His eyes opened wide at a glossy picture of a well tanned man wearing nothing but a thin leather string around his waist. His long penis also well tanned hanging loosely between his legs. Tony felt himself colour red, the magazine held high to hide his face was also held high enough to allow all the other people waiting there to see that it was a gay magazine. He closed it fast, looking at the cover to confirm that it was as he dreaded. Throwing it down on the table and quickly picking up a car magazine with which to hide behind.

"Mr. Davis?"

Tony sat behind the pages.

"Mr. Davis?"

He remembered that he was Mr. Davis and jumped up, returning the magazine and once again drawing attention to himself.

Once inside the room with the councillor he was safe from the people outside.

He was asked for his appointment card and his number was checked with that on the file.

He sat waiting, a silence followed.

"You'll be pleased to hear that this test was negative." He breathed a sigh of relief.

"You'll have to have another test in three months, just to rule out human error and to cover for the previous three months prior to this test."

"So I haven't got AIDS!"

"There was no sign of any HIV antibodies in the tests but if you have been exposed to the virus in the past three months it probably would not show up. That's why it's important for you to have another test in three months."

Tony could only hear that he did not have the virus in his blood, assuming that if it didn't yet show then he was safe. At least that was what he wanted to believe. That was what he needed to believe. He couldn't cope with the thought that maybe he did have the kiss of death. He couldn't put himself through another test just in case the next one came back positive, he couldn't accept that alone. He could not handle that without a friend to turn to. He left the hospital relieved, but frightened by what if... Now, with the fear lifted from his mind; at least temporarily, his only desire was to get out of Melbourne. He had run from Sydney, then Canberra and now he needed, yes he needed, to put distance between himself and this city. He booked himself onto the night bus with the two English boys with whom he had spent many hours drinking during the past few days. Next stop the pub, then Adelaide.

* * * * *

Al woke to another cold grey morning and he did not want to leave his sleeping bag. It reminded him of the camping holidays he and Steven used to have. Neither would want to get up in the mornings though it was usually he who ventured out first, always reluctant to leave Steven's warm body behind. He lay there looking up at the dampness outside and wondered why Gary had been so kind to him? Why had he let him stay in his house with an endless supply of hot water? Nine o'clock came and went as he thought about whether he should stay here and be lazy for another day, or whether he should move on? A lazy day was a day with his head stuck in his German book, trying to master the difficult throaty sounds.

"It's the Queen's birthday today. I wonder if I'll be able to get a lift? Why the hell do these Aussies get a holiday for the Queen's birthday when they hate us and the Queen?"

Eventually he got up and packed, leaving the house just after ten thirty. The drizzle had stopped, or was it the mist that had cleared?

Whichever it was, it was still cold and grey to the point of that miserable dampness that gets under your skin and makes your bones ache unhealthily. He was not sure of which direction to take, so he chose downhill rather than uphill. Ahead, two old women stood talking over the garden fencing. They stopped their conversation and stared at him as he approached.

"Good morning." Al said as cheerfully as he could.

They looked suspiciously at him before responding, curtly.

"Could you tell me which way I need to go in order to get back to the Pacific highway, towards Sydney?"

Again they looked at him as if they were suspicious of all strangers. Al felt that they had some dark secret to hide and did not want the outside world finding out and the short and impolite response he got to his question seemed to confirm that for him.

"Right at the end of the road," said the one within the garden. Her eyes, the eyes of someone transfixed by his presence. He pressed on and was relieved to be outside the village. He looked back once at the grey drizzle falling softly onto the houses, but where he now found himself was sunny, a blue sky with puffy cotton-wool clouds billowing around above him.

"Is this my imagination, or is this weird?" He kept walking, putting as much distance between himself and that dark and foreboding place.

Just two hours later he found himself in the north west of Sydney. He walked along the highway which ran south and tried to get a lift as he went. In the distance to the east he could see downtown Sydney, tall and modern it stood, sunlight beaming down through a break in the cloud, lighting it up like a model city under a spotlight. Taking a rest for a while in a bus shelter Al had something to eat and drink and wondered where it was he would go today.

"Maybe Tony is still in Sydney, living in a hostel, working, drinking? I'd love to see him again." He thought about his friend, he missed him far more than he had realised he ever could.

"I don't want to go into Sydney though." Looking over to the city, which did actually look appealing to him, he decided to avoid the risk of panicking by not going there. "If I get there and don't find Tony I will panic, I know I will. If I did go there it would only be to look for Tony, no matter what I try to tell myself."

He had been to four of the five major cities in Australia during the past six weeks and he did not really want to face another one just now. He looked at his map and decided that Canberra was neither too far, nor was it too big, so he packed his food away and started to walk.

The houses and gardens in this hilly suburb were on a grand scale. Only the rich lived here. Only the rich wanted views over the tops of the suburbs to the city way out on the horizon.

"Very Rushmere Road," he thought disapprovingly. "People who think that they've made it, but haven't!"

The road carried a constant flow of traffic, but this did not mean that it was easy getting a lift. Al would never have dreamt of trying to get a lift in Greater London, but here in Sydney he thought nothing of walking along the side of the road with a thumb and sign sticking out towards the endlessly moving traffic. It was two hours before a car finally stopped.

Phil was in his early twenties, good looking and going all the way to Canberra, returning from Newcastle after a friend's wedding. Al was pleased that he was able to go four hundred kilometres with just two lifts and he settled into the car for the journey.

The suburbs of Sydney seemed endless, but weren't and once out of the urban sprawl they were in gentle hill country. Green grass and almost, not exactly, but almost, with a little imagination, like home.

They talked as Australia whizzed past the window with little interest for Al, he watched Phil as he spoke. He watched his soft lips move to form soft sounds, ordinary words, but spoken in a way that made them special. He felt good to be with him, as he had with Gary and Stefan. Why? He asked himself again and again. The thought that he had been guided to these people, or they to him sounded like an absurd cliché. Could it really be just chance meetings? And as for the way he was feeling? Was that just because he felt good in the company of these people, was it because he fancied them, or was it something else that he couldn't understand?

The waters of Lake George were lapping against the road in several places after all the rain that there had been.

"It's not normally like that," Phil said. "It's been a wet year."

"That sounds familiar," Al joked and smiled to Phil.

"Where are you going to stay once we get to Canberra?" Phil asked, turning to look at Al as he drove along a reasonably straight piece of road. His eyes shone blue-green to Al. Al melted in his gaze before answering.

"I don't know yet. I'll have to find a camp site or hostel when I get there." Al answered, regaining his composure.

"If you like you can come and stay at my place for a few days."

Al did not even hesitate at this offer and immediately said, "yes please, that's very kind of you." He couldn't believe his luck. After all this time in Australia he was now meeting real Australians and staying in their homes. For a brief moment after he had said yes, he had a twinge of doubt in his mind about Phil's motives, dismissing them as nonsense after spending a night with Gary, though he didn't realise it, he was beginning to learn to trust again. Had he for one moment thought that he was trusting someone, he would have declined the offer. How could he ever trust anyone again? No. Never.

"It's a big house and there's just me and John there. There's so much room and John won't mind."

Al wondered who John was. Phil gave nothing away on what sort of relationship they had. Maybe they were lovers? The thought of that possibility aroused Al's hopes. Hopes that he could be somewhere and not have to pretend. Be with people who would understand. Maybe even help? He tried not to assume what was and what wasn't. He tried not to judge things that he knew nothing about, but he could not stop himself from hoping.

It was not long before dark when they arrived at the house in the north west of the city. Phil was right, it was a large house, built on five different levels, with stairs going up or down and sometimes both, on each floor.

"Bring your things in Al." Phil said leading him in. "You can sleep here, here, or there," he said, pointing towards three different rooms, each with a sofa. Al looked.

"Would you like a cup of tea?"

"Oh yes, I'd love one, Phil."

They stood in the kitchen and talked. Al examined every word that was said, every sound, every movement of body language. There was something that made Phil seem a little depressed, or was it the effect of Al being there? Had something happened at the wedding in Newcastle? He wasn't a nervous person, but he didn't like looking directly at Al; unlike many other Australians, not because he found him repulsive, but for some other reason. Al was aware that Phil looked in his direction whenever Al looked around at the room.

"I'll take you for a tour of the city while we still have some daylight left." Phil said, almost as if he had to say something in order to stop Al asking questions of him.

Al was pleasantly surprised by this, but also a little embarrassed. He didn't know this young man, but he liked being with him. They headed towards the centre of the city. It was so far, yet there was less than a quarter of a million people living here. Phil showed him where the shopping areas were, where he worked and then took him to the view point on Mt. Ainsle.

Al thought of Steven and he felt guilty, though he couldn't work out why. Maybe he didn't just think that Phil was good looking, but he actually found him attractive. He thought about all the mountains that he and Steven had climbed together. It reminded him about the time they climbed Scafell in the Lake District. All morning they had climbed, first one peak, then a second, before the final ascent up the peak they were heading for. All morning it had been grey and breezy and damp, a miserable day, an uncomfortable day. Not the sort of day that they had wanted to climb in. The sort of day that they would have been happier lying in the sleeping bag until late in the morning and then heading off to a little coffee shop for a few hours. They had decided to climb because the forecast had been good and they prayed that the sky would begin to clear and the mountains would bath in sunlight, but it grew darker and colder and at any moment they would feel the start of the rainfall.

They reached the summit and sat behind a huge boulder, sheltering from the chill of the wind while they ate. Within minutes, where there had only been dark grey now there was sunshine. The view was spectacular. To the south they could see North Wales and the mountains of Snowdonia. To the north, the Southern Uplands of Scotland. Behind them in central England the Pennines and in the west across the sea, Snaefell on the Isle of Man. They may have even seen some hills in Ulster and not even realised it. It was a magnificent sight and a magnificent memory; and also painful.

Now, he found himself in the Capital of Australia with Phil. Why? What reasons were there? He longed to be here with Steven, or in Britain with Steven, but that could not be. He was here with Phil, both uncomfortable, both content, both wary of their actions. Unknown to Al, Phil was homosexual, inexperienced and alone.

Desperate to reach out and touch someone, feel someone, love someone. Desperate to be loved. Terrified to be found out. He had seen Al at the side of the road, dark and slim. A stranger, safety in someone unknown. Someone who couldn't tell anyone about him and the way he was. For years Phil had fought against his feelings, but he knew what he was. He wanted to be loved by a man, touched by a man, have sex with a man. He had stopped for Al in the faint and terrifying hope that he too was homosexual. He was, but how could Phil have known that? How could Al know that Phil was desperate for him to touch him and say that he liked him? It was a sad moment, two people so desperate for physical closeness, if not sex. Two people, who would have been so well suited, but for the fact that neither of them could say how they felt. Pain screamed so loudly in the silence between them.

Canberra lay on the plain below and a curtain wall of mountains held it in their arms. Protecting it from all that lay beyond. Al was Canberra and the mountains were his friends. They looked at the view. Al was impressed, Phil had seen it so many times before, though always alone. He would spend hours here and cry at his loneliness and confusion. He looked to Al, hoping for a sign, hoping that Al would take the initiative and say, or do, something, anything, everything. Occasionally their eyes met. They both saw the pain there, they felt it. Phil too scared to speak, Al too scared to admit that he could like someone so much and that it could be someone other than Steven.

They shivered and looked. They shivered and spoke. They shivered and were silent. Time passed too quickly. Time was cruel to bring them together at a moment when neither was ready for this meeting.

"Come on, it's getting too cold." Phil said.

They walked to the car. Al hoped that they would sit and talk and not drive off immediately. He struggled for something to say. Something which would be interesting, anything to keep them here a little longer and maybe, just maybe, one of them would, could, steer the conversation around to make it obvious how they were both feeling. Al said something uninspiring and Phil answered briefly. The nervousness in his voice was so obvious, as it was in Al's, but neither wanted to risk being wrong about the other.

Phil cooked dinner for them both and they ate. Al had not got used to Australian generosity and was embarrassed and quiet. Inside he was screaming Phil! Phil! Phil! Close to despair, Phil cried in his heart at his lack of courage. He could not lose now. If he was wrong about Al then the worse thing that could happen would be that Al would leave, he would never see him again. He tried to say the words, ask the question. Are you gay? Nothing came out. Al, I am gay. Nothing.

If Phil had had the courage to say what he was thinking then the moment for that was lost. He knew that it would have to be him who would have to say something, it was he who was on home ground, not Al. But it was too late as John and some of his friends arrived home. Phil introduced them to him and they chatted to each other and put the television on. Al could see that Phil was uncomfortable with them here. He was so unlike the rabble who had just arrived. Al looked over at the television. The news was on and the Iron Lady was shooting down Neil once again.

"Go on Maggie! That's my girl." Al cheered.

"I thought most people hated her!" Brett asked.

"A lot do, but not most. Some people forget that although things aren't great, they are better now than they were."

"But she got rid of all your unions."

"No, she just crushed them a little and now they have to be real unions and leave politics to politicians. So the next time we get a Labour Government it can't be blackmailed by them and that has to be better for Britain."

The conversation continued for some time before Brett, John and Jason got fed up with the discussion and disappeared into the basement. A few minutes later the sound of some old Sex Pistol songs; badly played, drifted up from below.

"I'll show you where the bathroom and toilet are," Phil said sadly. "I hope you'll be comfortable on the sofa, whichever one you choose."

"I'm used to hard ground in my tent. I'm sure the sofa will be great." Al said, thinking that that was the wrong thing to say.

Phil took him up the stairs, then up another flight and showed him his room.

"Is this an invitation?" Al wondered. "Nice big bed," he said.

"It's a water bed."

"Don't you get sea-sick?"

"No, it doesn't make waves."
"Isn't it soft?"
"No, nice and firm. It's so restful."
"I've never slept in one. I couldn't imagine it."
"You'd love it, the best."

Al could think of nothing else to say about the bed. If an invitation to sit on it was going to come, then it wasn't coming now and certainly no invitation to share it. But what would he have done if he was asked to sit on it? To try it? Would he have steered the conversation on in order to make it easy for Phil to offer to share it? And what if Phil had offered to share it, would he be able to accept? Or, as he would have expected, would he pretend to be horrified and decline the offer? The longer the time that Al and Phil spent together, the more certain that Al was that Phil was homosexual, but something; he didn't know what, made him doubt and that made him decide to pull back a bit. Al returned downstairs and studied his German until late in the evening, only able to concentrate partially. His mind was on Phil. Phil was in bed, he tried to read, but couldn't. He tried to write, but couldn't. His hand stretched out to his side, the bed was cold and large and empty. So much space, room for Al. Tears rolled down his face at the thought that he would always be alone. Never to touch, or to be touched by another man. He would never have the courage to say what it was he felt. Those dirty words of I love you.

"Oh Al. I want you here. Come up and ask me something. Come into my room and touch me, show me how to love. Make me feel good, please."

Al was happy to see the sun rise. Morning had arrived clear, bright and dry, even if it was cold. He dressed and waited for Phil as he drank a coffee.

"I wonder how he slept? Was he thinking the thoughts that I dreamt?"

Phil arrived. He still looked troubled. Al still could not figure him out. He didn't know that it was the wedding of his best friend in Newcastle that was hurting him. The last of his college friends was now married. There was only him left. He faced two days of, "Well Phil, you're the last one now. Your turn next, and when are you going to get yourself a girlfriend?"

He did not want to be alone. He wanted someone to lay next to.

He wanted Al. Al made him a coffee. Phil watched his movements. He loved everything about Al, his slim body, his small sexy bum, his dark eyes and hair. If only he could have been sure.

Phil drove into the city. Al went with him.

"If you want a lift home at five thirty, just make your way back to the car. I'll give you my work number, just in case you get lost."

They arrived in the car park at the office where Phil worked. He scribbled down his telephone number and gave it to Al.

"If you find work then you are more than welcome to stay at the house." Al thought that he could hear 'please find and job and stay.' He did, but Phil could not say that.

"You can have the top room for seventy dollars a week and you can always grab a lift in with me.

"Thanks Phil, you've been really good to me." Al looked for a sign of hope in his eyes. It was there, he could see it, but what to do about it?

"That's alright Al."

Al walked into the centre. He felt good about being in this city and the thought of finding work and staying was an idea that he liked. All he needed was a job. He searched the job centre and looked in the local paper. Walking in and out of shops, supermarkets and offices. It was depressing being told no all the time and it dented the small amount of confidence he had. But he kept going, driven on by the thought of being with Phil, by the thought that he was not wrong about him. The thought of a relationship frightened him, that was something that he wanted, but didn't need. Or did need, but didn't want, he wasn't sure which. Sex did not interest him. When was the last time he had an erection? Certainly not from the thought of Phil. All he wanted was to have someone to hold, to sleep next to. Someone to laugh with and talk with. To share life with.

Eventually he had enough of job hunting in the city and he caught a bus to Belconnen, which was the local centre for his part of the city. For an hour he looked again for work before buying some food and walking for an hour to get back to the house. Once again he had to brave some dogs that were wandering around. Once again he panicked and hated, vehemently hated the animals and their owners.

Once he arrived home he shaved and showered before letting himself loose in the kitchen. He had spent almost three days' money on food, he wanted to give back a little of the kindness that had been shown to him. He was happy as he cooked. He looked forward to Phil's return from work. Happy as a puppy waiting for his master. He knew that these feelings were totally irrational. However much he liked Phil nothing was going to come of this relationship, which was not even a relationship.

Unfortunately the 'Sex Pistols' arrived home and demolished a large portion of the food. Phil was late and more food went. Eventually he came home and there was little of it left, Al was apologetic.

"Did you really make this?"

"Yes, I wanted to show you that I appreciate what you've done for me."

"That's alright Al. You're more than welcome." There was another little line to pick up on. Why should Al be more than welcome when Phil hardly knew him.

"I normally grab something out of the freezer, something idiot proof! I can't cook to save my life."

Phil tucked into his food, enjoying food which did not have to be taken out of a packet and cooked from frozen.

"I really like cooking, not that I get much chance while I'm travelling and it's not much fun cooking for one. It's better if you have someone to cook for, someone who you can eat with. I hate eating alone."

Al waited for Phil to pick up on that, but he didn't. They sat together and chatted idle chat. Phil was unhappy. Inside he was so unhappy and Al could see and feel it. He wanted to reach out and touch him, as Stefan had touched him in Brisbane, but he was concerned about the reaction he might have got had he been wrong. The fear of being wrong plagued him and he let the moment pass.

John had made up the fire downstairs and they all found themselves sitting around gazing into the flames and talking.

"This is so good," Al said. "The last time I sat around like this was January '87 when it snowed and we couldn't get out of town."

"Isn't it like that every year?" Jason asked.

"Oh God no! We only get snow that settles every three or four years, even the it doesn't last very long."

"But you get snow at Christmas don't you?"

"Not that I'm aware of. I think the last time that happened was 1962... the year I was born!"

"I thought it was always cold over there, even in the summer."

"Yeah, and I thought it was always hot and dry here!" Al snapped at the ignorant Australians' misconception of what the British Isles were and were not, as he moved nearer the fire as the night grew colder and colder.

"Surely it never gets hot?" Brett asked with genuine doubt.

"It's a different type of heat over there from what I had in W.A. Summers are around twenty one to twenty five degrees. Luckily it rarely goes over twenty eight as that's my point of suffering. I remember when it hit thirty six, it was hell."

"Never! Not in England? If you think that that is hot you ought to try the summer here."

"It will be so wonderful there now. It's been a bit hot, but I really miss the long hours of daylight."

"What long hours of daylight."

Al felt like a teacher with a group of disbelieving youngsters. No matter what he could say he knew that they had already decided what Britain was like and nothing was going to change that view in their minds.

"Well, now in East Anglia it will be getting light about three thirty in the morning and it will start to get darkish about half nine, ten. Up in Scotland they get a lot more light. It's great sitting out in the garden until well into the night, drinking, having a barbecue."

Al was bored with the conversation. It made him miss home. It made him miss his friends. It made him want Phil even more, he wanted a substitute for Steven. Phil sat quietly, deep in thought, listening to Al's voice, but not to the words he spoke. The words were not of any importance, they were merely words. He listened to the tone, deep and nervous. Al was not as self-assured as he pretended to be, not by a long way. He could feel Phil's gaze upon him, hesitated a little before looking over. Phil blushed and looked into the fire.

"I'm going to bed," he said, getting up. "Do you want a lift into the city again Al?"

"Please Phil."

He left, Al's heart sank a little as he gazed into the flames. Shortly after Jason suggested that they go and visit a friend, so they left and Al was alone by the fire looking into his German book, but not reading it. Al could not stop thinking about Phil. He knew what

Phil was feeling, it was as clear as daylight on a mountain in summer. He put his book down and stared hard at the fire. A tear rolled from his eye, was it for himself, Steven or Phil? He got up, climbed one flight of stairs, then a second, then a third and stood outside Phil's bedroom. Phil had gone to bed over half an hour ago, Al hesitated. What would he say? Why was he here? He swallowed hard and knocked softly on the wood. He waited. Silence.

Inside the room Phil sat in bed, quietly, but his heart was pounding away. He knew it was Al, he hoped it was Al, but he was terrified that it could be Al. Looking down at the gap at the bottom of the door Al could see that there was a light on, not a bright one, obviously a bedside lamp. He knocked again, a little louder. Phil shook.

"Come in."

Al opened the door, Phil sat in bed, naked from the waist up. His skin so white and soft. Al looked and entered the room. Their eyes were firmly locked onto each other as he walked in just over halfway between the door and where Phil sat. A moment passed and neither said anything. Both nervous with fear and anticipation.

"If I can't get a job tomorrow, or at least a good chance of one, I'll leave the next day." Al faltered.

Phil looked down from Al and said nothing. A tense silence hung in the room.

"You've been good to me Phil. I wish there was something I could do for you."

"It's alright." Phil answered, his voice heavy with emotion. Al walked nearer, then sat on the bed.

"Phil?"

Phil still looked down, away from Al. "Tell me Phil, please."

Phil shook his head.

"Phil?"

He looked up, his eyes full of tears. Blue-green washed with pain. Al moved one hand up to Phil's shoulder and touched him gently. Phil cried. Al moved closer, closer, close, putting his arms around Phil and held him tight, so tight that he could feel the vibration of his heartbeat. Phil cried and Al said nothing. Al held him in silence. Phil slowly raised his arms and held Al, lightly at first, but then tighter.

They sat together for ten minutes or more, Phil's crying stopped. Al stroked his hair and kissed his head.

"It's alright Phil. I understand. I'm here."

"I love you Al," Phil said nervously and sincerely.

Al wondered for a minute about what sort of answer he should give. He wanted to do everything right. He wanted to be here for Phil.

"I know Phil, I know."

Phil looked up at Al. He was so relieved that at the age of twenty two he had finally had the courage to tell someone how he felt. An hour passed, with such emotional intensity, both with the words they said and with the words which were left unsaid. Phil didn't ask Al to spend the night with him, he expected it. Al did not assume that he would, it just should be. He closed the door and undressed. Phil watched his every move. An experience and sight that he had never expected, but always hoped to see. Al sat naked next to him and kissed him tenderly. Phil was so nervous as Al pulled at the quilt and revealed Phil's full nakedness, getting in bed beside him. They lay together in silence. Chest against chest, legs against legs. Touching, looking.

"You can do whatever you want Al. I want it to be good for you. I love you."

Inside, Al cried at the words, I love you, I love you, I love you. It turned over in his mind and wrenched at his heart. He wanted Phil to be Steven.

"No Phil. You're not ready to give yourself to anyone. You've got a lot of thinking to do and when you're ready you'll find someone. Don't be so trusting and don't be too eager to believe in love, nice though it is."

"But I know I love you."

"I know Phil, but I can't love you. I'm not ready for all that again. You are so handsome and you've got my heart flapping about and your beautiful body is so hot next to mine..."

"Then why not?"

"I love someone else. Someone who doesn't want me anymore. It hurts Phil..."

Phil went to speak and Al put a finger to his lips and stopped him.

"You're gorgeous, Phil. Here I am in bed with the best looking man that I have ever seen, both of us naked, both longing, but only you have an erection. Something happened when Steven and me split up, my head is in such a mess and I guess my body is too."

Phil rested his head on Al's chest and eventually fell into a deep and comfortable sleep. Al remained awake most of the night, protecting Phil with his love and tormented by the desire to be with someone else. What could he do? He wanted to stay here in Canberra with Phil. Time was a good healer and with Phil at his side things could be good again. No. he couldn't stay in Australia forever, he had to get a job and what if it all went wrong again? It frightened him.

After another day in the city Al returned to the house alone before it became dark. He tried to study, but his thoughts were only of Phil. He sat looking at the clock, waiting for him to return home. It was getting late and still no Phil. He sat downstairs, staring out of the window at the multitude of stars which decorated the darkness above the city, thinking about the possibilities ahead. He couldn't take the chance. It wouldn't be fair on Phil anyway. Sure, Al found him attractive, but that wasn't the basis of a relationship; it wasn't before. It could not be fair to be with someone and still long to be with someone else.

Phil sat in his car at the top of Mt. Ainsle, looking out onto the same stars which Al was gazing out at, tormented by the thought that for the first time in his life he had met someone else who was like himself. The first time he had been able to talk about the way he felt. The first time he had touched another man. He wanted to go back to the house and be with Al, but he didn't want to be with him and know that Al was going to leave.

"Maybe he has found himself a job? Maybe I can talk him into staying? I know he likes me."

Al was still alone when Phil finally returned around eight thirty. He met Phil at the door. Their eyes met and each understood the other's thoughts and feelings.

"I was a bit worried about you. Are you alright?" Al asked. Phil nodded, but said nothing.

"Come and sit down with me, we need to talk." Al took Phil's hand and led him down and they sat together silently for a while. Eventually Phil asked the question that he knew he didn't want an answer to. He knew the answer wasn't going to be the one that he wanted.

"Are you still going tomorrow?"

"Yes Phil. I'm sorry, but I can't stay with you."

"If you're worried about money then don't. I earn enough for both of us. You'll get a job eventually."

"No Phil... Yes I need money, but I can't stay in Australia. What happens when my visa runs out? I either have to leave you and that will be harder then, or I have to stay illegally and then what happens if things go wrong between us? What happens if I'm caught?"

Phil said nothing.

"And if all that isn't enough, what about my feelings for Steven? How are you going to deal with that?"

Phil had no answers and Al was searching for obstacles.

There was no chance for them.

"I'm tired. I'm going to bed Al. Will you sleep with me again?"

Al wanted to say no, but the hurt in Phil's eyes was too much for him to bear and he could only say yes, even though he felt that it wasn't the right thing to do.

They undressed and lay down together. No more words passed their lips. Bodies entwined. They slept.

Morning came around; as it always does, far too quickly. Al woke just before dawn and found Phil hugging him. He lightly stroked Phil's hair and gently kissed him. He enjoyed the touch of Phil's soft warm body against his skin. He wanted to stay so very much, but the rational side of him remained strong and reminded him that ahead lay even more pain if he did stay.

Phil woke, looked at Al and lovingly stroked his face as someone who understands that certain things must come to pass even if one does not want them to happen.

"I'm going to miss you Al."

"And I, you."

"I know you're right, or at least I understand why, but..." He said no more for fear of hurting them both. Instead, just holding on to the last few minutes that they had together. They eventually rose, ate some toast and drank a tea without much conversation. The atmosphere tense between them. The few words they spoke trembled from their lips and to make the most of being together Phil offered to take Al out to the edge of the city, which Al declined. He wanted to get this goodbye out of the way and put it behind him before he tried to get a lift.

"I'll be here if you decide to come back," Phil whispered in Al's

ear as they hugged.
"Look after yourself Phil."
Phil nodded, swallowed hard, briefly looked at him and left quickly as the tears began to form in his eyes. The door shut. Al waited till the sound of the car faded, cried, then left.

The air was chilly, a light frost had melted and the sun began to warm the day. Al had a lift within half an hour as far as the main highway, where he only had to wait a few minutes before a truck stopped. It was going to be a long and slow journey to Adelaide and he decided to make it a two day trip, rather than arrive in the city around midnight. Al was amused to be at Wagga Wagga. In his mind he could hear his mother saying what he had heard a dozen times or more. "I've been to Wagga Wagga; and there's only a dirt track out there; and they're always drunk; and fighting!"

"Well mum, they have tarmac out here now. It looks like a typical small Australian town to me. It certainly doesn't look much, God knows what it must have been like when you came."

Few of the buildings looked as if they were over forty or fifty years old and he wondered at how much it must have changed since his mother had visited. It must have been a tiny settlement back in whatever millennium she had made that now very historic trek.

By late afternoon they stopped at a roadhouse several kilometres from Balranald. Al thought that it was time that he got his tent set up for the night, so he headed off along the highway and disappeared into the bush. No sooner had he set up and began to cook, when it started to rain lightly. It was warm and the air was still. He felt almost good, but for his thoughts of Phil and Steven.

"Poor Phil, I hope he'll be alright. It wasn't very kind of me to leave so soon, but it would have been worse in a few months from now. I could not have loved him, I still love Steven. God I miss him!"

He slept long that night, deeply and soundly. Dreams of Phil. Dreams of maybes and could haves. Comforting dreams of hope and love. He slept.

> *I dream of East Anglian countryside,*
> *The beauty of my home,*
> *The Stour, Orwell and Deben,*

Of heath, coast, wood and fen,
I see images of Gainsborough and Constable,
Images of the land for which my heart yearns,
Will I ever see such beauty again?

The rains fall heavy on my little tent,
I lose myself in dreams,
There is beauty in this barren land,
But no heath, coast, wood or fen,
Seasons turn and I grow old,
But Madam le Brun will remain elegant,
Time cannot age her now.

A dream, once dreamt is fading fast in my mind,
This dream I once dreamt is leaving me behind,
This dream, I once dreamt can never be recaptured,
A dream, once dreamt, is forever lost to me.

Days drag past so quickly now,
East Anglia is only months away,
So many lifetimes I've lived since then,
Yet there are still mountains left to climb,
The southern sky is not familiar,
Though Scorpio lights my nights,
I long to see the Aurora in the northern sky.

A warm hand, a warm heart,
Mine still have not turned cold,
I tell myself I have a special friend,
And I'll not climb the mountains alone,
I plan so I can run forever,
Forever no longer seems too long,
But I dream to see the beauty again.

A dream, once dreamt is fading fast in my mind,
This dream, I once dreamt is leaving me behind,
This dream, I once dreamt can never be recaptured,
A dream, once dreamt, is forever lost to me.

It was a bright and warm morning and he did not entirely mind having to walk so far into town. A few cars passed, none stopped. Standing on a bridge over the Murrumbidgee he stopped and looked at the dark green water swirling below. The tress grew tall and wild. Mosses and vines hanging from withered branches. Cooler air down by the water held pockets of mist, it drifted gently, but went nowhere. The scene looked as if it was part of a film set for a feature called 'The Ghost From The Swamp', or some such thing, such was the eeriness of the place. He moved on, eventually reaching the township, sleepy, dusty and warm. Life hardly stirred, though it was by now half nine or ten. A store was open and he bought some bread and fruit then walked to the edge of the town to await a lift to Adelaide. He remembered that he had to pass through a fruit checkpoint so he had to eat or dump his fruit. He thought about this for a while.

"Hey God, are you listening?" He waited for a reply, none came. "I guess you are and I guess you know what I'm going to say. I'm not going to throw this fruit away, not with millions of people in this world starving every day. And I'm not going to take fruit into an area that I'm not supposed to. I'm a horticulturist and I know what that could lead to. So, I will eat it, it's not that I don't care what you said... Oh why am I saying this? You know exactly what I'm thinking and feeling. I'll end up believing that I am mad if I carry on like this."

He sat at the side of the empty road and waited. Nothing happened, so he peeled the fruit and ate it. It was bitter, the most bitter fruit that he had ever tasted.

"Yuck!"

The sky did not darken and erupt into a violent storm, reaping havoc on the land. No Earthquake shook the Earth. But why should it? That was the God of religions and religions are man-made.

"I don't understand why I met Phil? It was a bit unfair to say the least. I don't need the chance of being loved by anyone else. I want to be with Steven. Oh that's sour!" His eyes closed, his face screwed itself up at the taste of the fruit that he wanted to throw away, but couldn't. "No, that wasn't fair. I liked him. I liked him a lot, he was a gorgeous hunk, but I can't love anyone else. And what about Phil? He's so frightened and alone and he needed me, he did love me. I could have been everything to him and I wouldn't have had such a bad deal. Maybe in time I could have loved him, but we wouldn't have had much time."

"Hey mate! Where ya goin'" A car had pulled up across the road and Al had not noticed. An Aborigine had got out and called over to him.

"Adelaide," Al shouted back.

"We're not goin' that far. 'Bout eighty Ks up the road." He said as he helped Al with his backpack.

Al got in and they turned the car in the opposite direction and floored the accelerator pedal.

"We're not even goin' that way!" The other man said. They laughed.

"What have I let myself in for?" Al thought.

"Don't worry mate, we're just goin' to get some grog." They stopped at the bottle shop. Al was amused by the fact that no matter how small a town or settlement was, there was always a bottle shop and a well stocked one at that. The driver's companion asked for a slab of beer and the man serving took the money from them before getting their drink. Al found that unacceptable and blatant racism. He'd seen this before and he began to despise white Australia for their treatment of the country's indigenous people. They got their beer and headed west at high speed.

"At least I'll be out of the car before they're drunk." Al thought with relief.

The driving was fast and erratic and from the back of the car came a strange noise. Al said nothing. The two men drank and talked loudly over the noise of the radio, they heard nothing. Then the car began to pull violently to the left and they stopped and all got out. Al could see a slight bulge in the tyre, he knew what to look for after his experience with Oliver on the journey to Port Augusta. The two men didn't notice and Al said nothing to them. He didn't feel very comfortable; was this him being racist? They continued for another ten kilometres and the noise continued. They could do nothing out here so there was no point in Al saying anything. So he didn't. The car got faster and faster. Part of Al was frightened because they were not in control of themselves; let alone the car, but part of him was glad as it meant that he was nearer to his destination. Again the car pulled to the left. Again they stopped and again they got out and saw nothing. They argued for a while before continuing the journey.

They were a good fifty kilometres from Balranald when the car screeched to a halt, turned around and left the road along a dirt track into the bush. Al looked ahead, there were two other cars there and a half dozen or more Aborigines who were so obviously close to drunkenness. Al sank back into the seat and made himself as near to invisible as he could. This did not feel good. The driver and his friend got out and went over to the group. All around in the trees at the edge of the clearing were empty bottles. Al sat quietly in the car. He could hear laughing and shouting. He wanted to be gone.

"Stay and drink with us," someone shouted.

Ten minutes passed, then fifteen.

"We have to go. We've got a hitch-hiker to drop off as well." Al could hear the driver telling the group. A few seconds passed and a dark round face appeared at the window, smiling, teeth various shades of black and white, some missing.

"Come on out white boy," he said, dribbling, grinning.

Al felt threatened like never before, his heart pounding. He sat upright, trying to appear as relaxed and in control as he could.

"No thanks. I'm alright here."

"He's shy!" The fat man shouted to the group. They laughed.

"Come on white boy, don't be shy, give me a nice little kiss."

How the hell did Al get himself in this situation? He could hear the laughter from the crowd, it grew louder. The fat slob tried to reach in to Al. Al threw his fist at him and desperately tried to look as threatening as he could.

"Oh! That's not very friendly is it? All I want is a nice little kiss."

Al punched at him again, but he caught Al's arm and tried to pull him from the car. He was too strong for Al to resist. He fought the fat bastard and broke free, but found that two others had rushed up and were holding him. No matter how hard he tried, he was caught. The fat man laughed, they all laughed, but somehow this was no longer just having a bit of fun with a lone white boy, the tone of their laughter had changed, this was more serious.

"Look at this white boy." The fat man called as he held his penis in his hand, rubbing himself. "How would you like this? I've never had a white boy before. How would you like an Abo cock?"

"Fuck off you bastard! I'll kill you first." Al screamed, pulled, pushed and kicked. He felt his right arm twist behind him. He felt hands on his legs. A hand rubbed at his penis through his jeans.

"Oh white boy. That's not very friendly is it?" His eyes were the eyes of a frenzied animal as he managed to give himself an erection. "Get his pants off!"

Al struggled, but could barely move. His jeans were unzipped and pulled down, his pants followed. Shaking and sweating he was forced heavily to the ground. His arm hurt so much it felt broken as he landed on it, a possible broken arm meant little to him right now. The red sand of the Australian outback was in his mouth, nose and ears as he felt the weight of the fat man bearing down onto him. A sharp pain shot through his body and mind as the fat man forced himself inside Al. They still held him, though Al could not fight anymore. His head echoed with the sound of the fat man's breathing as he shot his load inside him. Al was no longer there, he didn't feel the fat man get off and laugh as someone else forced himself into his body.

Al could only see the tiny grains of ochre sand by his eyes. He could only feel the sharpness of those grains on his skin as a third Abo bore down onto him. Al's eyes met with the driver who had brought him here. The smile fell from his face as Al cried out for help with dry eyes, lost eyes, vacant eyes. For a moment he stood staring at Al, it felt like hours to Al. The driver ran, as if in slow motion, running towards him. He pulled the man from Al. The Abo holding Al's arm dropped it, it fell heavily to the ground.

"Hey! It's my turn now."

"Go and wank yourself off!" the driver shouted.

There was a scuffle. A bottle smashed. A boot stood heavily on Al's legs. Al lay on the ground, unable to move. The driver and his friend picked Al from the sand. He screamed with the pain from his arm.

"Get your clothes on!" The driver shouted at Al.

Al struggled with his trousers. His right arm hung lifeless at his side. They helped him to the car. Pushing him in, then reversed at high speed through the bush and onto the highway. The car spun around and tore off along the road. They spoke to Al, but he couldn't hear what they said. He held his arm as life began, slowly, to return to it. His head full of nothing. He couldn't even feel pain or disgust. There was nothing there.

Fifteen minutes further along the road they stopped and got Al's luggage out of the boot. They were disgusted with what had happened and frightened by the thought of Al going to the police. Surely he would? They were party to what had happened. They could have stopped it.

"We turn off here. The town is a few Ks up the road." Al took no notice. He struggled to lift his pack, they helped him. He walked off, uneasily, unsteady on his feet. They called after him, but he didn't know what they said. He stared, tunnel visioned, at the road ahead. There was nothing to see, there was nothing here. He could see no town, just a straight road across a flat open and barren landscape with only a few trees here and there along the side of it.

ADELAIDE

Euston, 16th June 1989

Behind him, the car doors slammed shut and the tyres lost tread as they screeched away. A pale grey-black puff of smoke rose as rubber burned. Al kept walking though it was difficult to muster the energy. He had to walk and keep walking. There was nothing here, not a soul in sight in any direction. He left the road and hid himself behind a few trees and sat for some minutes in silence as he gently brushed the sand from his face and clothes. He stood up sharply and held onto a tree as he vomited, rough bark beneath his hand, a firm tree. There was so little in his stomach to bring up, but his stomach was drained. Flies buzzed. He felt numb as he expelled everything he could from his body and as he emptied himself of their vile fluids he could only think of Steven, he couldn't understand why he was not with him right now. Now, when more than ever he needed him. He was bleeding, but he could not feel any physical pain, he just felt dirty. So dirty. So alone.

"I must get to Adelaide. It will be alright when I get to Adelaide. I know that city. I'll be safe there." He tidied himself up, swallowed hard, cried.

"How do I expect I'm going to get a lift if I'm not presentable?" The bush seemed to hide him in his shame; though he had done nothing wrong. It hid him in his disgust. It hid him from eyes that were not there to see him.

He returned to the road and carried on walking, the tarmac stretched out forever. He wished this was Suffolk, a mile or two between villages. In the distance he could see some buildings.

"A farm. Dogs! So what?"

After half an hour he walked into the township of Euston.

"Damn! I can't get a train to Suffolk from here." He sat down at the side of the road and waited, there was so little traffic, nothing had yet passed him and when a few cars did come he stood up and held out his sign, only to sit down as they drove past and into the distance, towards Adelaide, towards safety.

"You have to smile, no one will pick you up if you don't smile."

He smiled for the next car and it stopped. In it were a man and woman, Maori, they were going to Mildura. He tried to make conversation, but most of the time he sat and looked at the dry land, the hateful barren land. He hated it. The scenery changed into groves of citrus fruit, rows of trees which were heavy with bright orange berries and although he had never seen such a sight before he wasn't much interested in it now. They crossed the Murray River and were now in Victoria, a little nearer safety. Mildura was a big town and he found out just how big when he was dropped in the centre, then had to walk out to the edge towards Adelaide, he didn't have the energy to make short work of it. He stopped at a dairy and bought a bottle of soda water, to settle his stomach. Around him, dozens of school kids, screaming, shouting, laughing. He looked at the faces, they shone, their mouths open, he heard very little sound as they filled the air with their riotous noises. Faces spinning. Faces of joy and youth and no worries mate, she'll be alright!

He waited for a few hours in the warm sun by the side of the road. Time was not on his mind, it was unimportant. Flies buzzed. They were unimportant now. He had to get to Adelaide. He had to.

"Oh Christopher," he spoke to a cloudless sky. He waited for an answer. None came.

"I wish I could talk to you now, but how can I tell you about this?" He needed his friend now, like never before. "I'm alone here. On my own and I've only myself to rely on. I guess I had better get used to that pretty damned quick... I miss you Christopher. I've never told you that I love you. I always write it and I know that you know it, but I've never had the courage to say it to you. I'm sorry brother."

It was hours before a young lad stopped. He was going through to Adelaide. Al sighed. He was pleased that he had a lift and he didn't care that it was taking forever as they drove through fruit town after fruit town, then bush and more bush and by the time they reached the hills it was already dark. He didn't give a damn. He was heading to safety; a place that was familiar; somewhere he recognised; almost as home.

Eventually, hours later, they reached the outer edges of the urban sprawl. Al was dropped off at the side of the road near to a petrol station. Aware that he was some way out from the centre; a minor problem, but at least he was here. He went into the garage and asked for directions to the nearest bus stop.

"It's right across there mate, on the other tide of the road, but I wouldn't have a clue if they still run this time of the evening," the attendant said.

"Do you know if they only accept the right fare, or do they give change?" Al asked because he only had ten and twenty dollar notes on him.

"No, you're alright. They give change on the bus."

It took him a while to cross the busy road and he sat waiting in the shelter, which he hadn't noticed before. It was cold, but he was safe. There was no timetable so he had no way of knowing if there were indeed any more buses this evening. He sat and waited, his mind drifting between Steven, Christopher, Phil and nothing at all. Almost half an hour passed when a group of young boys arrived, he was pleased about that as it meant that there would be a bus some time soon. Another fifteen minutes passed and Al could hear some girls laughing from somewhere behind the shelter, two teenage girls and a young woman came into view, the boys stood up and made room for them. Some more time passed as the girls whispered and the boys played up to their audience.

"Oh the boy/girl world," Al thought. He felt bitter.

"Here it comes," one of the girls said, then left the woman alone.

The bus stopped and the three boys waited for Al to get on.

"No, you go first, I've got to carry my pack on."

The boys got on.

"Do you know how much it costs to get downtown?" The woman asked Al.

"No, sorry. I've just arrived in Adelaide myself." He looked at her as if she was from another planet. She had such a strong cockney accent and it had taken him quite by surprise, it was one of the last sounds that he thought he would hear.

Al struggled on with his bag and pack and sat behind the woman.

"Do you know how far it is into the city?" Al asked.

"It takes about twenty minutes," she replied.

"What part of London are you from?" Al questioned her.

"London? No, I'm an Australian. I was born here in Elizabeth and I've only ever been outside South Australia once in my life and that was only to Sydney!" She laughed.

She may not have been a Londoner, but she did have the gift of the gab and by the time the bus broke down in King William Street Al felt that he knew everything that there was to know about her. Three kids, divorced, boyfriend who she was meeting for dinner, a car in the garage, a large house, courtesy of the social and a weekly wage from the Government! Luckily for Al the bus had broken down just where it did, as it was on the corner of North Terrace and he knew where he was. He was safe now. Adelaide.

It was only a few minutes walk to the hostel and he knocked on the door of the little cottage at the back of the main building. A young well-spoken and well-dressed English girl opened it.

"Hi, is Pat about?"

"No, he's not."

"Is there room here?"

"Yes."

"Can I leave my pack here while I go and phone him?" Al said as he pushed his way in, not giving her time to answer.

"It's a strange set up isn't it!" Al said, though he did not feel like talking, he could see that she was nervous.

"Yes, I'd never been in a hostel until I came to Australia and these mixed dorms take a little getting use to," she admitted.

"Yes, it came as a surprise to me. I've only spent four nights in hostels and I still feel a bit uncomfortable." Al left her and went to find a telephone. It took him a further twenty minutes to pluck up the courage to ask a stranger if they could change a fifty cent piece so he could make the call! Contact with strangers always being an impossible task to achieve for him.

"God help me if I ever get to Germany," he mused.

After making the phone call he returned to the hostel and introduced himself to this rich excuse for a traveller.

"Travelling on daddy's credit card no doubt." He bitched to himself half-heartedly.

"Is there anyone else staying here?"

"Yes, a Geordie called Steve."

"Can you understand him?"

"Yes, but it takes a little time." The thought of one very posh young girl and a Geordie having a conversation struck Al as quite amusing.

"I'll go upstairs and sort myself out." He didn't want to make polite small talk, he was longing for a shower, longing to cleanse his body.

Disappearing up the stairs, he felt ill, his stomach and mind in turmoil, he went for a long hot shower, scrubbing at his body like it had never been scrubbed before, the water so hot he could barely stand under it. He wanted to cry, but would not allow himself that weakness, that luxury. He could not allow himself to shed a single tear. Where would self pity get him? He dried himself carefully, his skin spotlessly clean, but still so dirty.

As Al descended the stairs into the kitchen Steve arrived back and Kathleen let him in.

"Oh hello," Steve said in a really thick northern accent, which was both amusing and strange to Al's ears.

"Hello, I've never met anyone from your part of the world before," Al said, as if Tyneside was somewhere in central South America.

"Are you ready, Kathleen?" Steve asked. "We're going to the casino, would you like to come with us?"

"No thanks, I don't have the right clothes, the right money or the right frame of mind at the moment."

Had he known that Tony was in the same city as him and was to be found in the very place Steve and Kathleen were heading, he would have gone. Al needed a friend like Tony and he in his turn needed a friend like Al. Together they could prop up each other's weaknesses and maybe some good would come out of being in Australia. They were both lost, each in his own screwed up way. Each were searching for the answers to questions that they were not yet aware of. Yes there were questions, but what were they? There were answers to those questions, but where could they be found? Steve and Kathleen left and Al sat to study his German.

"I will achieve something with my life. I will." His German would also help to keep his mind occupied.

* * * * *

Tony was drunk, not totally, but reasonably well plastered. Standing in the pub with the friends he had made in the hostel in Melbourne and with whom he had quite unexpectedly travelled with here to Adelaide.

The following morning Tony was heading towards Perth, while his friends returned to Sydney; it was the end of their four months and were just biding their time until they flew out to Auckland. They had grown tired of Australia and were longing for a change; New Zealand, Fiji, Hawaii, Canada and the States, then home for Christmas.

"We're really going to miss our drinking sessions, Tony," David said, buying another round, the last one before he and John were off to the casino.

"Are you sure you won't come out for a little flutter? A little black jack maybe?"

"I'd like to, but money is getting a bit tight now. I've got to get work in the next two or three weeks."

"Oh you will, there's plenty of work about. Come on Tony, you won't have to spend much. Ten or twenty dollars." John tried twisting Tony's arm. Tony gave in. He was reluctant, even if he wanted to go. He always enjoyed fun.

"O.K. But I'm not going to spend much and if I lose, then I won't keep losing."

"Good one Tony. We'll leave with a splash at the casino! Show these Aussies what us Brits are made of!" John spouted out.

Tony knew that he couldn't just spend a little money. Tony? Spend a little money? It was a contradiction in terminology. Tony and alcohol mixed far too easily; and not much better than Al and alcohol, and when that happened money just disappeared like water in a desert.

The walk from the pub to the casino sobered all three of them up, so the first thing to do was to get some more beer inside of themselves. Another twenty dollars gone and not even one go at roulette!

David and Tony fancied their chances on the wheel. The temptation of winning a decent amount was too much for them. Things were looking good, after a couple of minor setbacks Tony found himself sixty dollars up on the evening; excluding drinks, which ate into half of that by now.

"Stop while you're ahead Tony." John said.

"Don't be silly John, he's got luck on his side. It will be a hundred soon."

"Yeah John. You should be having some of this," Tony smiled.

Tony laid his next bet. Twenty dollars, black five. He was running, just as Al was, but he couldn't see it yet; his girlfriend now in America, little money left; needing to find work soon; no work to go home to; in fact nothing to go home to and to top it all, his dependence on alcohol, cannabis and nicotine. How could he stop it?

"Bad luck Tony."

By eleven o'clock Tony, John and David had each lost a hundred or so dollars as well as spending a large amount on alcohol. Tony was now down to two weeks money... at a push. For part of the evening Steve and Tony had stood next to each other at the same roulette table, both losing a lot of money, before Steve and Kathleen left the casino around the same time as Tony, John and David. Tony noticed Steve and Kathleen at the table, they spoke, but how could Tony have guessed that they were heading back to a hostel in which Al was lying in a bed feeling lost. He was calm, his mind had blanked out the horrors of the morning. His mind void of any real thoughts or feelings. His eyes focused on the ceiling above in the darkness.

On the walk back to the hostel Tony thought of Al. He couldn't imagine Al getting himself in a situation where he could be mugged and beaten up in Sydney, or evening getting anywhere close to the end of his money and having to find work.

"Yeah, Al will be near a warm tropical beach with lots of trees about him and few people... still wanting to be with Steven. Such a waste, it's over Al, it's over. You've got to get on with life, wherever you are. You can't do anything about the past except learn from it." Tony spoke to himself as if he was communicating with Al at his side. Wise words which he himself would have been wise to listen to.

"Tony?" John pushed him.

"What?"

"You weren't listening to a word I said were you?"

"Sorry mate, miles away."

"Tropical beach, lots of women and booze!" David and John laughed.

"Beach? Yes, but my friend Al. I couldn't help thinking that he is so sensible in so many ways, apart from when it comes to his ex-boyfriend, he just falls to pieces in the saddest of ways."

"Shouldn't worry about him, he's probably found some other queer and they've both got sore arses by now!" The two friends laughed, Tony wasn't impressed. "He's only a poof, Tony, he can't really be a friend to you, he probably wants to bum you."

Tony swung around at John, hitting him in the face.

"He may be gay, screwed up and unable to enjoy himself, but he's my friend and a better person than you are!" Tony was incensed by their ignorance. He hated the thought of Al being treated by society in this way all the time. John held his face, luckily Tony was too drunk to hit him really well.

"Alright Tony, I'm sorry. I didn't think that he was that much of a friend."

David stepped in between them. "Come on you two, let's not fall out over this on our last night."

Tony's fist slowly opened and they walked in strained silence back to the hostel.

The following morning Tony said goodbye to John and David and headed out to a transport depot and found a lift to Perth. He didn't really want to travel by truck after his previous crossing of the Nullarbor with a truck driver who popped pills to keep awake all the way from Norseman to Port Augusta, but now with less than three hundred dollars he had to get across as quickly and as cheaply as he could. He spent a week in a hostel in Perth, looking for work every day and drinking every night and then the money ran out. He continued to sleep in the hostel, on the floor. He was well liked by the people in the dorm and none of them were going to say anything to the managers. There were others who were nearing the end of their money and had phoned home for some more. Tony had no one to phone home to for money and things were desperate.

It was luck, good luck indeed that he had been in a pub early the previous week and got himself drunk with some Australians. One of them said that he could get him a job and although Tony thought at the time that it was all talk, he was now desperate enough to clasp at any straw, so he returned to the pub to meet Brad. To his surprise Brad had kept his word and gave Tony a piece of paper with a name and a telephone number scribbled on it.

"He's expecting you in two days, so that gives you plenty of time to get there. It's hard work, but bloody good money and Glenn's a good bloke."

Tony breathed a sigh of relief, this couldn't have happened at a more desperate time in his life.

* * * * *

Days began to drift past and Al did not want to go anywhere. Kathleen left and Steve and Al got on really well and took to running the place, unofficially. When people arrived that they didn't like the look of, they sent them to another hostel. The horror of having all five beds full was not what either of them wanted. Steve found himself a job in a threading factory which was only for two weeks. He hated the job, but needed the money too much to turn it down. Al got himself into a routine of early mornings. Steve relied on Al to wake him up for work each morning, then Al sat and studied his German, drank coffee and ate. Later in the morning he would spend a couple of hours in the botanic garden across the road and try to consolidate his knowledge of Australian plants. He had a talent for something and he used it to occupy his thoughts for a while. He also enjoyed the winter sunshine and while it was dry and light he wanted to be out in the open air sounded by plants. Mid afternoons were spent watching an old black and white movie, providing it wasn't Shirley Temple; he felt like pulling his hair out every time he heard that horrible squeaky voice.

Dawn arrived from Canada and Ute from Denmark, with a cold. They seemed to stay for weeks, but in reality it was only a few days. In the evening the four travellers huddled together on the sofa, wrapped in sleeping bags, trying to keep warm in the cold building as they watched television. Each time someone got up to go to the toilet, or to get a drink there would be a chorus of "put the toaster on." The toaster was the only source of warmth, even if in a building of that size it was only psychological.

The days passed too quickly and what would have been Al and Steven's fifth anniversary hurt a great deal. He felt more betrayed now than he had for a long time, but not bitter, he had passed that. The hurt was from loneliness and longing for that someone who had been special for so long. Someone who was no longer there.

> *"This is love,*
> *this is pain disguised as a dream, memories,*
> *are guaranteed to break your heart."*

"I wonder where you are today Steven? I bet you don't even remember do you? There's someone else in your bed, so why should you remember me? I'm not part of your life anymore. I'm nothing to you now, but then I've been nothing to you for a long time haven't I?"

Steve's job finished and he and Al spend much of their time together, they were almost inseparable, but Al was afraid of this, becoming dependent on yet another person who would one day say goodbye and then leave. Steve became an object of stability as they got to know each other better and better. They watched the black and whites together, sat together in the park, in the sunshine, shopped for bargains together and froze together in the evenings.

Ute left and Sue arrived, she was a Kiwi, but lived in Melbourne. They welcomed her into their little house which she used as a base for a major shopping expedition everyday. Then Dawn was ready to leave, on her last day Steve and Al went with her on a trip to Port Adelaide to visit the old historic port. They searched for it, but could not find much which held any interest for them. None of them were too impressed. For Dawn, old meant over two hundred years old and for Steve and Al at least twice that. None of them had been in Australia long enough to appreciate that late eighteen hundreds, early nineteen hundreds was old.

People came and went and a whole host of new faces arrived. The main building was reopened and they had to move into it. At least they had a colour television, ready for Wimbledon. Steve and Al would sit up well into the early hours of the morning watching the tennis and sunshine from London. Days flew past and neither Al nor Steve kept track of how many slipped away, such was their contentment. Then it was time for Sue to leave, returning to Melbourne the next morning. She struggled to pack her many new belongings ready for the coach journey home, it had been a good shopping spree for her. The gang that had formed in the cottage decided that they should go out to celebrate and commiserate the event. After a few drinks, then a few more, followed by a few more, sometime after midnight they were asked to leave the otherwise empty pub, which they did so reluctantly.

They walked through the city under the starlit sky; as well as under the influence of alcohol. Steve and Al were both well pissed by this time, singing and shouting. They came across a pub in which there was a party alive and well up on its first floor. There were people on the balcony, drinking, laughing, dancing.

"Hey can we come and join in?" Al shouted up to them.

"Yeah, can we come?" Steve and Sue called in unison.
Half a bottle of lager was poured down and someone shouted, "Have a drink on us!"
"Let's have a couple of tinnies, or a bottle of wine." Sue asked. For her trouble and cheek she got a carton of wine, which although it wasn't full, it wasn't empty either. They were all beginning to sober up in the chilly air and no one wanted to go back to the hostel. Al had spent half of the evening trying to keep awake and now he was ready to stay out all night. The streets of Adelaide seemed full of promise of something more, something to do, some excitement, though there was nothing happening. They stumbled upon a pub that was still open and in they went. More drinks, then Sue left, David went a few minutes later. Steve disappeared to the toilet and was gone a long time.

"Do you think you should go and see if he's alright?" Kylie asked.

Al was reluctant to go looking in the gents for Steve, it seemed too much like cottaging and Al did not want to be misread by anyone. He certainly was not out to be laid, nor laid out! But Steve had checked on him in the other pub, so he headed into the crowd. He was glad to get away from Kylie who was going on about her very rocky relationship with her selfish and arrogant boyfriend David. He had left them in a foul mood because he did not want Kylie to stay out if he wasn't staying. Al forced his way slowly into a crush of people and found Steve talking to a couple of girls.

"I was just coming to see if you were alright, obviously you are."

"Yeah, I'm fine. Is she still going on about Dork-head?"

"Yeah."

"Don't it just piss you off, she ought to leave the wanker." Steve said in his broad northern accent, which Al only now noticed when Steve or himself had been drinking, but being with so many Aussies and other non northerners didn't appear to weaken his accent at all.

"I'm going back to the hostel now, I just can't be bothered anymore."

"Oh don't go Al, don't leave me here with her."

"I don't reckon she'll stay much longer either." Al left the pub and although he wasn't sure where it was he still managed to find the hostel and sat watching the tennis, there was no one else about. Kylie wasn't much longer and she went straight upstairs. Half an hour later Steve came in, right off his face and collapsed into the chair next to him.

"Hit the bloody ball then!" He shouted at the television. Al laughed, he was glad that Steve was in a worse state than himself. They watched the tennis and after a few minutes Steve jumped up, only to fall back down again.

"I'm going to the toilet." He announced and staggering into the kitchen, looking around, confused.

"Steve, that's the kitchen." Al smirked, not too unkindly.

"I thought it looked familiar." He headed off along the hall to the front door and started swearing at it.

"What are you doing Steve?"

"I can't open the fucking stupid door."

"It would help if you pull it towards you, not push at it." Al opened the door for him and Steve fell out and down the steps into the cold darkness of the night. The rest of the hostel was in darkness, the tiny rear courtyard, empty, cold and concrete.

"Where's the toilet gone?"

Al laughed loudly, then covered his mouth when he realised just how much noise could travel in the early hours when amplified by the surrounding walls. Steve was so funny to watch. He brought him back into the house and led him to the foot of the stairs. Steve tried to get up the first step, but kept missing it.

"This isn't going to be easy Steve, you just lift your feet up and down and I'll push you up. O.K.?"

Steve nodded and started to move his feet up and down before he was going anywhere. Then Al held his shoulders and pushed forward, Steve moved his feet and they began to ascend the flight of stairs. It wasn't easy and each time Steve leaned backwards Al struggled to push his weight forward again. After a few hair-raising moments they reached the top, Al pushed him into the toilet and put the light on for him.

"You're an your own now Steve." He said pulling the door shut.

Al returned to watch the tennis, not thinking Steve would be silly enough to follow. He was wrong. Steve came stomping and staggering back down again before Al could even move from his seat and get there to help. They met at the bottom of the stairs. Eyes met, Steve looking deeply into Al's, or was he so drunk that he was looking straight through him? Unable to focus on the person stood in front of him Steve grinned, then went and sat down.

"Do you want some toast Steve?" Al asked as he walked into the kitchen. There was no answer, Steve was flat out asleep. Al felt quite paternal towards him and went upstairs and quietly took his sleeping bag from the dorm, bringing it back down and covering him. He looked lovingly at Steve lying asleep like a baby, a smile on his face, at one with the world; totally oblivious to it! Al felt closer to him than he had to anyone for a long time, he loved his funny new northern friend. He patted the feather filled quilt which covered Steve, stroked his short blond hair.

"Sleep well my friend." He could not remember when he had laughed so much, or indeed when he last had had reason to laugh. Steve was still young and silly, good looking and normal; whatever normal really meant? What would Steve had said if he knew his new friend was a poof? How would he feel if he knew the man covering him and caring for him right now was the other way? By not telling Steve he was being dishonest, but why should he have to confess his sexuality? It should not have been an issue and by discussing it, it would make it into one and therefore it was better that it was not discussed.

"I like you a lot my funny drunken Geordie. Surely there's nothing wrong in that?"

Behind him, his toast popped up out of the toaster and announced its presence with that just caught smell of toast, black at the edges. He patted Steve gently on the arm; like a real man would do, then walked to the kitchen and buttered his toast. The butter melted into the grains of bread, dressing it in a golden sheen which was wonderfully sensual to his taste buds. The aroma from the hot buttered toast made his mouth water, he could eat all night! The tennis was a close game and held Al firmly awake. The summer's sun; alluring, enviable, covetable; all that warmth in Britain while he froze in Australia. The heat which parched the grass on the court until it turned yellow, one of the drawbacks with long hot summers in Britain, not enough rain to keep it green and beautiful. It was three o'clock when Steve awoke. He searched the room, taking a moment to get his bearings, remembered where he was. Looked to Al, the television, his sleeping bag, than without a word he was off up the stairs, fast, furious, like lightning and almost as silent.

"I hope you get in the right bed Steve."

Sue had gone. Steve and Al were back in the botanic gardens, lying by the lake, feeding the ducks and black swans as well as themselves. It was just warm enough to be outside in their sheltered spot by the water. The sun was pleasant and they hadn't seen rain for nearly two weeks, but the daytime sun and warmth were deceiving, it was still winter and the evenings, nights and early mornings reminded them only too well. The ducks squabbled over an occasional piece of bread they would throw to them. A mass of feathers racing across water, mini tidal waves lapped the banks and spread in concentric circles across the lake, broken by the bodies of the larger and more elegant black swans.

"We aren't going to be able to stay here forever Al," Steve said, though he would have been quite happy to carry on as they were.

"I know, but I don't really want to move anywhere. I really needed to be here Steve, to stay put and have friendly faces around." He looked at Steve and saw that he didn't understand. How could he? Why should he? He hadn't been raped. He hadn't had the person he loved abuse him. No, the puzzlement on his face was well and aptly worn.

"It's not the same in the big hostel. Far too many people around." Al didn't answer, but nodded his head in agreement.

"We're going to have to get some jobs soon."

Al sighed heavily. Steve was right, unfortunately. They watched the birds on the water, lost in their contentment with each other's company and their surroundings. They made full use of the gardens as they were free, also the museum and the art gallery. There was a Gainsborough in the gallery, in his later style, which Al found far superior to the works which made Gainsborough a famous and a much sought-after portraitist. Madam le Brun was a link to East Anglia and more specifically to his home town on the Stour. So often, almost daily he would see copies of Constable's Haywain or Willy Lot's Cottage. The warmth he felt when seeing them lifted his spirits. Suddenly the world wasn't so big after all. Home was closer than he had realised.

Between them they had five hundred pounds, that wasn't going to last very long at all, so to take their minds off the problem of their cash flow shortage they decided to spend some in the pub.

"Only one though Steve." Al said, not sure that he wanted to go.

"Yeah, only one." Steve answered.

A few hours later and several beers downed, they returned to the hostel. The lounge was full of tourists of all nationalities, watching some American film which was supposed to be funny, but Al found rather silly.

"I'm hungry. Do you want some noodles with me?" he asked the German girl sitting by his side.

Noodles are the travellers friend, they are cheap, light and easy to cook and if at first you don't like them you soon acquire the taste as your wallet gets lighter and lighter. Within a few minutes they were sat eating the oriental flavoured noodles, then Al got up to leave.

"Where are you going Al?" Steve asked.

"To find a party." He smiled and left.

Al was well past half cut as he wandered into Rundle Mall, he was not behaving normally, whatever that was. The air was mild, a thin layer of cloud trapped the heat from the city. The air was exciting, charged with a promise of something more than an evening in front of the television. Ahead, a crowd of young people; Al did not consider himself so young anymore, emitted a lot of noise into the street. He went over to see what was going on. He was drunk, he would never have approached them had he been sober. The kids were arguing over nothing in particular, the way kids do. No one noticed, least of all Al, when a police car pulled up silently near them. Two young policemen walked towards the crowd of noisy youths and asked what was going on, then told them to move away from town and to not even think about coming back. Al stood there grinning as the kids had a moan and then began to leave.

"Well? What are you waiting for? And what is it that you find so funny?" The tall, blond, and frightfully good looking officer asked him.

"What? Me? I'm not with them," Al answered, somewhat surprised to be included with the rabble.

"You were with them when we arrived so you can move on with them as well."

"But I wasn't doing anything!" He was protesting his innocence in this situation.

"Where do you live?" the cute one asked. Al was glad it wasn't the ugly, stubby one; who had a bigger nose than his own, doing the questioning.

"In the hostel, around the corner," he said pointing towards the hostel in a vague random manner.

"Oh, you're a tourist are you?"

"Yeah, that's right..." He almost said dear, but wasn't so without his wits and he stopped himself in time.

"And a drunken tourist at that?" Al stood silently now. "I think you had better go now."

"Oh come on possum, I'm not hurting anyone, just taking in the evening air."

"You can be taking a ride down to the station and spending the night in a cell if you're not careful," he said in an agitated tone.

"Um," Al thought, "if I was spending the night with you I might be tempted, but not in a cell, that sounds a bit kinky." He wasn't tempted by his offer, but he still stood there grinning. The conversation was happening just a little too fast for him and he was only just keeping up with things.

"What's your name?"

"Al."

"Come on Al, you've had too much to drink and you don't really want to spend part of your holiday in a police cell do you?" Al didn't answer, he was listening to the change of tone in the policeman's voice. The tough voice of authority had been replaced by a soft, friendly, and very sensual sound. Soft, powder-blue eyes shone at Al as he stared deeply into them.

"Your hostel or the station? Where do you want to go?"

Al was still half grinning, he was quite enjoying this as sweety pie put his hand on Al's back and led him, willingly, to the police car. Al was put in the back and the door was closed. Ugly drove, and Al's beauty sat in the passenger seat with his back to him and he explored his short blond hair and smooth pink neck. He looked so handsome in his uniform, but what did he look like out of it?

"How long have you been in Australia Al?"

"Since the end of April," he couldn't work out how many weeks that was.

"And how long have you got left?"

"Oh, whatever. I want to stay." Maths wasn't his forte at the best of times.

"Most people do. You're English aren't you?"

"No I am not! You cheeky sodding colonial. I'm East Anglian."

Al's blond bombshell turned to look at him, laughing, not angry. He'd never heard anyone deny being English before, or claim to be an East Anglian.

"I was born in Thetford. Is that anywhere near you?"

"A fellow East Anglian! Oh possum, what a small world! That's less than thirty miles from my home town. Can you get me residency here? You have to look after your own sort you know!" Al wondered if this beautiful hunk of a policeman was his own sort? The policeman laughed.

"I'm Australian, I grew up here, don't remember anything of England."

"I don't blame you possum, but don't you remember East Anglia? Born an East Anglian, always an East Anglian!"

"No Al," he laughed as the car slowed to a halt outside the botanic gardens.

"Here we are, my fellow East Anglian. Here's your hostel. Try not to drink so much in the future and keep yourself out of trouble. Please." He got out of the car and let Al out. He stood tall next to Al, slim, but solid. Al grinned like he knew what the joke was, but no one else did.

"Thanks for the lift possum."

"And you can't go around calling people possum here in Australia Al," he leaned nearer to Al and whispered, "no matter how much you fancy them, or they fancy you." He got back into the car. "Be good!" He said, eyes smiling as they began to drive off.

"Oh I am Possum, I am! If only you would find out."

It was the alcohol talking and not Al. He would have run a mile if the chance of sex had risen, or anything else had risen for that matter!

There's flashing lights in the street tonight,
Cold air and bright neons,
I'm hot and it's cold and I don't worry,
There's flashing in my mind, in my mind, in my mind.

Oh I'm in love with Adelaide,
Can I really feel at home,
Am I in love with Adelaide,
My old friend, my new friend and a pretty face,

Peace and understanding haven't come my way.

I'll shy away from total truth,
Like cold air it brings more pain,
Life's like a knife, cutting me deep and much deeper,
And I don't want to be alone anymore.

Oh I'm in love with Adelaide,
Can I really feel at home,
Am I in love with Adelaide,
My old friend, my new friend and a pretty face,
Peace and understanding haven't come my way.

Stained in grey, is my life,
Where is the black and white from before,
I need comfort, but not warm flesh,
Chase this confusion from my head.

Oh I'm in love with Adelaide,
Can I really feel at home,
Am I in love with Adelaide,
My old friend, my new friend and a pretty face,
Peace and understanding haven't come my way.

The policemen don't like to be called possum here,
But I need your face to chase the dark shadows,
The policemen don't like to be called possum here,
And I want your face to rid me of my isolation,
The policemen don't like to be called possum here,
And I need those eyes to burn out my memories.

"What are you up to Al?" Steve asked.
"Nothing Steve, nothing. Just having a pleasant evening."
"I was going to come after you, I'd not seen you like that before."
"Now that is a sign of friendship," Al thought, though he was glad that Steve hadn't done that. Al was in one of his highly unpredictable moods and within ten minutes he was back out into the street, this time looking for policemen; or to be more precise, one in particular.

The following day Steve and Al decided that they would leave Adelaide later that week. They would make their fortunes picking oranges and Al knew where to head for, he had seen millions of them not too many weeks ago. Steve only wanted to get five hundred dollars and then move back to Sydney, so Al knew that it would not be long before he was once again on his own. Neither really wanted to leave this city, their existence was quite amiable and to change life was not so much a desire, as much as it was a necessity.

So it was they found themselves at the side of the road in Berri, a small fruit town on the Murray River, watching the bus turn the corner as they got their bearings. They soon had their tents pitched and went off in search of work, unfortunately it did not; unlike oranges, grow on trees.

On the river near the camp site there were two barges, which formed the only river crossing for miles around. All day they plied to and fro across the green-brown water. Along a short distance, an empty paddle steamer was tied up to the bank. It added a little of a ye olde worlde charm and atmosphere to the place. A left over from the days when the river provided the life line for the towns people and their wares, now all it carried were overweight and over loud Australian pensioners, time on their hands and too much money, just waiting for lives to expire.

Just along the road from the camp site was a pub and this was bad news for both of them, because the nights were bitterly cold they had an excuse; as if they needed one, to have a drink or two in order to fight it off.

They had been in Berri for a few days and still had not found any work. They spent most of their days in the sun and looked only occasionally for work. They were still spending money and not earning any, something had to change. Sitting in Al's tent, the sun having just gone down, along with the temperature, they waited for the water to boil so they could cook their delicious two minute noodles and tell each other how wonderful they were.

"Hey Al," Steve sounded concerned as he rubbed his arm. "Look at these, they weren't there before." Steve showed Al his arm, two moles, large and black had grown, apparently recently.

"Are there any on my back?" He said taking his shirt off to reveal his naked silky flesh. Al felt uncomfortable as his eyes scanned over Steve's back. Would Steve have asked him to look if he had known that Al was homosexual? Interrupting his thoughts and fears Steve asked, "are there any?"

"You've got a couple."

"Where about are they?"

Al nervously touched Steve's body near each mole. Steve wasn't sure if they were new or not, so the following day he would go to the doctor and have them removed. He worried if he had not over done the sun bathing in Queensland... the cancer state after all.

After the visit to the doctor they had to try a farm for work, this was their last hope before moving on. They packed and headed for the River Murray Berri Ferry, crossing the river and walking off across the flood plain. No one stopped to give them a lift. It wasn't long before Steve shouted in horror, "Look at that!" In front of them was a massive hill, stretching like Jack's beanstalk, towards the sky itself.

"We'll have a rest at the bottom of it, before we go up." Al said, trying to make it sound less insurmountable. At the bottom they stopped and rested, but the hill looked even bigger now and neither wanted to be the one who said let's go up now, or let's turn back. The problem didn't arise as a truck stopped and that brought a smile to both their faces.

"Where ya going?"

"Lameroo Farm," Steve answered.

"Oh yeah! We used to work there," the chap said.

"Yeah, we used to work there," a girl called from inside the vehicle. "I'm half Aborigine."

Steve looked at Al, Al at Steve. "So fucking what?" They both thought.

There was a large cage on the back of the truck into which they pushed their packs and then climbed, somewhat dubiously, into. They were each given a can of beer and watched happily as the hill drifted away behind them.

"It wasn't so big after all." Steve said, safe in the knowledge that they didn't have to walk up it.

At the farm the manager told them to come back on Monday to start work.

"There's no way I'm going all the way back to Berri and then back here on Monday." Steve said to Al as they walked back through the groves to where they had left their packs. He was right of course, so they set up camp close to some other tents of people who had been picking for some time.

Over the next few days they would get used to a routine that did not alter from morning to morning. From within a marquee that stood to their left there would come the early morning call of a loud New Zealand woman.

"Get up you lazy bastard! I get up early to cook you a fried breakfast and you're too fucking lazy to get up and eat it! I'm not going to do it anymore you lazy bastard! Come on! Get up! I want to be out in the fields before half past seven!"

This was followed by several groans from him as she kicked him until he crawled out of his bed and every morning they would leave for the fields before it was light.

To the right of Steve and Al were a young couple with a baby and a dog, there were lots of dogs here, much to Al's horror. The baby was well behaved, but the dogs would play chase around the tents, tripping over the ropes and chewing through them. Neither Al nor Steve were pleased by this, so they took to feeding the mangy mutts some disgustingly hot salami which neither of them could stomach, it had the desired effect of keeping the dogs quiet, even if only for a short time.

Monday morning arrived and they were eager to earn their fortunes before lunch.

"Steve," Al called from his tent. "It's quarter to seven."

"O.K." He called back.

It was still dark and Al lit the lamp, it was also cold. Steve came into Al's tent for his breakfast and cuppa and it was soon warm and cosy. They left the tent reluctantly and headed for the fields and were put to work on mandarins and after tasting one they lost no more time eating the fruit, which were bitter, dry and small. It was far too cold to stand around and eat fruit anyway. The attraction of earning money made both of them forget their mutual fear of heights. and they raced up the ladders, cutting at every orange berry in sight. Their spirits were high and they cheered each other along until Al emptied his first bucket into the bin. The fruit spilled out across the base of the large wooden box, they barely covered a quarter of it.

"Oh my God, this will take forever," he said under his breath.

By lunch it was quite hot and sunny and despite only having half the bin filled they kept each other reasonably happy.

"This is shit Al. I hope that we'll get faster."

"You're so right. It's not as if we've stopped and started all morning is it?"

Between moments when their ladders disappeared into the trees, falling towards the ground, with them following, they struggled on. By the end of the day they had just filled the bin and earned a massive forty dollars, between them! The second day was a repeat of the first and they were rapidly becoming disheartened and disillusioned, their arms covered in scratches from the thorns on the mandarin trees.

If the days were bad, then the nights were worse, long, dark and bitterly cold. They spent their evenings in Al's tent, Steve drinking tea and Al coffee and trying to look forward to their two minute noodles with anticipation. It wasn't much food, but it was enough and it was something hot to eat. Al studied a little German while Steve lay there listening to the radio, everytime Bedroom Eyes; his favourite song, played, a broad grin would stretch across his face and he would break out in song with the chorus. There was little else to do and boredom soon fell heavily upon them.

"We need a game to play." Steve announced.

Al thought about that for a second or two, what could they play?

"I know!" Al said excitedly. "You make a spinning top with some paper and a match stick, number it one to six and I'll draw a map of Europe and we'll have a game of war. It will be like you're back on the Rhine!" They laughed a dark sick laugh.

There was nothing else to do, so they invented their new game of Bomb The Shit Out Of You! They shared out the countries and marked on the map the size of the armies, there was one person for every million in real population, thus France had fifty five, West Germany had sixty five and so on. The object of the game was obviously to capture your opponent's countries by wiping out the entire population. The number killed was determined by the number on the spinning top and to make it a little more interesting some countries had nuclear weapons and when these were used the number spun was multiplied by ten. Once a country had been captured the victor received half the original number of people of that country to bolster his own armies. It was a crazy game, but they were cold and bored and there was nothing else to do on those long dark evenings.

The third day was to be their last day at fruit picking. They moved onto oranges and at first they were really excited by this. Psychologically it would make things easier as they would see the bins filling up much more quickly. However, the first hour was sheer hell, hands clasped around perfectly formed oranges which were firmly encrusted in a layer of ice. They could not use their fingers, they were too cold to bend. With teeth chattering and bodies frozen they tried to remove the fruit from the trees. By mid morning they were overjoyed by the temperature which was rapidly approaching twenty degrees, it was now a totally different experience. They were quite happy when by the time they had stopped for lunch the third bin was half full. The fourth was finished by late afternoon.

"That's enough Al. I just want a nice little factory job where you know exactly what you've earned before you even start. Fuck all this fruit nonsense."

"You're right Steve, forty eight dollars between two of us for a day's work is not enough.

"Let's leave when we get our wages."

With the decision made that they would be doing no more fruit picking they stayed up until midnight, keeping warm in Al's tent, Steve drinking his tea and Al his coffee, playing their war game. It still seemed strange to Al that he was lying in a tent with someone who was a complete stranger little over a month ago, now it felt natural to be spending so many hours together, it felt good to have a stable influence. Steve didn't panic, he was calm, he didn't let anything get him down for long and best of all, just like Al, he didn't really know what he was going to do with himself when the time came to leave Australia.

Steve didn't get up until he was sure the frost would have melted and the day had begun to warm, he came through to Al's tent about nine o'clock for his breakfast and cuppa; Al was already on his third cup, having got up an hour earlier and settled to his German. He had progressed from ich bin to konnen Sie mir empfehlen, wo man am besten isst? Good progress as far as he was concerned.

"It's so good not having to get up early and head off into the glaciated wastelands of Australia to pick oranges." Steve proclaimed his freedom from such poorly paid work. Forever.

Al smiled and smugly thought how good he felt at the moment.

Steve made him laugh, that northern accent still brought a grin to his face, though he was sure that none of this would be happening if he had known of Al's homosexuality, yes Al was sure of that. Society was so unfair to attach such a stigma to being different in the way that Al was different. It should have made no difference to him as a person as far as friendship was concerned. He wasn't after whatever Steve had hidden in his boxer-shorts. It wasn't any different to what Al had, he knew his biology. Just the thought of a homosexual is enough for so many people to assume that if you don't keep your backs covered you'd have one up you before you know about it. Was this really what Al was supposed to be like? Had something gone wrong with him that made him uninterested in screwing everything he could? Is that really what people thought of when they found out about his homosexuality? If it was then it would explain a lot about the reactions he had seen over the years. The pressure from society, straight and gay was pressure that Al could not deal with. He would not conform to anything that anyone might tell him he should be, how he should behave. Daily he had to question what it was to be homosexual, not because he had any doubts in his mind about himself, but because of the outside pressure, the supposed accountability and acceptability.

"We'll head into town soon, I hope we don't have to walk for long." Steve broke into Al's thoughts.

"O.K. then Steve. First stop skin cancer results." He liked Steve and decided that he would not tell him. If he didn't want it to be an issue, why make it into one by talking about it? It was a catch twenty two situation, guilt for not telling and guilt for telling. Why did the heterosexual world not understand? They were the people who produced homosexuals after all!

They set off for Berri and they did not have to walk far before they got a lift from a chap from Liverpool. He lived in Loxton which was fifteen Ks south of the farm and was adamant that he was staying in Australia. Neither Al nor Steve could imagine the change from Liverpool to a remote dusty little town in Australia, hundreds of miles from the nearest real town.

Steve was relieved to find that there was nothing cancerous in the moles which had grown on him. Al too was pleased. They walked back into town with nothing to do and no reason to return to the farm. So they strolled around the supermarket buying a few bits and pieces that they needed as well as a packet of custard cream biscuits, as a treat. Sitting by the river in the sun, drinking milk and eating biscuits, the little town quiet beside them, they relaxed and were comfortable in each other's company. The wooden bench and table absorbed the heat from the midday sun, under which they were both convinced they could improve their tans without the risk of cancer. The winter weather, once the morning frost had gone, was quite pleasant and neither of them would have wanted to be here in the heat of the summer, with millions of flies and thousands of city dwellers who, invaded the area at Christmas. The water of the Murray flowed past, greenish-yuck in colour, much like the Stour, but still a beautiful river. The paddle steamer was tied up. It looked like something out of Gone With The Wind. A survivor from an age of travel and way of life long since gone. The Proud Mary rocked gently in the current.

"This is the life Steve," Al stretched and felt the sun warm his chest.

"Yeah. I could do this forever," he answered wistfully, longing for life to be so straightforward and easy, to always have just enough money to never have to worry about anything.

In the office, the wages were being handed out, all hell had broken out when several people found themselves to be underpaid. Al and Steve quietly walked in and collected their pay cheque. One hundred and twenty eight dollars wasn't exactly a lot, but they had not paid tax or camp site fees. At long last the amount of money in their pockets grew, even if it would not last long.

Happier than they normally were during the cold dark evenings they played their game and knew that in the morning they would be on their way to Mildura. The thought of moving on felt good to them both, even if it meant no more free oranges, of which they had stuffed into their faces as many as they could bear.

It was early when they began to pack and when they were on the road walking towards town they had a lift in less than a minute with a man from Rumania. He had escaped from there four years ago after carefully planning his escape for a year before that.

"What kind of country was it that you had to escape from?" Al tried to imagine it, but could not. He had not escaped East Anglia, his was self imposed exile. A kind of hell in the middle of freedom.

Crossing the "rivermurrayberriferry"; as Steve liked to say it; as one word and as fast as he could, for the last time Al felt a little nostalgic about moving on from here, though he couldn't for the life of him work out why? It was a pleasant little town, but nothing more than that.

On the highway once again, they sorted themselves out and prepared to walk when another car stopped for them.

"We're going out to Renmark if that's any help to you two lads?"

"Yes!" Al answered somewhat surprised, not even having had time to hold out the sign and loving being called a lad. "That would be great. It's on our route."

Steve was wondering why hadn't he tried hitching earlier on in this visit, it was so easy. Berri now lay behind them, though there were still oranges to be seen, contrasting bright orange against the grey-blue of the Eucalyptus scrub. Within fifteen minutes they were once again at the side of the road, this time there was no immediate lift. Al walked further along and left Steve to take the first ride, whenever that would come.

An hour passed and Steve was totally pissed off, Al was used to it, though it had been some time since he had last played the waiting game. Two hours ticked slowly past and finally a car stopped and Steve went past, a smile of relief and a wave as he sailed past Al.

"At least he'll be in Mildura in a couple of hours." Al said to himself.

He stood waiting for a car to stop, never doubting for a moment that someone would pick him up. It was a sunny, but a cool day to be standing at the side of the road and today Al did not really want to do anything. He wanted to be away from other people, even Steve; not that he was bored with his company, he just needed time to be still with himself and re-think the events of the past few weeks. He wanted time to sit quietly and study his German, uninterrupted. To turn his thoughts to Tony, Christopher, Steven and Phil and away from himself. A car stopped. It was only going to be a short lift, as far as the next village, but it all helped.

On a wide dusty verge, at the edge of some small settlement Al could see Steve, waiting, longing for a lift to Mildura.

"Fancy seeing you here."

"Yes fancy that!" Steve was not happy. "I can't believe how long this is taking, Al."

Al just laughed, it was not news to him, but almost a way of life.

They chatted for a while, then Al moved further along the road. Hadn't he been thinking how he wanted to be alone for a while? Now he was thinking how lucky he was to be with Steve. It was good to share a joke, some good times, some not so good times. It was good that at the end of the day he was not alone, not a stranger in a crowded hostel, camp site or town. He had a friend with whom to share the events of the day that had passed. Steve was someone to see new sights with, hadn't that been what Al had so often yearned for? Someone to share time with.

A car stopped by Al, it was sleek, red and sporty. Inside, a young man, about Al's age, looked intently into Al's eyes as he leaned into the open window.

"I'm only going about fifteen Ks up the road. You're welcome to a ride." He was giving Al the feeling that sex was the type of ride he was after.

Al wondered why he had stopped for him and not for Steve? In other circumstances he would have accepted the lift and not worried how far he got or where he found himself, but something inside his head told him to stick with Steve and he thanked the driver, but refused. Al watched the car disappear out of sight. He was sure that he knew what the driver wanted, he was naive, but not that naive!

"He was quite dishy, I suppose... Um, that's enough of a reason to refuse a lift, one never knows where that might lead." Al only wanted a lift and definitely not a ride!

The air began to cool as a breeze got up, red dust swirled in an eddy of air and danced on the warm tarmac before dying amongst some trees. The sun, midday now gone, began to fall in the sky. It would be late afternoon when they would get to Mildura, if they got that far. Steve kicked at the red sand beneath his feet, he was so bored and very impatient of waiting. It seemed like he had always been waiting for a lift in this depressingly quiet part of Australia. Things began to happen an hour or so later when a car finally stopped. Al watched a man and woman get out to help Steve put his pack in the boot of the car. It was such a small car, but it was a lift. Steve was smiling as they talked, then he called to Al. They were both going to get a lift. Al picked up his pack and ran as fast as he could with the weight. Soon they were on their way. Squashed in the rear of the car Steve and Al were happy. The man driving was a real dip-stick; arrogant and obnoxious, totally condescending towards the woman who appeared to be frightened of him, too frightened to answer him back. The bush drifted along and the engine of the little car screamed as it tried to climb the hills. Barely thirty kilometres from Renmark the engine, rebelling against the punishing treatment being given to it, died. The car rolled to a halt close to the top of a hill and the stones beneath the tyres crunched. It stopped. Steve and Al looked at each other and both thought it was not really surprising. The bloke was a complete and utter waste of time and he proceeded to emit a continuous stream of obscenities from his mouth. No one else said a word, but all thought, "what a plonker!"

"We'll have to walk back to the roadhouse we passed at the border and phone for a tow truck," the woman said to the travellers. "What will you do?"

"We'll just have to try and get a lift from here." Al answered.

"I'm sure you'll get a lift, no one would leave you out here."

Al wasn't so sure about that and quite frankly he didn't care, he was so glad to be out of the car, and in a few seconds he knew he would be free of that male chauvinist arse hole.

Steve and Al walked up to the top of the hill. The couple walked back to the service station. Who knew how far back it was? Who cared? There were a few cars on the road, but only a few and none stopped. An hour passed, then two. It was all pretty hopeless.

* * * * *

Tony had arrived in Geraldton, he was totally unimpressed with the hick town in which he stood. He looked around, small-town mentality was written across the faces of the people who were on the streets. He stood looking, he was tired from the four hundred kilometre journey up from Perth, a journey which he did not desperately want to make, he did it out of necessity. The necessity was a job, money, food, survival. Unshaven and not having eaten a real meal for six days, scrounging from other tourists what he could, stealing fruit from a shop whenever the opportunity arose, he was surviving. He picked up his pack and walked long the street to where he could see a telephone box from where he would call the number which was scribbled on a piece of paper stuffed into the top pocket of his jacket, the number which would supply him with somewhere to sleep, work, food and money. The number was that of a slaughter house.

He dialled the number and spoke to Glenn. He was expected and all was well. He had to wait where he was and he would be collected in fifteen minutes or so. He sat on the kerb, resting his back against the phone box, oblivious to the sound of a woman making a phone call inside the booth. It was dry, the sun setting red in the west, cool. The road still had puddles of water from a heavy shower earlier today. Tony looked deeply into one, lost in his thoughts. He recalled seeing Al looking into the Gipping from the bridge on Princes Street, so many months ago. He had looked so depressed then, now Tony knew something of how he must have been feeling as he himself, now at a low ebb in his life, was having similar thoughts.

"Life's a bitch," he said spitting into the puddle, a series of ripples expanded out and across the surface of the water and lapped at the dirt on the tarmac, knocking at it again and again, just like life knocked at anyone it could, again and again until there was no more resistance.

"I hope Al is alright. I hope he hasn't done anything stupid... No, he would have been dead before Port Augusta if he was going to kill himself." he sighed with relief. "But you never know with him. I've never met anyone so unpredictable and irrational before. God it pisses me off, when you think that you know someone and they go and do something totally unexpected."

Glenn arrived, Tony got into the shaky old truck and they got to know each other a little as they drove back to what was to be Tony's new home for the foreseeable future.

"Brad says you're a good bloke and that's good enough for me, even if you are a Pom!" Glenn said.

Tony hated the way that Australians seemed to think that they were better than everyone else. It appeared that being British was being the fourth lowest life form in existence; the next three down being kiwis, Orientals in general and Japanese in particular, it was amusing to think that the Japanese were buying Australia from the Aussies who were willing to sell anything for a quick profit and then piss it all up against the wall. The lowest of all life forms was a live Abo, dead ones being better than live Poms anyday! The longer Tony stayed in Australia the deeper his contempt for Australians grew. Life was so easy and so good for them and it seemed that they were the only ones who didn't know it.

Weeks passed and Tony got used to the sight of frightened, dying and dead animals. He got used to the blood and guts. He got used to the feeling of meat which was hot, but uncooked, but never got used to the stench of death, or being the bringer of death on such a massive scale. He had killed rabbits and pheasants when he was a gamekeeper, he had killed vermin. He had killed and blood was on his hands, but the slaughter he now witnessed and was party to was different. He lost count of how many animals he butchered, he tried not to think about it, thinking instead of having a beer or two at the end of the shift. It was the only sanity for him.

So it was that he had a job and he had certainly needed it. He had a bed; in fact his own little room, basic, but comfortable and his own. He had as much food as he could eat and he had lots of money to spend on beer. Day after day, week after week he drank and drank and at the end of a month he had only saved two hundred dollars. He drank too much and his wages just lasted longer than a week.

At night he woke up thinking of blooded animals, hot and stinking and in amongst the dead warm flesh he could see his own naked body, blood stained in heap of meat, drowning in a pool of blood. He called for his girlfriend, frustrated that it had been so long since he had seen her; the only girl whom he had ever loved. Frustrated that it had been a couple of months since he had last had sex. He masturbated, but from it came no relief. Frightened since spending that week in Sydney having sex with a girl who injected for her kicks and that girl in Perth who didn't need to be talked into sex, so easy. Yes he had had the H.I.V. test in Melbourne and it was negative, but didn't they say that it could take up to three months to show infection? What if he had got it? The nightmares continued, sex, dead animals and the ever growing need for more alcohol. Why?

Weeks had passed like this and he expected it every night, but every night it was just as horrifying as the first nightmare had been. Waking up dripping with cold sweat, uncomfortable, frightened, confused; he would smoke a joint, but it didn't help. He would masturbate, but that gave no relief and even less comfort and now even alcohol wasn't doing its job because each time he needed more and more before it would have any effect.

He ran a towel gently down his body, lifting the sweat and cum from his flesh. He could do with a friend now, he needed help. There was no one.

"I've got to get out of here. I can't..." Tony could see how being here was affecting his physical and mental health, he could only take so much. His resolve to escape this situation was strong, such was the torment he was in. He knew that there was no point just leaving and ending up in Perth in a state where he had to take whatever job came along, that could lead him into a worse situation, though he couldn't quite think of a worse one than the one he was in now. He finished drying himself.

"Two weeks, then I'll go. No more drink until I get out of here."

His problems were not down to the horrors of the slaughter house. It just aggravated his fears and allowed him to focus on himself too intently. Alcohol was his biggest enemy and he saw it for what it was, but was not strong enough to do anything about it for long.

For two weeks he suffered from no alcohol. The nightmares still continued, slaughtered animals, the cold sweats, thoughts of his girlfriend, the girls he had screwed, AIDS, masturbation, cannabis. Anything that held a little comfort he grabbed at, a wank or a smoke, but he resisted alcohol until the last day of the two weeks then he could resist no more.

He woke from a drunken stupor a full day afterwards. He was feeling more than a little rough, more than a little fragile, but despite his present incapacity he packed his things and walked the eight kilometres into town. He stopped for an hour in a little café for a pot of coffee and something light to eat before walking through town trying to hitch a lift south.

* * * * *

The two tents stood close together, in front of which a large fire was burning. Al poured the water into their mugs, tea for Steve, coffee for himself. It was routine now. The fire lit the bush around them, the sounds of burning wood broke the stillness of the night. Behind the bright orange-yellow of the flames the shadows of the trees merged into blackness and nothing. Insects were lit up by the light, but were kept away by the heat and smoke. Al sat on a stone by the front of his tent and Steve lay in his with only his head and arms bathing in the warmth, he was stripping the bark from a supple forked stick, with which he was going to cook some toast.

"I could get used to this Steve." Al said dream-like, gazing at the dancing flames.

"Yeah. I know what you mean." He pushed a slice of bread onto the end of his stick and held it in front of the fire. The aroma of toasted bread floated around them as it quickly cooked. Steve bit into a slice and passed the stick to Al.

"How about staying here tomorrow?"

Steve thought about Al's suggestion, they were both disappointed by the day's hitching, it had not been successful to say the least.

"Why not?" Steve answered after some thought and after another slice of toast.

For hours after dusk had fallen they stayed by the fire, occasionally talking, but mainly in silence and thought, eyes captured by the flames which grew smaller as the hours passed. The mountain of embers glowed as brightly as the moon which was full and when the fire had died to little more than a few small flames the two travellers retired for the night. It was not such an unsuccessful day after all.

Al slept soundly, waking only a couple of times in the early hours of the morning before finally getting up about eight. Peeling open the flysheet he eased his head out into the crisp freshness of a new morning. The litter on the soil from the trees above glistened with a million tiny droplets of moisture, leaves, twigs and soil alike. It wouldn't be warm for another hour, so the first thing to do was remake the fire. Scrapping away at the grey ashes to reveal the centre of the fire, a still glowing heart, pumping heat out at Al like his heart pumping blood around his body. Picking up a pile of damp sticks, he rebuilt the fire and sat and watched it steam and smoke, there was no breeze and it rose vertically through the branches which over hung their camp. He felt the warmth and remembered two years previous; during the week when it had snowed so much and then drifted even more. The week East Anglia came to a standstill. Ipswich was cut off from the outside world. Al could not get to college, Steven could not get to school. For a week they sat by the fire, reading, listening to music, watching the flames, watching each other, making love. Flames of fire were as sensual as flames of love. Al could smell and taste Steven's body within the burning wood here in the Australian bush, Eucalyptus smelt sweet as apple. He could still feel his hot flesh next to his own.

"Yes please, I'd love a cuppa." Steve called from his tent when he heard Al pouring the water into the saucepan; interrupting his thought; dangerous thoughts of times past.

"Water's on." Al thought how lucky he was to be with Steve. He was glad of heterosexual company. There was nothing to be afraid of with him, no misreading the situation. No pressure. Though there was the deceit and that was difficult for Al to cope with. He wanted to have no secrets from his friend.

"I'm having a fried breakfast. Toasted salami, fried bread and toast with cheese melted all over it!" He drawled on the all.

Steve got up at the sound and smell of food. Al stuffed his face and drank his coffee.

"I could murder some bacon."

"Oh Steve! Did you have to go and say that? I kept imagining that I could smell some beautiful smoked Danish back and it was really depressing to accept that we hadn't got any."

Steve laughed, with Al, not at him; he understood only too well, he licked his lips, he could taste bacon. Imagination can be so cruel.

"It's a pity you can't do this in Britain, isn't it Steve."

"Yeah. There's always someone telling you not to do this, you can't do that. It really pisses me off."

This was as near to freedom that Steve and Al had ever come, All they needed was food and water and they could have done this for weeks, unfortunately, food and water were several kilometres away and one of them would have to make that trek today. Steve said that he would make the journey to the roadhouse and Al would collect enough firewood for the rest of the day and night.

It was obviously further to the roadhouse than either had realised and Steve was gone a long time. A mountainous pile of wood was stacked close to the tents by the time he did return and it was once again time to eat, this made Al reasonably happy. It was here that Al invented his triple Cooper burger, which consisted of layers of toast, cheese, fried bread, toasted salami, more toast, cheese, fried bread, more salami and finally toast! The Cooper came from Cooper's Ale of Adelaide, Steve's favourite drink.

"Each layer freshly cooked by my own fair hands, on an open fire in the middle of nowhere in particular. This is what I call good bush tucker!" Al exclaimed before sinking his teeth into the mountain of food held firmly with a deathlike grip, he was risking dropping none of it.

"How the hell do you manage to fit all that into your mouth?" You eat so much and yet you're so thin. There must be an army of tapeworms in your stomach."

"I'm a growing lad, besides, I don't eat anywhere near the amount that I used to eat."

Steve couldn't imagine anyone being able to eat more than Al without being twenty eight stone overweight.

They ate and drank their way through the day and well into the evening. In the distance they could hear the sound of cows mooing. Above them another crystal clear sky, a million, or maybe several millions of stars shone down onto a world falling into sleep. Through the tree tops a light breeze blew and on the air was carried a faint scent of Eucalyptus oils. The cows came close to the fence and Steve was unnerved by them.

"Go away! Go on, go away you stupid animals. Don't you come here. Look at that lovely big field you've got. Why don't you go and explore it?" Steve shouted at them and Al thought it was funny to listen to his northern accent. He loved that sound, he was fascinated by it. He wondered if the cattle had ever heard such a sound before? They were not particularly impressed by Steve's display and came closer to the fence. Steve was more than a little upset by their refusal to move and he gave a deep sigh as he grabbed a large stick from the fire; which was burning at one end, he waved it about, above his head. The flame, swaying back and forth through the blackness of night looked ten times bigger than it really was and the cows moved back at the sight of it. Then, to Al's horror, Steve threw it into the air. The orange-yellow flaming stick spun around and around as it rose higher and higher into the blackness. Spinning, spinning, up and up it went, almost in a slow frame-by-frame movement. Al caught hold of his breath and couldn't let it go, eyes fixed onto the stick which continued to somersault as it climbed. The cows turned, a few hundred hooves thumped together onto the hard sand and grass as they turned and ran into the night, away from the danger of fire. Reaching as high as it could go, the burning stick seemed to stop for a brief moment as it changed direction and began its descent to Earth. It fell heavily, less gracefully than it had risen, an uncontrolled collapse followed by a thud as it hit the ground, a puff of smoke billowed up, grey and white, a soft sizzle of fire and water as the moisture held onto the blades of grass after an earlier light shower extinguished the flame.

Steve returned to his tent and calmed down now that the cows had gone. Al was left with a cold feeling. What Steve had done was so stupid and potentially dangerous. Hadn't he seen a herd of cattle before? Didn't he understand the risks of fire in this country?

"Let's stay here tomorrow, Al. It's not costing anything to be here."

Al didn't need any convincing, he thought that it was an excellent idea, the best thing Steve had said in the six weeks that they had been together.

It was into another cool morning that Al crawled out to from his warm tent. He sat by the fire and although it again looked dead, even the sand around it radiated out heat. He sat still, in contemplation of being where he was. On the one hand it seemed like the most natural thing to be in the bush, at the edge of a cattle ranch, at the beginning of a wilderness, but on the other hand it was so alien to everything he had known during the previous twenty six years of his life. He longed to see Wolves Wood again, to smell the rich scents of the humus filled leaf litter, the scent of young leaves in the spring after a heavy shower. To hear the Nightingale's song fill the air, rising above the symphony of sound from a host of other singing birds. A movement below ground of a mole pushing up soil from its tunnels, a shrew darting amongst wet grasses in search of something tasty to eat. Pale yellow of primrose, purple of orchid. Lush green shoots of fresh grass racing towards the light in a bid to seed before rabbit and deer arrive. The smooth bark of young hornbeam, strong, firm, sensual, its grey-green bark cool and satin-like to his touch. The sway of oak canopy, still leafless after the winter, buds fat, ready to burst any day. Bugle and ground ivy rambling across the mud. Ponds full, water dark, a splash, a frog jumping. The drumming of a not too distant lesser-spotted woodpecker announcing its presence so clearly through the thick coppice stands. The squeal of a rabbit, taken by fox.

"Haven't you got the fire going yet?" Steve was watching Al as he lost himself in his world of East Anglian woodland. Al smiled to Steve and proceeded to dig a hole in the centre of the ashes, which still glowed red. He sat the pan of water on it and soon steam rose up and the water boiled. They ate for an hour or so, then collected their towels and headed off to the roadhouse. It took over an hour to walk there, a couple of cars had passed, neither stopped. As soon as they arrived they rushed into the showers. It felt wonderful to have hot water flowing over their bodies again, like kids playing in the rain, laughing beneath the dancing water, the dust and smoke rinsed away, silky smooth skin, soft hair, freshness. Heaven. They left the showers as three livestock trucks arrived, loaded with sheep. Stench filled the air. Al and Steve went into the shop and bought some milk and sat drinking while they mustered the energy for the walk back. The young lad at the counter filled their water bottles for them and they sat listening to the conversations of the people who had driven past them earlier in the morning. Their cars were prisons in which they were safe from the outside world, safe from all harm by murderous hitch-hikers, now in the café they were less smug, less superior, they shared the space around themselves, but they were not at any risk. Could they not see that their fears created a world of expanding fears, a world of contracting freedoms. Cars, mobile prisons.

> *"Here in my car,*
> *I feel safest of all,*
> *I can lock all my doors,*
> *It's the only way to live,*
> *In cars."*

Steve sat staring at these selfish people who could so easily drive past someone walking in a remote area.

"No offer of help, not even a kiss my arse! How would they feel if their car had broken down and no one stopped to help them? They'd see life from a different angle then!"

The door opened and a whiff of sheep shit swirled into the café riding on the air turbulence caused by the opening door. The three truck drivers ordered some food and gave Al and Steve disapproving looks, sending some unfriendly comments about using all the hot water. Al and Steve spoke quietly and waited another ten minutes before starting on the long walk back to the tents.

Clean, fresh and feeling generally good, they took their time as they walked back, not wanting to work up a sweat as they were loaded with water and wet towels, extra weight. There was nothing to hurry back for, only food and relaxation.

It seemed strange to need a break from travelling, from not working, but the life style that they had both slipped into was mentally draining as neither were willing travellers. Al running from his past and Steve running from not being able to get a job in the depressed northeast after five years in the army. The reality of the real world of civilian life in recession hit Britain was not easy for him to deal with.

They relaxed, they ate, they talked. Steve telling Al about the things he would get up to in the army in Germany, all on tax payers money while supposedly defending the realm. It was through the army that he came to be in Australia, during a stint on night duty and being absolutely bored he made up a number and phoned Australia, simply because it was daytime there. He got through to a company in Sydney and was passed from department to department until he got through to a girl called Joni who could not believe that he was in the British army in Germany and was phoning just to pass the time of day, or rather night. It was an invitation from her that put the idea of a trip to Oz in Steve's head and the economy of Britain which motivated him into going. A few months later he was here.

Early, but not too early; Steve was not a morning person, unlike Al, they packed and walked through the trees and back to the road. Neither wanted to leave, but they needed to get a job some time and that was the driving force within them now. Gone, the lazy evenings of gazing into the fire in the darkness of night. Gone the freedom of putting their tents up in the bush to wonder at the stars above. Gone. Heading back towards the roadhouse, from where they hoped it would prove easier to get a lift than it would be out in no man's land, a car passed at high speed, two young girls looked out at them.

"Oh come on girls, we won't hurt you." Al said.

"They won't stop."

"They will." Al answered as they turned to watch the car continue along the road and into the distance. They walked. A car slowed from behind them, then turned and stopped at the side of the road. The girls had come back!

Within the hour they were in Mildura, within two they were in a camp site and Al went for a shower.

"Al! They've got a bath. I haven't had a bath for so long I'm going for a long hot soak."

"I'll be in the laundry when you get out."

You can be on holiday for as long as you like, but there were always jobs to be done and washing clothes would rarely wait and he rubbed at his shirt collars before putting them into a machine. A tall, slightly heavy young woman started to chat to him and after a couple of minutes he realised that he was being chatted up. The smiles and glances flew in his direction. At first Al wasn't quite sure how to react, so he played it as innocently as he could. This excited the woman, she had a good catch here, a young lad, so obviously not very experienced. Al had never been chatted up by a woman before, he still didn't realise that Grete had been after him. It felt completely alien, unnatural, improper. She was not unattractive, but not attractive either, but did nothing to excite Al. What would he do with a woman? He felt a little disgusted at the thought of having sex with the opposite sex, just as he imagined many people felt about two people of the same sex having sex together. His world was so different from mainstream life. She continued to try to lead him on. She became more obvious, then blatantly obvious.

"Why don't you come over for a glass of wine after you finish here? I'm in number five."

"Oh, that would be very nice. I'd like that."

"Good. I'll send the kids out to play in the park for a while. I've got two kids, single parent. My ex is up in Queensland."

"I'll just get my washing out on the line then I'll be over."

"I'll be waiting." She said, smiled and left.

Al tried to contain his laughter as he waited for his washing to finish.

Steve came into the laundry after finishing his bath. Now had Steve been the one to chat him up he might have been a little more responsive, though only a little. A sexual relationship, long term, short term or just a quick screw was the last thing he needed in his life. No, even if it had been a man, a good looking man, Al would not have been so impressed.

"That was so good Al. I can't remember the last time I had a bath."

"It was a pleasant experience was it?"

"Decidedly so."

"I've just been invited around for a glass of wine by a woman from one of the vans. Fancy a glass of wine?"

"Yeah. I'll not say no to free alcohol."

"That's what I thought you'd say."

"You didn't waste much time chatting up the local talent."

"Talent she is not; and it was she who did the chatting up. I didn't tell her I was with you, but you may as well come along. It will teach her a lesson and maybe she'll be a little less eager to pick up young men!"

Steve put his washing into a machine and Al hung his on the line to dry. It was late morning when Al knocked on the door of the caravan. The sun was warming the day up nicely, shorts and T-shirt weather again. The door opened. The smile that was worn by Julie fell from her face when she saw two people at her door. Al quickly introduced Steve and added how kind it was of her to invite them around for a drink, thus catching her off guard. Had he mentioned this blond haired boy to her? Had she told him to bring him too? She didn't think so, she couldn't remember. She looked at the table, two glasses stood there, one clean, one empty apart from the telltale signs of wine recently having filled it, but since drunk. They went in. She got another glass out of the cupboard.

"It's alright kids, you don't have to go out if you don't want to." Her tone conveyed her disappointment, she wasn't going to be rooted; as it's so politely put in Australia, this morning.

A short silence and uneasiness hung over them while she sorted out what was happening, then proceeded to tell them how nicely she was doing living from social welfare. She ran a car, smoked and drank heavily, enjoyed evenings out regularly and saved a good amount each week.

"If I run out of cash I just go to St. Vinies and say that I can't feed the kids. I get enough from them to pay for my cigarettes and booze! You ought to try it, I'm going over there this afternoon if you want to come along?"

Al and Steve thought they had nothing to lose, so they said they'd give it a go. Neither of them liked the idea, but money was disappearing too fast to be proud. Steve went to hang his sleeping bag on the line, so it would be dry by the time that they got back. Upon opening the washing machine a mass of feathers flew out at him, his bag had split. It looked like the duck hunting season had begun and he was not pleased about it, or Al's almost hysterical laughter.

They stood in the charity shop, uncomfortably looking at the racks of clothing, silent. They waited while Julie marched her kids into the office and sat pleading poverty. Ten minutes later she came out smiling.

"I'll see you back at the park," she whispered as she passed them without looking at them.

Steve went in next and after just a few minutes he came out, quite unhappy. He was controlling his excitement really well, Al thought as it was his turn to be led into the office. His stomach sank as he began to plead poverty, not having to lie outright, just stretching the truth to its limits.

"I only got five dollars Steve," Al said as soon as they were a safe distance from the shop.

"I didn't get anything!"

"What?"

"He told me to go to the refuge!"

Al laughed. "It's you rich northerners! You look far too healthy and everyone knows that all the money is up that way."

"Huh! And you reckon that there's no north/south divide."

"There isn't. Some of US are meant to have money and some of YOU are not! It's very simple really."

"You jammy bastard."

"I know. Life's so unfair isn't it!"

They found no work in Mildura; not to say that they looked very hard. So two days later they were standing at the side of the road once again. Destination Bendigo. Steve felt like he had been hitch-hiking forever, Al just took it in his stride and didn't think about it. It took a few hours for Steve to get a lift and another hour before Al was on his way. It was going to be one of those days again. A young woman from New Zealand took Al a few miles further on and was very apologetic that she could not take him any further.

"It all helps," he said, "a few less kilometres to walk if that's what it comes to."

Half an hour later another car stopped.

"You haven't got very far have you?"

"No not really." Al responded to the man's cheerful face.

"I saw you and your mate this morning when I came into town. If we see him along the road I'll pick him up."

Ninety kilometres to the south, Al saw Steve standing at the side of the road, watching a man paste up an advertisement on a huge roadside board. They stopped and Steve swapped cars. Shortly after dark they were dropped off at a camp site at Marong. Steve and Al thought that this was an outer suburb of Bendigo, they were later to find out that they were fifteen kilometres north of the city centre.

Al went into the office to pay while Steve unloaded their things from the car. Saying thanks and goodbye to the driver they walked into the chilly darkness of the camp site and found somewhere to pitch.

"It's going to be minus two tonight Steve."

"What? Are you sure?"

"I heard it on the radio, it was definitely minus two."

"God, even two above sounds cold."

The past two weeks had been colder than the Australia they both had got used to.

"You can sleep in my tent if you want Steve. It will be warmer with two people in one tent, especially for someone who has lost half of their feathers from their sleeping bag." Al laughed, he couldn't help but picture the sight of flying feathers in the laundry.

"Yeah alright, you don't have to rub it in."

"You must admit it was funny when you opened the washing machine and all those feathers came flying out."

"No! You wouldn't be laughing if it happened to you."

"I know! That's why I'm laughing now...Quack quack!"

"Oh Arse holes to you!"

It was a cold evening, so after a hot shower they ran back to the tent, which was not too cool after many hours of burning butane. Al undressed and slipped into his sleeping bag, barely two feet from where another man was undressing ready for the coming night. He was a little nervous of this. Steve was nearly as ill at ease as Al was and that took the pressure off Al. Al stripped and slipped into his sleeping bag, safe in the knowledge that Steve wasn't after sex.

Steve kept his boxers on, he wasn't totally sure, but this helped Al feel safer.

"What would Steve do right now if he did know I'm a poof?" Al thought and an image of horror flashed through his mind, before he could dispel it. He was glad to think of Steve as an old friend, he felt almost safe in his company. The short passage of time in which their friendship had existed, was quality time, understanding and helpful time. Years of getting to know another human being had been crammed into a month and a half.

"Thank God for Steve being heterosexual," Al thought as he stretched out in his sleeping bag. It gave him a warm feeling. "It would be nice to be able to do this with Christopher, maybe have a holiday together." It would never happen though, no matter how much Christopher cared for Al he would never find himself in the situation of going away for a holiday or short break, let alone sharing a tent with him. If Steve knew the truth he would be in his own tent now, freezing alone rather than sharing with a poof, that's what it all boiled down to when all is said and done. A poof is a poof is a poof and not to be trusted, they are all after the same thing and how could any self respecting heterosexual man knowingly put himself in such a dangerous situation as sleeping in the same room, or tent, as one of them?

"It feels like I've always been in Australia now," Steve said. Al thought he sounded as if he was reflecting on something he was missing.

"Do you miss home Steve?" Al asked, helping to keep the silence away just a little longer.

"No. I miss my friends though," he paused and searched his feelings, held them in check. "I wish they were here with me. I don't like many of the Aussies that I've met, wankers, rich wankers who don't know how lucky they are. Brits are far more down to Earth."

"Knowing that you're so far from your friends is hard. Not knowing if you will ever see them again..." Would he ever return to East Anglia? "It sounds like you miss some of them a lot, Steve?" Al tried to be tactful.

"I think I'll asked Joni if she'll marry me so I never have to go back," Steve said with an air of urgency. Didn't he want to go back to his friends? Al had scratched at a sore nerve and it was evident that there was pain there, though he had no idea what the cause of it was and Steve had no desire to talk about it.

The night was not as cold as they feared, two people in a tent help to keep the temperature up. The morning however, most definitely was. Al got dressed, Steve was still half asleep and Al tried to be quiet as he unzipped the inner tent. A rush of cold air fell in towards him, it was much colder outside. He reached for the zip on the flysheet and it ran along the teeth to the top. The nylon stood rigid,

Al pushed, it cracked, falling back on itself, rigid with hoar frost. Overnight it had dropped to minus two, if not lower. His green tent sat white under a heavy frost, his footsteps crushed a trail in the grass behind him. His breath rushed forth as the smoke from a monster steam engine, express through East Anglia on the mainline towards Scotland. It was bloody cold.

They kept themselves busy until mid morning, drinking hot tea and coffee, Steve listening to his radio, Al studying his German; lesson six, progress, slow, but progress. They went to the main road and waited for a bus to take them into town, none came, so they hitched in and it was now that they realised how far they were from town.

Central Bendigo was a pleasant surprise, it had many fine examples of good Victorian and Edwardian architecture. It had character and charm of a sort which Al liked, a charm that most towns in Australia seemed to lack. Al wanted to spend time, as long as it took; a day, days, or a week, to explore, feel, see, to experience this old gold rush town that had not yet been destroyed by greed and progress, yes progress; where the almighty dollar is king. Any development is the way forward. Change for the sake of change and any loss is of no importance. Now he could deal with being alone. Now he could deal with his time and his self. They stumbled upon some progress in the form of a hideous building which served as the cathedral. Also some very typical Australian shops. Australia has these single storey flat roofed characterless boxes, Britain had the ignominy of the nineteen sixties. So much for world progress and development!

"Shall we see how much it costs to get to Melbourne by train?" Steve was thinking ahead, he didn't want to hitch again.

"Yeah O.K. Steve."

It was only two o'clock when they got to the station and as it was only thirteen dollars for the fare they decided to book their tickets for Sunday. That would mean staying another day in Marong; it would be cheaper to stay here rather than be in Melbourne, especially on a day on which they would not be able to do any job hunting. They continued to look around and time ticked past.

"Steve, it's four o'clock. We ought to be heading back now, in case it proves hard to get a lift." Al must have had a premonition of what was to come, though he gave it no more thought.

Walking through the town carrying two bags of shopping each, they were not totally surprised by the number of cars passing them by.

"Honestly! These fat Aussie wankers, they can see that we've been to the supermarket, they must realise that we're not going too far, but far enough to hitch a lift. Why won't the bastards stop?"

"Because they are rich and selfish Steve. Because everyone on this planet wants to steal their precious motor cars from them and rob them and kill them. The whole world is on the take except for themselves. They are too selfish and stupid to realise that the world is not as they have decided in their petty little minds that it is. In short, as you said, they are indeed wankers!"

Steve didn't want to walk more than a hundred metres, he demanded that some kind person should stop and give them a lift. If only life was that straightforward.

They walked for an hour, the dark was beginning to close in and the temperature was dropping rapidly. Their hands were cold, so cold that they hurt, their heavy plastic shopping bags cut into their fingers, tips blue from both cold and restricted circulation. They were not dressed for the coming evening.

"Fucking arse holes!" Steve shouted as another two cars passed them by. "Why don't they stop Al? Look at those fat bastards in their empty cars! Look at them! I hate these selfish bastards!"

Steve was suffering and if Al was cold then Steve was feeling even more so. So cold that he could have cried. The walking did not bother Al. He had walked a lot in the past few months. None of these cars owners were going to get to him, but Steve did bother him. Al felt confusion about the feelings he was having for Steve, who was not used to the walking game, who was not used to isolation and hardship of any sort. He had been having a five and a half year long piss-up. The knowledge that they were nowhere near to where they were heading, with bugger all chance of getting a lift as it grew darker and darker was something that Steve seemed unable to deal with. What could he do to help him?

"Come on Steve, you've got to walk faster, we must be halfway by now. No one is going to stop for us Steve. It's only us here and if we don't hurry we are going to freeze." Al didn't believe that they were anywhere near half way, but he couldn't tell Steve that.

It was night proper. It was cold. The thought of being out in the open with no tent, no sleeping bag, nothing, did not appeal to Al at all.

"I'm stopping here," Steve said, sounding utterly dejected and totally defeated. He stood at the side of the road, crushed by merely the thought of the task ahead, the selfish motorists, the cold.

Al felt lost, his fingers were so cold he wanted to cry with the pain, plastic digging deeper into numb fingers. He wanted to Steve to help him by walking and not standing broken on the road verge. The tall Eucalyptus stood still and silent above them, nothing in nature stirred.

"Come on Steve," he said softly, with love, compassion. You can't stay here, you have to keep moving. If we walk fast we'll be there in half an hour, it's much warmer to keep walking." Al put his bags down, relief from the weight on his arms, his fingers knew no difference, they were so cold. He stepped close to Steve, putting his arm around him. Why was he standing here getting colder trying to coax Steve into movement, instead of leaving him there to fend for himself ? If he really wanted to stay in the bush why didn't he leave him? He could not leave his friend. If Steve was determined to stay in the bush, which was absolute madness, then he would have to stay with him. He would not desert him. He could not desert his friend.

With his left arm around Steve and his shopping heavy in the other hand, he encouraged Steve to keep walking, urged him on with hopes of how they would soon be in a hot shower, hot tea, a warm tent and a warm sleeping bag. Words of friendship, of love. Al tried to understand how someone who had been in the army for five years could find it so mentally destroying to cover a mere fifteen kilometres now? He asked no questions of Steve, there was something that he did not understand and he did not want to open old wounds by an interrogation when Steve was at his weakest. He was here for him if he wanted to talk.

Al tried to set a pace for Steve to keep up with, he slowly moved ahead, but Steve did not walk faster in order to keep up, he merely dropped behind, so Al had to slow down every few dozen metres for fear that Steve might lose heart. They walked, it seemed like an hour for each minute that passed.

"Look Steve!" Al shouted, pointing into the darkness ahead. "The level crossing."

"What level crossing?" Steve said. "I can't see a fucking thing out here."

Al could see clearly the warning sign up ahead, about a hundred metres or so.

"I don't remember any level crossing when we came into town."

"I saw it on a map that I glanced at while we waited to cross a road." Al could not remember crossing any rail tracks this morning either and the horrific thought flashed through his head that they might be on the wrong road bounced around in his head, but it couldn't be, he remembered the map clearly, he saw it for at least ten seconds and he had a thing about maps, his mind retained that sort of information. He couldn't be wrong, could he?

"The village is just around the corner. We're here Steve, we're here." Al tried to sound enthusiastic to urge Steve on for the final few minutes.

"I still can't see a sodding thing and I don't know how you can." Steve wanted to believe Al more than anything he had ever wanted. Ever. Ever. Ever! But he couldn't see a thing, all he knew was that he was so cold it no longer hurt. He wanted to just sit down and not walk anymore.

Steve didn't see the level crossing until they were almost upon it, a relief to Al.

"It's not far now, just around the corner Steve."

The bend in the road continued around, it felt like it went a full three hundred and sixty degrees. The road straightened, there was the village. Al was so happy to be here, more for Steve than for himself. He had seen how Steve was suffering, but couldn't imagine it at all. Steve was now so happy he didn't know whether to laugh or cry. To jump up and down or to hug and dance with Al. How the hell had he got him to keep walking?

"I bet I have a longer hot shower than you do, Al."

"I don't doubt you, Steve. I don't doubt you at all."

Saturday came and went and they never left the security of the tent for more than half an hour at a time. Sunday dawned, just as cold, just as unfriendly and by ten o'clock they were standing at the side of the road waiting for a lift into town. They thought that they should start early, so there was plenty of time to walk, if it came to that. It turned out to be as easy to get a lift as it had been in Berri and they sat in the station for six hours waiting for the train to Melbourne.

"I'm sure Steve is going to find Melbourne harder to cope with than I did all those months ago." Al shivered at his thoughts, his memories of panic and his fears of what would happen this time.

The journey was slow, two and a half hours, an average speed of forty kilometres an hour and this was an intercity train, maybe that's why the train fare was so cheap? They were bored and pissed off by the thick ex army Australian who sat next to them and attempted to speak German when he saw Al's text book. Al recognised not a single word, it certainly sounded nothing like the voices on his tapes. Steve, after a couple of years in Germany had learned some of the language, but was totally baffled by this idiot.

"What a name for a suburb, Sunshine! Look at the state of it. Give me Brixton or Toxteth any day." Steve said with a look of total horror on his face. Had it really been his idea to come to Melbourne?

TWISTED MIND, WASTED LIFE

Melbourne, 23rd July 1989

The train slowed to a halt at Spencer Street Station. Al was unaware that there were two main stations in Melbourne. After his previous visit, when he had stumbled upon Flinders Street; the other station, he assumed they had to take a short walk straight ahead and they would then arrive in the main street of the city centre. Luckily for them they were in the street they were heading for, even if they were further away. The evening was cool, but they kept warm by walking with their heavy packs, they neared the centre. They found it busy and it wasn't as late as it felt to them, only the long hours of darkness and the tiring journey made it feel so.

"Oh my God! Look at all these wogs!" Steve cursed.

Al looked at him in disbelief. How could Steve make such a racist comment? Al and his sisters had been 'wogs' in Sudbury for people like Steve, just because of their foreign names and slightly darker, but not dark skins.

"What about me? Aren't I one of these wogs?"

"You're not a wog, you're British."

"I'm an East Anglian, but my father is Cypriot and most of these wogs here were probably born in Australia, so they are no longer Greek, but Australians"

"That's different."

Al could not see Steve's logic and could not be bothered to argue the toss. They looked for a hostel and when they found one they decided that it wasn't the sort of place that they wanted to stay, but they stayed just the same. Once they unpacked they went for a wander around the city streets and Al was pleased that this time he was fairly relaxed. The streets and buildings seemed half familiar to him now and there was no need to panic. Had there been reason to panic last time? Steve, on the other hand was having similar feelings as Al had on his previous visit, though for Steve it was the overwhelming number of Greeks that were the problem. He did not know that Melbourne is the second largest Greek city, after Athens, until he arrived that is.

Al woke early in the unfriendly hostel. He lay on the top bunk and looked over to Steve who was fast asleep, buried below a rapidly disappearing down sleeping bag. Below them two unknown faces slept heavily. Al had not heard them come in early in the morning. Steve stirred and they got up and packed. Steve went off to the post office to collect any letters that might have caught up with him after being routed via Sydney, Perth and Adelaide. Al went off to find out about camp sites and work. He felt guilty as hell as he walked into the job centre and he felt sure that he would be caught trying to work illegally, even before he had earned a decent amount of cash which would allow him to remain fed and housed until he would leave this country. He need not have worried as the chap in the job centre could not have been more helpful, showing him on a map where the main industrial areas were and how to get there. He knew that Al was going to work illegally, but he did not care. If this tourist was prepared to work then good luck to him, there were too many lazy Aussies who did not want to work, sponging off the system.

"Your best bet is to try here in the east." He said pointing at the map. "Take the train to Dandenong and visit the C.E.S. out there, they'll be happy to help you and if you can't get work there then there isn't any in Australia!" He smiled.

Al returned to the hostel and waited for Steve, checking the map to see where the nearest camp site was to where they were going to work.   Steve came in smiling.

"I take it you got some letters then?"

"Some! Get a load of all this." He said grinning broadly as he waved a bundle of mail. He was so happy now, had this been the same person he had walked with from Bendigo one cold evening?

"How did you get on?"

"We've got to head out to this place, Dan..den..ong. Al struggled with the name and mispronounced it. Steve tried it and did just as badly.

"Why can't they speak proper English here?" Steve spoke as Al thought.

"It's not far from where Sue lives, so we'll get to see her again."

They walked through the city to the station and found themselves sitting on a train and passing through stations which made London seem positively clean.

"It's as bad as the Paris Metro." Al said.

"Bloody slope heads!" Steve answered. In Australia, Orientals are called slope heads and most of the graffiti was in Chinese characters and was sprayed onto the seats, windows and walls. Many of the seats had been slashed by knives, stuffing poured out from them like water boiling over from a pan of pasta. It was hard to imagine why anyone should want to do this. It was beyond ordinary comprehension.

It was a fifty minute trip to Dandenong and they then had to get a bus and made that connection easily enough. They asked the driver to let them out at the caravan park which he said he would, and they sat back to a bus journey that they couldn't believe.

"Can't these idiots drive?" Steve asked as he was hurled forward against the seat in front. Each time the bus driver used either his brake pedal or accelerator he pushed his foot to the floor instead of gradually applying pressure as a normal person would. Neither Al nor Steve were used to buses being driven at such high speed and coming to a sudden halt at the bus stop.

Six kilometres south of the town the bus tore past the camp site and came to a rapid halt when Steve and Al went to the front to get the driver to stop. Unfortunately they were to see quite a lot of this driver, whom they named Slobbo due to his fat waistline, blank facial expression and general slack attitude.

The weather was quite good as they walked into the cabin which they had rented for two nights. Steve wanted to get out of the tents for a little while, though Al thought sixty dollars was a little too expensive; they could have put the tent up for a week for the same amount, nonetheless Al agreed and it was good to be in such a large space, have a bed to sleep on, table and chairs to sit down to eat and a kitchen to cook in and not have to share with anyone else. Yes it was quite good, though there was no one to love. Al looked over at Steve lying on the top bunk watching television, 'Nightmare On Elm Street.' Steve was a good looking young man and Al knew that his total lack of desire had nothing to do with him not finding Steve attractive, though he didn't. It had everything to do with having no desire at all, even when he thought of Steven he didn't get an erection. There was more going on in Al's head than he could understand and where was Steven now? Would he always feel like this?

Al and Steve walked around the industrial estate going in and out of factories asking if there was any work and after getting over the initial shock of being told no a couple of times they soldiered on. Steve came across a fish processing plant and was told to turn up the following morning ready to start which he did, only to find that no fish arrived and therefore no work. The following morning he arrived early once again and the same thing happened. Steve was not impressed at all by this and did not turn up a third time to be made a fool of.

Apart from the day they arrived when it was sunny and pleasant, even though not exactly warm, it rained very heavily, on and off and during the following days, more on than off. They managed to find shelter during the downpours as they continued along each road asking for work. A few places said maybe and would contact them, but never did and as they were knocking off from another day of asking they made one last stop at a manufacturer of fire engines, ambulances and other such vehicles. To their surprise there were two job vacancies and the man they spoke to seemed satisfied that they were both what they had been looking for. Al had worked in diesel engineering at Lucas many years ago and Steve had just finished his five years in the army as a generator mechanic. They left there with the promise of jobs the following morning and although they had the feeling that it had been assumed that they were both highly skilled diesel mechanics; it had not been anything they had said that had led him to that assumption, they said nothing and hoped that between them they could get away with it, at least for a while!

The next morning they were soaked through walking to the factory and they sat in the office with the factory manager as he went through their application forms and explained to them what it was that they would be required to do. Both Al and Steve had a strange feeling that they were not able to do the work and wondered how they were going to get away with it. To their relief the manager left the room for a few minutes and it gave them a chance to talk.

"I can't do this Steve."

"Neither can I. I think we're going to have to tell him exactly what we can do. Aren't we?"

"Yeah, I suppose so. He has assumed that we can do things that I didn't even understand."

The manager came back after a few minutes and before he could carry on where he had left off, Steve told him that there had been a misunderstanding.

"My training in the army doesn't cover what I think you want. I repaired generators, but you want far more than that." Both Steve and Al felt about two inches tall.

"What about you? It says on your application form that you worked for Lucas in the production and quality control of diesel engines."

"Yes, that's right, but it was production line work."

They left the factory barely before the morning light had arrived, soaked through to the skin, they were not pleased that they had had to be too honest before even earning a dollar.

They went back to the tent and got out of their wet clothes, quite disillusioned with trying to find work. At least they were to strip some wallpaper in the camp site office and although it wasn't much money, it was almost enough to pay for putting the tent up for a week. They waited for half an hour or so to calm down and chatted while laying on their sleeping bags listening to the rain coming down.

"We've got to phone back to the tile factory this morning, we'll do that in a little while, after another tea." Steve grinned.

Al smiled back as he poured water into the saucepan and lit the stove. He really was enjoying Steve's company. They had shared some frustrating moments together, whether looking for work, picking mandarins or walking in freezing temperatures for hours in the dark, but there had also been some very precious moments, at least for Al if not for Steve; like lying in the botanic gardens in Adelaide; when Steve was really drunk that night in the hostel when Wimbledon was on and even during that bitter walk to Marong from Bendigo when Steve didn't want to walk anymore, when Al knew that if Steve stopped in the freezing bush then he would have to stay with him because he was his friend and he cared about him. He wondered about Tony, was he alright? It had been three months since their chance encounter at Port Augusta. That miracle of a meeting that had made Al so very happy. Happy because he had found his friend whom he had left behind so suddenly and so selfishly, but then devastated to watch him disappear in a car to Sydney without him. It would have been good if even for just a moment it was Tony lying by his side waiting for the water to boil. How long would it be before they would meet again? Where would it be? Would it be a chance meeting? Maybe here in Melbourne, maybe today? The water boiled and Al made a tea for Steve and a coffee for himself. They enjoyed the warmth in the tent as they drank their hot drinks.

"All I want to be is a tile stacker! That's all I want to be. I want to go to work every morning and know exactly how much I'm going to get at the end of each day, each week." Steve said.

"I take it you're ready to make the call."

"Yes, and you know what?" Al still laughed at Steve's northern accent, though now that he was used to it, it no longer sounded so strong. "We are going to be tile stackers!"

With that confident encouragement from Steve they left the tent and ran through the rain to the phone.

"O.K. then, tomorrow morning, seven thirty." Steve grinned like he had never done before and jumped punching the rain in victory. "Yes, we're going to be tile stackers!"

However much they wanted the money. However much they needed the money, it was not to be as easy as it sounded and the reasons why there just happened to be two vacancies and more, became painfully obvious as they struggled to stack the tiles as they came racing along a conveyor belt at what seemed like a really stupid speed. The idea was to grab every other pair and put them into a neat little row of twenty two pairs along and a butt of six pairs at the end. Each pair could weigh around ten kilos and the whole thing had to be done in just sixty three seconds. Both Al and Steve fought with those tiles and all too often the tiles won. Luckily for Al he had a much easier week than Steve and was only on the line for ten hours, Steve had more than double that. When Al was not fighting tiles and breaking their corners off, he was in the large shed mixing the colours which were used by the roofers to dye the mortar to match the colour of the tiles. It was a much easier job as he stood listening to the radio, alone. Quite a few hours he and Steve were sent out to the back of the factory to make new pallets on which the tiles were stacked. They didn't mind standing in the rain working, unlike the Australians they worked with. Anything had to be better than stacking tiles!

"You still want to be a tile stacker Steve?"

"No I fucking don't, it's shit! But I'm quite happy to do all the other jobs that they want me to do. Besides, I'm just thinking of the money and then once I've got five hundred dollars I'm off to Sydney."

They had been at work since Tuesday, four days and now it was certain that they would stick at this job. The reality of Steve's departure dawned on Al, very soon Steve would be gone. Soon Al would be alone again. It would be at least another week, but he would be going. It had seemed so natural to be with him, travel with him, talk with him, eat with him, even sleep with him and now he was almost ready to go. How was he going to cope with yet another goodbye?

They worked well together and got on with their work, occasionally popping into the lunch room to get a hot drink. Bob, the factory manager, would appear silently from around the corner from time to time and he would always find them working, not fast, but always working.

"I don't expect you to be out here in the rain." he said, surprised that they had put on waterproof clothing and were still working.

"In Britain, if you're lucky enough to have a job you do it!" Steve answered.

"I wish all these fuckers I've got on the line thought like that. Nothing but a load of lazy cunts, everyone of them!" He sounded like a desperate man. "Do you two want to work overtime tomorrow?"

They were both surprised and answered, "Yes please," together.

Bob turned to walk away then turned back towards them.

"I don't suppose you want to on Sunday as well?"

"Yes!"

Now it was Bob's turn to be surprised, though he realised that they were tourists who had got low on their money and would not be around forever.

This was the golden land that Al and Steve had heard of. So much work and ordinary working-class people lived more like middle-class people did back home. Their houses were big compared to the houses in East Anglia, the house prices lower and yet wages were higher. All too often they had heard the term whinging Poms and he knew that it would have been more correct to say whinging Aussies for they were always complaining how tough life was, when in reality it was just a case that they had no idea how lucky they were.

The first two weeks passed quite slowly and they worked thirteen out of fourteen days. Steve had saved his five hundred dollars and he was leaving for Sydney on the evening bus. He would call in to see

Sue on his way into the city. It had seemed like such a long time since Adelaide, though it was only six weeks since she had left. Al decided to stay and see if he could stick at the job. It was good money and it would give him something to do until he had to leave Australia. He left the tent with Steve sitting up in his sleeping bag.

Al went to work feeling guilty because Steve had left and not told Bob.

"When are you planning to leave?" Bob asked.

"I'd like to stay until the end of October if that's alright? If I can extend my visa, then through to mid November."

That was good enough for Bob and Al felt just a little less guilty about working illegally though he couldn't work out why?

After work Al walked slowly back to the camp site, he was not looking forward to being there without Steve. In the tent there was a crazy note from Steve and although it brought a half smile to his face, it also made him feel extremely alone and unhappy that his northern friend had gone.

A natural tile stacker Al certainly was not. This new skill was a hard one to master and he would miss as many as he caught. The ones he did manage to catch were often getting broken corners and therefore were scrap, though they were still put out in the yard with the good ones. He kept to himself as far as he could as he was not used to and did not like being with so many people for so many hours and now that Steve had gone he missed not having him around. They used to have a moan about work or the weather or Australian bus drivers and now after nine weeks he was not there. There was a gap in his life. He had nothing in common with his work mates and there was nothing to talk about. He got on well with Bob and Ken, the foreman and they treated him well. They liked having someone who was always on time for work and didn't keep taking sickies.

Al worked every Saturday and most Sundays as well as extra hours during the week. Now he had a routine to keep his life orderly and too much to do and not enough time to do it in. Every evening he would have to shower, cook, eat, then wash the pots and then usually did two or three hours studying his German before he slept. Life was taking on a stability that he needed now he was alone again. The only difficult thing was the weather. From the day after Steve and Al had arrived in Melbourne it had rained practically everyday through the end of July and August and now September was not much better. Al could only put up with being in a tent because he wanted the isolation, save as much money as he could and because he was so stubborn. It wasn't until his sixth week at work when he pulled a muscle in his back that he realised how impractical life in a tent was and wondered what he would do if he was really ill. He couldn't help but laugh when the doctor told him to sleep on a hard surface, but he didn't believe Al when he said that that would be easy as he lived in a tent.

Ken had been foreman there for a few years although he was only in his mid twenties and was, by birth, an East Anglian. What a small world it was! Ken lived for the factory and always wanted everything done yesterday. Here, he was king of all he surveyed and he gave the impression that he ran the whole place single-handedly. Other people in the factory would call him by such titles as our fearless leader or superhero, or pratt, such was the problem with his ego. Had they not been so stupid or shallow they would have realised that he just wanted to be liked. He wanted to have friends around him. He wanted to be loved. His loneliness made him very volatile and moody, too moody to achieve results with the people who worked there. Having said that, Al had no reason to reproach Ken. He kept in his good books and was rewarded by numerous cushy jobs and if there was overtime for only a few people then Ken and Bob would make sure that Al was one of the few. Al would get a little abuse from some of the most brain dead of his work mates for being what they saw as a crawler and an arse licker, but they were of no importance to Al. All he wanted was an easy life and money. He was getting both.

The weeks drifted past at a bearable rate, his back injury had healed, his bank balance was growing, but still his thoughts were of East Anglia, Christopher and of course, Steven. There were times that the stress caused by living within the confines of a tent would get to him and it was difficult to keep up the pretence of pleasure from being there. Within his little green bubble he needed to pretend to no one. Zipped up within its nylon shell the tears could roll from his heart and through his eyes because there were no eyes to see him.

Collapsing tent, collapsing life,
The end of my hopes, my dreams,

Fading lights, fading mind,
My diet of bread and cheese,
Telephone calls across the skies,
Not sure to stay or go,
Take my mind, take my life,
There's not really much to take at all.

Blackbird sings before the storm,
My back is hurting me,
The codeine is not helping much,
My eyes just want to sleep,
I hide inside my little tent,
Where the world cannot get me.

I only dream of East Anglia,
Auf deutsch, ich liebst du,
But now look at this collapsing wreak,
That I have now become,
It's so very dark and grey.

Twisted mind, wasted life,
Twisted mind, wasted life,
Twisted mind, wasted life.

By the end of September the weather had improved and it did not rain quite so often. He was not used to such wet winters and in the damp it felt so cold to him. Winter in East Anglia was usually much colder, but a dry cold from Siberia, a healthy cold, invigorating. Even now it was usually around sixteen or seventeen degrees, but it did not feel that warm to him. The trees had come into leaf, but it did not feel like spring and did not sound right to him as at home it would still be summer and autumn would soon be approaching. Each day at work he would check the temperature for London in the newspaper, so often it would be twenty five or more. It had been a long hot summer that he had missed and he knew East Anglia would be looking parched after such a dry winter and hot dry summer.

He kept in touch with home, writing four or more letters each week and after almost five months without news from home he was now getting a few letters via Sue.

Al received a letter from the Immigration Department asking him to come to the office and to bring his air ticket with him. He had applied for a five week extension on his visa so he could go to see the Grand Prix in Adelaide. Of course he had no intention of going to the Grand Prix, he wanted to stay in Melbourne and earn an extra five weeks money. He told Bob that he would be in late for work and dressed himself in his smartest, most tourist looking clothes and went early to the office. He went to reception and the chap told him to sit and wait until he was called.

They left him stewing for just over an hour and he sat reading a tourist newspaper; just for effect. He felt so guilty, just as he had done in London when he applied for the visa, then he had done nothing wrong, now he had. He was called to the counter.

"Why do you want an extension?"

"Because I want to go to the Grand Prix on the way home." Hadn't he put that on the form?

"Why didn't you arrange your visit to coincide with this instead of extending?"

"I didn't know anything about it until I stayed in Adelaide a few weeks ago. I've never been to Australia before, I didn't know what happens down here?"

"Can I have your ticket?"

Al handed it over to her.

"Why haven't you changed your ticket for the date you want your visa extended to?"

"I didn't want to change my ticket in case you won't let me stay an extra five weeks."

"I can't extend your visa unless you change your ticket."

"I'll go to the Qantas office and change it now. Does that mean I can have my extension?"

"Not necessarily."

"Why do you want me to change my ticket if you might not extend my visa? I'd have to change it again."

"What will you do if you cannot get booked onto the aeroplane on November the thirtieth?"

"I'll ask for the twenty ninth and if that's full, the twenty eighth. The last flight available in November."

"Go and change your ticket and then come back and ask for me."

"So I can go to the Grand Prix?"

"We'll see."

Al left the building totally confused by the lack of logic shown by the official, but walked across town to the Qantas office and asked for the latest flight available in November from Perth back to London. It took a few minutes to search the data displayed on the screen of the computer.

"I'm very sorry but the latest flight available is the twenty sixth. Everything after that is booked up."

"That's alright, can you book me on it please?" That was all very straightforward and he returned to the Immigration Department where the silly woman looked at his ticket then issued a visa until the end of November.

Al had got used to the idea of not using his ticket home, but instead flying to New Zealand for six months, but then Uncle Bob; as he was now calling Bob the production manager said that there would always be a job here for him if he wanted to come back. The possibility of going home to see Christopher for a few months and then maybe going to Amsterdam to see Nina and Anna and to Norway to see Stefan now seemed like a feasible idea. Maybe even working for the few months he was in East Anglia?

Obviously the small amount of effort that Al had put into punctuality and getting on with the work he was asked to do was paying off. So often on his way to work Uncle Bob would stop and give him a lift, even if Al was only twenty metres from the factory. To Al, Uncle Bob was a good chap, to the brain-dead lowlife he worked with, Bob was a fat cunt. He was large and silent as he walked around the factory not doing an awful lot, but not much escaped his attention and every now and then he would blow his top and the wrath of Bob would be felt. The whole factory fell silent. Even the machines seemed to run more quietly.

Al got the cushy jobs because he was a brown nose, his work mates said. Al said he had a privileged position of trust because he had a brain and used it to his advantage. It was easier and more advantageous to do the work than to do nothing and pretend to be working only to get caught out, as inevitably they did. Most of them didn't like Bob. They watched what they said and did when he was around, but Al pleased himself and got away with it every time. He was able to be cheeky, though never rude and this reinforced a better working relationship for him with the people who mattered.

One sunny day in early October Al was working with Simon making pallets. They were chatting away as they worked as Simon was one of a few who actually had a brain and could use it to talk about things other than sex, cars, alcohol; which is called piss in Australia, they had stopped working for about ten minutes because they had run out of nails for the nail gun, not that they needed an excuse to stop for a talk. Bob appeared, as he did, silently from around the corner of the building and startled them a little.

"Oh Uncle Bob! I was just on my way to find you or Ken."

"Why's that Al?" Bob grinned. He knew that they were jawing, but it didn't matter because they would get their work done, they wouldn't have been standing around doing nothing for as long as they could.

"I need some more bullets, I've run out!"

A huge grin which went almost from ear to ear was fixed on Bob's face and Simon shook his head in disbelief.

"Come with me Al and I'll get you some more...bullets." As Al and Uncle Bob walked off to the store Al looked back to Simon who was holding his head in his hands almost crying at Al's behaviour. Al just grinned like a schoolboy given a special treat by his favourite teacher. Ten minutes later Al returned with his bullets.

"You're off your fucking head you are," Simon said in pity and in amazement. "Fancy talking to Bob like that! Uncle Bob, have you got any more bullets?"

"I'm an East Anglian, I can do what I like!"

"You a bloody mad Pom that's what you fucking are. Calling people Uncle or possum, and living in a fucking tent!"

It was around this time in early October that Al started to get to know Paul, who was leading hand. Up until now it had only been the odd word during the course of work. He felt good when they had to work together as Paul wasn't out to impress him, or to put him down and score points from him. Al admired his relaxed attitude, so laid back, but not slack or sloppy; apart from his time-keeping; as was normal here. He was one of those people who everyone seemed to like and there seemed to be some sort of feeling that if you were seen talking to him then you had in some way made it. Paul's motto was "If you look busy, then you are busy." He had perfected the art form like no one else Al knew.

Occasionally Al made the mistake of asking him a question and he would be met with Paul's standard and well used answer of, "Don't ask me, I don't fucking know." Or "I don't know nothing, no one ever tells me nothing." In Australian English the verb 'to fuck' is very important and is used almost as much as 'to be'. A large proportion of Australians whom Al had either met or just listened to put one; and sometimes more, fuck or fucking into a large proportion of their sentences, depending on whether it was a main or subordinate clause. Al found it too complicated to try and learn the rules which governed its use. He found German far more straightforward and decided to stick with that!

Every few days there were new people starting work at the factory. It wasn't that the factory was expanding, merely that the work was very hard until your muscles got used to it and there were certainly easier ways of earning a buck in Australia. Quite strange was the fact that the two new starters who began the last week in September both stayed. One of them was also a foreigner to Melbourne, this was Mark, from Katoomba, in the Blue Mountains. He had run out of money while visiting his cousin for a couple of months and he wanted to rent a caravan for a few months and then return home once he had saved enough money. Mark did not want to pay the amount that they were asking and Al thought over what he had heard for a couple of minutes then asked him if he wanted to share. Mark seemed to think that it wasn't such a bad idea and the following day they toured all the caravan parks within a radius of fifteen kilometres of work. They settled on one eight Ks to the east and moved in the following Monday.

Al brought his backpack and a small shoulder bag and Mark brought in suitcase after suitcase, skis, ski boots and all manner of other things.

"Where's the kitchen sink?"

"I haven't got that much stuff."

"No?"

Al looked at the bed that Mark had bagged which was hidden by all his belongings and thought how there would be no more zipping and unzipping to get in and out. No more worries about high winds and heavy rain.

"Oh no." Al said as he opened the refrigerator. In it was a bag of mouldy broad beans and at the bottom there was dried blood.

"What's wrong?"

"Come and look."

"Bloody Victorians, they're dirty animals." Mark said when he saw it.

"Looks like we're going to have to have a clean up before we get settled in."

Summer was still going strong in East Anglia. Al loved hot Octobers; the year he had been at college it was twenty eight degrees on October the first. It was supposed to be autumn wasn't it? Here in the eastern suburbs spring was at long last in total command. The evenings and mornings were lighter and it almost made him feel a little positive about the things which still troubled his mind. The distraction of sharing with Mark was a blessing in disguise as Al could not allow himself to give in to his feelings, though it also meant that he had to bottle it up on those occasions when he felt it was all too much; being away from home, away from Christopher, apart from Steven.

The first few days in the caravan were a little unpleasant as they got used to each other. Al had spent far too long on his own and he found it a little unnerving to be with someone now, especially as they worked together all day as well. Mark did not want to talk about sex, cars, sport or beer as the majority of the others whom they worked with did, but they still found that they had very little in common, apart from two very important things which although they did not know at the time and would not know for almost two years helped to build a strong friendship which would not just stand the test of time, but improve. The two things that they had in common? The most obvious for two strangers temporarily stuck in a city in which they didn't want to be in and in a job neither really wanted to do, but still they worked all the hours they could get. They both wanted as much money that they could get in the remaining seven weeks that Al had left in Melbourne and Mark soon came to decide that he would leave the day after Al. They both wanted to go home, though Al still believed he would not be leaving for home, but for New Zealand.

For Al even the size of the caravan took a little time to get used to after living in a tent in which he could out stretch his arms and touch all sides without moving. Being with another person for so many hours of the day was difficult and it took a little while to understand the meaning of tolerance and patience, but somehow they muddled through the first week and it hadn't been so bad for either of them.

If Al had realised at the time that Mark was a stable influence on him they might have grown to be friends and not just good mates, but Al, for all his pretence, was too screwed up to think too deeply, or to look too hard or long at his current short term situation. In the evenings Al would sit at the table; it was so good to be able to sit at a table, and study his German and maybe write a letter. Mark would be in bed quite early and sit there reading his Garfield comic books. He was totally preoccupied and engrossed with them and in them and from the end of the caravan would come a continuous stream of chuckling and giggling, which Al thought was quite amusing even if he didn't understand the obsession, so Al took to calling Mark, Garfield, after his hero.

They shared the van, but lived almost separate lives within it. Their foods were quite different. Muesli, wholemeal bread, fish, fresh fruit and vegetables did not seem to be good tucker for Garfield. He preferred foods which were high in salt, sugar and fat and if possible, all three and highly processed. There was also the age difference to contend with. Garfield was just a kid and though Al was only eight years older, he felt that life had made him much older. Mark was much taller than Al. Most of the world was taller than Al! He had dark wavy hair and a silly little moustache which he shaved off soon after they moved in, much to Al's approval. Because of his height he also looked thinner than Al and his really dark eyes looked too dark, the eyes of a child, and made him look a little dopey.

Now that Al was living at Narre Warren he was on the main line into Melbourne and Sue and would make use of this new found freedom whenever he wasn't working. If he had wanted to go into the city on a Sunday from where he had been living he had a six kilometre walk to the station first, this was much more convenient. Another benefit from the move to Narre Warren was that Paul had been wanting to lay a patio and path using old bricks and wasn't quite sure how to go about it and as he knew that Al had once been a landscape gardener and asked if he wouldn't mind coming and helping. Al was more than happy to help. He had grown to like Paul quite a bit and had enjoyed his company whenever they worked together. Paul's mannerisms also reminded him of Christopher and that also made him feel good.

The evening before Al's first visit to Paul's house Garfield was less than happy.

"It's going to be so boring tomorrow. I've got nothing to do." He sulked.

"Why's that?" Al asked, knowing exactly what the answer was, but pretending otherwise.

"I'm going to be all alone, all day!"

"What about your cousin?"

"She's going out."

What Mark was trying to say was that he wanted to go to Paul's house with Al. Al was pleased that he hadn't been asked as they spent at least twenty two hours each day together and Al needed a break and surely Garfield must have longed for a few hours away from Al?

Sunday morning arrived bright and early and Al was awake and ready to go an hour before he needed to be. He felt like he was on holiday, going somewhere new, with someone he liked, it was great. Armed with a bottle of Beaujolais and six bottles of Coopers, he walked to the road with the sound of 'My Dying Machine' thumping through his headphones, he sang as he waited for Paul to arrive.

> *"Why give orders,*
> *Why make speeches,*
> *Give me a reason to die."*

As he sang along with his tape and danced a little on the stony road verge in the morning sunshine Paul arrived.

"We'll soon get that smile off your face when we get a spade in your hand Al my boy!"

Al grinned even more, he didn't think so. Today was his day.

Al loved the way Paul called him Al my boy, it made him feel more like an old friend than someone that he just happened to work with and though Paul could not admit to it; because Paul was a real man and a real Australian man could never admit affection on any level for another man, it was his way of saying the unspeakable and he was aware that Al read his unspoken words loud and clear. Yes, Paul liked Al as much as Al liked Paul. There was nothing obscene in that to his eyes, though society; dictated by old ladies with purple rinses and skeletons in their closets, busy minding other people's business instead of their own, would have something different to say.

Berwick is a hilly, leafy village which is sadly being swallowed up by the rapidly sprawling Melbourne. The city centre stood some twenty five miles away to the west and it wasn't stopping here. It continued like a cancerous growth far to the east of here, unabated.

"Well Al, this is the homestead." Paul grinned.

The house was bigger than Al was used to at home, but it was an ordinary four bedroom timber house in Australia. It stood back from the road about twenty metres, on a slope which ran along and away from it. All around there were tall trees and the air had a freshness that he had neither smelled nor tasted since being in Melbourne. It was almost countryside as he knew it.

"So where is this patio going?"

They walked up the slope towards the foot of the steps which led up to the large veranda.

"I thought here, from the house, across to the bank, maybe cut away some of that and then out here to the grass and have a path to the drive and one to the washing line with somewhere for Liz to stand when she's putting out the washing."

Paul stepped around, showing Al what he wanted.

"Do you want it flush to the lawn this side?" Al asked as he bent down to get a good look at the angle at which the grass rose.

"That's alright isn't it?"

"Yes that's fine. If we start up there and take it down eighteen inches and this side six inches."

"What? Why so much? Are you sure you know what you're doing?"

"Do you want it to be quite level?"

"Well yeah, but it sounds like a lot of work to me Al my old boy."

"It won't take long for us to dig it out."

"It won't take long if that good for nothing Trevor gets here. I bet he's still in bed, pissed!"

They got on with the digging and Al was enjoying being in a garden again, though he wished that they used proper spades in Australia.

"What's wrong with our spades you whinging Pommy?"

"They make it harder work than it needs to be. These went out with the Ark, but obviously not here in Oz or Central Africa."

"Cheeky sod!"

"Anyway, it's whinging East Anglian not Pommy!"

As they argued the worth of Australian tools and the difference between East Anglian and English Trevor arrived with a thick head from the night before.

"Thick head? He is bloody thick!" Paul laughed.

It was slow work, but they were achieving something, though Paul and Trevor weren't quite sure why they were digging so deep as they saw a mountain of waste soil begin to grow at the bottom of the garden.

"Are you ready for a cup of tea, or would you like a beer?" Liz called down to them.

Al was longing for a cup of tea, but did not want to seem a wet lettuce in the presence of these Australians, so he opted for a beer, much to Trevor's approval and the horror of Paul who also wanted a cup of tea but went along with the consensus. It had actually become a warm and sunny day and the alcohol inside Al was not going to do him much good and he knew it. He was lucky that they were shifting the soil down the slope as he would never have been able to push a wheelbarrow full of soil uphill once he had a couple of Coopers inside him. Indeed by the time that they were called in for lunch it was taking all his concentration to hold the barrow upright and allow it to pull him behind as it went.

They went inside the house and washed. It was large and pleasantly furnished and the smell of a roast dinner was the sweetest thing Al had ever smelt.

"You can't have your wine Al, there's no cork opener." Trevor called through from the kitchen.

"What? Don't be silly, you can't have a house that doesn't have a corkscrew. Can you?"

"We have got one Al, honest. But we never use it and I don't know where it is." Liz said apologetically.

"They haven't got one Al, don't listen to Liz's excuses." Trevor stirred.

"We have."

"I could push the cork in for you."

As Al screamed "no" the cork bobbed inside the bottle.

"You animal! Paul! He's corked my wine!"

Paul laughed as Al's eyes were wide open as he stared at a film of tiny pieces of cork on his Beaujolais.

"Australians!"

They sat down to eat, the smell of hot food filling the air and made Al melt with happiness and contentment. When had he last felt like this? Certainly not in the past ten months.

"You're not going to believe this, but this is the best thing that has happened to me this year."

They believed what he said, but couldn't understand how something as simple as the present situation could possibly be the highlight of anyone's year. Trevor thought he was just odd, well he had to be odd living in a tent for so long. Paul thought it was a bit pathetic, but he liked Al and thought it was sad for someone to have been so low for so long. Liz did not know what Al was on about, she had only met him a few hours ago, but could sense that he was hurting.

"No thanks Liz, I would love some dessert, but I couldn't fit it in. It's been a long time since I've eaten so much. I really miss not having a kitchen to play with. I can, and do cook quite a bit with my two camping stoves, but it's limited. It's been over six months since I've had roast chicken and potatoes."

They had a good laugh at him because none of them could ever imagine themselves travelling as he was. Running, as he corrected them.

Their lunch break ran well into its second hour, none of them wanted to move, especially Al who had had a couple of Coopers and half a bottle of wine too much! Eventually, they got back to work and within an hour the digging was over. The rest of the afternoon was spent in true Australian style, drinking and talking and then when Liz sent out for some pizzas, eating! It was quite late in the evening when Paul drove Al back to Narre Warren and after such an enjoyable day he would not have slept for hours, even if his head wasn't spinning around each time he laid it down!

Apart from the extra money gained from working on Saturdays, Al enjoyed the atmosphere which was much more relaxed and enjoyable, or maybe the thought of so many hours at time and a half and better still, double time was all that made it feel different. After the eight hour shift had passed Al often stayed back for a couple of hours extra with Paul, Ken, Simon and Trevor to clean up. It was more money and apart from Dean who wasn't there, they were the only ones who he could get on with without making an effort. They cleaned the machines, removing the waste colours and concrete, oiling moving parts and sweeping up. As they worked the light would go and the factory fell silent, or as near to silence as it ever could get in the factory. Al was, at moments like this, enjoying being in Melbourne and if he had been offered the chance to stay he would have taken it. The familiarity was now security. Routine was now more than a reason to stop moving on, but also the provider of future opportunities. Paul was now a trusted friend, one whom he had become very close to. No one could replace Christopher, but Paul had the same status in Al's head and heart as he held. At long last, so many miles from home, so many miles from his friends he had found new friends that made Melbourne take on a new image and atmosphere. A new possibility arose in his head that this could become a new home, though he knew it was not practical, next month he had to leave.

Al pushed out a wheelbarrow of waste towards the dump. The evening air was warm. Was this the same place where it seemed always to be cold and raining? He felt so good, relaxed, happy. The moon was full and close to the Earth.

"Oh Christopher..." His line of thought was interrupted by a warm inner feeling he had. A feeling of comfort, of love, of friendship; yes friendship, as if Christopher was here, as if a time had come to hug his friend with no fears of embarrassment.

"I know this feeling." He had felt like this twice before, though then he was deeply unhappy and alone. This was like Coober Pedy and Alice Springs. He put the wheelbarrow down and looked around.

"Are you here?" He whispered. "I can feel you, but where are you? I can't see you." There was no doubt of his feeling this time, was he really that much stronger? He looked around again and again and tried to remember anything that might give him a clue.

"You will see a sign, a sign that only you will recognise, you will have to look up for it when it feels right." It felt right now. He looked up towards the roof and then when that sounded absurd to him he looked into the night's sky, it seemed so obvious once he thought about it, but what was he looking for? The brightest and most obvious thing in the darkness was the full moon and there was his star sign, Scorpio and right in the heart of the Scorpion was Venus, his favourite planet. His favourite mainly because it was easy for him to identify it; with Jupiter and Mars he was never quite sure until a few nights had passed.

"Venus, goddess of love." He felt cold at the thought that this was what he had been waiting for, for such a long time. There was no question in his mind that this was it, no matter how absurd it would have sounded to anyone else; indeed how absurd it would have sounded to himself not too long ago, but he wasn't ready for it now, he didn't want it now, he wanted to stay here. He wanted more time. Despite the thoughts he was having, despite wanting to stay here longer he accepted what he now knew, it was time for him to go home, but why? He would go into Melbourne in the morning to make arrangements for his journey to Perth. It seemed so straightforward as if it had already been determined for him. He had never been one to accept anything at face value, but now it seemed quite natural to do so.

"What are you looking at Al?" Paul said to him as he walked out into the darkness and joined him at his side. Al looked at Paul and smiled, he was safe and so happy to have a friend at his side. He wanted to tell Paul everything, his love for Steven, how he felt about his brother Christopher, indeed, how he felt about him. He wanted to tell Paul what had happened in central Australia and right now and the horror which he could not bring himself to tell anyone when he hitchhiked once too often, but how could he tell any of it to Paul? Could Paul have understood anything of the words that he would have to have used? So many problems might arise if Al had said anything, so for once he said nothing and saying nothing this time was the right thing to do. He stood with Paul at his side and he knew that wherever he had a friend he would always be home. No matter where he could find himself he could never be alone because there were too many people who cared about him, loved him. Al's smile was infectious and Paul smiled with him. He did not know all that had happened, but in a short space of time he had got quite close to what was making Al tick and what it was that he feared. He knew that he had been through more than he was able to cope with, but somehow he had muddled through. Paul smiled because something was so obviously making Al feel good and he was happy for him. Al looked back towards the sky.

"It's beautiful isn't it Paul?"

"Yeah, top sky." He didn't sound too impressed.
"The full moon, Scorpio and Venus."
"What the fuck are you on about now?" Paul laughed and looked at Al in a rather dubious manner, shaking his head in disbelief the way he often did. "Sometimes Al... Sometimes I have no idea what is going on in your crazy head, and to be honest it's probably better that I don't!"

"Oh it's nothing Paul."

"Al my boy..." He laughed and left Al to finish off outside. "And hurry up if you want a lift home afterwards!" He called from beneath the lights of the factory to where Al stood in the darkness.

The following morning Al caught the train into the city, he needed to get out of the suburbs for a while and he wanted to find out about getting a train to Perth for later next month. The thought of crossing the Nullarbor was quite exciting as by road he had only seen a small part of it and it had been so long since he had been outside of Melbourne. The fare was $165 which was cheap for Al. He paid by credit card in order to make the most of the weakening pound. The unknown quantity of what he was going back to unnerved him a little, but he knew he had to face reality even if he didn't like it.

In his last few weeks in Melbourne the economy began to take a nose dive. There was less overtime and less money. Al did not mind too much as he had saved like a proverbial Jew and spent like a proverbial Scot for many months and now he had more time to visit the city, where he never managed to spend too much on a day out. This extra time also meant that he finally got to see Sue, though trying to pin her down to one spot took as much planning as a military campaign. He broke his return journey and finally found her in, briefly. She filled him in on what had been happening since Adelaide and made it seem such a long time with all the things that she crammed into her time.

"Oh Al, I've got some letters for you, somewhere?" She hunted around and found them. He smiled and looked at the handwriting to see who they were from.

"Mum, Mary, Stefan..." He was excited by the letter from Stefan, but the last two made him go silent and cold, his hands shook, they were from Steven. It had been six months since that fateful phone call from Perth which led him to run off into the Australian bush like an idiot, leaving Tony behind. He looked at the handwriting on the aerogrammes, unmistakably Steven's hand. Part of him was excited, part of him was terrified.

Sue was on her way out and Al had to leave to get his train. Again and again he read his first three letters, but it was quite some time before he could bring himself to open the first of Steven's. He read them slowly, but was confused by his words.

"I'm still optimistic about our future..."

"What does he mean?"

"I'm sure we can find a way to sort things out."

"Does he want me back? Is that what he's saying?" Al was angry about the confusion these words put into his head. Was he misreading them or was Steven saying exactly what Al was reading? Now he thought that maybe it had been a mistake to book his ticket ready for his return, but he did not have to use it. There was always New Zealand?

"Do I want to try again? No," he lied. "Yes of course I do, I love him..."

The train arrived and he sat by a graffiti covered window, the doors slid shut as the train eased out of the station.

"I don't know. Just because I still love him it doesn't mean we can make a go of it. My love wasn't enough before so why should it be now? I'd want more this time, not less. Oh what the fuck do you mean, Steven?"

The confusion caused by these two letters made him feel really alone. He needed to talk to someone about them, but who could he talk to? There was Liz and Paul, but would they want to know him if he said that he was homosexual? Was he being unjust by not giving them credit as intelligent people who could understand and accept him? He did not want to take that risk. If he was to lose their friendship where would he be? Alone.

Rushing back to the caravan at the end of each day and crossing out little boxes of days gone by and hundreds of dollars saved. October came and went. Al was now an old man of twenty-seven, he couldn't believe it. What had he done with all those years since he had left school just over a decade ago? Another chapter was now coming to a close as the time he had left in Melbourne flew past. He was running out of time, just when he was beginning to fit in and relax a little, just when he was beginning to think that he could fit into life down under. He sat at the table reading his German course and wrote a few letters. Mark was in bed, his head buried in a Garfield book, an occasional giggle floated around the cool caravan which distracted Al. He got up and made himself a coffee, as much for warmth as for something to drink.

"What are you doing tomorrow Al? S'pose you're going around to Paul's."

"No, they're going out. I thought that I'd go into the city again. I'd quite like to go to the zoo."

"Oh, good idea. I'll come too. I'd like to do that."

Al was a little annoyed as he wanted to have the time to himself, but he did not want to cause any ill feeling so he said nothing. Mark had a lot to put up with from Al. He wasn't very chatty and was so insular in his own little world which was dominated by Steven. If only they had had more in common. If there hadn't been the age difference, if only Al could put Steven out of his mind. Even the situation in which he shared the caravan seemed strange and new to him, not too many months ago he had never shared and it still made Al stand back with surprise sometimes.

The station was just a few minutes walk away, but Garfield insisted that they would drive there. He maintained that it was too far to walk and Al remembered how different this attitude was from home.

"Hurry up Garf', we're going to miss the train." Al was outside by the car waiting as Mark fussed around with something. He was never in any hurry when he should have been and when time was on his side he was always rushing.

"We've got plenty of time." He called from inside, just before he appeared at the door. They drove in typically Australian fashion - foot to the floor; and upon arriving at the car park the bells at the level crossing began to ring. They ran across the tracks before the gates closed and just beat the train to the platform.

"I hope you know where you're going?"

"Yeah. Haven't you been into the city before?"

"Yeah, once, but I wouldn't have a clue about all these trains and trams and things."

"I want to go and buy an album before we go to the zoo."

"What do you want a photo album for?"

"No, an L.P. I found a record shop up in Collins Street that had a Gary Numan picture disc that I haven't got. I should have bought it last week, but I didn't want to use my credit card again. It's five years old and I hadn't seen it before."

"What? Your credit card?" Garfield laughed as Al swung his jacket at him for his insolence.

He was too late, the record had been sold, so after a visit to the cash machine at the bank they jumped on a tram to the zoo.

"Domsheide, Hamburgerstrasse, Weserwier."

"What the fuck are you an about?"

"Just practising my tram stops for when I get back to Bremen."

"Stupid Pom."

"East Anglian! Stupid East Anglian!"

At the zoo Garfield joined in with the masses making silly noises at the animals. Al shook his head in amazement and the monkeys just sat there looking at the stupid humans, they were obviously the ones who should have been in the cage instead of themselves. Garfield borrowed Al's camera and was busy snapping away at anything that moved and Al screamed with delight when they found out that Mark had not loaded the film properly and it wasn't winding on. It was so good to be with someone who could do something as stupid as he himself had done when he first arrived in Australia.

"Fancy doing that! How daft do you feel?" Al gloated jokingly, before he told Garfield that he'd done the same six months previously.

Mark was sure that they walked a lot, Al wasn't so convinced. They sat and ate their packed lunch and Garfield bought some chips to go with it, but they were soggy and barely warm. The day was passing too fast and the sun left the city and the wind blew harder. Despite last night's dread of spending the day with Garfield in preference to his own company Al had enjoyed himself. Garfield could be fun to be with, when Al was more responsive to his presence and he was certainly far more tolerant than Al could see.

"I've had enough now, it's getting cold." Garfield whined.

"Garfield you're a pussy, but you're right!"

They were greeted with utter chaos when they arrived at the station. All the platforms had been altered and no one seemed to know what was going on. First they were told one platform and then another.

"Let's just take this one and if it's not right we can change at Richmond."

Garfield wasn't convinced by this, but went along because he didn't have a better idea. The train left Flinders Street in the opposite direction in which they needed to go, Al hoped this meant that it was going via the city loop. He stared out of the window as the train picked up speed. Hundreds of bewildered passengers stood around on the platforms. It reminded him of that horrible night in Edinburgh when he had travelled all afternoon to get there, so he could see Steven. It was a senseless thing to do, but he couldn't see it at the time. Now he shuddered at the thought of that journey. The realisation of the business being in serious trouble because he was owed nearly four thousand pounds by customers who did not want to pay had been the final straw. All the hard work had been for nothing. He could have kept trying, but saw no reason to. After an ugly scene in the streets of Edinburgh Al had been left to wander the cold dark streets. March in Scotland was decidedly colder than East Anglia. He had returned to the station just before midnight and bought a ticket to London on the overnight train. He could see the weariness on the faces of the crowd that night in the faces on platform five in Flinders Street and it stirred memories which he would rather have forgotten.

At Richmond Al broke his thoughts as he stepped off the train to check the T.V. monitor. They were on the correct train, so he sat back and let the trackside scenery drift past the window without much consideration. Half an hour later they had arrived at dreary old Dandenong. There was little of charm in the town apart from the town hall. They found an old broken bench out of the wind and waited for their connecting train back to Narre Warren. They waited and waited and got colder and colder and Garfield was definitely unimpressed.

"This is so typical of Melbourne! It wouldn't happen in Sydney." He complained. Al suspected that it would. It certainly would happen in Britain.

"Hey Garfield, see that train over there?" He pointed to the far platform. "Three coach trains don't go into the city, they only go to Pakenham. That's our train."

"Can't be. They'd tell us if they had changed it."

Al gave him a very suspect look and said, "Garfield, Garfield,

Garfield. You obviously are not a frequent train traveller are you? We, you and me, we are only members of the public, customers. What makes you think that they would tell us?"

Time was passing and they were getting colder and Garfield was becoming more and more irate with Melbourne and now Victoria in general.

"Are you waiting for the Pakenham train?" A signalman called across from the other platform.

"Yes." Al shouted back.

"Well it's this one here and it's about to go, so you had better run."

Before he had time to finish speaking Al had jumped down from the platform and onto the tracks, ran across both lines and was pulling himself up onto the other platform. He looked behind to see where Garfield was. He was still standing on the platform.

"Come on Garfield, just look as if you own the joint!" With a leap and a bound Garfield's long legs had caught up with Al and no sooner had they sat on the train than it moved out of the station.

"Victoria!" Garfield said disapprovingly.

"Australia!" Al said in return.

* * * * *

Luckily for Tony he arrived back in Perth a day before some fellow backpackers were heading south to pick tomatoes. Tony could handle this line of work. Picking fruit did not carry the same moral pressure as butchering livestock.

The following morning he travelled south to Bunbury with these four people, still feeling less than good about his physical condition; he felt as if his veins still carried a high content of alcohol instead of oxygen.

The first day of harvesting came and went without anything eventful happening and it was painfully clear that he would be earning a fraction of the money that he had been getting in Geraldton, but that was unimportant. Quality of life counted for a lot and even if it wasn't much money, it was still something to save for his return home.

He tried to keep to himself, but that was not easy as he was a gregarious person. He did manage to drink large quantities of alcohol only occasionally and he was pleased about that. It felt like an achievement.

September came and went and October rushed upon him before he realised it. He thought about Al a lot in these final few weeks, it helped him take his mind off his girlfriend, his behaviour in Australia and the nightmares which he still had occasionally, though they were not as bad as they had been.

On the twenty fourth he arrived back in Perth, ready for the flight in three days time. He would have stayed out of the city until the last minute, but he wanted to find Al before they departed and spend the last days relaxing with him as they had spent the first few days together six months earlier. Tony checked the camp sites, he phoned every one of them within twenty miles of the city centre, but Al was not in any of them. Thinking it unlikely that he would stay in a hostel he checked them just the same in case he was wrong. He wasn't surprised when he didn't find him.

He went to confirm his seat at the Qantas office.

"Can you tell me if a Mr. Yerem has confirmed his seat yet?" Tony asked.

"I'm sorry, but we're not allowed to give out passenger information."

"But he's my friend, we came out here together and I haven't seen him for over five months. I've got no way of knowing if he is alright. His ticket number would be either the one before mine or the next one after."

The woman behind the desk looked at Tony, she believed him, but rules were rules.

"I've tried every camp site and hostel in Perth and I can't find him. He might not be here yet, but he would have confirmed his seat before now. He's like that. It's his birthday tomorrow and I wanted to spend the day with him." Tony tried to convince her. "Please?"

"Give me your ticket again." She said to Tony.

Tony handed it to her and she punched the numbers into the computer. He waited for the results.

"He's not confirmed on your flight. I'll check to see if he's changed his date."

There was another short silence as Tony waited for her to find his friend.

"Yes, there he is. What's his first name?"

"Al. Arif."

"Yes, that him. He changed his flight."

"Oh that's alright, he's already at home." Tony said with relief.

"No, he's not already gone. He's extended his departure."

"What?" Tony was surprised, almost shocked. "When is he coming home?"

"I'm sorry, I can't give out any other information. I'm not supposed to tell you what I have."

"O.K. At least I know he's alright. He must be if he has extended. Can you say where he was when he extending his ticket?"

"No, I'm sorry, but it wasn't Perth if that's what you're thinking."

"The ticket runs out at the end of November so it will have to be before then. I wonder where he is?"

Tony sat at the bar in the airport waiting for the boarding call. He felt good knowing that tomorrow he would be back in East Anglia no matter what happened when he arrived. He had had enough of Australia and greed and it hadn't helped sort himself out, but he couldn't blame Australia for that. He looked across at the row of spirits which lined the bar. This could have been anywhere. He looked at his reflection in the mirror behind the bottles and thought that he had changed a little, though it was only six months and he couldn't work out why he should think he looked differently now. He sighed heavily and thought of Al. He felt positive that Al had sorted himself out otherwise he would not have extended for a month.

"He must have a job and be wanting to take back as much money as he can, that would be the reason behind that. At least he won't be alone. I wonder if he'll see Steven when he gets back? I hope he doesn't, he's wasting his time with him."

Tony heard his flight being called and he walked through to clear customs happy in the knowledge that he would soon be home.

* * * * *

With the recession beginning to bite deeper into the Australian economy there was less work to do and little chance of any more overtime. The last Saturday that Al worked Ken's friend brought in his sprint car in the evening. He wanted to clean it with the pressure hose and by the time he arrived most of the work had been done and

Al, Ken, Paul, Simon and Trevor sat down and had a drink or two, then a few more. It did not take much to get Al well under the influence and before too long he was feeling quite light headed.

"Hey Al, jump on a fork and grab those beers from the fridge in the back shed." Ken asked.

Al grinned.

"You want me to go and get the beer, on a fork lift?" He was not in full control of these machines at the best of times, let alone when half cut. Driving carefully at first, then once out of sight he put his foot to the floor and although it was not fast it was fast enough for someone not in control.

"So far, so good." He told himself when he arrived safely at the shed and went in to find the beer. Two of the six cans were missing and he used the empty holes in the plastic to give him a firm grip on the rest. He turned the fork, skidded into movement, aimed at the corner of a stack of tiles while holding the beer high above himself.

"Ye ha!" Had he been sober he would have slowed at the bend to round the corner and the tiles, had he been sober he would have been much further from the corner and had he been sober he would have seen the sprint car coming towards him. All he noticed was Ken further back on another fork lift with a look of extreme horror on his face. The sprint car, nice and clean after its wash veered off left and onto the dust, rubble and mud. Al turned hard on the wheel, the back of the fork skidded around as he slammed on the brakes, he stalled the engine and stopped centimetres from a pallet of tiles.

"You fucking idiot!" Ken shouted as he arrived.

Al grinned, not really aware of what had happened.

"I think that's what you would call grouse!" Ken looked at Al grinning like a demented fool and could say no more to him.

October had been and gone and Al was now counting down in days not weeks until he would leave Melbourne. Garfield and Al were getting on really well, though Al couldn't see it. He still longed to be alone, or better still with an old friend, Christopher, or an old lover, Steven. He still spent a day most weekends with Paul and Liz and the patio was almost finished. Melbourne Cup Day was supposed to be a day of working on the garden, but after a half-hearted attempt at work it rapidly became an excuse to sit and talk and of course drink! Paul and Liz had made Al so welcomed and he was dreading the day he would have to leave them behind. It would be like saying goodbye to Sarah and Christopher all those months before. He hated the thought of having to be without Paul or Christopher, there could never be a time when they could all be together; and what about the day when Al would have to tell Paul the whole truth. He wasn't looking forward to that. He was safe here and did not want anything to risk that feeling even though it meant deceiving his friend. He so desperately needed this love that had been given to him, this sanctuary of stability and caring. He belonged wherever he had friends, though it may not ever replace his homeland.

"I've got a special job for you today Al." Paul said, he was up to something, Al could tell by that grin of his. They drove down the road to an empty block of land.

"Which plants are worth taking?"

"We're going to pinch them in broad daylight?"

"Yeah, we'll be quick."

"Oh my God, I'm going to end up in an Australian jail today aren't I! I wonder if that will entitle me to Australian citizenship?"

"What?"

"I'll be a real criminal then, just like your ancestors?"

"Now don't get cheeky Al my boy."

There it was again, Paul referring to him as Al my boy, it was out of friendship and it felt good. The only other times anyone had used pet names was when he was called faggot or wog and Paul's address was decidedly preferable. They pruned the best roses hard and dug up the rootstock, filling the boot of the car before making their getaway.

"Dear Mum, I've spent the afternoon learning how to be a really good Aussie. Paul knows a thing or two about this, so I concluded that it must be in his blood."

"Cheeky fucking Pom."

"East Anglian! Cheeky fucking East Anglian!"

The evening was cool, but not cold; spring had a firm hold now, though the leaves had emerged many weeks before. The fresh mountain air fell into the leafy suburban gardens in Berwick and there was a gentle fragrance of succulent spring flowers hanging in the air and plenty of mosquitoes which made their presence felt. Al was bitten by what he assumed was some nasty arthropod as during the following week his body ached down his left side and he couldn't even remember if he stopped the night. Paul said it was too much alcohol, but Al never forgot too much of that!

There was a barbecue in Frankston at Elizabeth's parent's house. Her uncle and aunt had been over for a holiday and were returning to East Anglia during the week and as Al was now a self appointed family member, he was naturally invited along, much to his delight.

"Right Paul, I'm going now. I'll see you at mum's." Liz called down from the house.

"O.K. Liz. Have a good time."

"And don't be late!" She added.

"I won't be late." Paul said. Liz was well aware what Paul's time keeping was like and somehow she would believe his arriving on time when she saw it herself.

They finished the edges on the patio and sat and had a beer. They chatted and sat together on a bench and although Al was never serious when he told Paul that he was part of the family, he felt as if he was now. Not having any friends from school and coming from a less than close and supportive family it was easy for Al to confuse friendship with the idea of family. He longed to have family members as friends and friends as family members, but that was an alien thought that bore no reality to the family unit he belonged to. The friends he had come to know since leaving school took on the demanding status on both counts.

He enjoyed being with Paul, sitting here with him, quietly talking. He had never found himself in this situation with Christopher and felt that he had missed out on something. Would he have found himself in this situation had Paul known that the man sitting next to him was homosexual? Something inside Al did not want to find out, that something was called fear. Was his homosexuality the reason that he had never shared a moment like this with Christopher? It seemed unlikely to him, but maybe subconsciously that was the reason. Maybe, however unlikely it seemed to Al, Christopher couldn't accept Al as an equal as he would have had he been heterosexual. Paul was a good friend, though they had only known each other for so few weeks. Al respected him and envied Paul's normality and respectability. It was something he could pretend at being, but only pretend. He was not made like that.

"Paul," Al wanted to say how good a friend Paul was, how he wished he too could be normal, but he couldn't. He wanted to say that he was still in love with Steven, yes he was homosexual and could

Paul forgive him for being that way? He wanted to say he loved Paul and thank him for his friendship and the kindness that he had shown to him, but the only words that came out were, "we're late."

"What! Oh Jesus. It's all your fault, I'll tell Liz it was you." Paul said swallowing a mouthful of beer as he jumped up.

"She won't believe that, not of innocent little me. I'll just tell her the truth, that you did not want to spend the afternoon with her family!"

"Yeah, that will be bloody right! Shop your own mate wouldn't you. And you have the nerve to call me your brother!" He laughed.

They quickly cleared away the tools and washed.

"Come Al don't drag your feet!"

As they drove the twenty or so kilometres to Frankston Al felt like he could have been here for years. The vast flat open paddocks looked so familiar they appeared normal. The meadows at Sudbury, beautiful as they were now seemed little more than a pleasant dream. It was as if Paul and he had been friends for years and they had always lived just a few miles apart. The routine of a steady job which did not demand much thought, living somewhere that although was not Al's idea of a great place to live, it was not too bad either. Most of all to be near friends. Yes, he could easily stay here.

"I can't remember where it is." Paul said as they drove around a housing estate.

"You obviously come down here a lot don't you."

"Yeah, it's just that I've come a different way."

"Yeah, yeah, yeah, I believe you."

"Don't start or you'll be walking home!"

They parked the car and could hear Scottish accents coming from the back garden. Liz's family hailed from Glasgow.

"Listen Paul."

"Listen to what?"

"Real accents. British Islanders."

"I told you, don't start!" He had a look around for Liz's car, but she hadn't arrived yet.

"Good she isn't here and you can't get me into trouble!"

"Don't put money on that!"

They made their way into the garden and Paul introduced Al though he need not have bothered as everyone seemed to know who he was. One of Liz's brothers told him to make himself at home as he was one of the family now.

"Did you hear that Paul?"

"I heard, but you're nothing to do with me!"

Al's last Sunday in Melbourne came and went far too quickly. After a day with Paul and Liz he came back to the caravan to help Mark clean. He was looking forward to seeing the East Anglian countryside again and being with Christopher and Sarah. It was almost an eternity since he was last with them. But what about Steven? He had heard nothing from him for weeks and assumed that silence answered his own question. He did not want to leave now.

MEET ME AT HEATHROW

Melbourne, 20th November 1989

In but a blink of an eye, seven months had gone. It hardly felt possible that he had been in Australia that long, though so often it had felt like a life time; like a life sentence, deported with the first fleet. His crime? Love. The sun began to rise over the tops of the trees which stood at the back of the caravan park, the leaves swayed gently in the morning breeze. The tops of the caravans on the other side of the road shone as the sun reached them and Al heard the crack of metal as the steel warmed and expanded. The bells began to ring as a train approached the level crossing which was not too far away. He thought that that would be a sound that he would not miss, he was wrong, he would miss it. Not hearing the crossing bells would mean that he had left and suddenly the thought of leaving really hurt. The thought of returning to East Anglia, very suddenly and for the first time, held no comfort for him. He slipped out of his sleeping bag and got dressed, the mornings were no longer cold, no longer dark. It would soon be summer here and he was returning to yet another winter. His third this year! Garfield was still in bed as Al went out to their en suite shed to have a wash.

"En suite! Such a joke," he mocked.

The train rumbled past and the bells fell silent. The park was still. No movement or sound, save for a lone blackbird singing and the chirping of a few sparrows. Despite the difficulties of getting used to this situation, being in Australia, in a caravan, with Garfield, away from his old friends and all the familiar things with which he had grown up with, despite everything Al knew that he was going to miss this place. He would long for the things that had become familiar to him during the past four months. The places, the work, his new friends. He had had more than his fair share of goodbyes this year and wanted no more. He sighed heavily at the thought of moving on. His last day at work, the last day that he would see Paul. He was worried about what might lie ahead for him, but tried not to think that far, when anything could happen and probably would. The cold water hit his face and brought him into his last day with a shock. He didn't like this depressing little room which was rather grandly called an en suite. It was trivial, but it annoyed him and he was annoyed about being annoyed about it! It was little more than a converted hut.

"My last day of security," he pondered as he stood outside the caravan looking around at the trees and sky before going inside for his breakfast.

"I don't want to get up!" Garfield called from below his duvet.

"You never want to get up, Garfield."

"Yeah, well today I don't want to get up even more!"

It hit him how much he was going to miss Garfield, it came as a surprise, he had not noticed a friendship growing between them, but how could two people spend so much time together and not become friends, unless they hated each other? In Al's head time seemed to be standing still, but the hands on the clock were travelling at double time. They loaded the car and gave the van one last clean, then drove from the caravan park and both of them had misgivings.

"I can't believe it's my last day already, it seemed that it would never come," Al said, in part to himself and in part to Garfield.

"Yeah, I'm glad I'm going back to Katoomba on Wednesday morning. I can't wait to get out of this smog and into the mountains again."

"I'll be in Adelaide on Wednesday morning."

They spoke half in conversation, half wound up in their own fears and hopes, then saying no more as they travelled to work for the last time. Garfield also had misgivings about returning home. He would have liked a little longer, maybe until Christmas. It hadn't been as bad as each of them made out. There had been fun times, strangely, both thought about their daily ritual of crossing the days off their calendars as each one ended and how each week, when they got their pay slips, they worked out how such they could save and shaded in the appropriate number of one hundred dollar boxes. Smiles came to their faces as they recalled a dozen obscure and trivial things which somehow, oddly, they now found amusing. Along the road Al noticed more plants than he had previously been aware of and as they rounded the top of a hill they saw the pollution from the industrial estate and city hanging in the air ahead like a brown viscose solution. They arrived at work for the last time and as Al walked into the factory he practised his 'thank God it's my last day' and 'it's great to be getting out of here' routine. Inside of his head he was still running and he was well aware of the fact. Only Paul knew of his fear of returning, though not the full reason why.

The day was but a blur. Four o'clock rolled around in the factory far too quickly and all the pussies; as they called one another, went out to the car park and in little more than an hour consumed all the beer that Al had bought.

"I don't know why you're flying out from Perth back to Pommyland instead of Melbourne?" Gorilla asked. He was called Gorilla because of all the weird faces he pulled. God he was ugly! He was also an ex-pat and had no choice but to come to Australia, because his parents were here and not having been in Melbourne long enough to become Australian he made feeble attempt to sound like one by referring to Britain as Pommyland.

"I'm not. I'm flying to East Anglia, Heathrow is within the tenth century boundaries of my country. As for Perth? Well it was the cheapest place to fly to. Also I want to cross the Nullarbor, I'm really looking forward to it as it is the only thing on Earth like it."

Al took a walk into the office to say goodbye to Uncle Bob who was coming over to Europe in March.

"I'll see you in East Anglia in a few months then, take you to a real pub with timber frame, real ale, good food and an estuary; maybe even some Morris dancers!"

"I look forward to that Al, and don't forget that there will always be a job here for you. If I could get rid of all these fuck-wits and get in people like you I'd be a happy man!"

By the time Paul was ready to leave, Al was well under the influence of alcohol; nothing to eat at lunch time and then drinking in the open sun on what was a very hot afternoon did not do much for him. Paul and Al said little as they drove to Narre Warren. Al wasn't happy about the coming few weeks and Paul understood to a degree. The car stopped on the dusty verge where not too long ago Al danced and sang one morning while waiting for Paul to collect him. He wasn't so happy now. He looked at Paul and wanted so very much to be able to let him know the full details of why he was here. The fear that Paul would not have been such a good friend had he known tore Al in two directions. That thought was insulting to Paul, to think that he could have been such shallow person to allow a minor triviality such as Al's homosexuality to influence his friendship with him. On the other hand, what if Paul could not accept having a homosexual friend? Al was sure that he was not the only homosexual at the factory, but such things could not have been known openly. He could see the unhappiness that came with repression from society. The ultra macho society of Australia where there are no homosexuals outside of Adelaide and Sydney. It just did not happen in suburban Melbourne, even if Al could see it in the way he was looked at by men who were walking hand in hand with their wives in the shopping centres, kids in tow; outwardly heterosexual men, normal men, all of them given away by the way they looked at Al as if he was dinner.

"Well Al my boy, take care of yourself over there. I hope it all works out well for you." Paul said, offering his hand and smiling.

Al gripped his friend's hand, he did not want to let go.

Paul's hand was strong, it was friendship, the hand of a real man. There were a thousand words that Al wanted to say, but could not put them into a sensible order. He watched Paul drive away, swallowed hard and took a deep breath. He could really feel the alcohol when he picked up his pack, it was so heavy, he was totally unused to carrying it now.

"It wasn't very clean," the caretaker said.

"What? It was spotless! Not like the filthy state it was in when we moved in."

"Well we can have someone clean it tomorrow and take a charge out of your bond money."

"What's supposed to be wrong?"

The caretaker, the worst sort of ex-Englishman handed him a list. Al took it.

"I'll go over and do it now, then I can have my money back."

"Oh you can't have it now, you'll get a cheque in a week or so."

"I'm leaving for Perth tomorrow, flying to London in six days! When we moved in we explained this to the lady who was here and she said that we could have the bond money back the same day."

"Well I don't know about that."

"Well I do! That money is going to feed and house me for the next six days... and pay my departure tax!"

"Oh alright then, go over and do those things on the list and I'll let you have your money back."

Al left his pack by the office and walked over to the caravan where he sat with his face under the cold water tap. He was feeling worse now.

"Why do I do it? I know I'm no good with beer, one can and I'm half cut, two and I'm gone, but five?"

He sat in the caravan for fifteen minutes trying to allow his body time to adapt to the effects of the alcohol, then went back to the office without doing anything to the already clean caravan.

"Here are the keys. I'll wait outside while you go and check it."

"No. That's alright, it must be clean, you were over there long enough."

Al took his money, lifted his pack and walked around to the station. By the time he had got into Melbourne he had sobered up a little, but not much. The streets of Melbourne were still crowded with city workers heading home, against whom he had to fight his way through. In Collins Street he climbed the four flights of stairs to the hostel reception only to be told that there was no room. He was given directions to another hostel which was not so easy to find, but when he eventually did it was the same story. He knew that there were hostels in St. Kilda, but didn't know where. Taking a telephone number from the notice board he walked through the streets until he came to a phone box. It felt like the beginning of a nightmare, it too was full. His head was light from too much alcohol, he felt a little ill, also from too much alcohol, he was physically tired and hungry. He was beginning to panic, though he was too far gone to notice. He felt lost and alone and he didn't like that feeling at all. Al walked down the hill to the junction and then back up to the phone box.

"I'll phone Sue. She'll let me stay the night, I'm sure she will."

Eventually he phoned Sue and found that she wasn't in. Her flatmate said that he couldn't stay as a friend of her's was staying. Panic took a firm grip and for nigh on half an hour he walked trying to think what to do. He could not sleep on the station, it would be locked early in the morning and the streets themselves did not lend a feeling of safety. Time ticked past and he became agitated with himself for getting in the state that he was now in, which only served to make things worse. He thought about phoning Paul, but he was way out in Berwick. He did not want Paul to see or hear him in this state, but he was becoming desperate. He started to dial Paul's number, but hung up. He didn't want to rely on Paul, he couldn't rely on him. There had to be another way. He searched for a telephone book which was still intact. There wasn't one that he could find.

"Oh come on Al, Paul's your friend and if you can't turn to your friend for help what's the point in going on? What's your life worth?"

"Yeah, hello." Paul said. Al could hear the baby crying in the background and he felt bad.
"Hello Paul, it's me, Al."
"I thought you'd be in Melbourne by now. What do you want?"
"Paul, I can't find a hostel that isn't full and I can't stay with Sue," he paused, he hated asking for help and he wasn't very good at it. "I know I shouldn't ask, but can I stay at your house tonight? I don't know where else to go."
"Where are you now? Are you still in Narre?"
"No, I'm at Flinders Street. I'd sleep on the station, but they lock it later on."
"Oh you are in Melbourne. Is there a train out here soon?"
"Yes, they run every twenty minutes." Al was feeling so depressed, the alcohol was really making the situation he was in much worse than it needed to be.
"Yeah, alright Al, when you get into Berwick give us a call and I'll come and pick you up."
"Are you sure you don't mind?"
"No, it's alright. We can't have you sleeping on the streets can we? Let me know when you arrive."
"Thanks Paul."

Under other circumstances Al would have loved to stay with Paul and Liz, indeed he had the offer once before and could not work out why he had declined. Now, with the effects of the alcohol and the state of desperation he had got himself into, he cried help because he was in no fit state to look after himself. It was like Perth again, though then there was no alcohol involved, just the pain and confusion.

Al boarded the train to Berwick and slept fitfully during the hour long journey. More wrecked he had not felt. He stood on the dark platform at the edge of the town. It was like a country station back home and had he known that it was like that he could have spent the night there and not bothered Paul. He walked out of the station, the few people who had got off the train had gone by the time he got to the phone box. He told Paul that he was at the station and sat on the kerb waiting for him to arrive. In the quiet darkness his mind slipped through obscure thoughts of the coming week, the coming days, the coming hours and minutes. Time was so short and it dawned on him that in one week he would have already spent a whole day in East Anglia. It frightened him.

Along the road the head lamps of a car turned towards him and blinded him. Paul drove the car by Al, driving deliberately close in order to make him jump out of the way, but when he realised Al was not going to move he kept away from the kerb.

"What's the matter with you?" Paul laughed at him still sitting on the ground.

Al looked up to him, cold, tired and feeling decidedly grubby.

"I feel like a parasite," he had forgotten how hungry he had felt not so much earlier.

"Yeah, you look like one too!"

"Thanks Paul. I really needed to hear that!"

Paul laughed and Al told him what had happened in the city, then he laughed even more.

Berwick was empty, though it was only nine thirty.

Yellow-white lights shone out from behind drawn curtains. Leaves and branches of tall Eucalyptus swayed in the breeze, their grey-blue and silver danced ghost-like in the darkness above both sides of the road. The shingle on the drive crunched below the tyres and added another noise to break the evening's stillness.

They were greeted at the door by Nicky, Liz and Paul's two year old son. Liz was sitting in the kitchen.

"Hi Al, do you want a cup of tea?"

"No thanks Liz."

"Something to eat then?"

"No." He shook his head, not with his current situation at all.

"I've done a pooh mum." Nick said.

"No, I don't think you have Nick," she replied.

"But I have mum, I've done a pooh," he insisted.

"Come on Nicky, it's time you were in bed."

Liz took Nicky off to bed and Al thought how trivial his own problems were compared to Nicky's most fundamental of problems.

"I'll show you where you're going to sleep Al." Paul led Al to the toy room and pulled out a mattress and laid it on the floor.

"Oh my God, a mattress too!"

"Oh yeah, I forgot you're not used to such things are you?" Paul

The mundane title of humdrum conversation.

was really amused by the thought and Al gave a reluctant grin in return.

"I'll get you some sheets."

"No, it's alright. I've got a sleeping bag."

"O.K. then, there you are. Will you want a lift in the morning, or will that be too early for you?"

"Yeah, please."

"O.K. I'll give you a call in the morning Al. Oh and don't stay up all night playing with the toys," he laughed. "Good night Al."

"Good night Paul," Al answered, as Paul left the room.

"Paul?" Paul came back and looked around the corner of the open door.

"Yeah mate?"

There were a few seconds of silence as Al looked at Paul, wanting to say something, but wasn't quite sure of the words.

"Thanks Paul." It was not just a thank you for now, but for the past several weeks when Paul and Liz had been such a support for him in his confusion.

Paul shook his head and smiled.

"Good night Al," he said in a tone which told Al that he was with a friend who genuinely cared and understood his need.

"Time to get up mate."

Paul stood at the door and waited for a response from Al, who lifted his head slowly and looked at a collection of toys and dolls and for a second he forgot where he was. His vision was blurry, he was tired and his head felt less than one hundred percent.

"Time to get up Al." He looked behind him and could see Paul. Last night fell into place and he understood.

"Why don't you go and have a shower, you'll feel a lot better for it," he grinned. "You couldn't feel any worse!"

Al wanted to say thanks a lot, but could not manage it.

"I'll get you a towel."

He struggled out of his sleeping bag and dragged himself to the shower, after which he went through to the kitchen where Paul was having breakfast.

"How are you feeling now?"

"Better, not a lot, but better."

"Tea?"

"Oh yes please Paul."

"Feeling a little delicate are we?" Paul joked, as a friend who shared a tender moment with another friend.

"I don't know if we are, but I certainly am!"

Paul had a good laugh at Al and Al could not respond, defenceless in his present state. Paul made some toast and even buttered it for him. Was this out of friendship or a reflection on how helpless he looked?

"I hope you're not going to eat it for me as well."

"So what are you going to do today? Your train leaves this evening doesn't it?"

"Yes."

"And you won't be raging all day in town by the looks of you Al."

"You're all heart aren't you!" Al said and Paul grinned, Al did too, but it didn't show.

"I'll dump my pack at the station then I've got the morning to recover before meeting Sue for lunch, then I've got to come out to Dandenong to give Garfield his half of the bond money."

"I'll take that in for you. It will save you coming back out this way again."

Al tried to work out what half of one hundred and ninety three was, but couldn't.

"My God! You are in a mess aren't you."

"I'm glad you are getting a good laugh out of this Paul, because I don't feel too good at all."

"And you're going to cross Australia and then fly across the world on your own?"

Al ate his toast slowly, it would be a few more hours before he was in a fit state to start stuffing his face again. At least for a while no harm could come to him while he sat here with Paul. How could he enrich Liz and Paul's lives like they had his? Though Paul seemed to be getting quite a bit of pleasure from Al right now!

"Well Al my boy, we had better go. You had better go and pack."

"Yeah, I've already packed."

The hands on the clock ticked past seven o'clock.

"You're late for work Paul. Not the first time and I'd put money on it not being the last time either!"

"Now don't get cheeky, or you'll be walking to the station."

They left the house, Al knew, or was that he hoped that one day he would be back here. He didn't know how, when or the real reason why. That demanded more powers of logic and reason than he had at the best of times and certainly not now.

"Narre Warren or Dandenong Station?"

"Narre Warren. Dandenong is out of your way."

"No, not really. I always go along the Prince's Highway to work, even if I'm late. I'm never in any hurry to get there, only to get home!" They had a laugh together as Al thought Paul had never said a truer word.

Barely a few minutes passed and the car drew to a halt near the station. This was it. This was that final goodbye that Al thought he had got out of the way yesterday. He hated goodbyes. They were but an exclamation mark of pain in one's life that he would rather have done without.

"Thanks for everything you've done for me Paul," he emphasised the everything. "You've been a good friend, far more than you realise."

"That's alright mate. You just take good care of yourself and we'll probably see you next year."

"Yeah, either five months, or if things don't go so well, a couple of weeks."

Paul patted him on the shoulder. "You'll be alright. Just keep off the beer!" Together they grinned broad grins.

Al got out of the car and watched Paul drive away, waving from the open window as he went. Al waved back. A lump was in his throat as in his soberness he watched his friend disappear for the last time and who knew for how long?

"I hope so Paul, I hope so."

He wasn't feeling too energetic, so he left his luggage at the train station and got on a tram to Bundora. He wasn't going there for any reason, just because he had not been out that side of the city before and he wasn't up to doing anything else. It used up quite a chunk of the morning and he went off to get something to eat and drink before heading back into the city ready to get a train out to Carnegie to meet Sue for lunch.

He arrived as Sue came down the stairs to the street and they went off to a little café, taking their food outside to eat and sitting under an umbrella because it had turned out to be a really hot day.

"I'm going on safari in two weeks," Sue said with anticipation. "To Ayers Rock, the Olgas, Alice Springs of course and a couple of days in the bush. I'm really looking forward to it."

"Oh Sue. I envy you. You'll love it, but take lots of insect repellent."

"It's not that bad is it?"

"Believe me. You don't want to find out the hard way!" He bit into his large prawn salad roll, mayonnaise oozed out from the sides. "How come you get so many holidays? It's not that long since Adelaide."

"I save them up. At Christmas I'm off to New Zealand. I want to go home and I want to stay there this time." She thought heavily about whether she would fit back into life at home, whether she was going back expecting too much, whether it was really what she wanted? Al was having similar thoughts about his reasons for going home. Yes, he did have to face the past, but he still had a hope that he and Steven could work something out, just as Steven had written in his letter a few weeks earlier. Could he really stay there? He was expecting the worse and that was why he had more or less decided to return to Australia within a few months of leaving, though that was not what he wanted either.

"It's going to be difficult going back, isn't it?"

"Yeah, I guess it is Al. I just hope that I can get some work, there's not an awful lot in New Zealand."

"I'll get over there some day, late next year I suppose."

"Do you think that you will come back then?"

"Yes I think so. It all depends on what happens next week. I can't believe that it will go alright, though I'd like it too, naturally. I may as well be down here where I can earn lots of money and have enough space to sort myself out. Though I do miss home."

"Oh! I've just remembered," she searched her handbag which was overflowing with all manner of things. "A letter for you. I guess it will be the last you get, but if anymore come I'll redirect them to England.

"East Anglia!"

"Whatever."

Al looked at the handwriting, it was from Steven. What news did it enclose. No doubt news that he did not want; or did want, but didn't need. He folded it and pushed it into his pocket.

Sue and Al said goodbye outside her office and they parted, another goodbye that he could have done without. Along the road the level crossing barriers closed as he walked towards the station. He was in no hurry and he watched the train bogies roll along the track, across the tarmac, towards the city, Steven's letter firmly in his hand, fingers clenched tightly around it. The aerogramme crunched within his grip. The barrier opened, the lights fell dull and the bells silent, he continued onto the platform and waited for the next train. For ten minutes he sat without movement in the shade of the station building, thinking. He would miss Paul and Liz and Sue, even some of the idiots whom he did not particularly like at work, Garfield as well, funny little Garfield, how was he getting on with his last day at work? Was he also pretending that he was glad to be leaving, when in fact he too had reservations? But it would be so good to see Christopher again, how Al longed to see Christopher. It would be better than he could imagine.

"I want to hug him, as I hug my European friends. I have never had the courage to hug him before. I hate the British way."

A pair of rosellas chirped from high in a Eucalyptus tree, then flew; deeply swooping at the ground before rising again, along the railway track. Oh to see robins and finches and kestrels again. To see green trees, not the grey-blues of here; not that there would be many green trees when he would get back, apart from the multitude of conifers which were evergreen, a few Prunus, Cotoneaster and of course Ilex and Hedera.

He took Steven's letter out of his pocket and pressed it flat, tearing at the seals and opening it.

"My dear Al. I received your letter yesterday. It was good to finally hear that you had received mine, though from the questions you ask it is clear that you haven't had them all. I'm confused by what it is you have planned upon your return? You do not mention where you will stay, only that you don't want to go to your mum's. I can understand that, but I don't think it would be a good idea for you to come here, I'm not sure what you want from me. You say that you will be at Heathrow some time on Monday morning, but you don't say what time? Are you in some way testing me? Monday is difficult because of work. Wednesday would be better, can't you change your flight, so I can meet you? I don't want to be caught in some ugly public scene. My love, Steven."

Al sat by the Yarra in the heat of the hottest day he had had in seven months in Australia. Twenty nine degrees felt a little on the sticky side for him as he drunk from a can of fruit juice and had something else to eat. He had recovered from the fragile state he was in during the morning. He wrote out a postcard to Liz and Paul to say thanks and tell them how difficult his day was, sitting in the sun eating and drinking, with time to do nothing. He also sent a card to Steven. He had been left with the feeling that Steven's letter was a little cold, especially after the previous two which seemed to suggest the possibility of something, even if Al didn't know what?

"Dear Steven, I've just received your letter and I'll post this before I leave Melbourne today, you should get it before I leave Perth on Sunday? I don't really know what I expect from you, if anything. I am very confused about your previous two letters and the seemingly unbridgeable distance today's letter seems to convey. I'm not sure what time I'm due at Heathrow, I leave Perth 3.30 Sunday afternoon and I guess I land about 7ish on Monday. Wednesday is fully booked. I'm not trying to trick you, as is the impression I get from your letter. I don't know where I'm staying, I can't think that far ahead right now. I probably won't stay and will either fly on to Amsterdam or take the evening flight back down here. I don't really expect you to be at Heathrow and if you don't want to see me then please don't come. All my love, Al."

Dusk fell as the train to Adelaide left the city and trundled its way through the suburbs. Al recalled the time of his first arrival with Nina, Anna and Darryl. It was as if it was some distant year, half forgotten. It was so unlike now, bitterly cold, noisy, frightening. Now it was hot, quiet, but still frightening, though now for a different reason. This time he did not want to leave Melbourne, then, he could not get out quick enough. He tilted his seat back and studied some German and had a drink. For someone of his build the seats were large and comfortable and he stretched out.

An hour or so passed before the man next to him spoke. Al did not want to talk so had not initiated a conversation. Lost in his warm feelings of maybe seeing Christopher again, his loss of leaving Paul behind, his fear of seeing Steven, he had enough to keep himself occupied.

"I going to have a go at someone as soon as I arrive in Freemantle. I have to rejoin my ship and because of this bloody pilots strike I've had to come by train. I was supposed to have a first class sleeper and some idiot has put me in this poxy carriage!"

Al looked at the man next to him and thought how rotten history had been to merge, by force, his own country of East Anglia, with the other British countries and to group them all together as if they were one. The Liverpudlian next to him was going to be moaning all the way to Perth, Al just knew it! Al said little, put his book away and settled into his seat and slept. It had been a stressful day few days.

Meet me at Heathrow, if you really want to see me,
I'll be there some time Monday morning,
Meet me at Heathrow, though I don't really expect to see you,
I guess it's just something that I must do,
Meet me at Heathrow, the tears, the pain, the memories,
Will come flooding back I know.

And though I keep on running,
I know I'm getting old and tired,
I'm getting weary of this life,
And when the sun is shining,
It just makes me think of you,
I want to see that smile again,
And though it's been ten months now,
I still can't stop loving you,
Wish I was in your arms tonight.

Meet me at Heathrow, if you really want to see me,
I'll be there some time Monday morning,
Meet me at Heathrow, though I don't really expect to see you,
I guess it's just something that I must do,
Meet me at Heathrow, the tears, the pain, the memories,
Will come flooding back I know.

I've tried so hard to hate you,
And I've tried too hard to forget,

I still can't lose my past,
And when the rain is pouring,
It just tells me how lost I am,
I want to be with you,
Maybe in another ten months time,
I will stop loving you,
I won't dream of you at night.

Meet me at Heathrow, if you really want to see me,
I'll be there some time Monday morning,
Meet me at Heathrow, though I don't really expect to see you,
I guess it's just something that I must do,
Meet me at Heathrow, the tears, the pain, the memories,
Will come flooding back I know, to me.

If you're not at Heathrow,
I'll take the next plane back,
to Australia.

    Deeply asleep, Al could see Paul laughing at him after having his shower.
    "Feeling a little delicate are we?"
    He could taste the tea that he had drunk in Berwick this morning, happy thoughts.
    "I hope you're not going to eat that for me as well!"
    The train proceeded with its journey. Ballarat was now way behind.
    "You are in a mess aren't you!"
    "I'm glad you are getting a good laugh out of this!"
    "Now don't get cheeky."
    "I'm glad you are getting a good laugh out of this!"
    "That's alright mate."
    "I'm glad you are getting a good laugh out of this!"
    "You are in a mess aren't you'"
    "Feeling a little delicate are we?"
    "That's alright mate."
    "I hope so Paul."
    "That's alright mate."
    "I hope so Paul."

"You are in a mess aren't you!"
"That's alright mate."
"I hope so Paul."
"I hope so..."
"Paul?" Al woke with a start, a cold sweat on his face, neck and back. He was alone, he was scared. It took him a little time to return to the reality of the new day which was just beginning to dawn over the hills through which the train was snaking its way between. Its path twisted down the hills, through run-down stations that had not seen passengers for many a year. Disused, uncared for, unloved. Al stared at their empty shells like looking through a window into his own mind and heart. He tore himself away from the window and went for something to eat and drink.

Adelaide stretched out below and it would not be long before he would once again be in his most favourite of Australian cities. The city of parks and kind faces, of paintings from East Anglia which made him a little less of a stranger. The city where he had met Steve and Sue, where he had first arrived with Nina and Anna. The city to where he had run for safety after being raped in the Australian bush. He felt like he was coming home.

After a mad rush for the luggage Al went for a shave and shower before finding a locker for his pack and heading into the city. The Adelaide he had returned to was not the one that he had left over four months ago. It was now hot. Too hot for Al. At thirty six degrees and with no humidity it was painfully hot. With each breath that he took he felt that his lungs were on fire. He did not feel like doing anything other than sit in the botanic gardens by the lake, just as he had done so often in the past. Surrounded by food and drink he allowed the day to drift along and take him with it as he wrote another postcard to Liz and Paul.

By three o'clock he made his way to the station and caught a local train out to the interstate terminal. He was quite amused by the narrow gauge trains of the city, the broad gauge of the train on which he had travelled on up from Melbourne and now yet another gauge; standard, for the rest of the journey to Perth.

Hours passed quickly while appearing to stand still. He studied his German as the train made its way laboriously north. He fell asleep just before Port Pirie and woke for a couple of minutes to the sound of the train crossing a bridge which he recognised as Port Augusta. So much had happened since that brief encounter with Tony so long ago. He smirked at the thought of places in Australia actually appearing familiar to him. Had there been a time when he had not been in this country?

Over the tops of the dunes the sun lifted her head, they were broad and tall, between them the track lay in large curves and Al could see the front of the train as it twisted and turned along them; he was in the second from last coach and as the train was so very long he was able to count ten coaches and both engines before the rest merged into one nearer him. Al thought that he should have made sure that he had a seat on the right hand side of the train as where he was, he would be in the sun all day, then he remembered that this side was south and this being the southern hemisphere, it would mean that he was on the shady side after all. Seven months down under and it still did not seem right that the sun should not be to the south. They passed a junction in the middle of nothing much. It must have been Tarcoola. From here the line to Alice Springs veered off to the north and now the train was heading west onto the Nullarbor.

"We stopped for hours during the night on a siding waiting for another bloody train to pass!" Al had forgotten about the Englishman to his right who did not want to be on the train and was determined to hate every minute of the journey.

"Really?" Al said in a flat, uninterested tone. "I didn't notice. I slept all the way from Port Augusta." A distance of three hundred and fifty kilometres which had taken nearly ten hours. Al was more interested in having a shower before anyone else woke up and then getting some food and lastly watching the scenery as the train continued to weave in and out of the dunes which stood like vast Ochre mole hills; thinking on an Australian scale, on both sides.

By mid morning, after a hot shower; which Al was glad of, after a large breakfast; which he was also glad of, the turning had stopped. They had arrived on the Nullarbor Plain. A vast limestone plateau larger than the British Isles and not a tree in sight, hence its name. Here the track continued in a dead straight line for over three hundred miles. It was unnerving to think of the vastness which lay outside the windows on both sides of the air-conditioned carriage.

At Cook the train stopped for forty five minutes while it was refuelled. This led to a mass exodus of passengers who were desperate for any distraction. Cook was purely a railway service town. Town? A collection of wooden houses and a shop, which obviously did more trade with train passengers than with the locals. Al had a quick look in the shop, but it was so crowded he had to fight his way out again, then wandered out onto the plain, alone, while everyone else got crushed in the shop or stood outside waiting to get in. He didn't go far, there was no time, nor any need. It was largely untouched, dry and scrub covered. Seemingly timeless. He could be happy wandering around here for a few weeks. He could be alone here and safe from thousands of indifferent faces in the cities.

By early evening even Al was beginning to tire from the journey as the train reached the end of the Nullarbor, there were once again trees and Al couldn't quite believe his eyes when he saw his first wild kangaroos, huge, mainly reds; which are the largest species. They stood there like giant rats looking at the train before bouncing off, seemingly without any effort at all, gliding through the air, powered by those unbelievably strong legs, balance kept by long muscular tails. Once again it was dark and at nine the train stopped at Kalgoorlie. Al stepped off the train for five minutes to stretch his legs. The air was cold and he was quite happy to get back to his seat.

"Surely it was only a few weeks since I was last here?" Thoughts of Steven filled his head as he remembered that he would be in East Anglia in three days. Thoughts of the last time they had spoken, seven months ago, from that early morning airport building. Steven had sounded so cold to Al. Al had sounded so desperate to Steven and neither could have done or said anything unselfish or unhurting. What would be waiting for him upon his return home? He was as unsure as he had been about his arrival in Australia all those months ago; a reversal of fears. Kalgoorlie drifted past outside of the window and there was nothing more to see in the blackness on the other side of the glass. He slept.

> *"I want you as the dream,*
> *not the reality,*
> *that clumsy goodbye kiss could fool me,*
> *but I'm looking back over my shoulder,*
> *at you happy without me."*

The journey now over; at least for a couple of days, he collected his luggage and went to catch a local train into the city. He looked for a ticket office or a machine. There was neither. He didn't want to get on the train without a ticket, but a train was coming, so he had no choice but to travel without a ticket even if he felt guilty. He recalled how he would jump on the Sudbury train at Marks Tey without a ticket after getting from London without one. The local train would already be crowded with people from Colchester and he would find himself a window seat, near to other people and stare, fixed eyed, on the passing scenery as if he had been sitting there for the past six minutes since the start of the journey. It always worked, unlike the train up from London when once he had been caught. He never understood why he did it? Maybe because it was a challenge? Maybe he was inherently bad? It certainly was not to save money, he had plenty in those days and travelling on a railcard he had lots of change from a fiver on a day return to London.

Jumping the train was easy. Finding a hostel was not. It took him twenty minutes to get to one.

"Sorry, we're full," the girl said.

"Oh no, not again. Don't panic, Paul isn't here to help you this time."

He walked along the road to the next hostel, only to be told the same thing again. It was beginning to sound like a scratched record, one which he had never liked anyway. He was directed to the next nearest hostel and was told to wait an hour in case there was anyone checking out. Two hours later he had a bed for his last two nights. He sighed. He was pleased. No more to think about for a while. After a shower, he went up to the roof to do some washing before returning into the city for the day. Drifting from cake shop to cake shop, filling his face with chocolate cakes and coffee. It was a perfect day, or as near perfect as it was going to get two thousand miles from Paul, eight thousand miles from Christopher and with the likelihood of seeing Steven in three days.

"Geographically isolated or what?" He joked with himself and pushed another piece of death by chocolate in his ever hungry mouth. He was like a cuckoo chick in the springtime around chocolate cake, mouth gaping, always demanding. More! More! More!

At thirty four degrees Al felt positively comfortable, it was far more pleasant than thirty six in Adelaide or thirty in East Anglia.

Barely able to move to the next konditorei he decided to sit out the evening in the cinema, Bette Midler was on in Beaches and it appealed to him and he was not going to deny himself anything that he might want. Once the film finished it was time to go for something else to eat, have a coffee and write a postcard to Paul and Liz. While it lasted he would enjoy this.

"Dear Liz, Paul and kids, You may have perfected the art of pretending to look busy Paul, but I have perfected the art of over indulgence; though I call it survival! I've had a really hard day which started like my last evening in Melbourne when I tried to find a room, though this time I was sober! I hate it when I panic! It's 34 degrees and the chocolate cake is great. Seen a film and now I'm going to bed, lots of love Al. P.S. I saw my first plague of kangaroos yesterday, all ten of them!"

At the end he drew a smiling face and a very stylised kangaroo. He always drew on postcards or envelopes, it was his trademark, his signature.

Saturday. His last full day in Australia. He was up early, collected his washing from the roof, minus one white shirt, his best shirt, the one he was saving for his return home. Unable to get too upset, he went to the train station and caught the first train to Freemantle. Once it had been a separate city, but now it was part of the massive urban sprawl that all Australian cities rapidly developed into. The city centre seemed so old to Al after all this time in a new country. Many of the buildings dated from the late 1800's and one went as far back as 1830! In East Anglia it would have been old, but not noticeably so, but here he found it quite impressive. He started his day with croissants, which he dubbed the best outside of France. After such a good start to his day he was determined to enjoy the rest of it, even if it killed him! Cake shop, souvenir shop, cake shop, book shop, cake shop, rest, cake shop, post office... and thus continued his day. During the afternoon he noticed that his trainers had split, so he had to find a new pair. He found a shop that was having a sale; all Australian shops have sales every single day; it seemed apparent that no one ever has to pay the full price for anything. In he went and found a pair which were size six and in his price range.

"Do you want them?" A girl snapped rudely.

"Are these British or American sixes?" Al asked, not quite sure how much of a difference there was, but he knew that there was one.

"No, they're Australian sixes," the ignorant girl answered.

"Yes dear, but do you use the American or British system?"

"I don't know. I'm sure they are Australian." She maintained.

"I don't want to make things difficult, but do you know what Continental size they are? I can cope with the Continental system."

Now she was totally confused and Al could see that from her blank expression which stared out at him from the void within her head.

"I'll tell you what, I'll try these on and you go and get a pair of sevens just in case."

She seemed to understand that and slouched away to the store room. Al was a little pissed off with the silly blond bimbo. Maybe she was the one that Tony had had all those months ago? That would have explain a lot, with all that noise that had come from his tent he had obviously fucked her senseless.

She took her time coming back and Al decided on the sevens.

"I'll take them," he said grabbing them from out of her hands so she couldn't get them mixed up with the other pair.

"It's alright, I'll wear them now."

"That's forty dollars."

Hadn't she been taught to say please?

"No. It has a three and zero after the dollar sign. In East Anglia that means thirty and I think it means the same here?"

He had had enough of her stupidity and rudeness. Once escaping from the shop he just had to get something to eat; to calm his nerves after the ordeal with the girl with the void between her ears. He sat by the quay eating king prawns until he could eat no more. Looking down into the blue water which splashed against a small yacht he returned to reality and left his world of food and security behind. Tomorrow... Tomorrow he would be leaving this country. The country that he always thought strange, always thought that he didn't belong, now he needed this land where he had learned to live. He needed his factory job, Melbourne, his friends. The fear of Monday loomed larger on the horizon. Like a dark foreboding cloud, heavy with rain, moving closer to a land already suffering from floods.

His last night came and went. He was awake for most of it. He slept fitfully through the torment in his own head. It was six o'clock when he went for a shower. He was cold under the heat of the water. He was lonely as he talked to two young boys from Derbyshire as he packed. They had just arrived in Perth and had a year in front of them on a working holiday. They were friends, they were together, they were lovers, they were lucky. He knew he could not have stayed with Tony, even if he had not run off and left him all those months ago, even if Tony had not gone off to Sydney, leaving him behind at Port Augusta. God, how he wanted to be with someone, to share his time with someone. He hated the vulnerability which he felt with distance, with isolation in cities.

He was at the airport early, but was not allowed to check in and get rid of his pack, so he went upstairs for something to eat and drink, bought himself a copy of The Independent, even though it was a week old. It was still news. It distracted him. By the time he went down to check in there was an unbelievably long queue as if every passenger had arrived at the same time. He stood in silence as all around people talked.

"I'm sorry Sir. There is only smoking as far as Singapore. Non-smoking to London from there."

"But right at the back? Are there no seats at the front of the cabin?"

"I'm sorry, that's all there are."

He walked around the building, more than a little pissed off about being stuck with all the smelly old smokers. Foul creatures. Steven smoked and he even did that behind Al's back, after all those weeks of putting up with Steven's bad temper when he gave up as well! Another reason to add to the list of why he should not get on the flight. There were three flights going to Auckland today. There were seats available, he'd asked. He could go there, it would be safe. Safe from what? No. He had to face his past. He needed to return, but he was still scared.

The boarding light flashed and he continued to read his paper. He hadn't paid his departure tax and wondered if they would not let him leave if he refused to pay it? It was the final call before he got up and walked through to the departure lounge, clearing Security and Immigration.

He sat quietly on the plane and dutifully ate the food that he was brought. Paul, Christopher, Steven, filled his head. Australia, East Anglia, New Zealand?

"Dear Liz and Paul, I'm in Singapore waiting for my next flight.

I really don't know why I'm making this journey. I'm sure it's a mistake. Thanks for your friendship, I don't deserve such good friends and I miss you more than you know. Tomorrow morning I'll be at Heathrow. Then what??? See you soon, love Al."

He ate again and tried to sleep. Then ate again. Then walked around the terminal at Bahrain. Then ate again and tried to sleep. Then ate again as it began to get light; it had been dark since his arrival at Singapore. Now he could see the coast of East Anglia far below. Blocks of sodium lights lit up the towns as they crossed just south of Chelmsford. The M25 snaked its way around London and the little red plane on the video screen turned south.

"Ladies and gentlemen, we will shortly be landing at London Heathrow. The current temperature is minus one and the forecast is dry and cool..." The captain continued with his speech as the plane turned east on its final approach.

As the plane made a perfect landing Al wondered why it could not have crashed? What had happened to all the time since he had left here? What had happened to Tony? Had he come back a month ago? Now he was back in East Anglia he felt like a stranger, but that was stupid. He felt as if this would not be home for him again, but that was not so stupid. He could not bring himself to think further than the next couple of minutes, waiting for the plane to come to a halt at the gate.

The confusion he still felt and tried to hide, whirled around his head as he chased after it, to try and stop it. The plane came to a stop and the seat belt lights went out.

A rush of people stood in the gangway waiting to get out. He sat still in his seat, belt fastened. What was going to happen if Steven was here? No, he couldn't be? He had to go to school. Then what was going to happen if he wasn't here? He had no idea what it was that he was hoping to happen. What it was that he was fearing or even expecting to now happen.

"Oh Australia, my land of hope, my land of isolation, of opportunity. Where are you now?"